Praise for *The Canc*

'A pitch-perfect love lett
– honest, uplifting an
Jill Mansell, *It S*

'Brave, bold, Josie Lloyd has written an incredibly
important book. Every woman should read it'
Veronica Henry, *A Wedding at the Beach Hut*

'A searingly honest, but fiercely positive story about the
importance of friendship and the power of hope told
with Josie's characteristic warmth and humour'
Mike Gayle, *Half a World Away*

'I adore Josie Lloyd, I love her writing and you are in for an
amazing, heart-breaking, inspiring treat – read this book'
Jenny Colgan, *The Bookshop on the Shore*

'A story as honest as it is entertaining, and as funny
as it is fearless. It made me believe in life, in love and
in the power we all have to overcome the worst – an
unmissable, hopeful and life-changing read'
Katie Marsh, *The Rest of Me*

'This life-affirming book will make you weep – and jump for
joy. A heart-warming story about bravery and compassion,
friendship and family. Beautifully written, witty and moving'
Freya North, *The Turning Point*

'I thoroughly enjoyed this honest, no-holds-barred story.
It is by turns funny, inspiring and incredibly moving'
Kathryn Hughes, *The Letter*

'Beautiful and brave, powerful and emotional.
An incredibly special book'
Alex Brown, *A Postcard from Italy*

Praise for *The Cancer Ladies' Running Club*

'What an engaging and life-affirming story! A page-turner, too, with such wonderful characters. I loved it!'
Rachel Hore, *The Love Child*

'A gorgeously bittersweet novel, unflinching and heart-wrenching – you will need tissues – yet full of warmth, wit and joy. I was cheering on *The Cancer Ladies' Running Club* right to the finish line'
Eve Chase, *The Glass House*

'Wonderful. A gorgeous, moving read'
Cesca Major, *The Silent Hours*

'Josie has done a wonderful job of treating the subject matter with such honesty, and infusing the story with a great sense of courage and hope. A story of friendship, and love, and battling obstacles head on with a very uplifting dose of inspiration and warmth'
Celia Reynolds, *Finding Henry Applebee*

'Beautifully written with honesty, humour and fabulous characters – an inspiring story that's not afraid to tell the truth'
Jessica Ryn, *The Extraordinary Hope of Dawn Brightside*

'This inspirational, hard-hitting, warm, and funny book pulsated with truth and experience. I laughed, cried, learnt a lot, and could NOT put it down. This one will be a huge summer hit'
Louise Beech, *How to be Brave*

'I RACED through this warm, witty delight of a read about strength, endurance and friendship. A wonderful book'
Suzy K Quinn, *Bad Mother*

Josie Lloyd's first novel, *It Could Be You*, was published in 1997 and since then she has written fifteen bestselling novels (under various pen names), including the number one hit *Come Together*, which she co-authored with her husband, Emlyn Rees, which was number one for ten weeks, published in twenty-seven languages and made into a Working Title film. Josie has also written several bestselling parodies with Emlyn, including *We're Going On A Bar Hunt*, *The Very Hungover Caterpillar* and *The Teenager Who Came To Tea*. As Joanna Rees, she writes sweeping dramas, the latest of which is her *Stitch in Time* trilogy set in London, Paris, New York and LA in the 1920's.

When she's not writing, Josie likes nothing more than a good yomp along the beach or over the South Downs with Emlyn and their dog, Ziggy. She also swims in the sea, plays the piano and loves hanging out with her family and friends. You can find her on Twitter @josielloydbooks, on Instagram @josielloydwriter and you can get in touch via her Facebook page too, @JosieLloydWriter

THE
CANCER LADIES' RUNNING CLUB

JOSIE LLOYD

ONE PLACE. MANY STORIES

HQ
An imprint of HarperCollins*Publishers* Ltd
1 London Bridge Street
London SE1 9GF

www.harpercollins.co.uk

HarperCollins*Publishers*
1st Floor, Watermarque Building, Ringsend Road
Dublin 4, Ireland

This edition 2021

1

First published in Great Britain by
HQ, an imprint of HarperCollins*Publishers* Ltd 2021

ISBN: 978-0-00-837365-8
ANZ: 978-0-00-837362-7

MIX
Paper from
responsible sources
FSC™ C007454

This book is produced from independently certified FSC™ paper
to ensure responsible forest management.

For more information visit: www.harpercollins.co.uk/green

This book is set in 10.7/15.5 pt. Sabon

Printed and bound in Great Britain by
CPI Group (UK) Ltd, Croydon, CR0 4YY

For Birgit, Jane, Hannah, Maddie and Paula

New Year's Eve

'Quick! It's nearly time,' I shout, and we turn on the TV, just as Jools Holland is counting down to midnight. The kids run in from the lounge and I put my arms around Tilly, my eldest, and Jacob, my 13-year-old son, as we yell out the final three seconds at the top of our voices.

There are cheers and hugs as all twenty of us kiss each other happy new year and quickly form a rag-tag circle between the long wooden table and the wood-burning stove in the kitchen of Scout's Suffolk farmhouse. As we overlap hands to sing 'Auld Lang Syne', we are all half singing and half laughing as Pooch, our dog, earnestly wags his tail like he's trying to do a butt shimmy.

'We'll take a cup of kindness yet, for auld lang syne,' I bellow, bumping shoulders with the kids, my cheeks pink. Who knows what it means? It feels good to sing it.

Afterwards, we break apart and I fall into Tom's arms. In all the mayhem, I haven't been able to wish him happy new year yet.

'Steady on,' my husband laughs, holding me up. 'Have you been keeping up with Joss on the champagne?' We both know Joss can drink all of us under the table.

'Yep, but I love you,' I slur looking up into his familiar face. He wears thick framed glasses that make him look kind of distinguished and funky. His once lustrous hair has thinned so much he now shaves his head, but he's better looking to me than ever – and definitely improving with age.

'I love you too, my Keira.' He runs his hands over my hair and looks into my eyes, then kisses me tenderly, and my heart melts, as it always does.

'OK, OK, you two lovebirds, break it up,' Joss says. 'There are children present. Honestly, you're just as soppy as you were twenty years ago. You coming outside?' she asks me, in a meaningful way. A meaning not lost on Tom.

'Good idea to get some fresh air. I'll put Bea to bed,' Tom says, letting me go and nodding to our youngest, who is heading for the cosy window seat with Pooch. Joss grabs three glasses of champagne and my arm and we head for the back door. 'Have fun. I'll distract the teens,' Tom calls after us and winks at me.

Outside, Scout joins me and Joss as we sit on the stone wall outside the kitchen. The huge garden is bathed in silvery shadows and the stars twinkle in the black sky. Inside, through the steamed-up window, we can see Scout's husband, Mart, lining up tequila shots. It's going to be a long night.

'So a new year,' Joss says, lighting one of her thin menthol cigarettes. 'What are we all going to change? Apart from the no smoking – which starts at daybreak.'

Scout and I laugh. She and I have known each other since our school days, but we only became proper friends when we both wound up at the same uni and she, Joss and I were in halls together. The three of us became inseparable friends and we shared a flat in Ladbroke Grove when we graduated, partying together through the mid-Nineties. Scout and I stopped clubbing and smoking years ago when we got married and had babies, but Joss remains an eternal 25-year-old. Every new year, she swears she's going to give up, but she never does. I don't mind though, because it means I can still bum the occasional party cigarette off her. I check through the window to make sure that Tom really has distracted the teenagers. I can't risk being caught by Tilly.

'You know me, I hate change,' I say, as she hands the cigarette to me. I take a drag, squinting through the unfamiliar smoke. 'And anyway, everything is just fine and dandy.'

'Now that you're going to be Brightmouth's retailer of the year,' Joss says in an excited voice. She's referring back to the speech Tom gave over dinner, saying how proud he was that Wishwells, my shop, has been nominated for the award.

'Yes, well,' I say, handing the cigarette to Scout. 'I haven't actually won yet, but it's good to be recognised for what we've achieved.'

'You'll win it,' Joss says confidently, and I smile at her unwavering faith.

'What about you, Scouty? You happy living the dream?' I ask.

Scout left a high-flying city job five years ago and moved up here to this lovely patch of Suffolk to start a new life as a farmer. You'd never know from looking at her. She's small with a blonde bob and she looks lovely tonight in her ancient Karen Millen velvet dress. She blows a stream of smoke out thoughtfully.

'It's good, I think,' she says. 'But if I'm honest, it gets lonely sometimes with just the alpacas for company. I don't get to meet new people.' It's true that she's isolated up here and

I worry about her. Mart still commutes to London, so he's away three nights a week, and her twin boys are in boarding school during term time.

'Oh, they're overrated,' Joss says, though for a second I'm not sure if she's referring to people or the alpacas. She works in a London PR agency and has to schmooze for a living. 'Right, K? New friends?' She pulls a face. 'Who has time for those?'

I nod and laugh in agreement. I already have a host of gorgeous women in my life – friends who I've known for twenty years, or even decades longer, like these two. Then there's the staff in the shop, not to mention my suppliers and all my regular customers. My days are full of people. I don't have room for anyone new.

'I get a lot of time alone to reflect,' Scout says, taking another drag and blowing a smoke ring towards the stars. She's the only one of us who could ever do that.

'Uh-oh,' Joss jokes, pulling a face at me. 'About what?'

'Well… don't you ever wonder if this is it? The peak point of our lives?'

'And it's all downhill from here?' I exclaim. 'Don't say that.'

'But we're all around halfway through.'

'We're not even fifty. We're going to be marching up mountains when we're ninety,' I remind her. 'Don't start talking like this is the beginning of the end.'

'Exactly. We've still got it, right?' Joss says and pulls a pout, looking at her reflection in the window, leaning forward to plump up her cleavage in her low-cut leather dress.

'Don't you ever want to do something big – that makes a difference?' Scout asks, handing the cigarette back to Joss. 'You know… don't you ever think about your legacy?'

4

'Your legacy will be a string of heartbroken toy boys,' I tease Joss.

'How exciting,' she says. She's recently single, having finally dumped her useless long-term partner, and has found Tinder. Scout's face falls. She has a tendency to go all existential when she's squiffy and me and Joss always undermine her, but we've gone too far and I relent.

'I know what you mean, Scout, but personally, I'm happy. I really, *really* don't want anything to change,' I tell her, grabbing her hand and Joss's and kissing their knuckles. They laugh, knowing how sentimental I am.

And I don't. Right here, right now, surrounded by my best friends, I feel drunk and content. And yes, of course there are things I *could* improve, but on the whole, I've made good choices, I reckon. I'm lucky. I want my life to stay just as it is.

1

3rd January

In the room on the fourth floor of the breast clinic, I'm flipping through Pinterest on my phone, searching for new ideas for the shop, when a WhatsApp pings up from Lisa, my ceramics supplier. *Check these out*, it says and I open her message to see the picture she's sent.

'Oh, they are lovely,' I gasp out loud, looking at the pretty batch of espresso cups she's made with our latest floral design. I can't wait to get back to the shop and show the girls.

I feel a glow of pride as I text Lisa back with effusive praise, and once again I thank my lucky stars that I found her when I had to outsource my ceramics all those years ago. She's been making teapots galore for me and it's lovely to see her hit the ground running this new year with renewed enthusiasm after our fantastic Christmas sales.

But as I send the message, I'm momentarily distracted by the vase of plastic yellow dahlias on the table which seem to throb in the shaft of sunlight coming through the slatted blind.

'Come on,' I sigh, tapping my foot. I really don't have time to be here. Lorna, my business partner, has scheduled a meeting this morning with our accountant, Miles. He's a dry old thing and I'm much more fond of him than Lorna is, so I need to be there to grease the wheels. He's been with us forever. He even used to do the books for Dad, when Wishwells was Dad's framing shop.

So, I don't want Lorna – or worse, Pierre – to have the meeting with Miles without me. Don't get me wrong, Pierre, Lorna's husband, has been very helpful over the last few months, and him re-vamping the office computer system with a much-needed upgrade was a job I would never have got around to. The problem is, I'm not sure how long he's going to stay 'helping'.

I said he could come in, as a favour to Lorna, really. He'd been sitting at home twiddling his thumbs since he got fired from his job in finance (unfairly apparently) at the end of last summer. Lorna made the good point that it's ridiculous to have someone with the business nous of Pierre at our disposal and not use him, so I said he could come in. But I can't help feeling that he's got his feet too far under the table and wants to change everything. And Lorna seems to dote on his every word.

The door opens and the nurse comes in. She's wearing a blue smock and she checks the dangling watch on her chest before smiling at me and sitting down in the chair with a sigh, as if it's good to be off her feet. 'So, Mrs Beck…'

'Oh please. Just call me Keira,' I say. I don't like being Mrs Beck. It gives me too much in common with my battle-axe of a mother-in-law. I kept my maiden name for the business and I'm used to being Keira Wishwell at work.

'Keira,' she smiles, 'thanks for waiting.'

'Do you know how long this will take?' I ask, looking at

my phone, as I slide it into my handbag on the floor. The big clock on the screensaver says 10.08, which means Lorna will almost certainly have to face Miles alone. *Shit*.

'Well that depends...'

'On what?'

She shuffles her bottom on the chair. 'Well you see, after your first mammogram, before Christmas, we've called you back because...'

Something in her tone makes my ears prick up like a prairie dog's. I'm under the impression I've been called back to the breast clinic as a routine kind of thing. That's what they said might happen. People get called back *all the time*.

She holds my gaze. '... because we can see some unusual breast tissue.'

Breast tissue?

BOOM!

I'm in the quiet room.

It only dawns on me now that she's brought me in here with the plastic dahlias to *deliver bad news*. Is this bad news?

'Unusual how?' My voice is squeaky and quivery, not like my voice at all.

Ten minutes later, still not having been told anything conclusive, I'm ushered through to the mammogram room and another lady introduces herself as Sinitta and it's on the tip of my tongue to start singing 'So Macho', that Eighties hit by the singer Sinitta, which *this* Sinitta is probably far too young to remember, or appreciate at all. She's also in a lab coat and has an intense stare as she looks at my notes.

I stand naked from the waist up feeling cold and exposed and trapped inside her ominous silence, whilst the lyrics 'He's got to be so macho, he's got to be big and strong enough to turn me on...' roll around my head. Of all things, how has that song and its ridiculous lyrics managed to lodge itself in the filing cabinet of my memory?

As she marks lines on my breast with a pen and adjusts the machine, she's concentrating so hard, I don't feel like I can talk. I have to forcibly gag Sinitta in my head.

She skilfully, clinically, manoeuvres my breast onto a cold plate in front of a giant white machine and the other plate comes down and squishes it. A sort of boob sandwich. It hurts. More than last time, back in December, when I was up to my eyeballs in work and my appointment was a quick in-and-out job and not like this at all.

After she's taken some shots and is squinting at the screen, I pipe up, 'Can I take a look?'

'Oh, are you medical?' she asks.

'No... er... no, just curious.'

She swings the screen round.

There's my left breast in dark outline, looking like a distant planet in outer space. Or it could be a scene from a *Planet Earth* programme about the deepest part of the ocean. Strange tendril-like white things float around. What are they? They are spidery and spindly and creepily floating. Are they milk ducts or something?

At no point in my life have I really paid attention to the internal workings of me. My cells, blood, organs, *tissue*. It's a shock to have a glimpse into this inner world, which is living, evolving, doing stuff all by itself. It's like seeing time-lapse photography of moss in close-up. It's a world that I own, except I don't. The machine does.

'Can you tell anything? From the images?' I ask Sinitta, but she lowers her eyes.

'I'm afraid it's not my job to interpret the data,' she says.

Data? Is that what I've become?

2

I'm told that there's probably at least a half-hour wait until I'm seen for the ultrasound, but I have to get out of here. I can't keep watching the women with clipboards going in and out of rooms as my panic mounts. I need some fresh air and a decent coffee and besides, there's no reception and I should call Lorna and grovel about my lateness. I queue and get an insipid Americano from the Hospi-Coff kiosk and walk over the road to the park. I feel profoundly discombobulated, like I've been temporarily air-lifted out of my life.

It occurs to me as I sit staring at the barren trees, that I haven't actually sat dog-less and alone on a park bench since I was a teenager. I had my first snog with Gary Stubbs on a park bench, just like this one. How long ago that seems now. When Sinitta was in the charts. That's how long ago.

So macho…

Shut the fuck up, Sinitta! Not now, OK?

My phone pings. It's a text from Lorna.

Er… Earth to Keira? Come in please…

I try and type a text to Lorna but delete it. I can't seem to focus. All I can think about is those tendrils and what they might be.

But until I've had the ultrasound, telling her anything – even where I am – seems a bit dramatic. Instead, I put my phone in my pocket and clutch the coffee in my hands for warmth, but my teeth chatter. There's a few clouds around and I watch the shadow gobbling up the grass.

'Bloody hell, Dad,' I say out loud, noticing how my breath clouds.

Dad died fifteen years ago, when his converted camper van collided with an articulated lorry. They said he died instantly and he wouldn't have suffered, but the shock and heartbreak of losing him so suddenly and unfairly remains to this day. I often talk to him – mostly when I'm muttering about the kids and their spectacular messiness and I need someone to be on my side, which he invariably was. Or when I'm in the shop and I need to find something – like scissors, or the electricity meter cupboard key. I quite often ask him to locate the said item and usually it turns up right in front of me in his old cabinet.

'Can you just fix it so that it's OK, please? I can't do this. Can't. Just can't.'

I'm far too busy to have a medical problem. I don't *do* medical problems. I'm robust. Healthy. I barely even have fillings, for God's sake!

I mean, it can't be serious, can it? I'm only 47. In my prime. Most women don't even get mammograms until they're 50 and I only got one as I was sent a letter saying they were doing a random pre-50 screening programme. I would have ignored the letter, except that Tom found it and told me I might as well go. Because of the dimple. The tiny weeny dimple in the bottom of my breast that I noticed...

how long ago now? A year ago? Not that I've been that worried about it.

Because *my GP said it was fine.*

But what if it isn't fine?

3

I wait for some sort of sign, but there's only the wind in the bare trees. I notice a woman running slowly along the path towards me. She's a terrible jogger. She might as well be walking. That's how *I'd* look if I was jogging. Not that I ever jog these days, despite all my good intentions. I think the last time I went running was about six months ago and it was so hard, I somehow never managed to get round to putting my trainers on again. I always joke with Tom that I'm built for comfort, not speed.

Besides, I have an issue with running – ever since sports day 1984, which is indelibly marked as possibly the most humiliating experience of my life. After a long, involved campaign to snare the attention of heart-throb (and Danny from *Grease* dead-ringer) Ollie Redfern, I had lost weight and taken up fitness and – breasts plumped up with socks in my bra – thought I looked pretty irresistible as I limbered up for the 800 metres.

All was going well as I came up to the finishing line. I could see Ollie in the stands cheering, but as I sped up, what I didn't see was that my left breast had bounced free of my low-cut bra. And, as I triumphantly crossed the finish line, I only realised when I heard the laughter of the whole school ringing out. And, dying of mortification, saw that Ollie Redfern was cheering the loudest and whistling – but for all the wrong reasons. Ugh. Still makes me shudder.

As the runner gets nearer, I see that her chest is heaving. She's making a rasping sound as she tries to breathe in. She's fairly covered up by logoed running kit, but I can see that she's got tattoos over her neck beneath her jet black hair. I know everyone has them these days, but I really don't get the appeal of tattoos and I'm immediately a bit judgemental about her. *Maybe she's on drugs.*

Oh, for God's sake! I sound like my mother-in-law – even to myself.

As she reaches the bench where I'm sitting, she stops, leans forward and puts her hands on her knees and pulls in air. She's just metres away and I can see that her fingers are covered in chunky silver rings. She looks slim and fairly fit, so it's a surprise she seems to be having difficulties. Her eyes are closed – as if she's in pain. She's not having a cardiac arrest is she?

I'm jolted from my own potential medical crisis into her very real one.

'Are you OK?' I ask, getting up, feeling slightly panicked about my lack of first aid know-how. 'You want to sit down for a minute?'

She nods and I help her over to the bench. She sits, her eyes still closed. She seems to be concentrating very hard – almost as if she's meditating. She has deathly pale skin, which I see now is white make-up, and thick black flicky eyeliner which has smudged a bit. Her lips, which I thought had gone blue through lack of oxygen are actually that shade because of her metallic lipstick. Her black hair which pokes out beneath her Nike cap is very obviously dyed and makes her look even paler. She has multiple piercings in her ears.

But the most surprising thing is that she must be my

age, *at least*. I tell myself off for being a bit prejudiced about her being a druggie. But then, a full-on elder goth runner is a bit of an anomaly.

'Thank you,' she says, eventually, opening her eyes. They are a deep blue. Her voice is soft and low. 'You're very kind.'

'Can I get you anything?' I ask, although I don't have any water, so it's a fairly empty offer. I look down at the plastic lid of my coffee cup. It has pink lipstick around the little hole. She's not going to want that.

'*Christ!*... I hate how hard it is,' she says, shaking her head. She means the running.

'New year's resolution?' I ask because I've already made up her back story. She's a repentant punk. She's spent years getting stoned (and/or shooting up) whilst listening to dark music (*in* the dark obviously – or in the glow of a skull candle), but now, with the new year upon us, she's turned over a new leaf. She's out for the first bit of daylight exercise in years...

'No. I'm a long-distance runner.'

Oh.

That cancels out all that then. Has she just run a really, really long way? I'd be out of breath if I'd only run from the park gate to here.

'Well I used to be,' she says and there's a real bitterness in her laugh. She takes a deep deciding breath, then slapping her chunky ringed hands on her knees, gets back up again. 'Keep at it. It's the only way,' she says, as if to herself.

'Are you sure you're OK?'

'I'm not dead yet,' she says, smiling at me now. It's a wide smile – a proper cheeky Cheshire cat grin. There's something impressively defiant in her look and I immediately take back

16

all my pre-judgements. This is a woman with 'gumption and pluck', as my mother would say. I kind of like her.

'You waiting to go back in there?' she asks, before she goes. She rolls her eyes over towards the breast clinic over the road. Is it that obvious? Is this the bench where panicking middle-aged women sit? It frightens me that I'm not the first.

'How did you know?'

'Nobody in their right mind would get a coffee from that kiosk in there, unless they were stuck between appointments. I mean what muppet in branding thought of Hospi-Coff? It sounds like heated phlegm,' she says as she nods at my cardboard coffee cup with the logo of the kiosk on it and I laugh. 'Good luck,' she says and then she's off.

I sip my coffee and wince, thinking of it being heated phlegm, as I watch her lumber up the path out of the shadows and into the sunshine.

4

My encounter with the tenacious punk runner has cheered me up a bit and I muster up a gung-ho attitude as I'm shown into the ultrasound room. It's dark and womb-like and it reminds me of having the scans for the kids when they were babies. I remember seeing their little forms in black and white – their beating hearts, their spiky fingers, feeling overwhelmed with relief and joy. Jacob famously gave us a double thumbs up. I somehow know this won't be the same.

Another nurse lies me down on the bed and puts a sheet of scratchy paper over my naked breasts, whilst the radiographer looks at the screen and presses some buttons.

It's going to be fine. I know it's going to be fine. I'll be out of here in ten minutes, hot-foot it to the office, apologise to Lorna. Maybe take in cakes for everyone. Sod the new year's resolutions. Let's treat ourselves. I'll get those little donuts from Jennifer's café...

The radiographer has dark circles beneath her intelligent eyes, but the look she gives me is kind as she does the ultrasound. The jelly is warm, not cold like I'm expecting it to be. She tilts the screen and I can see another type of outer space, as she rakes the scanning wand over my breast again and again. I try to will it into performing real magic, into making everything OK.

But then I see her expression change and I know it, *just know it*. She's found something.

A lump.

I stare very hard at the dark grey mass she can see clearly on the screen, but that I can't make head nor tail of. Is it a lump?

I hardly hear the words as she explains that she'll have to do a biopsy and nods at the nurse. I tell myself in a steely internal voice that this is nothing. *This is a cyst. A little lump of nothing, right?*

The nurse applies local anaesthetic gel and I watch and flinch in pain as the needle pierces my skin on the screen. Talk about a jab in the wab! I've been warned that the needle will make a noise, but it sounds alarmingly like a staple gun. I'm reminded of Moira, our shop manager, putting shop rotas on the office noticeboard.

The radiographer does it twice, and each time I watch the needle on the screen shooting the dark matter. Then little samples of my alien planet growth is stored in a jar, then the nurse helps me to sit up.

'Can you just tell me what it is?' I ask, sounding confident and strong. The radiographer looks at me.

'I can't say for sure, until the test results are back,' she says.

'But you must know?' I probe. 'You don't have to soft soap me. I'd rather know.'

She glances at the nurse and I catch the look between them. This is not protocol, obviously.

'Please,' I urge. 'Just tell me. I can take it.'

The nurse looks at the box of tissues on the desk next to her and picks them up.

'Well, it's just an opinion, based on years of experience, but I'm afraid that it looks very much like cancer to me.'

5

I don't remember getting into the car, but I come to as I pull next to Lorna's Mini in the small car park we use behind the high street and notice that my hands are gripping the steering wheel so hard my knuckles have gone white. I look up at the back of Wishwells and the higgledy-piggledy black timber-framed building that is like a second home to me, and slowly relax.

The building hasn't changed much since I was a child and it was Grandpa's joinery shop, and I can still remember the smell of putty and sawdust and the sound of Grandpa whistling. Then later, when Dad turned it into a framing business, it still smelt of sawdust and I remember Crosby, Stills and Nash playing on the turntable as Dad chatted to the customers, always with a pencil behind his ear and a smile on his face.

That's what I need. I need to get inside and to forget what's just happened. I need to see Moira. Dear, wonderful Moira, who worked for Dad for ten years and stayed on to help me, although that makes her sound like an employee, when she's actually more like a second mother. It was Moira who encouraged me to do ceramics in the first place, Moira who knew that Tom was 'the one', Moira who helped look after each of my babies when they were newborns and kept the business afloat when Dad died. She's my rock, and right now all I want is to be engulfed in her soft, perfumed, jangly-wristed embrace. I need everything to be normal.

But Moira isn't in the shop. Ruby is in her place, folding the cashmere tartan blankets that are going in the January sale. We employed Ruby straight out of college and she's a good kid, although she dresses in shapeless black garments. Lorna is always – very unsubtly – trying to suggest that she goes on a diet. Seeing her, I remember now that I was going to stop and get donuts. But that was before.

It's like I'm experiencing everything through a weird Instagram filter. Everything is different. There is a *before* this morning and an *after*. Two distinct parts of my life. The person I was this morning belongs to the past. To the old me. This is new territory.

'Hey,' Ruby calls out, when she sees me in the stairwell by the back door. I see straight away from her face that something is wrong.

'Hi darling,' I say, although my voice sounds odd. 'Everything OK?' She shrugs, but I don't have time to winkle out the details of her latest problem. 'Where's Lorna?'

Ruby flicks her eyes towards the stairs in front of me and I make my way up the rickety wooden staircase touching the framed newspaper centrefold on the wall, a local press splash about Wishwells, when I first brought Lorna on as my partner.

Back then, she'd been my brother Billy's girlfriend and I gave her equal shares, thinking she might marry Billy and the business would have a lovely family symmetry. But then she split up with Billy, who surprised us all by moving to Australia, and Lorna married Pierre, who is just about the opposite of my brother in every way.

I can't knock her though. Like me, Lorna's lived the Wishwells brand and if it wasn't for her, I'd still be just doing ceramics, rather than expanding into the whole world of gifts. She's also made me take on venture capitalists so we could expand the business online – although, I have to admit, this latest thing with Jackson has grated a bit.

Jackson is Lorna's cross-breed pug, which as far as I can make out, doesn't have a brain cell in its head. Lorna did a loose doodle of him, and spurred on by the girls in the office, plastered the image on our various phone and iPad cases. Then this YouTuber who I'd never heard of – but is HUGE with the youth, I later found out from my own teen, Tilly – came into our shop and bought the phone case and then declared it her 'must have' for Christmas online, so then the demand went nuts.

Even so, I still can't stand Lorna's dog – who has now been elevated to celebrity status and has even been given his own Instagram account, FFS.

But then, boom! It hits me again like a brick – that Jackson, work, perhaps everything my entire life has been about up until this point, is no longer really important at all.

No. Don't. I can't just give in like this. Life must go on, right? Isn't that what they say? Think of the children. Of Tom. I've picked up the phone to call him ten times since leaving the clinic, but I couldn't… just couldn't find the words.

OK, so deep breath. Here goes. *Get your game face on, Keira.* It's time to face Lorna.

6

I push through the stairwell doors into the office, which has several desks and lots of yet-to-be labelled and sorted merchandise in boxes stacked around the place. Becca, our online manager, sits at the desk with headphones on staring at the giant Mac screen in front of her. She doesn't notice me.

Lorna is standing by the window, some bulky order folders in her arms. She's wearing orange trousers and a black roll-neck jumper, which accentuates her slim, toned body. She looks effortlessly stylish as usual. In comparison I feel shabby in my green tweedy coat.

'Afternoon! Where have *you* been?' Lorna says, trying and failing to pull off a comedy voice. She must see something in my harrowed look, because she doesn't continue. 'Oh. Right. You want a black coffee?'

This is our code for a 'power meeting' in the office kitchenette. She marches after me and shuts the door.

She knows something serious must have happened for me to have missed the meeting this morning and to have ignored her text, so I can see her scanning my face for clues. I have to make something up, I tell myself. Right now. I can't let her know the truth.

'Is it Tom? The kids? Is it Tilly? Don't tell me you've caught her taking drugs?' she says, in a low, worried voice.

Oh Jesus. This is actually what goes through her mind about my life.

I shake my head.

'What then?'

And that's when I know I can't lie. It's just too big… too momentous… I have to spit it out: The C-bomb. Here it comes…

'I've got breast cancer.'

It's the first time I've said it out loud and words fall between us like a guillotine. For once, Lorna is silenced.

Suddenly, the tears that have been shaking around inside all the way here arrive. Big, fat drops that now erupt like a burst water main. 'I j–j–j–just c–c–came from–m–m the c–c–c–clinic.'

Lorna envelops me in a hug. She smells of expensive Diptyque perfume.

'Oh, Keira. I'm so sorry.'

'I just can't believe it. What if I'm riddled?' I sob. 'What if I die?'

I haven't cried like this since… well, forever. I'm properly gasping. It's quite alarming.

Lorna grips me by the shoulders and leans in, her eyes fierce beneath her choppy fringe. 'Stop it,' she says in such a harsh tone, my tears stall. You're not going to die. This is a blip. A speed bump.'

She guides me into taking a few slow, deep breaths, before taking the tea towel from next to the microwave and dabbing it at my face. It smells, but I don't care.

'It's a–a–a bit of a b–b–bumpy speed bump,' I say, eventually. I've stopped the torrent of tears. It's embarrassing to have had such an outburst in front of Lorna. I blow out a deep breath, glad that the tears have receded for now, but I'm aware there are still more. Lots more.

'Have you told Tom?' she asks.

'I can't. He's in court. And it's that big case. This is just… this just couldn't be a worse time.'

'I don't think anyone schedules in a convenient time to get… you know… ' She can't say the word.

'I'll have to tell him later. I can't leave a voice message.'

I tell her what happened at the clinic and the biopsy and that I won't have any conclusive results for a week. I'm still doing that post-crying inadvertent hiccupy thing the kids used to do when they were little.

'So you don't know for sure, it's… you know…?'

Oh wow. She really *can't* say the word.

'The radiographer looked super experienced to me. She wouldn't tell me it was… you know… cancer… if it wasn't.'

'But she could be wrong?'

'Theoretically, yes.'

'OK, so there's no need to panic for a week.'

She's diarising her panic. Or rather, my panic. She's telling me to pull myself together. And maybe she's right? Because what good's panicking going to do either of us, anyway?

I let out another hiccupy thing and put my hand on my chest. My waterworks have left me feeling flooded, like you do when you've done a roly-poly in a pool and the water has gone up your nose.

She smiles at me, but her face has a look on it that I've never seen before – sort of abject pity. I try and ignore it. 'Lorna, please don't tell anyone. Not yet.'

'OK.' She nods, then her phone pings and she pulls it out of her pocket.

'Where's Moira anyway?' I ask, trying to keep her attention.

'Oh… er,' she says, distracted. 'I meant to tell you. She's not coming in. She's… er… it's… um… she's having a holiday,' Lorna says, looking at her phone and moving towards the door. 'I said it would be fine.'

'A *holiday*?'

'She got the chance to go on a cruise.'

This is certainly big news. Moira has hardly been away for a day from Wishwells for as long as I can remember.

'It just came up suddenly,' Lorna says, holding the kitchen door open for me to follow, but I'm still confused. Moira would have texted me, or told me something so exciting.

'How long will she be gone for?'

'I don't know – a month maybe?' Lorna says. 'It's fine though, right? We don't need her.'

That's not the point. *I* need her.

7

The whole atmosphere of Wishwells feels different now without Moira. Maybe I'm being paranoid, but I sense that there's something unspoken in the air… not just my cancer news. I suspect that something serious happened this morning with Miles, but Lorna won't discuss it.

Instead, she busies herself with arrangements for the Birmingham trade fair at the end of the month – even though that's usually my department. She's suddenly treating me like I'm fragile – like one of our teapots that might smash into a million pieces.

I wish I'd never said anything now. I wish I'd kept everything that happened this morning a secret.

Becca, however, is oblivious to how Lorna is treating me. She's Lorna's mini-me and is achingly trendy with a nose ring and half-shaved head. She openly marvels about the success of the latest online footage of Jackson chewing a sock and Lorna laughs indulgently over her shoulder, as they stare at the screen. I can't share their enthusiasm. In fact, the whole vacuousness of it makes me want to scream, when the word 'cancer' is pulsing through every single thought.

I retreat downstairs to the shop, but Ruby is still sulking. She seems to be nervous of me and it's not until I've gone over the road to Jennifer's café and brought back a mochaccino for each of us that I finally get to the bottom of what's going on.

'I do understand the company policy,' she says, like this is something she's given a lot of thought to. Her dark hair is piled up in a scrunchie on the top of her head and even though her pale skin is caked in foundation, she looks very young.

'Company policy? What are you talking about?'

'I overspent at Christmas and it's not payday for ages and I haven't got enough for the rent.' She looks close to tears. 'I asked for a sub.'

'Well, that's fine, surely?' I say, confused. I've never had a problem subbing the girls on their salaries before. I know how tough things are for everyone in January. And anyway, Ruby worked her socks off over Christmas. It's the least we can do to help her out.

'Lorna said no,' Ruby said.

'Er, Ruby… I hope you're not worrying Keira with your problems.' We both turn to see Pierre, Lorna's husband, by the till like he owns the place. He's obviously crept in through the back door. Jackson is tucked under the arm of his designer leather jacket.

Ruby goes bright red and I beckon Pierre back into the corridor, away from the shop. I instinctively put out my hand to pet Jackson's head, but the small dog lets out a low warning growl. Its brown bulbous eyes glare at me.

I want to challenge Pierre about interfering with my conversation with Ruby, but instead, he crouches down and lets Jackson go, with an '*Allez, allez*. Go find *Maman*,' and affectionately watches as the small dog snuffles up the back stairs to Lorna.

Pierre is tall, with black, coiffed hair that makes him look like a hairdresser's model. There's something a bit aloof and superior about him that means I'm never quite myself around him. He's not 'tribe' as Joss would put it. Or maybe it's just that he's French.

'Oh Keira, I heard your news,' he says, his thick eyebrows ruffling together, his face contorting into what he obviously thinks is a sympathetic look. The way he says it makes it sound like I've been shouting it from the rooftops, and I'm instantly cross that Lorna has broken her promise so soon.

There's a beat. He's obviously waiting for my reaction. I glance towards the shop to make sure Ruby hasn't heard.

'It's, um… actually… I'd rather not discuss it.'

'Well, I'm here for you,' he says, earnestly, squeezing my arm. I feel the urge to shake him off. 'Whatever you need. Anything at all.'

'Um… thank you,' I say, awkwardly. And this *is* awkward. I don't need anything from Pierre, only for him to mind his own bloody business.

'Do you know why Lorna refused to sub Ruby?' I ask, desperate to change the subject.

'Well, actually, *I* said no,' he says, then picking up on my look continues, 'we discussed this, didn't we? We agreed that I could streamline the finances.'

Did we? I remember the hurried conversation I had in the shop with Lorna just before Christmas and, with a jolt, remember that I did sort of agree to Pierre looking at the books, but *this*… this just feels too much. I've always liked to think of Wishwells as an extension of my family. And family help each other out, right?

'It's just about putting in a level of professionalism, Keira. That's all. I appreciate your soft style of management, but it's not healthy. Certainly not for the balance sheet. We're trying to grow a business here.'

I swallow down this barbed criticism and my shock at his casual use of 'we'.

'You know,' he says, looking directly down at me, but I find his eye contact very intimidating. 'I don't want you to be offended by this, but you look very tired and stressed. Why don't you go home early today? Nobody is going to mind if you need to take some time for yourself.'

8

I'm waiting for Tom in the hallway, almost the second he's through the door. I texted him to tell him to come home directly from the court rather than go back to Bryant and Woodruff, the solicitor's office where he works. It's important, I typed. I have to tell you IN PERSON. In capitals.

This is dramatic stuff and he knows it. And New Year wasn't supposed to be dramatic. This was supposed to be a batten down the hatches kind of a month, a month of healthy resolutions after the anarchic drinking and rich food blow-outs of December. Not to mention New Year and the colossal hangover we both had.

He also knows that I've never been able to keep a secret from him for more than a nano-second. He looks knackered as he chucks his keys on the hall table. He's working pro bono on a hideous trial involving a corrupt builder and it's all rather nasty. Today was the first hearing and I can tell from his demeanour that it didn't go well.

'Tell me,' he says. He has his game face on. *Lay it on me*, it says. *I can handle anything.*

This is my husband, my rock, my lover. The thought of what I'm about to say and how much it'll upset him seems so much that, for a second, I consider lying to him. I could tell him I've been banned from driving, perhaps, or that the business is folding. Both seem less dramatic.

The kids are in the kitchen. I can hear Tilly goading Jacob and Bea, egging them on. There'll be a fight in a minute. These moments are precious.

I'm dying to tell him about how awful it was with Pierre, but I can't tell him just how horrible today has been until he knows the facts.

'You know I told you I had to go back to the breast clinic?' He nods, his brow furrowing. 'You said it wasn't a big thing…'

'I didn't think it was, but…'

He pulls me into his arms. His bag slips down his arm and thuds to the painted floorboards. 'Oh baby,' he says. 'Come here.'

I bury my face in that patch of his chest that belongs just to me and for the first time all day, I feel some of the tension leave, but at the same time, telling him has made it even more real.

I recap, in a hushed whisper, what happened at the clinic.

'*It's cancer then?*' he says, his eyes wide. He looks terrified and this in itself makes me more scared than I've been all day.

'I'll know for sure in a week.'

'A week?' his voice says it all. Right now, that feels like a year.

'Please don't say anything to the kids. We can't say anything yet.'

He nods and I gulp back tears. How on earth am I ever going to tell them that I've got cancer? Tilly has watched *The Fault in Our Stars* – her generation's cancer equivalent to *Love Story*, about a hundred times. She'll go off the deep end.

'I love you,' he says, looking at me. 'Whatever happens, we'll face it together, OK? I've got you.' He leans down and kisses me.

'Gross. Get a room, you two.' It's Jacob behind us.

We pull apart, sharing a desperate look.

'Don't need a room, we've got a whole house, thank you,' I say, going past him to the kitchen, whilst Tom and our son do that shadow-boxing hello thing they do.

There's been a few articles I've spotted in the weekend supplements recently about the dubious moral nature of lying to your children. Personally, I think this is bollocks. I've been lying to them since they were born. About Father Christmas, the Tooth Fairy and then later… about how many people I've had sex with and various other bad behaviour from my youth. So lying now should be easy, except that it's not.

I already feel like a helium balloon floating away from them as we sit at the table, eating the casserole I've defrosted. I look down at myself with my precious tribe, seeing myself in the middle, like in a family portrait.

Beside me is Tilly, our brilliant kamikaze 16-year-old – all braces and bravado, full of nuggets of 'wisdom' from Snapchat and YouTube, but about to blossom. Jacob, my ray-of-sunshine boy, his foppish hair squashed down from where it's been under his baseball cap. And smiling at Tom, as he pours water into her glass, is my baby Bea, with her heart of gold and frizzy blonde curls, intent on saving the world even though she's only nine.

Pooch puts his chin on my lap under the table. He knows something is up. I look down at his doleful brown eyes and stroke his floppy salt-and-pepper ears.

What if I've taken all this for granted? My kids, my home, my happy family and now it's all going to be ripped away from me? Or worse, me away from them? Because that's closer to the truth, isn't it? It's me who could be gone. Just suddenly edited out of the family photo like in *Back to the Future*.

They don't notice I'm quiet over dinner – the kids are too busy bickering and then there's a tussle when I suggest they clear the table. Then Bea drops the green plate on the floor and it smashes.

There's a deathly hush.

The kids know that plate – the last of the dinner service I made for my final ceramics degree project – is of particular sentimental value and we all stare at it on the floor and then Bea looks up at me with frightened eyes.

'I'm sorry, Mum,' she says.

I nod, holding back a pent-up wail as I stoop down to pick up the three pieces of cracked china.

'That's the end of that, then,' I say, but my voice is no more than a whisper.

9

The kids scarper after that so Tom and I clear up the kitchen. I try and explain how Lorna treated me when I told her my news and how I felt her pity as a kind of diss, but I can tell he doesn't really get it.

'And Moira not being there is just bloody weird. I mean, why didn't she tell me she was going away?' I ask, shutting the dishwasher with unnecessary force.

'She told Lorna,' Tom says, reasonably. 'And anyway, you've been telling her to go on a holiday for years. You can't be pissed off now that she has.'

'I guess.'

'And Pierre is just trying to help, I'm sure. Listen to me,' Tom says, folding me into an embrace. 'You have other things to worry about. I don't want you getting stressed out at work, OK?' he says, pressing his face into my hair.

'OK,' I relent, glad to be in his embrace.

'Let's go to bed,' he whispers in my ear.

It's not that normal anymore for us to have a shag on a Tuesday, but upstairs in our room, Tom and I fall on each other and kiss with a defiant intensity. I guess we both need to feel alive and solid and 'us', but in the middle of it, we both start crying. I sit astride my husband, the duvet pulled up over my head so that it's like we're camping.

'I'm sorry,' he says.

'Don't,' I whisper.

'I can't believe it.'

'Neither can I.'

He cups his hand around my left breast. 'Is it sore?'

'Yes.' I look down at the plaster covering where the nurse did the biopsy. I can see a dried bloody stain on it. *Sexy!* 'What if I have to have it off?' I say, cupping my boob. 'What if they both have to go?'

As I stare down, this thought completely freaks me out. Tom loves my breasts. He looks stricken too.

'Let's not deal with the what ifs, let's just deal with the facts, OK?'

I nod and he sits up and I hold his face against my chest. I feel the dampness of what I think are his tears as I hold his head.

Eventually, he falls asleep – well, I think he's asleep, but I lie wide awake, staring at the bedroom ceiling, suddenly feeling totally lost, like I'm adrift in space.

My mind is a pinball machine, firing thoughts that ricochet around my skull. *I'm going to die. Maybe within the fortnight.* My tight chest is clearly an indicator of lung cancer too. I should never have had that cigarette with Joss and Scout at New Year.

Jesus, I've got so much to sort out before I die! I can't die and leave the utility room in its current state. And my cupboards, and my drawers… and I'll have to defrost the freezer. And I'll have to find my teenage diaries in the loft and burn them before anyone finds them.

And I'll have to write goodbye letters to the kids. Try and

give Jacob advice that he'll need in a couple of years, about respecting women and not becoming addicted to internet porn. And little Bea. She won't even remember me when she's a grown-up. I'll have to go to Boots and print out all the photos on my phone. Why didn't I do yearly photo albums, like I meant to? Why didn't I make the time? And what about going to Australia to see Billy and his kids? What if that always-talked-about trip never happens. What if I never get to see my baby brother again?

And my beautiful Tilly. My teenager, who needs me more now than ever. Who will be there for her when she has her heart broken for the first time? Who will fuss over her on her wedding day?

I'm properly welling up now. I take in a raggedy breath and blow it out slowly. Hot tears slide down my face.

I try and pull myself together, but the pinball machine blasts up again, firing out more horrible thoughts.

The fear of an operation. Any operation. Especially one that will take away a part of my body. What if I'm hideously scarred? What if I can never walk around naked again? Never take a bath with Bea? Never make love naked again? *That might just have been the last time*, I think, as the panic makes it impossible to breathe. And I'll never wear that lovely green ball dress with the plunging neckline again (not that I can do up the zip). It feels like proper grief.

For the first time in ten years, I feel like getting up and grabbing a bottle of whisky and going to find the packet of Marlboro Lights which I think are hidden in the toby jug Tom inherited from Great Uncle Jim on the top shelf in the garage. I'm tempted but then the fear of Pooch waking up and barking, and the fact that it's freezing in the garage, deters me. And what am I even thinking of anyway? Smoking and drinking? I need the opposite. I need to be healthy. I need to be well.

And then I see her, the punk runner with her Cheshire cat grin. And I wonder why she was finding the running so hard, but also why she was doing it anyway? And why did she wish me good luck?

I can't get her face out of my mind.

10

I've never been so relieved to see the dawn. With unusual calm, I make potato waffles and fried eggs for the kids and get them off to school. I walk in with Bea and stand by the other year five parents feeling like a fraud. Everyone chats just the same as usual, treats me just the same, but *can't they see the neon arrow pointing down at my head?*

I phone Wishwells and tell Becca that I'm going to be late. I feel too wobbly to face them all right now. I have a bath, although the nurse at the clinic told me that I can't get my boob plaster wet, so it's a bit tricky. Annoyed that I can't lie down, I get out and stare at my body in the mirror.

Generally speaking, I've always felt fairly body confident. Well, bits of it – my tummy mainly – I've had issues with over the years. And yes, I'll admit that quite often I've stood on the scales and made a solemn vow to go on a diet (a vow I usually break within the hour), but naked, I've felt fine. And of late, although I'm a little heavier than I once was, my body confidence is at an all-time high. I'm curvy and womanly. My breasts are perky and shapely, despite breast-feeding three babies. I have toned-ish thighs (from the front) and a big, peachy bum. OK, so a bit bumpy from the side, but I'm a good shape. I'm in proportion for me. And getting away with it (I thought) considering I really don't have an exercise regime apart from walking Pooch, although that hardly counts as exercise as he's so slow these days.

But now my body has gone and grown cancer, all by itself. *On my watch*.

It feels like a gross betrayal.

And sort of unbelievable, too. I mean, surely, if I had cancer I'd feel ill? Or I'd have been able to feel something? Seen something? How can I *not have noticed* cancer?

I take Pooch out for our usual slow amble around the park to try and clear my head. It's doing that fine January mist rain thing that gets you soaked through, and it's chilly. Pooch looks at me resentfully. He is, after all, over ten, which is pretty old for a cocker spaniel, and he'd much rather be in his basket in the warm patch in the kitchen listening to *Woman's Hour*. However, the weather suits my mood and I drag him up the path. I put the hood of my ancient parka up and call Scout.

'Hang on.' She's milking a goat, she explains. 'What's up, mucker?'

With squirting noises in the background, I tearfully tell her my news.

'It'll be nothing,' she says. 'I know loads of people who've had it. At worst, it'll most likely be a lumpectomy, followed by some radiotherapy. Bit un-comfy, according to my pal, but then job done. She's just done an iron man... or was it "woman", which it should be if it's not, because otherwise, it's a bit sexist, don't you think?'

I hear the milk sloshing around in the bucket. 'There you go, old girl,' she says – to the goat, not to me.

Her much-needed perspective instantly starts dissolving some of the worries that kept me awake last night.

'The thing is,' I say, 'and I hate to admit it, but it's just…'

'What? Come on. Out with it.'

'Oh, Scouty… I just can't *bear* it that I'm ill.'

This is why we are best friends – so that I can voice these vain, unpleasant thoughts without judgement. It feels so good to exorcise the night gremlins, holding them up to be zapped by my friend's wisdom.

'Everyone gets ill at some point. You've had a good run so far.'

She's right. I do need to get over myself. Life throws curve-balls at everyone and as I talk Scout through what I've been told at the clinic, the whole thing turns from being something terrifying into something practical.

'But I feel so labelled. So *judged*,' I tell her, glad to get it all off my chest.

'Judged how?'

'I don't know. It's just people look at you differently when you're ill.'

'Do they? I'm not judging, sweetheart. You're still you,' she says, which makes my eyes well up with tears.

But as I ring off, I realise that I don't want to be one of those people – either the judger or the judged. Because I know I'm guilty of it myself. I've always been a bit judgey around people being ill, moaning when Ruby takes days off work for period pain, secretly judging Rob, Mum's partner, and concluding that he puts on his sciatica just to make my mother scurry around him more. In fact, come to think of it, I'm deeply intolerant. And that's just over little things.

Cancer is a whole other level. Don't get me wrong – I'm not uncharitable (I donate to appeals on the TV all the time and Tom has a direct debit to Oxfam), but I hate to admit that I've crossed the road before to avoid people shaking buckets to collect for cancer charities. Like that's *other people's* business. Or, and this is the really weird thing – and probably the first time I've ever actually admitted it, even to myself – like if I don't cross the road and engage with them, and I don't say the word, like Lorna couldn't, then it might just be something that never affects me.

Oh!

Oh… I see what this is…

This is the universe biting me on the bum.

I'm brooding on this epiphany as I head back to the car. In the distance, I can see someone jogging on the far path, but they are too far away to see clearly. I feel my heart leap with anticipation. Could it be my punk runner? For a second, I'm almost tempted to start running myself, just to see.

But the fear of what I'd say stops me. She probably wouldn't even remember me, right? Why would she? I don't know why I'd even want to approach her. What do I want to say? Why is she on my mind?

I want to tell her that her determination was kind of inspiring, I guess. And to ask her if what I already suspect is true: that the reason she knew about the shitty coffee was because she's somehow been affected by cancer herself, or knows someone who has.

I was supposed to be getting fit, wasn't I? Well, *that* plan has certainly gone out of the window now. That my vague resolution has been crossed off my list – through no fault of my own – irks me. I feel suddenly like I'm in a crazy maze where doors keep locking – where choices that I'd taken for granted are now rapidly shutting down ahead of me.

I blip open the boot, and let Pooch jump up onto his muddy cushion. When I close it, a flyer falls from the back windscreen wiper to the ground and I pick it up. It's about the upcoming charity 10K race in April and how I should JOIN IN AND MAKE SOME MONEY FOR GOOD CAUSES. I feel a spark of anger, knowing that *I'm* the charity case now.

And then I feel a genuine shudder of terror. Where on earth will I be by April? Will I even *be* here? I turn the radio to Heart FM and crank up Madonna to drown out the fear.

11

In the café over the road from Wishwells, Jennifer shakes extra chocolate on my cappuccino and slides it across the counter.

'On the house,' she says.

'Don't be silly,' I tell her. 'Everyone's feeling the pinch in January.'

I hand over a fiver and then put my change in the tips pot and Jennifer smiles gratefully. She's wearing a denim apron with embroidered flowers on it and has rosy cheeks. Like the other shopkeepers on our patch of the high street, it feels right to support each other and I really value her friendship.

'You had a visit from the council yet about the redevelopment?' she asks.

'What redevelopment?' I ask, but at that moment, my phone rings and I see that it's Joss. I have to hold up my finger to Jennifer to tell her that the conversation will be continued and apologetically back out of the café.

'What the fuck, K? I mean, fucking, fucking, *fucking hell*!' Joss launches forth.

Scout must have told her and I feel a bit miffed that I've been gossiped about already. I don't blame Scout, though. We've never been good at keeping news to ourselves between the three of us.

'It's not fair. This shouldn't be happening to you. Not to you of all people.'

Joss is usually so buoyant and kick-ass, it breaks my heart to hear her so upset on account of me. I haven't heard her cry for years.

'No person deserves cancer more than another,' I tell her, remembering what it said in the leaflets the nurse at the hospital gave me. 'I mean, if it's one in eight that get breast cancer, then look at it this way: I've taken one for the team. You're all in the clear.'

She laughs through her tears. 'Jesus, you're being so brave. I knew you'd be brave about it. I'd be a jibbering wreck by now.'

'I'm working up to that,' I say. 'I'm sure I'll have my moments.'

I can feel her trying to stem her tears. 'Sorry, it's just that I'm in shock.'

'I know,' I say, sympathetically. *She's* in shock, just like Lorna was. Just like Tom. It's funny, but in a weird way, it helps that it's not just me.

'I'm OK, really. I promise. Try not to worry.'

'OK,' she says, blowing out a breath and composing herself. 'That's my girl. Now then. One important thing...'

'What?'

'If you die, can I wear your Vivienne Westwood dress to the funeral?' she asks, deadpan.

And despite everything, I laugh. One of her most redeeming qualities has always been her ability to go to the dark side.

'Sure, but only if you make everyone sing "Bohemian Rhapsody".'

'All of it?'

'Scaramouch and all.'

I look up at the familiar gold and black signage above the door of Wishwells, push against the door and take a deep breath. Dealing with everyone else's reactions to my cancer news is exhausting. But as the bell above me tinkles and I'm enveloped in the smell of our scented candles, I'm grateful to be back in the familiarity of my shop.

Because in here it's soft and lovely and calm and full of beautiful things that have nothing to do with illness or death. The walls are painted lavender and there are strings of fairy lights illuminating the rough wooden shelves that house the stock. There's all sorts on display: from our signature teapots and mugs, to cashmere throws, to pretty slippers and printed cotton robes we sourced from Delhi.

Portishead are on in the background, which means that 'Keira's Old Skool Playlist' – one of my particular favourites – is being beamed out from the iPad. Ruby is humming along, standing on the small steps dusting the shelves with a big pink feather duster. She looks round at me like a startled rabbit.

'What's all this?' I ask, seeing that the central table has been stacked high with the Jackson merchandise, rather than the sale items as I suggested. Moira would have a fit if she saw this.

'Lorna says we have to sell the things that are most popular online.'

'But I was going to put Lisa's new range of coffee cups out,' I protest.

'They'll have to go at the back,' Ruby says, nodding to a hidden-away shelf in the corner.

Her wide-eyed stare stays on me as I walk through the shop and the skin bristles on the back of my neck.

'I'll make you tea,' she says, jumping down off the steps and rushing towards the back of the shop, so that she can go up to the kitchen.

'I've got coffee already,' I say, holding up my cup.

She nods, panicked that she hasn't noticed. She looks between me and the coffee, her hands wringing the wooden handle of the duster. 'How you doing?'

Oh shit. She knows.

I can't bear the look on her face. She's supposed to be having her appraisal this week, but I can already tell she thinks I'm faulty. Different. Somehow not as capable as I might have been yesterday.

'I'm fine. Honestly.'

'It's just… you know my mum had cancer,' she says, her voice husky. 'She died.'

Died? Jesus. Is that what she thinks is going to happen to me?

I try not to show my shock, but I'm surprised too because despite Ruby's almost constant babble about the details of her life, this important fact – that she's lost her mum because of cancer – has somehow passed me by. Just like those people on the high street with the collection buckets. I've been trying to avoid it all this time, but actually, it's always been here, just a few steps away.

'Oh, Ruby,' I say, hugging her. 'I'm sorry. But look, I mean it… I'm fine, honestly. It's just bad luck and statistics,' I tell her. 'And besides, we don't even know for sure yet that I even *have* cancer.'

She nods, trying to pull herself together. 'I thought you were tough as old boots. That's all.'

'I *am* tough as old boots,' I tell her. 'Now more than ever.'

She nods, but she doesn't look like she believes me.

'Mum's was bowel cancer,' she says, pressing the cuff of her cardie into the corner of her eye and blinking up. 'It took her so fast. She only found out and then two months later... poof! Just like that... she was dead.'

This is a somewhat sobering conversation and one I'm not really equipped to deal with right at this moment. I can see that instinctively, she wants to share her own cancer experience with me as she thinks it might be reassuring, but it's *really not*. And worse, now I have to sympathise about the details of someone else's cancer. But even talking about it feels like it's bringing their cancer closer to me, when what I want is distance... huge distance from awful stories like this. I swallow hard, forcing myself to be the grown-up, to be the boss.

'I'm so sorry. That must have been so painful.'

'I was three. I don't really remember her.'

'Oh. Well, I'm sorry anyway.'

'They say treatment is much better these days,' she says, trying to be reassuring, but she doesn't sound it.

A memory surfaces of the playgroup I used to go to when Tilly was a baby. It was one of those ones where they make you hold a huge silk sheet and sing a silly song whilst the babies dribbled and giggled below it. I absolutely hated it. Every minute. I was envious of the other mothers who seemed to relish being part of this group, but I recoiled from it. I resented the fact that motherhood had been such a grand leveller. I'm not *the same* as you, I wanted to shout. I'm not *the same* just because we happened to have babies at roughly the same time.

But now I'm being labelled again. Only this time, not as a mummy, but as a sick person. And that's *not* all I am. It's *not*. And I want to scream it and shout it out loud. But somehow I already know that I would just be banging against soundproof glass – because everyone else has already *decided* what I am.

'As a matter of interest, how did you know? Did Lorna tell you?'

'No, I saw Becca's post,' Ruby says.

I pick up the iPad by the till, wondering what on earth she could mean. On our Wishwells Instagram account, Becca has mocked up a scene in the shop with lots of our scented candles – all of which have a click-through link. Underneath I read her comment, *calm vibes at work*, followed by a hashtag colleaguewithcancer and some crying emojis.

I can feel my cheeks burn with a new emotion that I can't name. They certainly don't have an emoji for this one.

12

Despite me trying to get a private moment to discuss Becca's post with Lorna, it's not until the end of the day that we are finally alone together on the shop floor.

I wait for the final customer to leave, before locking the door and turning the sign around to 'Closed'. The 'Sale' sign is emblazoned on the window. A street cleaner walks past and peers in the window. I can see Jennifer in her café across the cobbles and remember that I should go back and finish our conversation from this morning, but it's been a relentlessly long, annoying day.

'You OK?' Lorna asks. She's blowing out the scented candles. 'You look a bit... well you must be feeling...' I can tell she's trying to grope for the right word.

'To be honest, I'm fucking furious about Becca's post. Did you know about it?'

Earlier, I made Becca take down the post and she looked genuinely baffled that I was upset, but I didn't give her the chance to argue and I have deliberately ignored her for the rest of the day. She obviously hasn't discussed it with Lorna, though, because Lorna looks surprised.

'I said it was fine. You seem upset?'

'I just can't believe you would think that was OK. It's *my* news. Not anyone else's. And besides, my children follow our

Instagram feed and I haven't even told *them* yet – and now you've announced it to the world.'

'Oh,' Lorna says. 'Sorry, I didn't realise.'

'You didn't ask,' I snap, pointedly.

'Nobody named *you*, though,' she says, defensively. 'And nobody meant any harm. We all just want to help, Keira. You know there are no secrets around here.'

My fury slightly abates. I guess it's an apology of sorts. And she's right, it has always been impossible to keep secrets at Wishwells.

'Well, I made Becca take the post down, but I'd rather you leave any mention of my cancer out of any of the social media feeds in future.'

'Noted,' she says, with a smile, like I'm some kind of crazy person. 'But…' She cocks her head on one side. 'I'm just making an observation, Keira, but *perhaps* you're being a bit oversensitive?'

I let out a gargled, frustrated sigh. She really doesn't get it.

'Well maybe I am, but there's no rule book for how you feel when you get cancer,' I counter. It's on the tip of my tongue to add… *and when you get cancer or something dreadful happens, I'll be sure to come to you for your valuable advice, because you'll obviously deal with it perfectly…*

There's a beat.

'That's it? We're all good?' she asks.

'Well, no, actually, there's Ruby,' I say, forcing my tone to sound more reasonable. 'Why did you refuse to sub her? It's not like we can't afford it.'

I don't tell Lorna that I've lent Ruby money from my personal account. I won't tell Tom either, as I know he'll say it's not

51

ethical and that Ruby should sort her own problems out. Even as I was transferring the money, I knew it was the wrong thing to do, but I feel so sorry for Ruby. Who else has got her back?

But now, Lorna presses her lips together and looks at the floor as if deliberating something. I know her well enough to know something is up and it's bigger than Ruby asking for a sub. She puts her thumb and forefinger to her forehead.

'What? Just tell me what's going on.'

'I wasn't going to say anything and Pierre said I shouldn't, what with everything going on, but I might as well. Now that we're having this conversation...'

I feel an impending sense of dread. Is this why she's been avoiding me? What exactly is this conversation she's steeling herself to have with me?

'The thing is, there's been a mistake,' she starts.

'What mistake?'

'The Jackson phone and iPad cases weren't priced correctly. The mark-up was totally wrong.'

'But we sold hundreds,' I tell her, incredulously, my mind flitting back to November and how I'd signed off the pricing. Or did I? I can't remember properly.

'Yes, and we lost eighty pence on each sale of the phone case and more for the iPad cases.'

I feel my heart thumping and my cheeks go pink.

'If you don't believe me, I'll email you the spreadsheets Pierre corrected,' she says. 'But as far as profitability goes...?' She shrugs and fingers the pile of pink tissue paper next to the till. 'It's a giant fuck-up, if I'm being honest.'

I open my mouth to speak... to defend myself... to at least question her about how we could have got this so wrong – how

I could have – as she clearly thinks this is my fault, but instead I just feel my chest tighten and my eyes fill with tears.

'You should have told me,' I say, fighting back the tears… furious that I've reacted like this. It's business after all. I sort this stuff out *all the time*. Why am I being so wet?

'I didn't want to say anything. You've got enough on your plate. And anyway, it's not like we can go back and change it. It's done now.' She pauses and I see her biting her lips together again.

'What else?' I ask her and she sighs.

'We need to talk about Miles.'

'Miles? What's he got to do with it?'

'Well, he didn't spot it and Pierre did. And, since we now really need to streamline and cut our overheads, I think it makes sense to replace Miles and make Pierre Finance Director.'

'But—'

'We can't afford any more mistakes, Keira. And Miles is old. He's dead wood. Surely you can see that?'

Dead wood? That's surely Pierre talking, not Lorna?

'But he's been with Wishwells—'

'I know and I know the whole nostalgia thing you've got, but the thing is… we need to move forward, Keira. Not stay locked in the past. And anyway, we've discussed it and Miles has agreed to think about stepping down.'

'*What?*'

'He understood our position, once Pierre and I had explained.'

'You've talked to him?'

'Yes, at the meeting this morning.' She can see from my face that I'm outraged that they've had such a momentous discussion without me and she hurries on. 'If you'd texted me, I would have waited for you, but I'm afraid the moment was right and I just went ahead and dealt with it.'

Lorna goes upstairs and I wipe the tears from my eyes. Had she seen? I hope not. I feel ashamed. Not because of what she thinks I might have done, but because of how I've reacted. Jesus Christ! What the hell is going on? I feel like I'm falling apart.

I cash up the till on autopilot, still trying to make sense of what Lorna has just told me.

'Fucking Jackson,' I mutter, but I can already foresee the knock-on consequences and how this latest blow means the pressure is on. *On me*, that is. Right when I have just about the least brain space available. Right when I feel like I'm such a ticking time bomb, I'm like the crocodile in *Peter Pan* that has swallowed the clock.

Poor Miles. I picture his sweet old face and take out my phone, knowing I must call him, but instead I stare at the back screen picture of my kids, lost for words.

A long time ago, when we were students, our mate Zippo, Tom and I (after nearly an entire demijohn of particularly noxious home-brew, which may – I later found out – *may* have contained some magic mushrooms) experienced some big picture realisations that seemed utterly epic at the time. It was like we were tiny amoeba floating in the universe and nothing earthly actually mattered at all. It was a complete change in perspective – like looking behind the façade and seeing the scenery holding everything up.

Suddenly, standing in my shop, this feels similar. Like this whole cancer diagnosis is making me see things with new eyes.

Because the shop, Lorna, Miles… none of it is that important in the scheme of things. Not really. My brain suddenly feels like a train timetable board on a huge concourse, where all my petty worries are rattling around to CANCELLED. Because all that actually matters is that I get better and that I live to see my children grow up.

13

For the rest of the week, I make a big effort to stay professional. I don't want to be accused of being 'oversensitive' again and I go out of my way to close down conversations about cancer before they've started – especially from Ruby, who starts looking at me with her head on one side, her eyes squinting with concern. I'm reminded of Derek Zoolander doing the fashion look 'blue steel', but this is more like 'suffocating pity'. I don't say anything because I'm not allowed to make jokes anymore, it seems. The unspoken subtext seems to be that life has dealt me a serious blow and the only response is for me to deal with it seriously.

And, according to everyone else, I've also lost all my physical capabilities, just like that. On Wednesday, Lorna leaps across the office and rips a box from my arms.

'Sit down, sit down,' she says, in a shocked gasp. 'You shouldn't be lifting anything heavy.'

'I'm fine,' I snap, but she shakes her head.

'You've got to take it easy, Keira. Honestly, we really can manage.'

I've always found work to be a sanctuary – a place full of laughter and easy banter, but without Moira everything is different. It's only now that she's gone that I realise how in synch the two of us are, instinctively knowing what needs doing so that the shop runs smoothly and there's no stress. But with Lorna hovering and the results of my biopsy looming, by the end of the week I feel exposed and unsure of myself. Without Moira's unswerving back-up, I start second-guessing decisions that are normally automatic.

It doesn't help that when I look through the spreadsheets, my fuck-up is so glaringly obvious, I'm deeply ashamed that I missed it. Pierre is in all week, sorting out our email system and is charm itself, but his smarminess grates on my nerves.

But even Tom says that it makes good business sense for Pierre to become our FD and to take Miles's place on the board. Then Miles hands in his resignation and there's a separate card for me, wishing me well and telling me that he thinks Pierre is good news for Wishwells. But something about it all rankles.

I ring Scout on Wednesday lunchtime from the car for a bitch. It's the only place I can get any privacy.

'Have you got a minute? I need to vent,' I start, without even saying hello. She listens carefully as I blurt out all my anxiety about Pierre taking over.

'Why is he so keen to be FD of Wishwells,' Scout asks, 'when he was some high-flyer in the city?'

'Exactly!' I say, so relieved she understands. 'He obviously likes working with Lorna, but I can't stand him muscling in.'

'I wonder why he was fired,' she says. 'Do you want me to ask some of my old colleagues?'

I flush, feeling torn. Snooping around on Pierre behind his back feels a bit drastic, but she's right. Why is he hiding in Wishwells, if he's such a hot shot? Maybe I'm just being paranoid, though. I back-track, telling Scout that it doesn't matter. I can't risk Lorna or Pierre finding out that I don't trust them. Because I do trust them. I have to, right?

I try very hard to stay rational as I meet Tom for my appointment at the clinic to discuss the results of my biopsy, but a steadfast kind of denial has set in. After all, I haven't been told *for sure* that I have cancer. What if the radiographer misinterpreted what she was seeing on the scan? What if I don't have cancer at all and I've just made a bloody great big fuss over nothing?

Whilst Tom queues at the Hospi-Coff kiosk, I flick through a very old magazine, but I can't concentrate. I keep looking at all the nurses and doctors carrying clipboards.

Then I notice a door down the corridor open and a good-looking man with sandy-coloured hair coming out with his tie tucked inside his shirt, followed by someone familiar. It's the punk runner! At least I *think* it is.

She's in the process of tying a scarf around her head, but not before I see that she's completely bald. Without make-up, and what I realise now must have been a wig under her cap, her face still looks pale. Her features look shockingly naked without her painted on eyebrows and thick eyeliner. As she's tying the knot behind her head she looks up and catches my shocked double take.

Because I *am* shocked. *Bloody hell! Punk runner has cancer.* As in, isn't in a relationship with someone else who's got it – which is kind of what I assumed when she first revealed that she knew about the clinic – but has actually got it herself right now. Or is actually having treatment in any case.

She looks… well, like a cancer victim looks. Not that I've

ever known any, or not while they were going through treatment at least. She looks really ill – like the people in the adverts on the TV. People whose appearances are a stark reminder of our mortality. People who make us feel... as I feel right now – fear.

Is that what's going to happen to me? Is that what I'm going to look like?

She holds my gaze and then she juts her chin in recognition and I hate myself for being so judgemental. I'm doing *exactly* what I've hated other people doing to me all week. I've slapped the label 'victim' on her, without even thinking.

She breaks away from the doctor in front of her and walks quickly towards me. I get up and meet her.

'It's you,' she says. And there's the Cheshire cat grin.

'But you were running,' I manage. 'I didn't realise you were ill.' Although now, of course, it seems obvious. Her breathing, her exhaustion... everything. That's why she wished me luck. Because she's in the same boat.

'Technically I'm not ill... *anymore* that is,' she said. 'They cut the bastard cancer out. It's just the treatment. It's...' She stops herself, realising that maybe she's saying too much. I raise my eyebrows, willing her to go on, as a couple of nurses squeeze past us. 'It's a *motherfucker*,' she says forcefully and loudly. I laugh, because the way she's said it – with such defiance – is just, well, cool. But I can see she's ruffled the nurses, as one turns and frowns. 'That's why I run. Despite it all. *Because* of it. All I know is that the running helps.'

'Oh,' I say, amazed. 'Well, good for you.'

'I take it you're in here for all the wrong reasons.' She nods at the waiting room I've just come from.

I blush, adamant denial still rising. 'I'm not sure yet.'

'Well, my advice? Keep yourself healthy.'

'I… well… I'm not like you. I can't run. Well, not can't. I mean I don't—' I blunder.

'Anyone can run,' she says with a shrug.

'Tamsin?' It's the doctor behind her calling.

Tamsin. I wouldn't have had her down as a Tamsin.

'Coming.' She turns away, then smiles back at me. 'Sexy Phil. He's the best oncologist. Ask for him if you can.'

I open my mouth. I'm not even sure what an oncologist is. Will I be needing one?

'You should come running,' she says, her deep blue gaze challenging me. 'Meet me by that bench. I'm there most mornings at ten to nine.'

I smile back at her, but shake my head.

'Come on. It'll be good for you. I'll see you there,' she says, grinning at me. Then she turns to go.

14

'Who was *she*?' Tom asks, but I'm saved from explaining by a lady with nice blonde hair tied in a swishy ponytail who appears now and introduces herself and we both stand. She shakes my hand and explains that she's Sam, my breast cancer care nurse.

Unnecessary, I think, the denial really strong now. *I won't be needing you. I don't have cancer.* Because nobody's actually said it for definite yet, have they? It still might not be true.

She's extremely sweet with the nicest manner, which feels entirely natural, rather than something she's trained for. She takes us through to a consulting room where there's a bed and a chair and explains the consultant will see me and she'll give me a few moments to get undressed to my waist.

Tom sits down on the chair in the corner while I disrobe. I'm tempted to sing 'Patricia the Stripper'… *and with a lick of her lips, she started to strip, to tremendous applause, she took off her drawers…* but this might just be the un-sexiest striptease of all time. Tom doesn't look like he's in the mood for levity. He holds my coat, then my jacket, top and bra, but it's weird, like he's already playing the role of 'caring husband'.

I lie down on the table and it creaks disconcertingly. Sam comes back in and puts a scratchy piece of green paper over my chest.

The doctor comes in, but I don't catch his name. He's small with a nut-brown shiny crown with an edging of grey hair and a bushy grey moustache. He's rotund, his belly accentuated by the stripy shirt he's wearing. He seems very serious. The kind of man you imagine you might give a cup of tea to at a wedding rather than a glass of champagne.

There suddenly seems a lot of us in the room and something about it all makes me feel very self-conscious. I have to suppress the urge to giggle nervously.

He feels my breast, like he's testing bread to check it doesn't require more kneading, and says 'Hmmm' in a way that suggests everything beneath his fingers is confirming his very worst suspicions.

He goes just as fast as he came and Sam tells me to get up. Tom hands me my bra and top and I try and make conversation about the weather, but it feels all wrong.

Next door in the consulting room, the chair layout is all wrong, too. It's a narrow room with the desk wedged in a corner. A large computer monitor is on it showing the picture from the mammogram taken the other day. There she is: my orb planet.

Tom sits alongside me – slightly behind me and takes out a notebook and a pencil. We've agreed he's going to take notes, like he might in a courtroom. Like we then might be able to argue the facts round to a mutually beneficial conclusion for everyone involved. Sam sits by the door next to a sanitary bin.

The consultant opens a brown folder in front of him. I can see a scan picture paperclipped to the edge. He starts talking in hushed tones, in the kind of voice you'd expect a commentator to use when describing a sporting legend gearing up to take a shot: *and so much is resting on this. She steadies herself and...*

'The results have come in. I'm afraid you have grade two lobular breast cancer.'

Oh and she misses! The crowd gasps.

I haven't a clue what he means.

He explains that it's in my lobes, rather than ducts. *Lobes? Ducts?* Who knew I had either? And it's in several places and has grown to five centimetres. How did it get to be five? That's as long as my sodding finger! Why didn't I see it poking out?

So as far as treatment is concerned, it's not a lumpectomy, but a mastectomy. The whole lot has got to go.

He means my left breast.

I'm extremely calm and together. I'm glad my eyes are not in Tom's line of sight as I'm able to focus on the doctor. What does a mastectomy involve? Tom asks.

The doctor takes a piece of paper from the drawer of his desk, looks at the type on it, then turns it over to the blank side. He clicks a biro and then draws a massive breast with a nipple. Then he draws a line across it and says that they slit the breast from side to side. Hang on...

Slit?

Then they remove the tissue.

'What about my nipple?' I try not to sound as horrified as I feel. Surely I can keep it? After all, my nipple is not an insignificant factor. In fact, I'd say it was fairly major to me. The personality of my breast. Irreplaceable. One of a pair.

'We remove that too.'

Remove. Like a wardrobe you're taking to the dump.

He goes on to explain that the nipple depends on the

network of blood supply from the skin. When the skin is cut, the blood supply goes.

'You could keep your nipple, but there's a high chance it might wither and die,' he says, with a shake of his head.

Wither and die? Jesus!

We quickly move on to reconstruction which can be done at the time of my cancer-removing op, but there's some very confusing back and forthing between him and Sam about where this would take place and who would do it. Tom furiously scribbles in his notes. I don't think he's looked me in the eye since we came in.

I can have an implant at the same time, the consultant tells me, but in 25 per cent of cases radiotherapy makes the tissues around the implant go hard. What happens then, I ask? He says they go in and sort of chop up the implant.

Chop up...?

Or I can have reconstruction using my own fat cells. *Fat cells?* But that involves slitting open my stomach. *Again with the slitting.* He gestures right across his own gut, then mimes pulling out the fat cells out and putting them on his chest. 'So that roll would become a breast.' He points at my stomach and I clutch my hands over myself protectively.

Roll? Who said anything about a roll? He can't call my stomach a roll.

'Some women see it as a bonus tummy tuck,' Sam says brightly, trying to put a positive spin on it. I turn and face her in horror.

'But sometimes radiotherapy can, well, sort of zap the healthy cells,' the consultant says in a cautionary tone.

But that's not all. I'll need chemotherapy. I'm in a grey area, but it's probably recommended. Eighteen weeks' worth. Six sessions. Then a couple of weeks off, then radiotherapy. Daily zapping. Bish. Bash. Bosh. After that, hopefully, I'll be cured.

Hopefully.

I stare at the folder on his desk. The one with the scans in it.

'And you're positive,' I ask. 'As in 100 per cent positive?' I look from the folder to my chest and back again. 'There's no way that scan be wrong.'

'I'm afraid not,' he tells me, with a sad, slow shake of his head.

And then the appointment is over.

15

Tilly has just turned 16 and, despite spending many, many hours taking selfies and perfecting her eyebrows like she's a contender for *Love Island*, she's still a kid at heart. She comes bouncing down the stairs in a tiger onesie when we come in.

Tom and I have agreed in the car on the way home that we might as well tell the kids. There's no way we can pretend that nothing is up after what we've just been told. We need to somehow take it on. To 'own it', Tom said ironically – that awful phrase, like 'nailed it' and 'smashed it' that the kids use. But I know what he means. We need to take charge of what's going on. Even if the truth is that the decisions we're making are because we've got no other choice.

'Can we have a word?' Tom says, and she slows down and then hangs on to the bannister, her eyes narrowing suspiciously. Tom's never usually around in the day.

'Sure. What's up?'

'In here,' Tom says, gesturing towards the lounge.

On the rug between the TV and the sofa, she stands with her hands on her hips, looking between me and Tom. Her cheeks are starting to flush.

'We have some news,' he says.

'It's not about college is it?' she says, preparing for the

worst. 'Because if they've been in touch about attendance, I have been there—'

'No,' Tom cuts her off. 'It's about Mum.'

There's a pause, as she computes this. Me being in any other role than chef, chauffer and cashpoint to her is clearly confusing.

'We've just come from the clinic,' Tom continues.

'Oh my god,' she says slowly, her eyes wide and her mouth dropping open. 'You're not pregnant are you?'

A snort of laughter erupts from my nose.

'No. No, it's not that, darling,' Tom says, looking at me, laughing too, but he also looks like he wants to cry.

'Oh, thank goodness for that,' she says. 'You had me worried there.'

Clearly relieved, she crosses her arms and stares expectantly at me, wondering what it could be. And in that moment, I realise how totally unprepared she is for something shocking to enter her charmed, blissfully cosseted life. And it's this realisation that makes my laughter evaporate into thin air. I swallow hard. I'm determined to be strong, but this is, hands-down, the hardest thing I've ever had to say.

'I've just come from the *breast* clinic,' I explain.

'Eh?'

I look at Tom and he takes over. His eyes don't leave mine as he speaks. 'Mum had a mammogram and there's some unusual tissue.'

'A what?' Tilly asks.

'Where they X-ray your breasts,' Tom tries again. 'And they found… well it's complicated and it's going to be completely fine, but…'

'I've got breast cancer,' I finish for him.

Ker-paw! The C-bomb detonates.

'Cancer?' she gasps. 'Cancer?'

'Come here,' I say, folding her in a hug. 'It's just going to be a bit shit for a while, then I'll be fine.'

'Will it? Do you promise?'

'Yes.' I swallow.

Because, please God, it will be fine, right? It *has* to be. I'm not leaving her. I won't. I can't.

Her chin wobbles and she nods, but her hands shake as she sits down on the sofa. 'Oh my god,' she whispers. This is not one of her comedy Oh My Gods. She's utterly rocked to her core.

Tom and I sit either side of her and hug her together, squeezing her between us, like we did when she was a baby. Tom says soothing things about how strong I am, and how we'll get through this as a family. But all too soon, she breaks away.

The blue light on her phone is going off in her tiger pocket. Her hand clamps around it. I know that she's going to text her friends, like I've passed on a live grenade and she has to off-load it. But it's not just that. It's something more, as she backs away. I can see it in her eyes, even though she won't look at me anymore. It's like a blind being drawn, a door being closed, a lock being turned. On me.

16

It's impossible to find a moment to tell Jacob and I'm aware that the clock is ticking. It's only a matter of time before he finds out from Tilly and I want to be the one to tell him 'the news'.

Because the news is already out, the ripples spreading. Tom has had to go back to the office, having taken most of the day off, but I know he must have found time to contact Zippo, because my phone dings with a text:

Rubbish news. Have always loved your knockers. Am sending you a book. Love ya. Zippo. xxx

Zippo – real name Alex – is Tom's childhood friend, but my old university pal and the reason we met in the first place. He used to be a big cigarette smoker back in the day (hence his nickname), but in recent years has cleaned up his act, jacked in his marketing job, left his poisonous wife and now teaches tai chi, when he's not building yurts. He's on a very chilled vibe, so whatever book he's sending will probably be some hippy-ish tome about channelling energy. Still, I'll take anything. All help is welcome right now.

I am touched by his message, but I feel annoyed that he knows, although it's understandable that Tom wanted to tell him. It feels even more important that Jacob and Bea know as soon as possible, but Jacob won't stop playing Fortnite with Biffa, his mate. There's a moment, but then the door goes and it's a delivery of a bottle of posh gin from Joss. We've always resorted to gin in times of crisis. I don't have time to call and thank her, though, before it's time to pick up Bea from street dance at the community hall.

On the way, I call Lorna from the car.

'There you are, *at last*. I've been worried,' she says. 'What did they say at your appointment?'

I start to tell her about it, but just as I'm describing my shock at my impending mastectomy, I hear her whispering – probably to Becca, 'Yes, put it like that. No… no… that way… yes.'

I fizzle out, offended that she's not listening. There's a beat, when she realises I've stopped talking.

'The main thing is that you're OK,' she says, failing to grasp that I'm really not OK.

'The treatment sounds quite tough,' I say.

'You'll get through it,' she replies, 'you're strong.'

But am I? I don't feel it.

At school, I'm just about on time for pick-up and from the doorway of the hallway, I stare at Bea collecting her things. She's only small. Not even double digits. She waves at me, flashing her huge, innocent smile, her blonde ponytail swishing and my heart is breaking. Because I keep thinking, *this is the before. The before she knows.*

Because that's how it's going to be for all of them now, isn't it? Not just me. BC and AC. Before cancer and after. That's how the timeline of my precious little family will be seen from now on.

Mum calls when we get back in the car. She's been on holiday with Rob and she's ringing to say that they are in Alicante airport. The flight has been delayed.

I have a ridiculous conversation with her on the speaker phone about Rob trying to buy a ham sandwich and him thinking jamón was two words, 'jam' and 'on' and how that would be horrible with cheese. She thinks Rob's hilarious. I think he's a bit of a twat.

She talks to Bea about a jumper she's currently knitting and how annoying it is that she's had to put her knitting needles in the hold, when she has all this free time to knit. (She takes the security checks and her knitting very personally, outraged that her knitting needles are deemed dangerous weapons.) I feel a pang as I imagine her in the airport lounge. I'm dreading telling her my news.

Bea is full of the dance performance, tuning in her phone on Bluetooth to the car to play me the track she's dancing to. She's excited and I try and smile, but it's a rictus grin, my hands gripping the steering wheel. I feel sick to my core.

17

Eventually, after fish fingers and chips with Biffa and Jacob, I tell Bea when she's having a bath. After the practice run with Tilly, I try and be more straightforward, sticking to the facts. I think I've been as sensitive as I can be, stripping the phrases of the drama they imply, but she bursts into tears.

She gets out of the bath and I wrap her in a towel and sit on the chair in the bathroom, holding her on my lap, as she cries.

'You're not going to die, are you?' she asks. Her voice is small.

'No, don't be ridiculous. Of course I'm not.'

'Will you lose your hair, like they do in the adverts?'

'Probably. But it'll be OK,' I lie.

I remember Tamsin at the clinic. I'll look like that soon. It won't be bald in a cool Sinéad O'Connor singing 'Nothing Compares 2 U' type of bald. It'll be that other kind of bald. The bald that spells illness. The kind that makes people instantly recoil and judge – like I did. *The treatment is a motherfucker.* Tamsin's words echo in my head.

'I'll cut my hair off. You can have mine,' Bea says.

'Oh darling,' I say, squeezing her tight.

She wriggles on my lap, her hand reaching up to scratch behind her ear.

By the time I've combed out the latest batch of nits from Bea's hair and got her to bed, it's late and Jacob's already in bed. I say the words for the third time, but this time, I say it really fast all in one go.

'Oh, so, I had a bit of news today... it's nothing to worry about... but I've got breast cancer. I might have to have surgery and treatment, but it's no big deal. Just thought you should know.'

He stares at me.

'Do you want some fresh water?' I ask, as I do every night, nodding to the glass on his bedside table.

'Sure,' he says and I go to the bathroom and fill up his glass.

When I come back, he leaps out of bed and in two strides he reaches me, surprising me by squeezing me in a tight embrace.

'Oh, Mum, I'm so sorry,' he says.

I'm so touched by his empathy, I almost crumble, but I force myself to be the grown-up, even though tears spring from my eyes. I put down the glass of water and then hold his face and look into his eyes.

'Nothing is going to get me. Certainly not this,' I say and as I do, I know I absolutely believe it. Like the words, 'I'm going to be fine' are a tattoo through me, like the letters through a stick of rock.

'Does this mean I have to be nice to you?' he asks, as he gets back into bed.

'Yes, it bloody well does.'

'Are you going to make me do things? Like clean up my room? Because you've got cancer?'

I laugh and wipe away my tears. 'Most probably.'

'Do the others know?'

I nod. 'Be nice to your sisters, OK? You've all had a shock.'

We chat a bit more and then I tuck him in. I kiss him on the forehead. At the door, I switch off the overhead light.

'Mum?' he says.

'Yes?'

'You do know you are the best, right?'

I nod, swallowing back more tears. 'Thank you. I love you, peanut. Sleep tight.'

Down in the kitchen, Tom is back from work and has poured me a humungous gin from Joss's bottle.

'Well, that was a pretty shitty day,' he says, clinking glasses with me.

'It's up there. Although, we have got three incredible kids, so it's not all bad.'

Spotify is on random, and now Al Green's 'Let's Stay Together' comes on. It was the song we first snogged to in a field when we met at Zippo's 21st birthday party. I remember we'd talked all day and as the night fell and the stars came out, we sat around the fire on hay bales toasting marshmallows on sticks. Zippo had music playing on the stereo of his beaten up Land Rover and when that song came on, Tom pulled me up to dance.

It's always connected me to the younger, healthy, exuberant me, but that girl seems to fade away into the mist as Tom hugs me and then we dance slowly like we did all those years ago.

I don't want things to change. I don't want to be ill. I don't want to be weak and have no hair. The petulant small child in me is screaming: *I don't want it. I don't want it*, whilst throwing my toys out of the cot.

I breathe. Tell myself to be calm as I rest my head on Tom's chest. After all, life constantly evolves. Everything changes. Except that we have changed from new and good – over the years – to wise and flipping amazing with every shade of excellent in between.

This feels like falling off a cliff.

18

The next morning, I wake up resolving that I'll put my trainers on and meet Tamsin in the park before work. There's a part of me that really wants to seek her out, but as soon as I get up, I know it's not going to happen. I sense that my family needs me to be normal, but I'm not sure what that really feels like anymore. I try and make jokes over breakfast, but the kids look at me as if I'm speaking in poor taste. Oh yes, I'd forgotten. The sense of humour thing. Not allowed when you have cancer. Silly me.

We're all late and Tilly has her game face on and she heads off to college. I tell myself it's natural she's being testy, but she doesn't kiss me goodbye. She just leaves and the slammed door makes my heart jolt.

I make some calls before work – to the headmistress of Bea's school and Jacob's teacher to let them know what's going on. Then Sam from the clinic calls to give me the details of my appointment with the surgeon next Tuesday. They seem to be moving very fast for the NHS. But then, my cancer cells are doubling all the time. The race is on, but I'll be operated on by someone different to 'Mr Wither and Die' who examined me. There's been some muddle up with his lists, but I'm relieved there's a new surgeon in the offing.

It occurs to me that, so far, I've met very few female senior staff. Where are all the empathetic lady surgeons and physicians I wonder. Because, for now, I've been assigned another bloke to assess my knockers and she tells me his name: Mr Mabiyan.

I promised Tom I'd steer clear of going online and just listen to the real-life experts, but even as I said it, I'd kept my fingers crossed. Because I feel like I am one giant walking question mark at the moment. Or, when not that, an exclamation mark, living in fear. So any scraps of information I have, feel like food to a starving prisoner.

Of course it would be a lot easier if there was some sort of trusted portal, like TripAdvisor. Where is TitAdvisor when you need it?

I finally find some brief, but official information about Mr Mabiyan. In his photo, he looks reassuringly like a breast. There is definitely a boob-like quality to his round face. I wonder if surgeons grow to look like the body-part they operate on, rather like some people come to look like their dogs. Hmm, maybe a bit unfortunate if you're a dick doctor.

I should get into work, but I feel myself guiltily being drawn to the search bar, hungry for information about the new world I'm entering. Cancer World. Kind of like Disneyland Paris, only with a whole lot less people volunteering to queue up for the rides. I type in 'causes of breast cancer'. Because I have to know. Why has this happened?

More specifically… why has this happened to me?

But what becomes quickly apparent is that *nobody* knows for sure. And that's the biggest shock. Because all this time, I've been living with the assumption that there's a whole strata of much more clever grown-ups out there fixing the world. People I don't come across socially, because they are busy doing the kind of important medical research jobs, the names of which I can't even pronounce. So why haven't they found out what causes cancer? What have the much-more-intelligent people been doing?

But there are, of course, a lot of theories. Gemma from Connecticut on a forum in the US reckons nasty deodorants with aluminium in them definitely cause breast cancer. Lois from Idaho is equally adamant that dairy products are to blame. She cites the fact that Chinese women (who don't slurp lattes like us Westerners) have far less breast cancer.

A man called Dave, who, according to his blog was an agitator at Greenham Common says that the toxic chemicals I was exposed to growing up in Britain in the Seventies and Eighties could well be to blame, whilst Jedi2002 says aliens are to blame, with their random cosmic rays.

And it keeps getting more bizarre. Theodora, who recommends a healing site and has little crystal emojis next to her name, says cancer is an emotional response by the body and it's all to do with grief.

Lord! That had never occurred to me. Has Dad's untimely death caused these cells to mutate? Or has something else been festering for years? Did my break-up with Harvey – my first real love – damage me? But that was nearly thirty years ago. It's been pretty plain sailing since then. I mean, the odd upset, but nothing major. Since meeting Tom, who did, on a profound emotional level, save my life, I've been happy. Ridiculously happy.

So, is this punishment for having it all? A happy marriage, healthy kids, great boobs? Is it some celestial slight for my unthinking arrogant happiness?

Not that I don't count my blessings; I do. And, rising above the pinball machine of fear, I can be magnanimous. If I were to die today, or indeed any time soon, I'd die happy. Not delighted to be leaving everyone I love, of course, but in terms of life, I have hit the jackpot. I have loved and have been loved. I've set up a successful business and been fulfilled in my work. Not many people my age can say that. And I have laughed – a lot. And socialised. And eaten fine food and thoroughly mixed my drinks.

And there we have it. Booze. The only reason I can find that really applies to me is on one of the major well-known sites about the possible causes of breast cancer. There's no family history and, according to the consultant I saw, I don't have the BRCA gene, which is responsible for hereditary cancer. I don't smoke. Well, not anymore. Apart from on special occasions with Joss and Scout. And I'm not obese. Well, a bit overweight, yes, but not terribly so.

But now I'm wondering… have all those after-work pints and Saturday night tequilas finally come home to roost? I can think of a lot of people who drink more than me. Am I really that much worse than everyone else? Is this self-inflicted?

My phone pings. It's Lorna.

Are you coming in?

I close my laptop guiltily and look at the clock. Shit. I'm very late.

19

I'm just parking behind Wishwells, however, when I get a call from the matron's office at Jacob's school. It's a man. The kids call him the Man-tron. He's very sweet. He explains that Jacob has been involved in 'an incident'. I call Becca and ask her to apologise for me, as I turn around and drive back to Jacob's school.

In the Man-tron's office, Jacob is nursing a swollen eye with an ice pack. I sign him out.

'What happened?' I ask, once we're both safely in the car.

'It doesn't matter.'

He looks out of the window at the rain as I drive out of the school gates.

'Tell me,' I say gently, and he sighs.

'They were taking the piss because Biffa told them about you and they all started teasing me and one of them said you were going to die.' There's a hiccup in his voice.

'Who said?'

'That kid Nathan. You know. From year ten.'

'So, you thumped him?'

'Yes.'

'Good,' I say. Because as terrible a person as that makes me, I can't guarantee I wouldn't have done exactly the same thing.

Jacob looks at me. 'You're not cross?'

'No. Fuck him.'

Jacob grins at me swearing, but for once doesn't demand a contribution for the swear box. I stroke his hair. 'Come on, let's go home.'

I smile back, but inside, I want to roar. *I'm Mumma Bear. Nobody messes with my cubs.*

And, no, for the record, Jacob didn't do the right thing. It's not the way Tom and I brought him up. But for today, sticking up for us, defending us, almost makes me want to whoop.

I leave Jacob at home and head for work. It would be nice to grab a coffee from Jennifer's and have five minutes to decompress at work after the day I've had so far, but Lorna and Pierre are in the meeting room upstairs and as soon as I arrive in the office, she waves for me to come in.

'Sorry I'm late,' I say, although it's not like I don't have a good excuse. I know that if Pierre wasn't here, she'd be asking me how I'm holding up, having told the kids my news, but I'm not going to discuss anything personal with her. Not now. She looks at me guiltily. 'What have I missed?' I asked, sensing that I've come in mid-conversation.

'So… there's been a rent increase,' she says, pulling a grimace. She flaps a letter in her hand.

'Has there?' I ask, surprised, taking it. My stomach drops when I see the demand for the following year.

'Yes. As you can see… a complete hike. And it's just about the last thing we need.'

'The thing is,' Pierre cuts in, 'there was an email sent before Christmas offering us the chance to renegotiate, but…' he pauses and glances at Lorna, 'you didn't respond, Keira, so we're now rather over a barrel.'

'I didn't... what?' I ask, trying to compute this accusation. 'What email? I didn't see an email.'

'There was definitely an email,' Lorna says.

I march out of the open door to my desk and my fingers clatter over the keyboard. We've never had passwords, so I'm straight into my email account, but when I search for the landlord's management company, I see that the top email has been marked as read. I open it up.

'I swear I have never seen that before,' I protest, my cheeks flushing. Pierre and Lorna stand behind me. Because I'm really *sure* I haven't read that. Because if I had I'd have been straight on it, wouldn't I? And she should know this.

'You must have just scanned it and forgotten about it,' Pierre says, trying to offer a reasonable explanation on my behalf. 'You've had a lot to process.'

Pierre offers to write to the council, like this is something I'm completely incapable of and Lorna agrees that it's the best solution, like he's some kind of knight in fucking shining armour.

I sit at my desk and stare at the email. *Have* I read it before? I'm pretty sure I haven't, but maybe Pierre's right. Maybe I did just scan it and forget about it. I open my diary and check the date, realising that the night before the email was dated, it had been our office Christmas party, when I'd taken everyone out for a meal at our favourite little pizza place and I'd drunk a skinful of red wine, before leading the way to the karaoke bar. I think back to myself, slurrily draped around Moira at the end of the night, telling her how much I loved her.

It takes everything I have not to cry.

20

Tom and I usually take it in turns to plan meals and shop, but he's had so much on at work, I said I'd do the internet shopping, but feeling so scrutinised by Lorna and Pierre, I don't dare go online. Instead, I have to stop at the garage minimart to get food on the way to get Bea from school.

She comes out of the doors to the playground with a gaggle of year five girls around her, all vying to be the most sympathetic. Her teacher comes and finds me by the gate.

'I'm so sorry to hear your news, Keira,' she says, putting an affectionate hand on my arm. 'It happened to my best friend.'

'Oh. Well,' I say, trying to be chipper. 'It's very common. Is your friend alright now?' I ask.

'No, she died.'

Here we go again. Just like it was with Ruby. What is it with people wanting to share their morbid cancer stories? For fuck's sake. What am I? Some kind of cancer magnet?

'But my uncle,' she hurries on, realising how insensitive she's been, 'he's still going strong... well sort of strong. He was diagnosed with pancreatic cancer five years ago and the doctors wrote him off, but he's still alive, at least.'

'Oh.' I nod and give Bea a hug, as she runs into my arms.

'See, I told you Mum was fine,' the teacher says, touching

Bea's hair. She pulls a face at me. 'She was a bit upset earlier,' she whispers.

Bea looks up at me guiltily.

I put my arm around her to try and lead her away, but Grace, Molly's mum intercepts me. Molly and Bea used to be best friends, but there was a falling-out a little while ago, that I never got to the bottom of.

'Oh, Keira…' Grace says, putting her head on the side. She flips her purply-grey cashmere throw over her shoulder and I'm about to ask her when she got it from, when I see that her eyes are Bambi-wide with pity and, yes, gossip.

Because I can see all the other mums watching. Because that's what I now am. Gossip. News. I can feel my ears go red. I know they've probably been WhatsApping all day about me.

'I'm so, so sorry. We heard about the, you know…' She leans forward and now, in a nasal whisper, like she can't engage her vocal chords with the word, she says, '*ancer*.' Not cancer. 'Ancer. On an inhale. 'If there's anything I can do?'

I almost say, 'Yes, you can fuck off.' Because I don't want help. I don't *need* help.

'We'll help, you know. All of us. Through the chemo.'

'That's really helpful,' I say, summoning up a tight smile. It's the best I can do. I know she's not trying to be bitchy. Quite the reverse. She's not a nasty person. And I can see that she really does care. It's me with the problem. Not her. Why can't I be gracious and grateful? Why is the fact that she's clearly invoking the status of being the mum who is 'closest' to me – the epicentre of the drama – making me feel so angry? 'Thank you,' I manage.

'I mean, I suppose you'll have to change everything now.'

'How do you mean?'

'You know. No booze, no sugar. You can't eat any of that stuff. Cancer loves sugar,' she says, with a tittery laugh, like cancer is a real larker about.

I smile, confused, and lead Bea away to the car, where I dig out the packet of chocolate digestives from the shopping. I eat five.

21

On Thursday, I stay late in the shop, and then back at home, work until midnight on the laptop, contacting all the suppliers about this year's orders, so that on Friday, I can work from home. My anxiety about the rent disaster has only got worse and I haven't slept well. I know I have to get my ducks in a row for the upcoming board meeting, but I'm finding it very difficult to concentrate.

The shop has always been such a happy, friendly place and I've always harboured a sense of inclusivity, but I can't help feeling that there are secrets and resentments brewing. I've caught Lorna telling Becca a few times 'not to bother Keira'. Even Ruby is behaving oddly – like she knows something I don't. Or maybe she doesn't. Maybe this is all in my head and I'm being paranoid.

I call Moira, just to find out when she might be coming back, desperate to hear her familiar voice, but her phone goes straight to voicemail and I don't leave a message. I'm not sure what to say. That work feels dreadful without her?

But then I remind myself that I'm the boss and that would be deeply unprofessional. And anyway, what right have I to drop my work worries, or my personal ones onto her when she's on a well-deserved and long-overdue holiday?

At noon, the front doorbell rings and Pooch barks. It's

Mum, paying an unexpected visit and I inwardly groan. I've been putting off this moment.

'I was passing on the way back from the chiropodists,' she explains, flouncing in, her Per Una trench coat flapping. 'I'm not stopping. Rob's in the car. I'll take a cuppa out to him. He's listening to *Desert Island Discs* on the podcast. It's that cricketer… oh what's his name…?'

I look past her down our front path and beyond the gate to where Rob sits behind the wheel of his red Astra. I give him a wave and he gives a weak wave back. Mum had been a widow for a decade when she met him at the over-sixties singles cinema club that her best friend dragged her along to at the new art house place in town. I don't resent her having another partner after Dad, but I do think she could do better. I suppose anything is better than loneliness, though, and at least it means she has him to boss around first, rather than me.

She pushes past me into the hall and is about to continue, when she stops. 'What's with all the flowers?' she asks. 'Has someone died?'

I look around the living room. There are no less than three 'I'm sorry you've got cancer' bouquets from last week, to add to the other two that have already come this week – from Scout and from Tom's parents. I sound ungrateful and in any other circumstances, the flowers would be lovely, the messages of love and support heart-warming and sweet, but Mum's right – *en masse* they're starting to make the kitchen and living room look like a mausoleum.

And that's just the thing. No one has died. I'm still here. With life rushing every bit as fast and not taking a second off just because I've had bad news. The dog *still* hasn't had his injections, the builder still needs to be rung to book in a time for him to fix the leak in the conservatory roof, the kids clubs still need to be paid for, the washing, the shopping, the school pick-ups, not to mention all my work emails. And now my mother too.

'Er… there's something I've got to tell you. Let's get the kettle on.'

'I knew something was up,' she says.

I want to be sarcastic, like I would have been as a teenager: 'See it in your tea-leaves, did you?' I nearly say, but don't. She has this annoying habit of claiming that she already knew that something was going to happen before it happens. She is Queen of the Retrospective Foregone Conclusion. Billy, my brother, and I have always joked that we'll put 'I told you I was going to die' on her gravestone.

She comes into the kitchen and stands by the counter, scooping some crumbs off the surface with her hand. She still wears the wedding band Dad gave her, even though she's been living with Rob now for a year or more.

I almost tell her to stop it, as she continues tutting, sweeping the crumbs into the bin, but over recent years, Tom has helped me to see that being annoyed by her passive aggressive habits is entirely futile, as I'll never, ever change them. I stick my hands in the back pocket of my jeans.

'So… it seems that I've got a touch of breast cancer,' I say.

I don't know why I put the 'a touch of' in that sentence. I don't know why I'm playing it down. You don't get 'a touch' of cancer. You get a slap.

'Well, I'm not surprised,' she says.

Perhaps she realises she's been a bit harsh from my expression, because she hurries on. 'You burn the candle at both ends. And you work far too hard. Haven't I been saying that the stress is not good for you? It was bound to catch up with you sooner or later.'

Even though I kind of knew this would be her reaction, I still stick my tongue in my cheek and mentally count to five. She has never fully supported me taking over Wishwells when Dad died. She always resented him for spending all his time in the shop and she's never missed an opportunity to point out how alike he and I are.

And now here's her proof because she clearly thinks this is *my fault*. Self-inflicted. Like I've *chosen* to get cancer, because of the way I live my life. And is it? Because she might be right, mightn't she? Because I don't know. I might never know. In fact, all I do know is that other people telling me I'm to blame isn't helping me one little bit.

I almost lose it, but I don't. There's no point in arguing. She's only ever looked at me and seen fault, even when, all of my life I've been a good girl. It was Billy that shoplifted and smoked weed. Not me.

And that's what makes unbidden tears spring to my eyes. Because she can't see that what I need now isn't judgement or advice, just a hug.

Instead, I tell her where we're up to and what's happening.

'Did Tom come with you to the appointment?' she asks, in a way that suggests he's unqualified for the job. 'I'll come with you next time.'

'You don't like hospitals, remember?'

'You'll be very bored.'

Boredom wasn't the kind of emotion I thought might come out of this whole experience.

'I'll keep you company,' she says.

'Thanks,' I manage. She finally gives me a hug and I cry a bit. 'I'm just… I feel… oh, Mum, I don't want to lose my breast. It'll be so weird having it chopped off.'

'You'll get used to it,' she says in a matter-of-fact way. 'People get used to anything.'

I nod and swallow back more tears. She's clearly not going to be my go-to sympathy person.

'Did I tell you that Rob's back is bad again?' she says. 'They say there's nothing worse than back pain.'

22

Tom has been given a new intern – a whipper-snapper called Janine, right when he's at his busiest with his case. The case Tom *has* to win, so that Andrew, his boss, will finally come good and promote him to partner.

I point out that Janine is a good thing, surely? She can share the workload, but when he's so snowed under, he's not convinced. There's a very straight-laced corporate culture at his office and it always seems to be a competition about who can be seen to put in the most hours. He knows as well as I do how unhealthy this working practice is, but his boss remains impervious to any suggestions of change. So I understand why he is annoyed that his colleague Dan has off-loaded Janine, rather than train her up himself which has meant Tom now has to catch up on the work he didn't get done over the weekend.

Even so, it irks me that my work isn't going well either, but I don't prioritise it on a family day and yet he does. I'm not quite sure when our Sundays together stopped becoming sacrosanct. I'm aware (with a slight sense of my own failure) that each member of my family is looking at a screen in a different room of the house.

How did that happen, I wonder? When did technology take over so thoroughly – seeping into my life and my home, despite my best intentions not to let it. As I do increasingly often, I wonder what would happen, if someone just unplugged the internet? Most people would go bananas and businesses would crash, I know, but personally, I would relish it. I can't help the feeling that in return we'd all receive time. And time is the one thing I want most of all.

That said, I wonder if my romantic notion of 'togetherness' would really work with my family. Or whether the kids would tear each other apart and everyone would get bored? Or would we embrace it – go on big adventures, look at big vistas, connect with nature? I guess I'll never know.

Maybe it's the red wine, but after lunch, I feel as if a weary dart has hit me and Tom tells me to go for a nap.

I never, ever nap in the day.

'Just go, Mum,' Bea says.

'Yeah, you got cancer,' Jacob adds. 'Make the most of it.'

Tilly thumps his arm.

'I'm just saying,' Jacob says defensively.

I hate being banished to bed, and upstairs, I try not to be grumpy and put out. I think about what Tamsin said and how it's so important to look after myself, but I'm not very good at it. I like being busy.

And for the last twenty years I've been *extremely* busy: Setting up a business, raising a family, running a home, socialising with friends, organising parties and making the arrangements that all of those things entail. I've lived by the mantra that if you want something done, ask a busy woman.

In a fairly delusional way, I've thought that constantly juggling all the balls in the air that make up my life has been a good thing – the stress of it being a badge of honour, almost. But the fall-out is that me-time has been absolutely on the bottom of my list, to the point that taking any time for myself or putting my needs first makes me feel like a fraud.

Huffily, I lie on the bed and pick up the book Zippo sent me and flick through it. But actually, it turns out to be very interesting. It's all about the power of the mind, as witnessed by the placebo effect in medical experiments. The science community have been kind of miffed about this in the past. The notion that our bodies will be affected if we *believe* we're taking something that will affect it. But now, science is waking up to the fact that the power of belief is mega. Turns out, there is truth in the old saying, mind over matter. Or that's what Zippo's book says anyway. And who knows? It might even be true.

And if it *is*, then so long as I believe I will make a full and speedy recovery, then I will. *Simples.*

Well, anything is worth a go…

I try and work on a visualisation, as the book suggests, but all I can think about is my cancer. Going on inside me. Right now.

My thoughts wander to when all this started. When did the first cell go rogue? Was there a moment – and this must have been a while back – that precipitated one cell to go to the dark side? This prompts some *Star Wars* imagery to start zipping around my imagination and my inner voice to go all deep, like a movie trailer: *One rogue cell… disgruntled… disenfranchised and rebellious… recruits others to his dark and deadly cause…*

Actually, I'm a bit cross about all of this. Because whilst I was on my summer holidays last year, larking about, those pesky cancer cells were probably already trying to outfox my white cells – like Al-Qaeda in the desert. And all that time – when I was dancing, camping, eating, going out, arranging things in the shop, they were *in* me. It's a weird thought. Frightening. That your body could be the host to a secret rebellion.

So I'm lucky I guess, because now they have been found out. What started as a rogue cell is now a fully equipped army with a dangerous spaceship, loaded with toxic weapons, ready to fire out cancer to all parts of my body.

Ha! But I see you. Here at central command, we've identified the threat. You are on the mothership's radar. So let the fight commence. You are going DOWN, motherfuckers.

Does this count as meditation? I'm not sure.

23

On Monday morning, I feel ridiculous for lying, but I don't tell Tom or the kids that I'm going to the park near the clinic before work. I don't even know if Tamsin will be there, but I've resolved to jog once around the perimeter anyway. I need to clear my head and I can't quite face Pierre and Lorna yet.

Besides, maybe running might be the key to powering up my internal cancer-fighting mothership. Of all the contradictory stuff I've read online about cancer, the one thing everyone agrees on is that keeping fit and healthy certainly won't do you any harm.

I park the car, feeling guilty for leaving Pooch, but he's not a good running companion and I don't want him to embarrass me with his squitty bottom. I haul up my leg onto the bumper and take a stretch forward. My legs feel (and look) like tree trunks.

I set off in the direction of the bench by the statue, but I can already see that Tamsin isn't there. *Of course she isn't*, I tell myself. After all, this is the worst non-arrangement in history. Why am I even here?

I'm about to leave to complete my jog alone, when I see another woman walking from the other direction. She stops on the path, just up from the bench and looks at her Fitbit. She's wearing a bright orange and red waterproof jacket and she has snazzy running leggings and jaunty pink trainers. She has dark croppy hair held in place by one of those funky headbands which covers her ears. She pulls out a Bluetooth earphone from underneath it.

'Are you waiting for Tamsin too?' she asks, seeing me. She has a plummy voice. Well spoken. Her skin is flawless.

'Yes, well, no. You know Tamsin?' I stumble.

The woman nods and smiles. She comes closer and I notice that she's really very pretty.

'Has she bamboozled you into running too?' she asks.

'Sort of. I've only met her once, but she mentioned that she runs. I thought I'd join her,' I say, but this sounds a bit pathetic. Like I'm a bit needy. But then again I am. Except that I'm not sure what it is I need, or what I'm looking for by being here.

'She's bullied me into it,' the woman confides, then puts out her hand. She's not wearing a wedding ring. 'Amma,' she says.

'Keira,' I introduce myself and we look at each other and smile. I wish I'd made more effort with my appearance, as Amma exudes glamour. There's something about her that's vaguely familiar.

'How do you know Tamsin?' I ask.

'Oh. I met her on the chemo ward when I was looking round,' Amma says, then laughs when she sees my eyes go wide.

'You're having chemo?'

'I will be. And yes, it's a wig,' she says, with a sideways glance at me. 'Not that I need it just yet. I still have hair, but I've cropped it short. I just thought I'd get used to the idea of this thing, so it won't be a shock when I really do have to wear it.'

'Good for you,' I tell her, impressed with how practical she's being. 'And for the record, I'd never have guessed it was a wig,' I tell her. And I wouldn't have.

'Good. Tamsin made me get this one. She came with me to the wig lady. I'm glad it's fooled you,' she says, fluffing up the bottom with her palm.

I smile. 'You'll have to give me tips,' I say. 'On wigs. When I start.'

'Oh no,' Amma says, with genuine concern. 'Not you too?'

I nod.

'How long?' she asks.

'I just found out,' I tell her. 'I'm seeing the surgeon tomorrow. I'm having a mastectomy, I think, then all the treatment.'

This unburdening to this glamorous woman, who clearly understands, feels good, but at the same time, spelling it out makes it all seem very real.

'Oh. We're the same. Only I'm just ahead of you.'

'You've had the operation?'

She nods. 'Oh yes. One boob down.'

'What's it like?'

She laughs. 'Like having your tit chopped off.' She registers my shock. 'Sorry... I scared you. It's worse in theory than in practice, I promise. I mean, fair play to the old girl,' she adds, looking down at her chest, 'she gave good service and I was very sorry to see her go, but I can manage without her for now. Then I'll have a fabulous reconstruction and get a proper perky rack.'

Listening to Amma being so frank and funny makes everything seem a little more bearable. It feels indescribably comforting that there's someone else in the same boat as me.

'And the chemo? Is it as bad?'

'I'm about to start, so I'll keep you posted. Do you know how much chemo you'll have to have?'

'Six lots, they say.'

'Me too. And what about your cancer?' she asks. 'What type is it?'

I try and remember what the doctor told me, but as I do, I realise that I haven't grasped the finer details. I've been in such shock that I've rolled over and taken the diagnosis, without really looking into what it actually means. I resolve to get in control and find out more and start fronting up to this thing properly.

Then, suddenly, she waves. 'Oh, there she is. It's Tamsin. She's here after all,' Amma says.

Tamsin is wearing her Nike cap, black wig and some impressive purple and silver eye make-up.

'You're here,' she says to me. 'And you've met?'

I laugh. 'Yes. I'm Keira by the way.'

'I know. I asked Sam about you. She wasn't supposed to tell me your name, but I found out anyway,' Tamsin says with her cheeky grin. 'You're from Wishwells.'

'That's it!' Amma exclaims, clicking her fingers and pointing at me. 'Wishwells. I knew I'd seen you before. That is absolutely my favourite shop in town.'

I flush with pride.

'Come on then, ladies. Let's get running. We can natter on the way,' Tamsin says. 'And, by the way, I'm loving the hair,' she tells Amma. 'It looks completely real.'

24

We set off around the park, but it's tough. Tamsin's pace is much faster than I'd normally run. Meaning she really must have just run a long way that first time I saw her. Shit, how far was she planning on making us run *now*?

It's funny how life can suddenly change. You can coast along for years doing the same thing and then plop, one day you're well, the next you've got cancer. Or you can be a couch potato and then – *poof!* – just like that you're running.

Except that it's hard. I'm way, way too unfit for this. Very soon, my head is screaming: *I can't do it. I can't do it. THIS IS SO HARD. I need to stop. I... have... to... stop... .*

At the top of the path, after about two hundred metres, I slow down, panting.

'Fucking hell, Dad. I had no idea it'd be this hard,' I say quietly, heaving forward, my hands on my knees.

Tamsin stops and comes back for me. Amma jogs on the spot. She's not even lightly perspiring.

'What's the matter?'

'I'm slowing you down. Please, go on without me.' I wave my hand to the path ahead. It's still hard to breathe.

'Nonsense,' she says.

I give her a look.

'How many times do you go upstairs a day? Or actually sit down to relax?'

She's got a point. I am on the go pretty much constantly at home, not to mention the fact that I never, ever sit down at work.

'Stop being up here, Keira.' She taps her head and her rings clank. 'Running is all mental, you see. Once you understand that, the rest is easy. It's one foot in front of the other. Just shut your head up and tell yourself you're going to do it. End of.'

I heave myself upright. 'Really? That's the trick?'

'Yes. It's simple. Just chop up the run into bite-sized pieces. Tell yourself that you're going to run to that bush, then that tree, then that pile of dog shit and each time you hit your marker, congratulate yourself. "Bloody well done me."'

I laugh at her effusiveness.

'I'm serious,' she continues. 'Tell yourself that if you really must, you can stop for a bit, but before you do, assess whether there's more juice in the tank. There always is, believe me. So then you go to your next marker and before you know it you'll see our bench and you'll have done something you couldn't do before. We're only doing 3K. That's all.'

'*All?*'

'Just believe you're going to do it. You might not enjoy it the first time, but next time you will. Come on. We'll chat. It'll be fine. You'll see.'

I nod, processing what she's just told me and run on with her and we catch Amma up.

'She head doctoring you?' Amma asks, with a grin. 'She's good, isn't she?'

On the second lap, I really can't believe I'm still going, but I am.

'Have you run all the way through your treatment?' I manage to ask Tamsin. I need to keep her talking, as I'm concentrating really hard on not stopping and getting to the bin at the end of this concrete stretch.

'Not as much as I'd like. The first three loads of chemo were fine, but they use a second drug and this batch is a bummer. Not that I want to put you off. Everyone reacts differently.'

She talks about it, like she's in the middle of a marathon. And I guess she is.

'What's been the worst bit so far?' I ask them both.

'For me, it was finding out. The shock of it. The bit you're going through now,' Amma says. Her honesty is oddly reassuring.

'I know! And it's so hard coping with everyone's reactions,' I tell her.

'Tell people you've got diabetes or heart disease and they just shrug and say they'll see you down the pub,' Tamsin says. 'Tell people you've got cancer and they act like you're going to die any second.'

'Exactly!' I say, laughing and panting. 'And people can't even say it,' I tell them both. 'Like Grace, this mum at my daughter's school. She's lovely and has been so kind, but she says 'ancer through her nose.'

'Oh, *her*, she's got…' Amma does a dramatic impression. '*Cancer.*'

She's so funny and we laugh a little more and then I'm out of breath and have to run a bit faster to keep up with them.

But soon we're on the downward path and I watch our shadows as we jog amiably. 'How you doing?' Tamsin asks me. 'This pace OK?'

I wonder if I've gone beetroot red. I feel like I have. My skin is doing that pulsing burning thing.

'Good,' I tell her. And it does feel good. Somehow, doing proper exercise is tethering me back to me. She's right. It does feel defiant. A two fingers up to cancer.

And, now my head clicks into a more familiar monologue that goes something like this: *This is so hard, but I'm going to feel so good when I've done it. But I must do it more. In fact, I'm making a vow right now to get fit. Fitter than this. Because this is just the start. Very soon, I'll be super fit and super skinny. I'll be a whole new me…*

Except that I have cancer, I remember. Very soon, this is going to be a whole lot harder.

Amma says, 'Are you doing that thing where you keep racking your brains for reasons that it's happened to you?' She looks at me like she already knows the answer.

I nod. 'All the time. But I guess we're just statistics.'

That we're a 'we' not an 'I' feels deeply comforting.

'Don't waste your time,' Tamsin says. 'Could be anything and nothing.'

'Or cosmic rays,' I say and she raises her painted eyebrows. 'There's a lot of stuff online.'

'Oh Christ. Don't go online, whatever you do,' Amma says.

'Personally, I reckon it's my tempestuous past catching up with me,' Tamsin says, matter-of-factly.

She goes on to tell us that she ran away from home when she was 16, then lived in a squat in London. She played in a punk band (lead singer and bass) but then fell out with everyone, including her parents when she met Ian, her partner. She thought he was worth the sacrifice, but he's been 'a total shit', and next to useless whilst she's been having her treatment. She doesn't mask the bitterness in her voice, but seeing our shocked faces, cracks a smile.

'Come on, girls. Sprint finish,' she says, chirpily. 'Let's run like the wind.'

There's fifty metres or so before we get to the bench. I'm ridiculously out of breath.

'Come on, Keira.'

'Oh but here she comes in the inside lane. Suck on this,' Amma says, speeding up and flicking me and Tamsin the bird. I let them go ahead and they race each other over the imaginary finish line by the bench and collapse laughing.

'I think I'm going to puke,' I say, catching up and heaving in breath.

'Nonsense. You'll know it when you need to puke,' Tamsin says, high-fiving me, and for the first time in ages, I feel like I'm part of a gang.

Amma and I both have cars, but Tamsin refuses a lift. 'So, how about we do this again?' she asks.

'I can do Friday,' Amma says.

'Friday it is. The Cancer Ladies' Running Club will convene again then.'

25

On the iPad at Wishwells I google Amma Khatri and realise immediately that I've seen her before. She's an actress and I've seen her in a production of *The Inspector Calls* at the Theatre Royal in town and she was in *The Bill* for a bit and then that online shopping TV advert. *That's* why I recognised her. It isn't just that she's one of our customers.

I can't help feeling a little starstruck when I see a profile piece about her from a magazine a few years ago. She trained with – and was flat-mates with – Isabel Monroe. Isabel Monroe. You know, *The* Isabel Monroe who is in everything. She's super-duper famous.

And now Amma Khatri *who is also friends with Isabel Monroe* wants to be my Facebook friend. I connect with her and feel fizzy with girly excitement. Fancy knowing an actual actress! I mean, how anyone could do that – put themselves out there – be on stage and TV in front of an audience, is completely beyond me. I would never have the confidence to do that.

You'd think actresses might be a little false, or a bit snooty, but Amma was so down to earth and lovely. And so open. I probably know more about her from our short meeting this morning than lots of her six hundred Facebook friends. She hasn't put anything up about having cancer, but then again, neither have I. But then, I'm a bit of a hypocrite about social media – happy to look through other people's posts, but reluctant to share anything about myself.

I shamelessly go through all her pictures on her Instagram feed, feeling a little inadequate as I see her at various gigs and festivals looking radiantly beautiful. She seems to be single, with no significant exes or even any kids, but I can't quite work out how old she is. She's got to be in her forties, I reckon, although she could pass for mid-thirties.

'Who's that?' Lorna asks, coming onto the shop floor and looking over my shoulder.

'No one,' I say, quickly closing down the screen. I don't want to tell her about Amma and Tamsin, or the reason for our new friendship.

I go back onto Spotify to find one of my playlists, but my Old Skool lists aren't there. I don't have time to question who might have deleted them, though, because Lorna is staring at me.

I look up and see her and Ruby at the till and remember we have a meeting upstairs.

'Are you OK? You look a bit red,' Ruby asks, as I pass.

I put my hands to my cheeks. 'Oh? Am I? It's because I went for a run this morning. About 3K,' I explain.

And all of it is worth it for the look of surprise on her face. Because it's like I've jumped out of the box she's put me in. The label she gave me has just peeled right off. And I can't help the swagger in my step as I walk upstairs towards the meeting room.

Becca brings in a tray of coffees and a plate of biscuits. I instinctively reach for one, but then catch Lorna looking at my hand and stop myself.

'So, the Birmingham trade fair,' she says.

'They've been on the phone about our stand,' Becca says. 'If we still want to keep it.'

I usually do the Birmingham fair and over the years I've got the noisy, hectic trade bun-fight down to a fine art. It's all about being able to recognise the dross from the products with mark-up potential. This year, however, Lorna wants to take a stand, too, to sell on the Jackson merch.

'It's in ten days,' Lorna points out. 'You might be having your op.'

The way she says it, makes it sound like it's an elective thing I've chosen to have at a particularly bad time.

'Not necessarily. And anyway, I can still work,' I say, shaking my head as if she's being ridiculous. 'I can always man the stand.' I feel invigorated by my run – a little bit of my own invincibility has come back.

Lorna and Becca exchange a look.

'You won't be able to go to Birmingham, Keira,' Lorna says. 'You know how busy it is there. You won't have the energy.'

'And in your current condition, you can't be exposed to all those germs,' Becca adds. 'You know, before you start chemo.'

'But—' I start, defensively, but already, it's become clear that I'm not the only one who's been busy with their internet research.

'We have to plan, just in case,' Lorna says. 'That's all. No one is having a go at you.'

But it feels like they are. It feels like I've let them all down.

'I can do it,' Becca says. 'With Ruby.'

I want to protest that they're not ready, but I can sense that my authority has already been undermined. I hate the way I'm being side-lined. I hate the way Lorna is making me feel – even though she's doing that pitying smile and saying things that are supposed to sound like she gives a shit.

The meeting carries on and we argue for a while over the pricing of Lisa's new espresso cup sets. Lorna wants to discount them heavily as she's doing some sort of online push.

'We have to capitalise on the momentum we've built and I really want to expand our online sales,' she says.

Her strategy declaration is news to me. This hasn't been discussed or agreed, but she smiles innocently at me.

'If you think that's best,' I say.

'I do. And so does Pierre. So can we all make ten tomorrow for a meeting to finalise a few things?'

'I can't. I've got a scan,' I say, remembering my appointment.

'Oh, *yeah*. OK, right. How long do you reckon it will take?'

'I don't know, but I'm seeing the surgeon in the afternoon. Then I'll come straight in.'

'We can manage without you,' she says. 'Your health is much more important.'

And this statement is, of course, true… so why do I get the feeling that she really doesn't mean it?

26

I told Tom that Mum could come with me to the scan appointment and that he should go to work, but he absolutely insists on taking the day off. He's jumpy and tense and I want to soothe him, to tell him it'll all be alright, but I'm not actually sure that it is going to be alright.

It feels like the start of the long journey ahead as we set off together in the car. All the way to the hospital, Tom takes a work call. His boss, Andrew, is super-stressed and taking it out on Tom.

Tom's mood only gets worse when it becomes clear that there are absolutely no spaces left in the exorbitantly expensive hospital car park. In the end, I leave my muttering husband doing yet another loop around the concrete pillars, and go into the hospital alone.

In the MRI scanning department, I fill in a few forms and then am asked to wait in the nice area with the coffee machine. No Hospi-Coff kiosk here.

I wait and wait and realise that this is what all this treatment now means: that I'm at the mercy of a system. I don't mean that in a nasty way. I'm not moaning. But the first rule of having any sort of medical condition is that from the second you walk through the automatic doors, your time is no longer your own. In exchange for treatment, you relinquish any rights at all – even to *ask* how long things might take.

I resolve to master the art of waiting, because clearly the queues are very long in Cancer World. Eventually, though, a man in nurse's uniform with very blue eyes comes to collect me. He tells me to go into the changing room and strip off to my waist and put the hospital gown on – the fastening at the front.

In the MRI room, the scanner's bed is pulled out and there's a pink paper sheet on it. I sit on the bed as the nurse fits me with a canula in my arm. I feel slightly queasy as the needle goes in and an angry little purple puncture wound appears on the inside of my elbow. It hurts as he tapes the plastic contraption to my skin. He explains that they'll be using it to pump in something called gadolinium to enhance the magnetic contrast. It sounds very serious. I recoil at the thought of these weird-sounding drugs entering my bloodstream, but I guess I'm going to have to get used to it.

I'm told to kneel on the bed and I see there's a hole for my breast to dangle through. Is this what it felt like going into the stocks in medieval times, I wonder. Well, from a tit's point of view, anyway.

I'm given earplugs and then headphones. My face goes into a padded hole, like I'm having a massage. I can see the nurse in a small mirror. I feel myself sliding into the machine.

I've noticed that people talk about MRI scans in a kind of revered way, like they talk about the latest iPhone, like it's 'big tech', so I am kind of curious about what's going to happen. I've been worried about feeling claustrophobic, but there's too much happening to feel afraid.

I can hear the song 'Budapest' through the headphones. I've opted for a compilation CD. The music cuts out now though, and it's the nurse's voice. 'We're going to start the first scan.' Then 'Budapest' is back on. Louder this time.

I'm not sure George Ezra intended his music to be listened to like this. I bet he thought, when his music producers sat with him in the room with all the twiddly dials and slidey buttons, that people would dance around to it. Young people. In cool rooftop bars. Not middle-aged, half-naked women in scanning machines.

There's a loud noise, like the kind you might hear on the shutting doors of a ferry. Then the machine starts to judder. It's a bit like when someone is digging up the road with a pneumatic drill and you kind of recoil at the noise and desperately want it to stop. George Ezra competes in the background.

My nose itches. There's a rogue hair tickling my eye and nostril, but I can't move.

I'm always worried that I have a rubbish memory, but now, out of nowhere, with George Ezra banging on over the sound of the road digger and when I can't move a muscle, my mind goes all by itself to a happy place.

In my mind's eye, I can see Tilly as a baby, hanging in her bouncer that Dad had rigged up on a beam above his workbench in the shop. I can see him tickling her feet and her giggling – all dribbly and gummy. To have such a glimpse into these rare archives feels like such a blessing, I gasp.

The music cuts out and it's the nurse. 'You OK in there?'

I open my eyes. My nose is screaming to be itched. I can see the snaking tube coming between my hands in front of me to my elbow, although I can't see my elbow. I can see fluid in the twisty tube and I suddenly feel hot and like I really, really need to pee. I squeeze my pelvic floor muscles in a panic.

I don't want to wet myself in a scanner. That would be very, very embarrassing.

Ed Sheeran is singing 'Shape of You,' but now the CD is jammed and he's repeating 'you, you, you, you, you, you, you'.

The noise is intolerable so I close my eyes tightly and will myself back to the Wishwells of the past. And here comes another happy memory – of Moira and I looking up at the sign-writer finishing the sign above the door. And I see myself, young and happy and content in the sunshine.

Eventually, the bed starts to move and I come out. My sternum aches and back in the changing room I see a huge red mark where I've been on my front on my chest and face. I look rumpled and worried and for a moment I think about reapplying some eyeliner, but it seems a bit pointless.

Tom is waiting for me outside, having only just got a parking space. He kisses the top of my head and I wish he'd gone to work.

'I wish you'd gone to work,' I say.

His eyebrows knit together. 'I want to be here for you.'

Then be here for me, I nearly say, but I don't.

27

Later on, after we've eaten a sandwich in the car, Tom and I head to a different maze of hospital corridors for our meeting with the consultant. Mr Mabiyan has a firm handshake and looks me in the eye. I like him immediately.

He explains that lobular cancer is 'tricky'. No more dangerous or potent than ductal cancer, only it's difficult to detect because it's not in lumps. For the second time in a week, a senior health professional unearths a bit of A4, clicks his biro and draws a huge breast. All this equipment and yet there's nothing to explain anything better than a pen and paper.

I ask about the nipple issue and he shakes his head. The nipple is an integral part of the breast – just on the outside. It's the roundabout of all these ducts and lobes and their pathways. It's not possible for her to stay. I like it that he's given my nipple a sex.

He explains that my cancer is growing and hardening the tissue in layers. He's looked at my mammograms and scan. He's seen this all before. He knows what's going on. I believe him.

What about the MRI I just had? What can he tell from that? He explains that he's asked for the results, but the facts are that it takes at least three hours for the 170 pictures the machine took to load to the computer and then another day for them to be sent through to be analysed. As soon as he has the MRI – later this week, he'll know exactly what surgery to perform.

We chat and chat and he gives us his full attention. He smiles gently when I ask him about diets and supplements.

'This is not a punishment, Keira,' he tells me. 'Don't deprive yourself. Enjoy life. Have everything you want. Just nothing in excess.' I'm literally hanging on his every word.

'Even wine?'

He chuckles. 'Even wine.'

I know drinking too much might well have been a contributing factor to what got me here, but it's a relief to hear him say this. Because my love of booze is still a part of me. The fun me, who goes out and can still raise a smile, even when times are bad.

We discuss treatment. He assures me they won't under treat me. This has to be a solution for the next thirty years. And whilst this is reassuring, it's the first time a health professional has ever discussed my life in terms of years left. It's certainly not something I've allowed myself to think about. For me, time has always been intriguingly stretchy, the future there, but around the corner, out of sight. I'm not brave enough to peep around the corner from this – the right-now – to contemplate the road ahead. Not even through my fingers.

But now we're talking about it. How, if the cancer came back, it won't be in the other breast, but an offshoot of this cancer. Next time, it'll be in my liver or bones. That sounds quite scary.

'But I want to climb up mountains when I'm ninety,' I tell him.

'Maybe eighty-nine,' he retorts.

He assures me that the surgery and treatment I'm about to have *will* be a solution for thirty years – so until I'm 77. That's do-able, I guess. I try and picture my 77-year-old self. I imagine Tom and I in our house, our walls covered in crayoned pictures our grandchildren have done.

I want that. I want that very much.

Mr Mabiyan examines me behind a curtain and the nurse comes in as a chaperone. Old Mabiyan knows his eggs. Or boobs. It's like he can 'see' what's beneath his fingertips and he gets me to have a good old prod of my left boob.

'See, there's a bit there. You can tell the tissue is hard,' he says, taking my fingers and feeling under his. I can feel some weird lumpy stuff. And it's very tender.

'But I think there's some over here too,' he says, moving my fingers towards my armpit. 'An area there. Like a sausage. So if I can I'll just remove this bit,' he says, drawing a wedge like a slice of cake, 'then rearrange the tissue inside. I'll sew it up and it'll be a bit smaller, but hardly recognisable as different. But maybe – probably – I'll do a mastectomy. In which case the scar will be like this…' He pulls the edge of the sheet taught across my breast. 'So you won't see it above a bikini or bra.'

This is a man, who up until five minutes ago, was a stranger. And now we're actually discussing the nuts and bolts of chopping off my whole breast. This has to go down as the weirdest chat of my entire life.

After I get dressed and we're about to leave, he gives a gentle squeeze on my arm. 'It's all going to be OK, Keira,' he says. 'But have you got plenty of support?'

'Of course,' I say.

'It might be worth joining a support group.'

I glance at Tom. We've had several conversations about how we can face this together and how we don't need anyone else. And while I know it might be really helpful for other people to sit in a room and share their experiences, the whole thought of it makes me want to run away. I am not staying in Cancer World, like people stay in Disneyland. I don't want to be immersed in the experience, thanks very much. I'll just pop in and out.

'She's joined a running group,' Tom says. It didn't seem like he approved when I told him about Tamsin and Amma, as though the whole thing might be some kind of betrayal of his ethos of us against the world, but now he sounds like he might be a little bit proud of me. Perhaps he can see the good in it after all. 'Of women, you know,' he continues. 'Who are going through treatment.'

'A splendid idea,' Mr Mabiyan says. 'Tell me all about it next time we meet.'

'You think it's a good idea to run?' I ask him.

'Absolutely,' he says. 'Enjoy every stride.'

28

So there we have it. I do have a support group. Completely by accident. Because Tamsin texts to ask how my appointment went. My other friends have texted too, but somehow her concern seems the most palatable. It's not tinged with pity, just genuine interest. I tell her what they've said at the clinic. She texts back.

Onwards and upwards. One foot in front of the other, remember. Believe it will be OK.

I hold my phone to my chest and smile, hearing her saying it in my head. I'm so grateful for my new friends, especially when Amma texts and tells me to call her if I fancy a chat. And, feeling nervous, but excited, I call her.

Considering we've only just met, I find nattering to her on the phone surprisingly easy, like we've been mates forever. Maybe it's because there's an imbalance with all my other friends – because I'm the sick one and they are being sympathetic, but being in the same boat as Amma sweeps aside all the drama. I'm able to be myself. And it's such a relief to talk to someone who understands, when Lorna and the girls at work really don't.

I've been made to feel so guilty for taking the time off for my scan today, but I tell myself I'm going to bloody well eke it out before I go in. I need to process what's just happened before I deal with work. And it's not as if I'm not going to be working extra hard, with the board meeting tomorrow.

I sit in the kitchen, my slippers up on the table and defiantly rummage through one of the 'I'm sorry you've got cancer' boxes of chocolates I've received, squinting at the chart to see if I like the fillings.

Soon Amma and I are on to what Mr Mabiyan said about wine.

'I'm so confused about the whole lifestyle thing. Food in particular,' I admit, discarding the cherry liqueur chocolate and putting it back. 'I mean, I thought I was healthy, but I then I bloody well got cancer. And now I'm wondering whether I should go on a diet.'

'Don't ask me. I've always been conflicted over that stuff,' she admits. 'One always is as an actress. I've done bulimia, anorexia, the lot. It doesn't help that I'm a Monday dieter.'

'A Monday dieter? What's that?' I ask, wondering if that's a guru's book for the inside elite.

'Well, you see on a Monday, I'm Gwyneth Paltrow. Seriously. I am clean. My body is a temple. I am full of new resolutions. In fact, if you meet me on a Monday, I'll bore you stupid about the new me. No booze, no… no… no… never again. I'm juicing and making nourishing superfood bites to take with me to my extra-long hot yoga session, because *Deliciously Ella* is my new bible.'

I can't help laughing. I'm a bit like that too.

'But by Wednesday, I'm bored of being so virtuous. And then maybe there'll be a "totally legitimate excuse" for a glass of wine.' I can picture her doing quotations in the air. 'And that's my downfall, because it turns out that I'm excellent at legitimate excuses.'

'Aren't we all.'

'But one excuse always leads to another and then before I know it, it's Friday and I've turned into Keith Richards and I'm dragging Gwyneth round who is clutching onto my ankle, as I drag her across the bar and order shots. And by the early hours of Saturday, I've unshackled myself completely. Gwyneth has been banished and I'm dancing on the bar. Don't laugh, Keira.'

'I'm only laughing because I'm exactly the same. Except the dancing on the bar. Not with these bunions.'

We laugh some more and then she continues.

'I'm exaggerating a bit, of course, but the tragic thing is that I always think I look amazing. And that everyone loves me for being so outrageous. I guess that being the life and soul of the party makes me feel free. And like I'm sticking two fingers up to the man.'

'Or to Gwyneth Paltrow.'

'Exactly.'

'But…' She pauses dramatically. 'And this is a shocking newsflash – it turns out that I'm responsible for my health 24-7.'

'Who knew?' I say.

I close the box of chocolates and shove them under the cushion of the kitchen bench. I'll throw them out later, when Tom won't find the evidence of my gluttony.

As I drive to work, I reflect on my conversation with Amma. Like her, the shut-off-then-binge switch is kind of hard wired in me. Somewhere, somehow, there's an internal voice that has developed – since my teens probably – that has a long-established narrative: that looking after myself is boring. That being healthy is square. That being virtuous is uncool. That recklessly eating and drinking means I'm having fun. And having fun equals being young.

It's interesting to unravel all this stuff, but at the same time, I make myself remember what my surgeon has said: that this isn't a punishment.

Even so, it's dawning on me that perhaps I really need to change my ways.

29

There's a brand new Jag and Porsche Cayenne filling up the Wishwells spaces in the car park and, annoyed that these imposters have taken my usual space, I have to go and park in the multi-storey. Ruby taps her wrist at me as I walk in through the door.

'You're really late, Keira,' she says. 'Lorna's freaking out.'

I'm confused. Lorna knows that I had my scan and appointment today and I knew she wants to have a meeting to discuss her online strategy, but I get an impending sense of dread as I go through the shop and walk upstairs.

Lorna looks up at me through the glass of the meeting room. Pierre is sitting at the head of the table, laughing with Richard and Clive – our two non-exec directors, who were appointed by the private equity company six years ago to sit on our board. They are both in their early sixties and, between them, have run some fairly big organisations and it's only now that it hits me that the cars in our car park belong to them.

'I thought the board meeting was tomorrow,' I hurriedly say, walking in and shrugging off my coat. The board meeting *is* tomorrow. Lorna must have rescheduled it for today. And I was at home talking to Amma on the phone, with my feet up, eating chocolates and they were *here*, waiting for me. Although from the look of the notes on the pad in front of Lorna, they haven't waited.

'I emailed,' Lorna says. 'Last night. I thought you'd got the message.'

'But—'

'Yes, well, as we've just been hearing, Keira isn't very good at reading her emails,' Clive says, as if this is a joke. I see Richard raise his eyebrows, as if this is some kind of gross understatement.

'Fortunately, we've also been hearing about how Pierre has done some renegotiation on the rent,' Clive says.

'How much have I missed?' I ask, flabbergasted. How long have they been discussing my business without me?

'Don't panic,' Lorna says, as if I'm being embarrassing. 'It's not a biggie. You can read the minutes afterwards.'

'Just before we finish with the rent, I gather there's a break clause in the lease coming up,' Richard says, looking through his half-moon glasses at the papers in front of him.

'That's not an issue,' I counter. 'We'll just renew, as usual.'

'Let's agree to defer the decision,' Clive says. 'See where we are in a few months.'

He looks at me and I can tell that Lorna and Pierre have told them about my diagnosis. They've all been talking about me and they aren't going to divulge the details, but I sense that some kind of decision has been made in my absence.

'Well, it's not as if we're going anywhere. There's no reason to think anything might change,' I say, my voice catching.

'Well, I'm sure you're right,' Clive says. I look at Lorna, but she won't meet my eye. 'I know you're in capable hands with Pierre here.'

The meeting ends shortly afterwards, Clive and Richard no

doubt keen to get back to their respective golf clubs. I watch Pierre laughing and joking with them, slapping Clive on the back.

At my desk, I go through my emails and there's one from late last night about the board meeting being today, but I definitely didn't see it on my phone.

'This is all to do with this new-fangled computer system,' I say desperately to Lorna. 'I would never have—'

'You're not blaming Pierre are you?' Lorna asks, folding her arms. 'Just because you didn't read your emails.' She looks at me and shakes her head. 'Look, there's no point in getting het up about it. We sorted out what we needed to.'

'But what did you discuss?' I sound whiney and needy and I hate it, just hate it that she's taken this control away from me.

'You don't have to be so suspicious,' she counters. 'You should be pleased we're expanding online. That's where the real money is. Pierre was showing Clive and Richard our projections and how we are going to aggressively market our site content.'

'But we can't suddenly produce more product out of thin air. Lisa is at full capacity as it is with the ceramics.'

'We don't need her. Pierre has found a supplier in China who can make the teapots for a fraction of the cost.'

'China?' As in mass-produced rubbish, not made by local artisans, which is *the whole point* of Wishwells!

'He sent one of the teapots out before Christmas to a contact he has.'

They are not 'the' teapots, though. They are *my* teapots. *My* design. Although I realise now, with a sinking sense of horror that I've never registered any kind of intellectual property or copyright. Pierre and Lorna's dodgy Chinese suppliers can copy anything they want and I don't have a leg to stand on.

30

But, back at home, after I've unleashed a half-hour verbal tirade about the board meeting, Tom seems to think that expanding online is a good idea and that maybe I should listen to Lorna's plan. When I tell him that I definitely didn't see the email about the board meeting change, he gives me one of the looks he gives the kids.

'You think someone has been deliberately tampering with your email?' he asks.

'It's possible, isn't it?'

'But highly unlikely,' he counters, picking up an apple from the fruit bowl and biting into it.

I'm pleased when he leaves for work the next morning. He just doesn't seem to understand how pushed out I feel by Pierre and Lorna. How they are using my cancer diagnosis against me.

Or maybe Lorna's right and I am just stuck in the past – terrified of anything changing. And maybe I'm really not as sharp as I should be with so much on my mind.

In Jennifer's café when I go to get my coffee, she bustles around the counter, her face beaming.

'Oh, perfect timing,' she says, squeezing my arm. 'Sian's here.'

With a sinking sense of dread, I remember that when I told her my news the other day, she said she'd introduce me to her sister, who has just been through breast cancer. And, trying to be nice, I agreed that it would be good to meet a veteran. However, meeting someone else who is dealing with 'The Big C' is the last thing I have energy for right now.

But there's no way out of it and she walks me over to the window table. 'Sian, Keira, Keira, Sian. Both of you with breast cancer,' Jennifer says, like we're lucky winners of a competition. 'Well, not now,' she says, seeing my face and Sian's narrowed eyebrows. 'But *so* much in common, going through the same thing.'

She leaves me and Sian alone, with the promise to get us both coffee.

'Wow!' Sian says. 'She's about as subtle as a brick.'

Sian has short, boyish dark brown hair and is wearing trendy glasses. She has nice features, I notice, with big brown eyes that make her look studious and owl-like.

'It's OK,' I say, laughing. I know Jennifer doesn't have a bad bone in her body.

'She used to do this when she tried to set me up with men. "Oh, look at you two, you'll just love each other because you've both got blue jeans on. So much in common."'

I laugh – mainly because I like her for being so honest, but also because she does a really good impression of her sister. She gestures to the seat opposite her and I sit down. Through the fogged-up window, I can see Lorna in Wishwells, her face suspicious as she looks out onto the street. I wonder if she's waiting for me.

'Anyway, sorry to hear about...' Sian waves her hand vaguely in the direction of my chest.

'It's OK. Thank you. And you too.'

I try not to look at her chest, but it's hard not to. She has small breasts beneath a fairly tight purple polo neck jumper. If she's had an operation like I'm about to have, then you'd never know.

'Where are you up to with it all?' she asks and I tell her that I'm about to have my op and then I'll have all the treatment.

'Sounds similar to me. Although, I'm out the other side... so they say.'

'You must be glad it's over?'

'I am, of course. It's just going back to my old life... everything about it. It's hard. I've changed, but I don't really know how.'

I've been trying to be so cheerful, so positive, so determined that I'll get through this, get the op and treatment done and then be back to normal, but talking to Sian makes me realise that going back to normal afterwards might not be so easy. I hadn't really considered the long-term psychological impact of cancer before now.

'How do you mean?'

'You go through all this treatment and then you're sent on your way, just like that,' Sian says. 'Like you should just be able to pick up and carry on like nothing has ever happened. All the appointments stop, the contact, the care.' She sounds bitter. 'Sorry, I probably shouldn't be telling you this.'

I can tell, though, that as I did with Amma and Tamsin, she feels good unburdening herself to someone who might be able to understand.

'And that's not all. There's the hormone drugs I'm taking,' Sian says, with a nervous laugh.

'What about them?' I ask. 'Are there bad side effects?'

She pulls a face. 'It's not marvellous. The drug I'm on, Tamoxifen, seems to have crashed me head first into the menopause. Hot flushes, night sweats, exhaustion, aching bones, dry skin, dry… well… everything. Sorry! That's a big overshare, when we've only just met.'

'It's OK,' I laugh.

'But I guess you just have to put up with it. They say it's a life-saving drug.'

I nod, because she's right: it's not like we really have a choice about what we're going through. This is the first time I've even thought about the hormone treatment that will follow my radiotherapy. This trip to Cancer World is going to be very, very long, by the looks of things. The trip of a lifetime.

'Anyway, I'm waffling on. I should just get on with it, get back in the swing of things. I guess I should think about finding another job.'

'What do you do for a living?'

'Oh,' she says, flapping her hand. 'It's too boring to describe. Accounts, computers, that sort of thing. I was with a team in Bracknell, but I moved back here to be near Jen and Mum when I got ill.'

'Why don't you go back?'

She shakes her head. 'It's not that easy.'

She seems such a genuinely nice person and I'm sad for her that she's obviously in such limbo. 'And there are other things I can be doing. I mean, I keep meaning to get fit, but I keep finding excuses not to,' she confesses.

I tell her about Tamsin and Amma and how I've started running in the park. 'There's always room for more in the Cancer Ladies' Running Club,' I say in a funny voice, smiling at the silly-sounding name Tamsin has given us. 'Why don't you come and join us?' I offer, wondering the moment I've said it whether this will be OK with the others. But I'm sure they'd like Sian too.

'That's funny,' she says.

'What is?'

'That name. The Cancer Ladies' Running Club… because it sounds like exactly the kind of club you wouldn't want to ever have to join, but you know what?'

'What?'

'Maybe I will.'

31

On Thursday night, I stay for the late-night shopping, but our stretch of the high street is very quiet.

Jennifer comes over with some leftover pies from the café. We talk about Sian for a while and I tell her how much we got on. Jennifer says that Sian is definitely up for running with us and I'm glad I've been able to inspire her to get her trainers out. We talk for a while about business being slow.

'Oh, I meant to ask, did Brian pop in with a poster?'

Brian runs the shoe shop two doors down.

'What poster?'

'He wants us to join his campaign to stop this redevelopment they're planning for this stretch of Brightmouth high street.'

'You mentioned that the other day,' I say, remembering our conversation. Usually, I would have been straight over to talk to Jennifer about it, but I guess I've had other things on my mind.

'The council have put a tender up to flatten all the buildings and build new offices.'

'What? They can't do that,' I say, outraged.

'Haven't you seen the letters about it?'

'No!' I exclaim, because I haven't. This is the first I've heard of it.

'Brian is up in arms. I mean he's been suffering just like the rest of us. He said his Christmas sales were terrible this year, because everyone is buying online, but it's the principle that counts. It's bad enough fighting off the chains, but now the council want to get rid of us altogether.'

'It's never going to happen. We're carrying on with the lease,' I tell her.

'That's good,' she says, clearly relieved. 'As long as Wishwells stays, then they can't do anything.'

After she's gone, I find the poster rolled up on the shelf below the till. I'm annoyed that Lorna hasn't put the poster up in the window of the shop. So I do.

That must be why the landlord put up the rent, I think, as I start cashing up. Well, I'm glad it's sorted out now, because there's no way anyone is getting their hands on Wishwells. It infuriates me that the council aren't supporting our small businesses, when shops like ours – as I plan to say if we get this Retailer of The Year award – *are the lifeblood of this community*. If we stop human interaction, then we're screwed. That's what I reckon, anyway.

But I can't think about it more, because the phone rings. It's Mr Mabiyan from the hospital. It seems that my MRI scan has confirmed everything he suspected at my appointment. He's had a cancellation, so my operation will be two weeks on Wednesday. 'Is that OK with you?' he asks. *Like I have a choice.*

Man. That's soon. The NHS is supposed to be grindingly slow, so I'm impressed – and a little alarmed – that they're acting so fast. I ring off and my phone pings immediately.

It's Billy, my brother, who seems to have a sixth sense about when news comes through, so I message back, telling him about my operation. He's been in pretty much constant contact since I told him about the cancer, and now, knowing there's a date for the op, he wants to come over from Australia to see me. I'm so touched he'd even consider it, but I tell him not to come. He's busy with his job running a windsurfing school and besides, if he came to stay with Mum, it'd only cause stress. He's not as relaxed about Mum moving on from Dad and living with Rob, as I am.

I look for the office diary to mark the days I'll be in hospital, as I try and wrap my head around my operation. It's a silly thing to worry about, but my immediate thoughts are about all the dresses in my wardrobe that I'll never wear again after my op. I wonder if the awards dinner will be before or after I'm boobless.

Then it dawns on me that Lorna was right after all. There's no way I can go to Birmingham. My mind races with how we'll work out the cover needed in the shop with me out of action and Moira still away.

I picture Moira on a big cruise ship in the Caribbean and feel a pang of something that feels like indignant longing. How can she be away and not have a clue what's happening to me?

32

It's a gloriously clear day, with a promise of spring when we meet for our Friday run. Sian is waiting for me in the car park and I jog with her over to the bench and introduce her to Amma and Tamsin.

If Sian is remotely judgemental about Tamsin's appearance, like I was at first, she doesn't show it.

'Ooo, I love your web,' she says, admiring Tamsin's chest. 'That's amazing. I've got a bat, on my hip.'

'A bat? Oh, I *love* bats.' Tamsin is clearly won over. She grins at me and leads us to the grassy patch for some warm-ups.

'So look! We're now up to a grand total of four,' I say, feeling oddly pleased about our burgeoning numbers. Because it's not just the cancer that's multiplying, is it? It's us too. And we're here to kick its arse.

'At this rate, we'll have nearly enough for a football team by the end of the year,' Tamsin says.

'So long as nobody dies,' Amma reminds us.

'Yes, there is always that.'

'Yes, and bollocks to that too,' Tamsin says. 'And one of us could get hit by a bus anyway, so there's no point in worrying about it. Not that there is ever a bus at our bus stop when I need one.'

'Or mine,' Amma says, although I can't imagine her ever

getting the bus. She just seems too glamorous for public transport.

'I'll be slow today, I warn you,' Tamsin says, but despite this, the fire is in her eyes as she puts us through toe presses and knee raises, like a fierce, but loved army drill sergeant.

'Not as slow as me,' Sian says. 'I haven't done any exercise for ages.'

I tell her how far I've come in just a few short weeks. Where I used to dread even putting on my trainers, I look forward to each run now. And I'm certainly fitter than I was all of last year, which is ironic, given what else is going on with my health.

'You'll be fine,' I tell her, remembering Tamsin's valuable advice. 'It's all mental. Just tell yourself you're going to do it. One foot in front of the other.'

We run the first lap together slowly. I have Pooch with me and I keep having to stop to call him to catch up. To my embarrassment, he keeps scooching his bottom across the tarmac. I must give him his worming pill. And *goddammit*, I haven't taken him for his injections.

The roofers wolf whistle as we go past the loo block. 'Aye, aye, a new one,' one of them shouts. 'Nice pins, love.'

'Ignore them,' I tell Sian.

'It's the first compliment I've had for a while,' she says, laughing. 'I'll take it.'

'Err, ladies… can we not just remember that we're feminists? At least I hope we are? Me too, and all that, eh?' Amma says. She's teasing, but there's an edge to her voice. 'We shouldn't have to put up with that shit – from anyone. I don't mean to be rude, Sian, but nobody needs a leery builder to give them self-confidence.'

Amma tells Sian about how she's an actress. She mentions a few things she's been in and Sian says she's addicted to a new crime drama on the BBC. 'What's it called? Oh... oh... it's got that actress in it... you know, she's in everything...'

'Isabel Monroe?' Amma suggests, not masking the scorn in her voice.

'You know her, right?' I ask. 'I wasn't snooping, I promise, but I saw on Facebook that you were friends.'

'Ha,' Amma says. 'Some friend. We used to be so close. Closer than sisters, but then we both went up for the same movie. And it was so exciting – that we were going to get our first big break together. But then she got the part and I didn't. And then Evan poached her from her agent.'

'Evan?' I ask.

'*My* agent. Evan Harding. You won't have heard of him, but he's kind of big in agenting circles. Anyway, he took a shine to Isabel and put her up for all the good auditions instead of me. Well, that's how it felt at the time, anyway. And then she got so busy that she had no time for me anymore.'

'Ouch,' Sian says.

'I know. Believe me, the pain of an estranged friend is somehow worse than everything else. I mean, she's married now and has a child that I haven't even met.'

'Surely you could tell her what's happening to you?' I suggest. 'I'm sure you could patch things up? I mean, surely she'd want to help if she knew what you are going through?'

I think of Joss and Scout and how supportive they've been, even though they are both so far away. There hasn't been a day when one or other of them haven't texted or sent an encouraging WhatsApp message.

'No. Absolutely not,' Amma says, shaking her head. 'Never. She must never know.'

We talk about friendships for a while and how they change and I get on to talking about Lorna. Before I know it, I'm in full flow about how horrible this week's board meeting was.

'This Pierre sounds *awful*,' Tamsin says, outraged on my behalf.

I feel a swell of gratitude. She's the first person who's seen Pierre's behaviour from my point of view. I expand a bit and tell them how Lorna treated me about the rent email issue.

'The thing is... I'm pretty positive I didn't see that email. I *never* make mistakes. Not like that, but now they are making out I'm too fragile to know my own mind.'

'Even if you did make a mistake,' Tamsin reasons, 'they didn't have to be so condescending about it.'

I could honestly kiss her.

'Tom says I'm making too much out of it. But it's not just Lorna and Pierre. It's the others too. Since they found out about the cancer, I hate them all being so...'

'Pious? Patronising?' Tamsin offers.

'Both,' I say gratefully.

'That's why I haven't told anyone,' Amma says.

I stare at her and then Tamsin says, 'She's a right piece of work, this one.'

'You haven't told anyone? Why not?' Sian sounds incredulous.

'Because it's hard enough being an Asian actress as it is, but it was career suicide to move out of London, which I only did because I stupidly thought there was a future in a relationship I was in. More fool me. Everyone told me not to move and they were right, because my agent is only capable of thinking about his clients inside zones one and two.'

I feel for her, but it's also reassuring to know I'm not the only one with work issues. I feel sad for her, too, that her relationship didn't work out.

'I'm serious. In terms of acting, this is a terrible move. If word gets out about the fact I've got…' she takes in a breath and does the dramatic, '*cancer*, then I'm doomed. You think you've been side-lined and judged – I'd be dead to them.'

'Well, you think that's bad. I'm still getting snarky emails from my boss,' Tamsin says. She works in the HR department of the council. 'I think a male boss would be much more understanding. Some women can't stand other women being weak. It's like we've let down the side.'

'I know what you mean,' Sian chips in. 'I loved my job, but when I got cancer, they couldn't wait to get rid of me. My boss – this awful woman Lianne – even asked me not to tell anyone at work… like it might be catching. Like a virus. She was so horrible about it, I had no choice but to leave. I dread to think what she told the team.'

Tamsin nods in agreement. 'The thought of going through all of this and then going back there… back to *her* bossing me about… well, you're very lucky running your own business, Keira,' she tells me. 'Don't forget that. Don't let anyone undermine you.'

33

Being with Sian, Amma and Tamsin has bolstered my esteem levels no end, and later, as I go into work, I feel better than I have done all week. Tamsin's right: I should stand my ground with Lorna. I look in the rear-view mirror of the car and say out loud, 'You're the boss, kiddo,' and as I get out of the car, I add for good measure, 'back me up, OK, Dad? I need a bit of support today.'

I stop for a cup of tea at the café and Jennifer is delighted that Sian has come running with us.

'It's good to see her with a bit of get up and go at last,' Jennifer confides. 'She's been so low and you've really brought her out of herself.'

'I can't claim to have done that, but I'm glad the running has helped.'

'She's so bright, you know. She does the odd day working here for me, but it's not enough. It's just like she's treading water...' She smiles at me and flaps her hand. 'There I go again. I can't help myself trying to interfere.'

'She seems like a lovely person,' I tell Jennifer, honestly. 'I'm sure she'll find her feet soon enough.'

'And you? How are you doing? Only I was thinking... why don't you book in a massage at the weekend? Treat yourself. I've got a voucher for that Thai place. You can have it,' she says. She's so kind to even offer me the voucher. I know it's worth quite a bit of money.

'No, honestly, I couldn't.'

But Jennifer won't take no for an answer and gives me the voucher, watching me whilst I dial the number to book an appointment.

I wave goodbye to her whilst I'm waiting to get through and walk across the road to Wishwells. I see that Brian's poster has been taken down. *Bloody hell.*

The woman on the phone is very friendly, and books me in for Sunday afternoon, but then she says, 'Oh, sorry, one more thing. It's just a formality. Any medical conditions?'

'No. No, nothing,' I say, then I pause. 'Well, actually, I have just had a diagnosis for breast cancer.'

I hear her recoil at the words. Her tone changes and her voice lowers into an urgent whisper. 'Oh, well, in that case, no. I'm afraid a massage is out of the question.'

'What? Why?

'Our therapists won't work with people with...' she pauses, like she can't bear to invoke the bogey-man, '... *cancer.*'

'Won't? Why not?'

'Well, it's... it's very dangerous,' she says.

I'm not sure what's dangerous. The massage for the masseur, or me.

I feel slightly deflated after this call, but mercifully, Lorna isn't in work. Ruby shrugs when I ask her what happened to the poster. It's odd that it's just disappeared, but Ruby isn't in a talkative mood today. I resolve to ask Brian for another one.

I spend the afternoon arranging the new pieces that

Lisa brings in, but I can't quite reconcile the new ceramics with Lorna's Jackson stuff. The shop just looks messy and I miss Moira and her magic touch. She can always make everything look just right.

In the end, remembering that the table can divide, I split the central table into its two parts and put the ceramics on one and cram the Jackson stuff onto the other table. That's compromise enough. I feel pleased with my handiwork.

Maybe it's off-loading my worries to my running friends, or maybe it's just that without Pierre and Lorna in Wishwells, pottering around my shop feels restorative. And it's nice to have a chat with a few of our regular customers. Even so, I'm tired by six and when Ruby suggests I go home early and that she'll settle up, I'm very grateful.

On the way home I pick up some lovely food for supper. Tom says he'll cook a risotto whilst I have a bath.

Up in the bathroom, I tell myself that I must stay positive. Because there *are* a lot of positives. Firstly, the cancer is contained. It's going to be sorted. That it's just a little op. That if you're going to lose a part of your body, then a boob is probably the most dispensable. It's not an eye, or leg, or even a toe. Nobody will notice. It's been good meeting Sian and seeing that it is possible to *look* completely normal at the end of treatment, even if she doesn't feel it inside.

'You OK?' Tom asks, as he comes into the bathroom with a glass of white wine for me.

'I'm trying to look on the bright side,' I tell him. 'After all, you never know, maybe there might be advantages to having one breast.'

'Such as?'

'Well… I don't know, maybe I can finally play pool. Or do that magic trick where I can produce a long silk scarf from my bra and it'll keep on coming.'

Tom laughs. 'You might be on to something,' he says. 'I mean, think of all the myths about the Ancient Greek Amazons. They chopped off one of their breasts so they would be better at archery.'

'Exactly. You may address me in future as Keira, Warrior Princess,' I tell him.

'You could still opt to have reconstruction at the same time as the mastectomy,' he says. We've discussed the pros and cons of this quite a bit.

'I don't want one perky one and one nearly-fifty one,' I tell him, which is silly, I know, because plenty of people go down this route and are perfectly fine with the results. But for me… right now… I'm just not ready to make that kind of decision. The thought of my operation is freaking me out enough already, without piling the pressure of a tummy tuck and reconstruction into the mix as well.

'I'm sure they try and even them up,' Tom says.

'But what if they don't get it right and they want to start chopping up my healthy one?' I say, cupping my right breast protectively. 'I can see why people go for it, but it's not for me.'

He grabs me from behind and wraps his arms around me. Then we stare at our heads side by side in the mirror. 'I love you,' he says. 'It'll be OK. I promise. We'll make it OK.'

'I know.'

We stay, smiling at one another, but then my phone pings from the bedroom.

'Leave it,' Tom says. 'Have your bath.'

'But it might be Tilly. I texted her to tell her to be back for supper,' I say, breaking away.

But it's not Tilly. It's a WhatsApp from Becca at work. I open it up to see a piece of video footage with the words WE WON emblazoned across the clip. I click on the play arrow and I can hear applause and see some wobbly footage of Lorna, dressed in a slinky evening dress standing up and smiling at Pierre, who looks suave in his black tie get-up. And then I realise where they are.

They're at the awards ceremony.

They're at the awards ceremony and they didn't invite me.

34

On Monday morning I'm in Wishwells early. I've been festering all weekend, but have failed to speak to Lorna in person, so she doesn't have any idea of my thunderous mood. Tom doesn't get why I'm so upset, but then he's someone who absolutely hates public events. He thinks I should be happy that we won the gong and I was saved the hassle of collecting it in person. I know he's putting down my hysterical crying to fear about my impending operation, but it's really not that. And now I feel yet more indignant tears rising as I hear Lorna on the stairs, talking to Jackson in that baby voice she does.

'You didn't even tell me it was on. I could have been there,' I say, as she makes it into the office. I sound unhinged – even to myself. She looks baffled by my verbal assault. 'You went on Friday. To the awards ceremony. Without me,' I clarify.

She looks at me, like you might a petulant child. 'Oh *that*. Look, I didn't want you to have to worry about it,' she says. 'You've got so much on your plate with your operation coming up. I thought it'd be better if we went and saved you the bother. Aren't you happy that we won?'

'Of course I am, I just wish I'd been there, that's all. I didn't even know the event was on Friday.'

'Didn't you?' Lorna says, surprised. 'There was lots of stuff online about it. And Becca posted on Jackson's Instagram.'

I try and stand my ground, but I feel it slipping away beneath me. I was too busy pottering around in the shop to bother checking Instagram. I can't bear having images of Jackson stuffed down my throat.

'If I'd known about it, I would have said something, wouldn't I?' I wipe away a tear, furious that it's fallen.

Lorna sighs and puts down her bag on her desk. 'Keira, you're being ridiculous,' she says. 'And… frankly, I know you're stressed, but getting yourself worked up like this over some little awards thing…' She trails off, her head cocked with condescending pity. 'You have to believe that we really only have your best interests at heart.'

I gawp at her, my fury popping like a punctured balloon. There is no point in trying to explain the level of betrayal I feel. And not just from her. From Ruby too, who was with me all day on Friday and didn't breathe a word of what was going on. But she must have known. She must have been primed by Lorna to keep me in the dark.

Well *fuck them*, I think. *Fuck them all.*

It's weird – this new feeling – that I really can't trust any of my staff, so I'm glad to have an excuse to leave the building at lunchtime. I need to buy new pyjamas for my hospital stay, as mine are all awful and nighties are no good as I might not be able to get them over my head if my armpit is sore. Armpit? Ha! Who am I kidding? It's not just my ruddy armpit that's going to be sore.

And I've been advised to buy a post-operation mastectomy

bra – something I didn't even know existed until a couple of weeks ago. Mum has insisted that she wants to come with me.

The department store in the shopping centre doesn't stock mastectomy bras. Even asking for one induces a look of fear in the assistant's eyes and she runs across the store – runs! – to ask her manager. There's some very hushed apologies.

In the next posh bra shop, I actually see the assistant recoil. I feel like I've got the plague. Or the Cheese Touch, that game the kids play.

We carry on the search, heading to the glitzy store at the end, but as we pass all the mannequins in the window, I can't help lamenting the death of my lingerie-wearing days – although to be fair, it's been quite a long time since I've got it together to wear matching undies. I used to love buying sexy pants and bras when I was young. I remember the first 'Hello Boys' Eva Herzigová advert for the Wonderbra in the middle of the roundabout at Shepherd's Bush just near the flat Joss, Scout and I shared. Suddenly, the Nineties skinny grunge look was out and curves were in, and we could all get curves just like Eva's. We all rushed out and bought a Wonderbra, but now I feel irrationally sad that I'll never again achieve such epic cleavage.

In the store, Mum scowls as she inspects the bras and knickers on the stand. 'It's just two pieces of material,' she says, holding up a thong. For a second, I worry that she's going to ping it at me. 'And look at the price.' Her voice is loud. Too loud. I scoop her up and frog march her to M&S.

A lovely sales assistant shows me to a whole stand of mastectomy bras and generally makes me feel much less like I have the Cheese Touch. She invites me along to a pampering session for the 'post-op' ladies in the area. Is breast cancer that popular? It must be. It's rather worrying that there are enough of us for the store to put on a whole event.

'Oh, and before I go, do you have any sports bras?' I ask.

'What?' Mum asks.

'I've taken up running,' I tell her.

'No she hasn't,' Mum says, rolling her eyes as if I'm insane.

'Yes I have. In fact, I need a new running bra and leggings too.'

Tom saves the day with a well-timed call. I know he's ringing to check up on me and to find out what happened when I tackled Lorna about Friday night. He sounds relieved that I'm with Mum.

Wanting to make the peace and prove I'm not just a hysterical wife, I agree to nip in quickly to the office and bring him a sandwich. He says he can't wait to see my new purchases, but I know he's being kind. My beige post-mastectomy bra is really not the stuff of anyone's sexual fantasies.

I'm glad I'm not single. I mean, there must be women going through this cancer malarkey who don't have a Tom at home and, as I nip over to his office in the car, I feel a genuine pang for them. How would I get through this without my husband loving me like he does?

In the reception of Bryant and Woodruff, it's unusually quiet. I call out, but the secretary who has worked there forever is nowhere to be seen. Now a young woman comes from the back room to the desk, carrying a cup of herbal tea. She smiles, her teeth a dazzling white.

'Hi,' she says. 'Can I help?'

'I'm here to see Tom,' I say, confused. Who is this person? She's wearing a slinky, figure-hugging dress, that leaves nothing to the imagination. 'I'm his wife.'

I can't stop staring at her. She's ridiculously nubile and young. Like she might have just stepped off a podium, having won the first prize cup in a Miss Gorgeous competition.

'Oh, you must be Keira,' she says, happily. 'Mrs Beck, I mean. Sorry.' She laughs, charmingly. 'Tom's told me all about you. I'm Janine.'

35

In all of our marriage, I've never once felt insecure. Tom has certainly never given me cause to doubt his commitment or love, but now I can't stop thinking that Janine is flaunting herself in front of my husband and I feel jealous.

It's an old, old emotion. Like letting a ghost out of a cupboard. I know it's ridiculous and based on absolutely nothing, just an irrational distress at her youth, health and gorgeous plump breasts and it feels doubly bad because I'm so ashamed of feeling it.

It's like whack a mole. As soon as I've stamped on one unpleasant emotion, another appears. Self-pity: thwack. Anger: thwack thwack and now Jealousy: thwack thwack thwack.

I stew on it until we're unpacking the car on Thursday evening. I've insisted on doing a whopping supermarket shop so that Tom doesn't have to do it after my operation. He's banned me from talking any more about Lorna going to the awards ceremony without me, but he knows me well enough to know that there's a lot on my mind.

'So is this Janine of yours married?' I ask him, trying to make it sound like an innocent question.

'I don't think so. Why do you ask?'

'She's very beautiful.'

'Is she?' He pulls a 'you're being ridiculous' face at me.

'She's got great knockers,' I say, but my voice breaks and he is about to protest, but then he sees that I'm upset and dumps the bags back in the boot.

'Come here,' he says. He holds me tight. 'It's going to be OK. OK?'

But I don't feel as reassured as I want to.

Upstairs, when I get ready for bed, I examine my left breast which is now very tender and officially looking poorly. The bruise from the biopsy has gone green. Bruise green. Not a colour used in fashion much. You wouldn't want a jumper that colour.

My sense of body betrayal has gone and in its place is a kind of sad sympathy for my poor, poor boob. Just like Amma's lost breast, my girl has given such great service. And now she's for the chop. Imminently.

I feel regret now, that I didn't *do* more with my breasts in general. I can't really qualify that with reasoning. It's just a feeling. I remember when Billy and I used to go to London as kids and coming up the steps at Piccadilly Circus and being shocked by the postcard stands full of pictures of naked breasts with silly drawings of mice on them.

Why didn't I ever paint a mouse on my breast? Or put lipstick on my nipples like they do in erotic novels?

OK, so I dabbled in nipple tassels once – a present Joss gave me for a joke. But they had far more comic than erotic value. I was fascinated about how you could bounce up and down on your toes and the nipple tassels would circle one way and then the other. Tom found the whole escapade terrifying. He's frightened by all of that burlesquey kind of stuff.

It's bad enough that the bulk of my breast is going to have to go, but the bit that gets me is losing my nipple. They've always been such a big part of me. My babies suckled them. What other part of my body, apart from my brain has performed such incredible acts? They are amazing. And they are so much part of my sexuality. One tweak, one lick, or, better still, a little suction and I'm in ecstasy. They are the gateway to me feeling horny. The dials to getting my juices flowing. But not for much longer.

I feel like a woman at Cape Canaveral who is on the verge of sending a child into space in a rocket. I know they are doing something noble. Taking one for humanity, so to speak, but I know I won't see them again, until they have been through a giant, traumatic experience. I have to be stoic and brave, but that's my baby rocketing into space. And the ship may explode. I have to be all smiles and wave for the cameras, but inside… ugh. Dreadful.

'What are you doing up here?' Tom asks, coming into the bedroom. 'What's the matter?'

'What if you don't fancy me anymore?' I ask. My voice sounds pathetic.

'You're being ridiculous. I'll fancy you no matter what. Anyway, you'll still be you.'

As if to prove it, later on, we make love, but it feels like we're both silently saying goodbye to my body as we've known it. Somehow the 'me' I always took so much for granted doesn't feel so solid. Like my vital essence has sprung a leak, like one of Jacob's footballs that Pooch has punctured in the garden.

36

Tom's reassurance has done me the world of good, but even so, I find myself counting the minutes until my Friday run with the girls. I'm wearing my new leggings and I have also co-opted Jacob's old football jacket and gloves. When we meet by the bench, I'm delighted to see Sian jogging from the car park.

We do some of Tamsin's warm-up exercises and set off. Amma is full of news and tells us all about how she's been up to London for an audition.

'What was it for?' I ask, slightly glamour-struck.

'Something I'll never get in a month of Sundays,' she says, 'although it's a shame, because it's a for a Netflix series.' She sips from her water bottle. 'A conflicted female politician. You have no idea how much I could sink my teeth into that one.' She sounds wistful.

'Well… well done for going,' I say.

'I only went just to keep onside with Evan. It's the first decent audition he's got me in over a year.'

'And you wore your wig?' Tamsin asks.

'Oh yes… and full make-up. They didn't twig anything was wrong at all.'

I think she's so brave to have gone for it and for not letting cancer stand in her way. I mean, maybe, just *maybe*, her way of dealing with all this works. Maybe stoically getting through it and not telling anyone could be the way to go. It's too late for me, of course, but now I wonder whether I'd have been able to front it out in Wishwells, because I *so* wish Lorna and Pierre didn't know about what is happening to me.

When it gets to my turn to share, it's not long before I'm into the saga of Lorna going to the awards ceremony without me. It's so good they all know about my situation at work and I can launch straight in and get it off my chest.

'So let me get this straight? You were up for an award for retailer of the year and they went to the ceremony without you? They didn't even tell you they were going?' Tamsin asks.

'Nope. They kept it all under wraps.'

'What a fucking bitch,' Amma says. 'That's outrageous. Wishwells is yours. That was *your* award to collect.'

Exactly. She's *exactly right*.

'Tom thinks I shouldn't be upset,' I tell them, feeling awful for slagging him off, but righteous too. I *haven't* been going mad if this is their reaction.

'Lorna thinks she was doing me a favour.'

'Wow. What a *cow*,' Tamsin says.

'I cried all weekend,' I admit.

'I'm not surprised,' Sian says. 'I would have too.'

Once again, talking to the girls during our run makes me feel empowered and I go into work determined that Lorna and Pierre aren't going to undermine me, but it's not that easy, especially as Lorna has re-assembled the table in the shop, and filled it with the re-priced Jackson stuff, confining Lisa's gorgeous cups to the back shelf. And, not only that, the poster on the door window has been taken down again.

I try to mention it over the following days, but Lorna is in too big a whirlwind preparing to go to Birmingham. She makes me feel that I've caused her untold stress by not going too – even though she's the one that has banned me from going herself.

She doesn't mention my impending operation at all. Instead, on Tuesday, she smooches Jackson and tells Pierre she'll miss him, before actually snogging him in the office. I stare at her as she leaves, but she ignores me and doesn't wish me luck.

Wondering if they've actually forgotten that I'm having a major operation, I remind Pierre that I'll be off for the next few days.

'Oh yes, you must take all the time you need, Keira,' he says. 'We'll be fine here.'

I watch him sit at his laptop in the meeting room, suspicion racing through me. I'm worried about leaving him in charge with the Saturday girls for extra cover. I simply don't trust him. I call Moira, but she must have lost her phone, because now her number is dead.

Downstairs, before I leave, I stand in the shop, wanting the familiarity of it to fill me with the confidence, but all I can think about is that tomorrow they are going to slit me open and take away my breast.

And what if I don't survive the operation? What if I'm allergic to the general anaesthetic? I've never had a general anaesthetic. How do they know I'll be OK?

And the scalpels. They are going to cut off my boob. *SLIT*. With the sharpest knife. Sharper than our crazy sharp kitchen knife. And my nipple. What will they do with my nipple? They're going to put it in a bag. In a bin. Thrown out with less ceremony than the scrapings from last year's Christmas dinner into the recycling.

'Oh, Dad,' I whisper. 'This is really scary.'

37

When Bea wakes us up the following morning, she looks all little and frightened and I hate the fact that it's *me* who's making her scared. It feels all wrong: Parents aren't supposed to terrify their children. That's kind of a basic rule.

'Pinch, punch first of the month, no returns, white rabbit,' she says, heralding the first day of the month.

'A flick and a kick for being so quick,' I tell her gently, pulling her into my arms. I bury my face into her hair, breathing her in. Her eyes well up when she looks at me.

'It won't hurt, darling, I promise,' I tell her. 'They'll give me lots of painkillers. You can see me right after school.'

In the hospital, I have to fill out a long medical questionnaire. I tick 'no' in so many boxes. No diseases. No history. Nada. I'm a picture of health – except I have cancer. It really feels like it's happening to someone else. Tom and I wait and eventually a nice nurse in outpatients takes my blood, height and weight and swabs me for MRSA. I have to poke a cotton bud along my bikini line.

Then, the matron comes in. She's wearing a plum coloured dress in which she looks very appealing. I notice Tom looking her up and down, but any glimmer of jealousy is negated by the fact that she's possibly one of the nicest people I've ever met. She explains what will happen to me in great detail. There's some new bits I hadn't realised. Like the fact they'll artificially respirate me during the operation, so I'll have a big tube down my throat. They'll also do a weird pump thing on my calves to keep my circulation going. But most bizarrely of all, they will inject me with blue dye, so that it'll show up in my lymph nodes. 'You may get blue tears afterwards,' she says.

And I'm *consenting* to this? Apparently I am, because I sign the forms, which I suspect is some kind of waiver that they're not really responsible if I die.

I get undressed and into the hospital gown, which I'm told to put on so the ties are at the front. Mr Mabiyan, my surgeon, visits and says it's all very simple and straightforward and I'll only be under for a couple of hours, like it's no big deal. And I guess, compared to so many operations, it's really not. Who am I to be such a wimp, when people have to face so much worse?

Tom says he's going to wait, but I'd rather he picked up Bea from school. He can bring the kids in later.

I nip to the loo and meet my eyes in the mirror, because in a few hours' time – if I wake up – I'll be completely different. This is the Cape Canaveral moment. 'I can do this thing,' I tell myself out loud. 'I will be marching up mountains when I'm ninety.'

I squeeze my boobs together and look down at my cleavage for the very last time. I read once that the actress, Scarlett Johansson calls her breasts 'The Girls' and I've always related to that. I stare at my left breast.

'Goodbye darling,' I whisper.

Back in the room, Tom looks like he's trying to be really brave.

'So this is it,' I tell him.

He holds my hair away from my face. 'I'll see you later,' he says. 'Don't do anything crazy.'

'I'll be fine,' I tell him, knowing instinctively that I have to be strong in this moment. If I crumble now, it'll be terrible for him. 'I love you,' I whisper.

Then Sam, my breast cancer nurse, is there. 'All set?' she says. Tom and I hug tightly before I get into the wheelchair they'll wheel me away in.

38

Clack, clack, clack.

I come to.

There's beeping. And clacking.

Mum. She's here.

And then I think, with an inward smile, *of course she's here.*

I turn my head to see her deeply concentrating as she knits by my bedside. It's fiddly by the look of it. Something in fawn wool. She's consulting a pattern that is leant up against the bar on the side of my bed.

Oh no. Not something else for Jacob. He's got five of Mum's creations at the back of his wardrobe.

I try and speak, but my mouth feels gluey. I try again.

'What are you making?' I manage.

Mum doesn't look up from the pattern. 'I'm knitting you a breast,' she says. 'A knitted knocker.' She turns the paper pattern towards me. 'I found it in a magazine.'

I nod and close my eyes and smile. 'I like that. A knitted knocker.'

I'm floating on the clouds, but a second later, I feel her familiar cool hand stroke the hair away from my forehead and I make a sigh as Mum's lips kiss me very gently.

'My brave girl,' she whispers.

When I come round again, I've been moved from the recovery room to a ward. Mum is still clacking away doggedly by my side, determined to keep guard until Tom and the kids arrive.

Eventually, I ask her to go downstairs and get me something to eat. I know the big M&S in the entrance lobby is catnip to her and she won't be able to resist my request.

Alone for the first time, I breathe out slowly. I feel fuzzy, but in a good way. I can't believe it's all over.

I lift up the sheet and peep down the front of my hospital gown. My skin is yellow where it's been washed with iodine, something they told me they'd do. There's a large rectangular plaster over the area that was once my left breast. My scar tissue is fairly swollen so it just looks like a smaller breast with a plaster on. I notice that I'm wired up to a tube coming from beneath the plaster. I follow the tube down to where a bag of what looks like raspberry coulis is tucked under a sheet.

And then I look up and see someone talking to the nurse, who points in my direction. It's Amma. She's carrying a bunch of pink roses already in a vase.

'Aha! You're awake,' she says, beaming a smile. She's wearing a funky red cashmere jumper and red lipstick and an elaborate turban with huge earrings.

'It's good to see you,' I slur.

'You like my Gypsy Rose Lee?' she asks, putting her hand under her chin and doing a funny pout. 'I come to tell your fortune, Lady,' she says in a silly accent.

She puts the roses down on the Formica cabinet next to my bed, kisses my cheek and then delves inside her cloth bag. 'I was passing and I won't stay, but I bought you ear plugs,' she says, depositing things on the hospital blanket. 'And an eye mask. Believe me. You'll need them. It's impossible to sleep in this place. She takes my hand and peers down at me. 'How you doing?'

'I'm off my tit,' I say. 'In fact, I'm totally off my knocker.'

'Good,' she says, laughing at my joke. 'Ah, dear, sweet morphine. It's a marvellous feeling. Get them to keep you topped up, since this is the only time you'll get to do that shit without feeling guilty, or getting arrested.'

We're both laughing when Tom and the kids arrive.

'Hey,' Tom says, looking a little put out to see a stranger holding my hand. Tilly, Jacob and Bea run to my side. They are loaded up with flowers which are nowhere near as nice as Amma's, but the kids have homemade cards for me. I feel my heart aching when I look at them, admiring Bea's card with a tissue-paper blue butterfly.

'Tom, this is Amma,' I tell him and they shake hands across my bed. She says hello to the kids and Jacob stares at her with an open mouth, like a groupie. He probably recognises her from TV.

'I'll leave you to it,' she says. 'I'm in on Friday for my first chemo so if you're still here, I'll come and find you. Nice to meet you all.'

She leaves and Tom leans in to kiss me. 'I thought you didn't want any visitors?' he says. We had a long chat about how it would be after my operation and how he'd have to fend off Joss and everyone else who had expressed an interest in coming to see me the second I came to.

'She just turned up,' I tell him.

'Who was she?' Bea asks.

'She's one of my running friends,' I tell her, stroking her hair.

It's only a few hours since I saw her this morning, but Bea's gorgeousness takes my breath away.

'I like her,' Bea announces.

'She's very glamorous,' Tilly says. 'Do we know her from somewhere?'

'She's an actress, mainly theatre, but she's done a bit of TV,' I tell Jacob, as he leans in and I kiss him.

I'm glad we have something to talk about other than the fact that I'm lying helpless in a hospital bed.

39

Time slips and slides over the next twenty-four hours, no doubt because of the morphine. There are no blue tears, but I do have crazy dreams. In one particularly vivid one, I find myself running across that beach with that pack of handsome men at the beginning of *Chariots of Fire*, with the Vangelis music pulsing out. And I'm getting faster and faster, racing through the pack, until I'm running neck and neck at the front with Nigel Havers, and he turns to me and grins and says that wonderful line in the film, 'with hope in our hearts and wings on our heels'.

And I've no idea what it means. Maybe just that deep down I secretly fancy Nigel Havers. But when I wake up, it really stays with me – along with the urge to get back out there as soon as possible… to get running. As though it's something I don't just want to do, but something I now need. Because Amma, Tamsin and Sian seem to be able to make me feel more like me than anyone else at the moment.

All of which, of course, makes me now determined to leave the hospital as soon as possible. Amma's right: There's also so much bleeping and so many interruptions, that once I'm off the morphine, I just can't sleep. And the food is not exactly terrible – just unidentifiable – apart from the peach melba yoghurt.

During the small hours, I chat with the lovely nurse about

her old life in Bulgaria, her boyfriend problems and also about our dogs. She has a crazy Pomeranian, but then she gets all excited when she realises my connection to Jackson, of whom she's an avid Instagram follower.

But the talk of dogs makes me miss Pooch. In fact, I miss everything. I miss Wishwells. And I know I'm lucky that I've had so many visitors and that Tom is more than capable of looking after the kids and Mum's on hand to help, but I can't help feeling that I need to be back on my feet. NOW. Still in charge.

Mr Mabiyan does his rounds and he assures me that he's got good margins – the amount of healthy flesh he cut out around my tumour. I've done my homework and I know that it's vital to have good margins, so it's a relief to hear this.

He inspects me and says the nurse can remove the bag of raspberry coulis and that the tube can come out of the wound. It all happens very fast and I don't get to inspect the damage, before I'm re-bandaged and told to keep a close eye on whether my non-breast fills up with fluid. It's all so visceral… so blood, guts and gore. I just want to be in my own bedroom and out of here.

Eventually, late on Friday, they set me free.

When I get home, Pooch is overwhelmed to see me. He does three hundred and sixty degree circles and wees a little bit on my Ugg boot. Force of habit drives me into the kitchen, where I immediately start emptying the dishwasher. Tom gets cross and takes it as a criticism and, backed up by the kids, I'm banished up to the bedroom.

I'm touched to see that someone has changed our bed linen

and there's flowers by my side of the bed. There's a card next to them and I see it's from Pierre, Lorna and the staff at Wishwells.

The flowers are lovely and the thought is there, but the message annoys me. Wishwells isn't some giant corporate conglomerate. And when did Pierre get top billing?

In the bathroom, I look in the mirror and my body looks and feels strange. My hands and inner elbows are battered and bruised with puncture wounds. In fact, I feel quite beaten up.

I stare at the big rectangular plaster on my chest. The swelling on that side has gone down and my chest is flat and it's so weird to see my left rib cage. It's like a corner of me has been chopped off and I'm all odd angles, like someone has selfishly cut the nose off the big Christmas brie. I put on my favourite, oldest buttoned-up shirt. In the past, I've worn it over a bikini on the beach, thinking that I look kind of sexy, but I don't feel sexy in it now. I feel flattened, in every sense.

Tom and the kids come in with a tray and we all sit on our bed to eat dinner. It feels like we're all on a boat together. Everyone seems super happy that the cancer has gone and want me to be happy too, but my smiles feel false. I feel like a frost-bitten polar explorer returning home – not quite able to believe it's all over.

When they all disappear to do the washing up, I text Amma to ask how her chemo went.

A: Still high on the steroids. I'll start to feel shit on Sunday.

Me: Shall I come and visit you?

A: Only if you're up and about, but don't worry. How you feeling?

Me: Tearful.

A: That's the anaesthetic.

Me: … and angry.

A: Normal. Why wouldn't you be angry? It's a brutal operation.

Her text makes me cry. It's just such a relief to be given permission to feel like I do.

Me: It feels medieval.

A: I know. But it won't feel like that for long. Welcome to the OBC (One Boob Club).

I laugh, but it's not really that funny having one boob. I stare down at my right breast below my shirt. Alone, she looks like an exhausted udder. I wonder if she misses her sister. I wonder if I'll get phantom nipple itch, like amputees get.

40

I'm not sure how the Victorians mastered the art of convalescing. They'd get ill, then repair to take the sea air for a month or so to recover, sitting in airy conservatories with rugs over their knees, with nothing to do, except drink healthy tonics, read the paper and snooze. But I just can't do it. I feel indolent and anxious sitting in bed, but then I get up and do too much and feel weepy and exhausted.

I also can't help fretting about Ruby and Becca in Birmingham and what level of tat they might be spending our precious resources on. I'm not convinced by this new online drive of Lorna's. I know I should trust her judgement, but I feel increasingly anxious about the direction she wants Wishwells to take.

I text her, but she sends a reply saying that the shop is covered and that my time would be better spent trying to get better rather than micromanaging her.

Chastened, I snuggle up with Bea on the sofa and watch comfort movies – silly family favourites, we usually reserve for Christmas: *E.T.*, *Home Alone*, *Overboard*, whilst trying not to think about what has happened to me.

On Saturday Zippo rings. He's in the vicinity, having been to a gig, and it's nice to hear Tom laughing on the phone, the way only Zippo can make him laugh.

'He wants to know if he can stay the night?' Tom says, putting his hands over the phone. He makes a grimace. 'Is it too soon?'

'No. No, it's fine,' I tell him. 'It'll be nice to see him.'

I hoof myself off the sofa, thoughts crowding in about cleaning the bathroom and getting the ironing pile off the spare room bed. Then I remember that Tilly has commandeered the spare room for her art project. We are not remotely visitor-ready, but Tom reminds me of the squat he lived in with Zippo back in the day. Of all people, Zippo can put up with our shabby ways.

I'm excited about seeing my old friend and I get dressed for the first time in days and put make-up on, but it's only when I open the door and see that he's brought his latest girlfriend, Lucy, with him that I know I'm not resilient enough to entertain strangers.

Tom looks at me and raises his eyebrows in amusement because Lucy is at least fifteen years younger than Zippo. In fact, she's a nubile, hippyish, 30-something, who lollops on Zippo and stares at him with puppy-dog adoration. That's when she's not doing lazy (and yet somehow ostentatious) yoga stretches, which reveal that she's not wearing a bra.

He looks relaxed and tanned from a month in Kerala at Christmas and is wearing harem pants and biker boots and she's in a matching outfit. His hair is thinning and it's an unflattering shoulder length, but Lucy doesn't seem to mind. Zippo clearly adores her too and they show us their matching tattoos.

I watch them smoking roll-ups at the back door, resentful of the smoky draft that comes into the kitchen, even though only a short time ago, if the kids weren't around, I might have joined them. They down bottles of beer, one after the other, whilst chowing down on crisps, which I don't eat, because I'm trying very hard not to eat too much processed stuff. I feel separate, not just to them and all the guiltless, harmless fun they're having, but separate to me, the old me, the BC one who isn't here anymore.

Pull yourself together, I tell myself, and for a while I do. Because, yes, not everything about my first post-op social outing is terrible. I find it refreshing, for example, not to be talking about me or my cancer, but as the evening wears on and it's never mentioned, I start to wonder if it's because Zippo hasn't told Lucy? I don't get the chance to find out, but the question fizzes on the end of my tongue.

I conclude that Lucy is only interested in herself and Zippo. That said, she doesn't really understand his jokes at all, or any of our references to the good old days of the Nineties, when we were clubbing and she was practically still in nappies. Supper gets later and later and eventually I go to the kitchen to retrieve the lasagne from the oven. Tom is too busy laughing with Zippo and I'm annoyed, because he'd promised that I wouldn't have to lift a finger if Zippo came.

Lucy refuses a plate, when I start serving the food.

'Maybe you should go vegan,' she tells me, authoritatively, watching a forkful of lasagne enter my mouth. 'I've heard it's *sooo* much better for you.'

Oh! So she *does* know about the cancer. She must do to make comments like that. But what exactly does she mean? That if I'd just eaten a bit more healthily, then I wouldn't have got sick? She's smiling when she says it and I realise that she doesn't mean any harm, that she's just trying to make conversation, but even so, it smarts.

It smarts, too, that she moves the conversation on and starts evangelising Zippo, who happily reaches out for a third hunk of garlic bread. He grins at her, clearly enthralled by her youthful ways... or maybe just her pert, cellulite-free bottom.

And there it is, I'm doing it again. Thinking mean thoughts. Being jealous. Not being myself. I feel a wave of tiredness coming over me and escape to the kitchen with Tilly.

'What a baby hunter,' she says disparagingly.

'You think?'

'It's so obvious.'

'Surely not? Zippo is nearly fifty. He's far too old to start having kids now.'

'No he's not. You know, I read a thing about internet dating.' I watch her remove the remnants from a tub of Philadelphia with her finger. 'This survey said that all men – regardless of age – think their ideal woman is twenty-one. Maybe mid-twenties at a push,' she continues, chucking the pot in the bin.

'How very depressing. Can you wash and recycle that, please?'

She rolls her eyes at me, in a 'get with the programme, Mum – and can you get off my back whilst you're at it' kind of a way. Surely her dubious statistic can't be right? I mean, all the women I know in their forties and fifties are amazing. Why wouldn't Zippo find one of us attractive? Someone his own age? What is wrong with the world? What is this obsession with youth, when it turns out that old age is really the only prize worth having?

In the small hours, we hear Lucy and Zippo having noisy sex on the sofa bed downstairs as I get ready for bed and it makes me feel even more ancient.

Tom and I lie in bed listening for a minute and I'm about to launch forth and tell him exactly how I feel, when his phone rings. I watch him lean over and put on his glasses. This better not be a work call, because he's too drunk to take it. Or *her*. Janine. Christ. When did she start becoming a *her*?

But maybe, like Zippo, Tom can't help himself being attracted to a younger woman. And she him? Working late on a weekend, getting in his good books? I see where this is going…

'Let it go to answer machine,' I tell him.

He pulls a face as he looks at the caller ID. 'It's Mum,' he says, clicking the green button and I groan and roll over.

41

With her usual spectacular timing, my dear mother-in-law, Hilary, has chosen this inopportune moment to 'have a fall'. I nod, tight-lipped as Tom gets up early the next morning and explains that he has no choice but to make the five-hour drive to Devon. This is not the first time his mother has 'had a turn' in order to get Tom to come and see her, when there's been absolutely nothing wrong.

'It sounds serious,' he says.

'Well, if it is, wouldn't she be in hospital?'

'Don't be like that.'

'Like what?'

He gives me a look.

'I'll be back as soon as I can. She sounded really shaken up on the phone and Dad is not fit enough to help,' he says.

The only good news is that he gives Zippo and Lucy a lift back down to Devon. Zippo's yurt-making business is only a few miles from Tom's parents, so I wave them off, and gratefully head back to bed.

With Tom away, however, my convalescence comes to an abrupt end. At first, I'm happy to be up and about, but the kids refuse to go out in the rain and I have to take Pooch out, but I'm not quite ready for the elements. When I call Scout to tell her I'm on a walk, she's horrified and demands that I turn around and go back inside.

On the way home, I call Tom. It turns out his mother really *has* had a serious fall and has torn some ligaments in her knee, so I have to be contrite and sympathetic. And yes, OK, I feel suitably chastened and guilty too.

I sense that Tom wants me to be more understanding about how tough this is on him, particularly as his dad's mental state is much worse than he'd thought. We've suspected that he's been losing it for a while, but Tom reckons he definitely has dementia.

In the absence of anyone else, his mum is off-loading on him about how the new painkillers have ruined her bowels and caused her to need a 'manual evacuation'. The mind boggles.

'TMI,' I tell Tom, but he can't see that my laugh is one of horror. He's miffed that I'm not engaging more with how awful it is, but I'm unusually low on sympathy. And that really *is* too much information. When did it become acceptable for Hilary to talk about her toilet habits with her son?

Mum comes round to tell me off for doing too much, but then won't leave herself. I'm so exhausted that I completely fail to sleep.

On Tuesday, I'm a bit tearful and wobbly, but force myself into work for a bit. I'm really hoping Moira will be back from her holiday. I need to see her friendly face and explain what's happened to me. I can almost recite how our conversation will go – how she'll be mortified that she hasn't been here for me when I tell her everything she's missed. But I'll forgive her immediately and then… then the Wishwells boat won't feel so rocky.

But as soon as I walk in through the shop door, Lorna seems offended by my visit and wants to know why I'm in, when they can manage perfectly well without me. I would have thought she might have asked how my operation went. If she'd been the one in hospital, I'd have gone to visit.

But she's been busy. I notice that a new clothes rail has been installed at the back of the shop. I've never wanted to do many clothes – instinctively feeling that this would be treading on the toes of Joelle's shop, a few doors down.

It seems that they've all been on a major spending spree in Birmingham. Ruby holds up two samples of cashmere-mix jumpers she's picked out for the spring collection and wants me to make a choice between them, but I can't. It's too much to take in.

There's also a new member of staff in the shop, who I've never met and Lorna explains that Tyra is a new member of 'the team'. She tells me proudly that Tyra is from a fashion background, like this is a proper asset to Wishwells and I'm sure, in some ways it probably is. Tyra seems like a nice young woman, with immaculate skin and a nose piercing, but she treats Lorna like she's the boss and not me. I offer to show her how things are done, but Lorna insists that they have it covered and I see her reaching out to stop me from tidying. She tells me more forcefully to go home.

'But I want to stay,' I tell her.

'But you really don't look very well, Keira,' she says, before looking me up and down. I notice now that both Ruby and Tyra are both very smartly dressed and Lorna herself is in a designer button-down dress. I feel shabby in my Ugg boots and jeans and I remember that I didn't put very much make-up on and haven't washed my hair.

I think about apologising and then stop myself. I don't have to apologise for having had a mastectomy, surely?

'Don't be offended,' she says. 'It's just that we're *trying* to be aspirational, that's all.'

Oh! And my haggard look doesn't cut it. I get it.

42

Back at home, Bea is in tears as I've failed to order her the right hoodie for her street dance performance, Jacob has trampled mud throughout the house after football, Pooch has been sick in his bed, the conservatory roof has leaked onto the new iPad and then to top it all off, I get a sniffy text message from the attendance secretary at Tilly's college saying she's bunked off lessons.

I stomp upstairs, ignoring the sensible Keira in my head, who is wind-milling her arms, trying to get my attention… trying desperately to make me remember all the parenting blogs I've read, but suddenly, I'm a juggernaut of stress with no brakes and without knocking, I fling open Tilly's bedroom door. She's getting ready to go to her friend Destiny's, but I'm not going to let her go now.

'So… the attendance people rang. Where did you go? Huh? You think it's OK to bunk off?' I demand. 'Just because Dad's not here?'

She hastily shuts her make-up case and gets up. 'No.'

There's an odd smell in her room. Has she been smoking?

'Have you been *smoking*?' My voice is shrill.

'For fuck's sake,' she mutters.

'Don't you use that language with me, young lady.'

She barges past me, out of her room and stomps down the stairs, jolting my shoulder. A sharp pain sears through my scar.

'Ow,' I yelp.

'Oh stop milking it, Mother,' she says, and I gulp, stunned that she could be so nasty.

'Come back here and apologise.'

'No,' she shouts. And then the front door slams.

The noise reverberates around the house. Jacob comes out of his room, slowly clapping his hands. 'And mother of the year goes to…'

'Oh, shut up,' I snap, biting my urge to say something much more profane.

'You know she hasn't been bunking off, Mum. That's just her college being useless. She's been out of lessons because she's been doing her volunteering at St Margaret's. For her Duke of Edinburgh Award. Remember?'

Oh…

SHIT.

'She didn't say anything,' I say, weakly, thinking what an idiot I've been.

I go into Tilly's room, feeling her residual hatred like it's a pulsing energy. The smell has definitely got worse. And then I see the culprit: Her hair straighteners are on, scorching a mark in the melamine dressing table. She hadn't been smoking at all.

I pick them up and drop them, burning myself in the process. And then I do swear. I shout 'Fuck' so loudly, I hear the pigeons fly off the roof and Pooch starts barking.

43

I feel wretched about Tilly and when Tom calls, he's too frazzled to cope with me.

'Why did you have to be so confrontational with her?' he asks. 'You know what Tilly is like.'

I resent him telling me off.

'I know, but—'

'Look, I'll come back tomorrow,' he says, as if he's the only one who can parent.

'I can deal with it.'

'Clearly not,' he says and I practically slam down the phone. The burn on my thumb throbs.

Then the doorbell goes and I jump up. That must be Tilly.

But it's not Tilly. It's Sian.

She's holding a large dish covered in foil.

'I brought you a curry from the café,' she says, lifting the dish. 'I was helping in the kitchen there today. It's not too hot. I think the kids will like it.'

'That's very kind.' A tear spills. 'Sorry,' I tell her. 'You caught me at a bit of a bad moment.'

She follows me into the kitchen and puts the dish on the stove.

Then she steps towards me and folds me into a gentle embrace, careful not to hurt my bandaged chest.

'I'm sorry,' I tell her, as I cry.

'Don't be.' She smiles at me. 'Keira, you don't have to be superwoman.'

'I seem to be getting everything wrong. And I was so good at my life, you know?' I confess, grateful she's here and lending a sympathetic ear.

'Look, you won't always feel like this. Your life, from what I can see is *still* great. You have all the stuff that matters. And even a job that you love.'

'I suppose.'

'This cancer is not going to define you, Keira. Don't let it.'

We chat a while longer and I'm grateful for her perspective – for her simple kind act of holding up a mirror and reminding me of myself. She's right. I do have so much to be grateful for.

'Are you missing your job?' I ask her, getting a sense that she's not feeling so defined herself.

'Yes, but I can't get another one doing what I do without a reference and Lianne, my old team leader… she won't say anything nice about me, so there's no point in asking her.'

'Why not?'

She sighs. 'Because I left so suddenly. Let's just say, I didn't exactly follow the protocol.'

'What happened?'

'I kind of lost my rag, swore at her and left. Not very professional, I know, but I'd had enough by then.'

'Well, I don't blame you. This whole thing is all rather stressful. And she sounds awful.'

'She was. But you can't just walk out and expect to be treated like a grown-up afterwards, it seems.'

Compared to that, I guess Lorna really isn't so bad.

Tilly comes back at half eleven. Her eyes are red-rimmed and I wonder, for a moment, whether she's stoned as well as upset. *Stand down*, I tell myself, because I've already accused her of bunking off and smoking today.

'Listen, I'm really sorry,' I tell her, intercepting her just inside the front door. 'I completely forgot that you'd been volunteering.'

She looks at the carpet and scuffs the toe of her trainer on the first stair. Pooch waddles over and she ruffles his ears.

'I'm sorry too. I was mean,' she says.

I step closer. 'How did it go, anyway?' I ask, although as Jacob has already pointed out, it's way too late to ask this question.

She shrugs. 'It was OK.'

'Only OK? I thought you'd been looking forward to St Margaret's?'

'It's a hospice, Mum. Most of the people there are going to die any second.'

I take a step closer and lift her chin and what I see in her face is… I don't know… fear? Resentment? Or something more complex than that? She's growing up so fast, growing away so fast, I can't bear it. And what if I'm making it worse? What if what I've been through – am going through – is going to wreck our relationship? No, I won't let that happen. I won't let this drive us apart.

'Come here,' I tell her, pulling her into my arms. Her shoulders shake silently as she cries.

Afterwards, I make us both a hot chocolate and she asks me how I feel.

'Like I'm the worst mother in the world,' I tell her, and she laughs.

'At least you're being honest with yourself,' she teases.

'I don't know… I just want my life back,' I tell her and then her arms go round me.

'Oh, Mum. Come on. It's going to be fine,' she reassures me. But is it?

44

I'm very nervous about my appointment with Mr Mabiyan to discuss what they found when he did my operation. For the first time, it dawns on me that the news might be bad. As in really bad. As in screwed.

Mum wants to come, but I tell her that Tom – who has absolutely promised to be back in time from Devon to come with me – is coming, so she can go to aqua aerobics with Rob. But then Tom gets stuck in traffic, and without a car, I have to get a cab to the hospital alone. On the way, the driver regales me with the finer details of his mother's slow, torturous death from breast cancer.

I'm getting used to this now, this need people have to share their cancer stories with me, but you never get the good ones. Never the ones where, say, someone gets cancer and it inspires them to reassess their life and go into politics and bring about everlasting world peace… no, never that.

Or maybe there really aren't any good news cancer stories at all?

Mr Mabiyan is his usual jolly self and he's about to talk to me, when he's called away to a medical emergency in another room. Left alone in his office, I can't help noticing that there's a brown cardboard folder on his desk with my name printed on the label on the front. I do a fake whistle and look at the ceiling and then slide the folder towards me and open it.

The first page is my pathology report. My stomach jolts as I squint at it, trying to decipher the medical speak, but what becomes apparent is that my breast – including 110mm of my skin and my nipple – was sent to the lab, where a histopathologist called Dr Pedro Sousa took the specimen and chopped it up 'into 17 slices from medial to lateral'. *Seventeen slices. Wow.*

I imagine Doctor Pedro. He's in his thirties. Swarthy. South American maybe. In my mind's eye he's in a lab coat and eating a sandwich as he nonchalantly looks down the microscope at my tit slices. 'Nipple is in slices nine and ten.'

Oh dear God! I feel a little bit of sick pop into my mouth. This is why they don't let you see your medical notes.

I hear a noise and hastily shut the folder. The door opens and Tom rushes in, full of apologies. I've been so cross with him for being away and for being late, but I'm so glad he's here now. I hold on to his hand tightly, as Mr Mabiyan arrives. I don't tell Tom about slices nine and ten. I wish I could un-see that report.

Mr Mabiyan lays me down on the bed and the nurse comes in too. He gently takes off the large plaster covering my breast. He snips off some rogue stitches and looks at me, his head on the side, like he's a hairdresser.

Then I get up so that I can see for myself in the hazy plastic mirror on the wall. Tom comes over and puts his arm around my shoulder.

I have been dreading this moment, but it's not panning out at all how I'd imagined it, not with the surgeon and Tom and me all staring at the innocent line that was once my breast. It's like a block of flats has been dynamited and we're all staring at the flattened pile of rubble, trying to remember what the flats looked like.

'You're healing nicely,' Mr Mabiyan tells me, as if it's no big deal.

I meet Tom's eyes in the mirror and he looks away. I can't tell what he thinks. 'Can you tell us what you found?' Tom asks.

When you chopped up my breast like a gala pie at a picnic, I nearly say.

'Ah yes. Get dressed and come and sit down,' Mr Mabiyan says.

Back on the other side of the curtain, he sits in his leather chair which makes a hiss, then flips open the folder. He turns to me and laces his fingers, looking into my eyes as he delivers the verdict.

It's short and to the point. It's in line with what they suspected at the start, and the feeling that I'm on a conveyor belt and this is all very standard continues. There were cancerous cells in the lymph nodes they took out, so they're going to do six rounds of chemotherapy, radiotherapy and hormone treatment.

'Does that sound OK?' he asks, again, like I have a choice.

I've been warned there would be treatment, so I shouldn't be so shocked, but I am. Tom grips my hand.

Why does this feeling that I've been through enough persist? It's like I've been on a horrible ride in Cancer World and I really, really want to get off. Only it turns out, they don't let you off the ride – in fact, woo hoo, lookee now, they're jolting me straight round onto the big dipper.

45

On the night of Bea's street dance performance, Tom very nearly misses it because he's late back from work – even though it's been on the calendar for ages. Everyone is tense in the car and when I bump into the wall when I'm reversing into the last parking space in the school, Tom shouts at me.

'Bloody hell, watch out!'

'Calm down,' I yell back, but I'm furious that he's over-reacted. After all, I'm the good parker in the family. I'm the one with an unblemished record. And besides, there's no damage to the car – which has plenty of scratches and dinks on it, none of them attributable to me. I get out and slam the door and hardly get to wish Bea luck. She looks between me and Tom.

'Nice one, Mum,' Tilly says, kissing her sister, like this bad atmosphere is my fault.

Inside the hall, once we're seated, Tom looks down at his phone. I see a message from Janine on the screen. There's a kiss at the end of it.

A kiss. Who puts a kiss at the end of a message?

I frown at him and he puts his phone away, turning it off. I hate it that we're scratchy and tense with each other. I read his look and knowing him as well as I do, identify that there are at least three reasons for this current atmosphere.

Firstly – and most importantly – he's annoyed that what I'm

not saying is that I'm annoyed that he's working so much with Janine – although we both know this is the issue. He's caught me making a few snide under-my-breath comments about her when he's been singing her praises. It's very childish, I know, but I can't help myself. I resent him having someone else in his life who gives him an 'out' from the spider's web of cancer, which seems to have ensnared every part of my life.

Secondly, I am annoyed that he's having to put in the hours he missed because he was with his parents. And not only that, he's committed us all to going down to see them at the weekend – even though he's only just been.

Thirdly, he's annoyed that in the past few weeks I've become so disempowered at work – so unable to tell Pierre and Lorna what I want, resorting instead, to ranting about the situation at Wishwells at home. For every new rant, Tom has patiently offered plausible explanations and solutions, all of which I have batted away. I know his patience is wearing thin.

Bea's dance, however, takes my mind of it. Looking up on the stage, seeing my little girl tumbling and turning, I feel myself puffing up with pride as I watch her and her friends perform. They're so tight, so together and it's only now that it occurs to me that she's been practising this whilst all of the other stuff has been going on at home. The fact that she's out there, putting a brave face on, being exuberant and part of a team touches me in a way I hadn't expected and when the dance is over, I spring to my feet and clap enthusiastically, prompting a baffled standing ovation from our row.

Afterwards, Bea comes over – her cheeks still pink from the exertion of her dance.

'You were amazing,' I tell her, hugging her tightly and closing my eyes as I kiss the top of her head. What I don't express is that I'm so glad I was here for her. So glad I got to see her dance. So very grateful that even though we were all rowing on the way here, it's so precious to be here with my family to see her and support her. That I will do whatever it takes to always be there for her. No matter what.

Molly, Bea's friend from school is in front of me and is nearest and I reach out to touch her. 'You too, poppet,' I say, smiling. 'I could never do that. That was fantastic. Honestly.'

But to my surprise, Molly won't meet my eye. Instead, she twists the fabric of her hoodie over her hand, as if to protect herself from my touch. Bea looks embarrassed and I remove my hand, feeling burnt.

Grace, Molly's mum is suddenly there. 'Oh, Keira,' she says, her head cocked on one side. 'I'm so glad you're here. So glad you made it,' she says, leaning in, in order to be confidential. 'Now, don't forget to email me that schedule for your chemo and I'll set up the rota for meals,' she says. 'Everyone at school wants to help. I know what you're going through is so hard. *So* hard,' she emphasizes.

'That's very kind,' I say, then eyeball Bea. 'Shall we get our things together to go home?'

I'm more shaken up by Molly's reaction to me than I want to be. I hate feeling that she thinks I'm infectious and I can't help feeling that Grace is to blame for Molly's attitude and I'm annoyed that she's clearly talking to all the other school mums about me. Just as I did at the beginning, I still hate being treated as different. Different to what, though? Different to the old me, I suppose. The old me that was having a lark at

New Year. *That* old me. I think back to being outside Scout's kitchen, revelling in my smugness at my perfect life.

But that was then. And this is, well, this is where I am now. I suddenly start to understand what Sian was saying. About how she'd changed, but didn't know how. Because already, I'm different and I can see the shore of the island of Old Keira receding as I sail further and further away from myself. Lord knows how I'll feel when I've got through all the treatment.

Back at home, I'm exhausted and want to head to bed, but the washing machine is beeping to signal that it's ended the cycle, so I go into the utility room.

'Tilly, can you come and help?' I call, waiting for her response. After all, she's the one that needs her black shirt to be dry for the morning. I'm a bit annoyed she didn't think of hanging out the washing herself earlier, without being asked.

How have I raised children that are so thoughtless, I wonder? Not thoughtless, exactly. I mean, they're wonderful, but pretty happy to be waited on hand and foot. I see now – with blinding clarity – that this is my own fault. For the sake of efficiency, I have done everything for them, but in doing so have made them totally reliant on me.

My mother never treated me and Billy the way I treat our kids. We were latchkey children, used to heating up a tin of something with lumps in it for tea and counting ourselves lucky to get three television channels and content to watch the test card whilst waiting for them to start. If I wanted something new for going out, I'd get inventive, repurposing something old. I was resourceful and frugal and proud of it, but somehow, I haven't managed to bring up my kids with the same values.

'Out you go,' I tell Pooch, opening the back door. He looks up at me and stands steadfastly by the back door. 'Go on. Go and have a wee.' I boot him out.

'What is it?' Tilly says, arriving in the utility room, a har-rumph in her voice.

'When I start chemo, I won't be able to hang out the washing all the time. You'll have to help,' I tell her. 'And you'll have to empty the dishwasher too. That sort of thing.'

'Alright. Don't have a go.'

'I'm not having a go,' I say.

We hang up the damp washing in silence. I know I've over-done it, humping the wet washing in the washing basket. My arm and my scar throbs.

'Did you notice how Molly was with me?' I ask.

'No,' Tilly says. 'Why?'

'She was just… I don't know. She acted like I was infectious or something.'

'Take no notice. They're just little kids.'

I take one of Tilly's lacy bras and hang it on the wooden struts and a pang runs through me for what I've lost and my hand lingers on it.

'How are you feeling about it?' she asks. 'Is it still sore… the… I don't know… what do you call it?'

'The boobless boob?'

'Is that what you're calling it?'

'What else would you suggest?'

'How about the stump?'

'The *stump*? Fucking hell, Tilly,' I say and she laughs at her own insensitivity and my swearing.

'Sorry. That sounds all wrong.'

46

I have the hot bath that Bea has vacated, and Tom comes in with a herbal tea, just as I'm getting out. Maybe Tilly has told him about her stump comment. Perhaps it only hurt so much because it's true. My chest does feel stumpy and bereft, like I've lost something precious. My railcard, or wallet, or... oh yes, my tit.

He puts the tea down and I know him well enough to know that this is an apology. I wrap the towel around me.

'I bought you some Bio Oil,' he says. 'I was in the supermarket and I remembered,' he says, pulling a bottle of orange liquid out of his back pocket. 'Mr Mabiyan said to rub it in every night,' he reminds me. 'Then the scar won't be too bad.'

He pulls my towel down gently.

'Don't look at it,' I tell him.

'Why?'

'Because...'

Janine has gorgeous plump breasts. And she's young and healthy. And it turns out that health is the only real currency that counts. And she has it in abundance and I've got cancer.

'Keira, you've had an operation,' he says. 'That's all.'

I'm silent.

'You're still you. You're still beautiful,' he says and kisses me. He takes the oil and puts some in his hand. 'Come on. Let's have a rub, shall we?'

I relent, but it feels oddly intimate having him touch my scar. There's some sensation, but mostly numbness.

'Don't. It feels too... I don't know...' I tell him, putting my hand over his.

He looks into my eyes. 'I love your scar,' he tells me. 'Do you hear me? I love it because it means you're still here with me. Right where you should be. And if I love it, can't you learn to love it too?'

I nod and blow out a tearful breath.

'Come on. We can do this,' he says, chivvying me along.

I've got what I've found out is called cording in my armpit, which is a side-effect of the operation, when Mr Mabiyan chopped out my lymph nodes. There's long rope-like knotty ridges in the soft tissue beneath my skin which hurt when Tom helps me lift my arm up. Despite feeling squeamish about my scar, I can't deny how good it feels for Tom to massage the knots.

'Of all the things I thought might go wrong with my body, I never thought we'd end up focused on my left armpit,' I tell him.

'Me neither,' he says. 'But I kind of like your armpit. It's a very attractive armpit, as armpits go.'

47

Amma is already by the bench on Friday morning. She has been vacillating on our WhatsApp chat this morning, unsure of whether she'd feel well enough to come and meet us after her chemo, but Tamsin demanded that she 'get off her whingeing tuches', so I'm delighted to see her.

I kind of admire Tamsin. It's really difficult to disobey her. She'd be much better suited to being a motivational coach than working in her office. Or running the country. Yeah, she'd be pretty good at that. I can see Tamsin and Sian deep in conversation as they come from the other end of the park. When they arrive, I see that Tamsin is wearing glittery emerald green eye make-up and silvery lipstick.

I kiss them all. 'How are you feeling?' I ask Amma. I've been checking in with her daily, mostly to give her moral support, but also to know what to expect when I start chemo – although we all know that everyone reacts differently. Encouragingly, Amma looks radiantly healthy for someone who is processing a load of chemicals.

'Not dead yet, as the wise one says,' she replies, nodding her head towards Tamsin.

'That's the spirit,' Tamsin says. 'Feel good to be out?' she asks me.

I nod. 'Nervous. First time since the op.'

'You'll be lighter without that breast, so potentially you might go faster,' she teases, before we set off. 'Let's see if you can beat your time. I'm feeling OK today, so I reckon we should do two and a half laps. Maybe three. What d'you say? Amma? You think you can manage it?'

'If you can, I can,' Amma says.

Three laps of the park seems like a crazily long way, but as I look between Amma, Tamsin and Sian, I see there's no choice. If they can do it, then so must I. I adjust my top. I have Mum's knitted knocker stuffed down one pouch of my exercise bra and looking down at my T-shirt, everything looks like normal. I stretch up my arm, checking my cording isn't too tight.

'That's good to keep it moving,' Sian tells me as we set off, and it's reassuring to find out from her that what I'm experiencing is completely normal and will simmer down.

'Aye, aye, it's Morticia,' one of the builders says, as we pass them.

'Drop dead,' Tamsin says, flipping a finger at them.

'Oooo!' The builders tease, glad to get a rise out of her.

Amma looks glamorous in a blue turban and I tell her how stylish it is, admiring her fringe and how much it suits her.

'Oh this thing. This is a tuck in,' she says, matter-of-factly pulling out a little bit of hair attached to a band from underneath her turban.

'That's so clever,' I tell her, holding the fringe in my hands. 'It looks so realistic.'

'We'll get you one,' Tamsin says although I haven't had a fringe since the early Noughties. 'I'll take you to see Amanda the hairdresser and we'll fit you out for wigs.' She says it proprietorially, as if this is her role.

'Thank you,' I laugh.

'Sooner rather than later,' she says. 'I'll ring and make an appointment.'

'I'm not sure I'll be like Amma, though,' I say. 'You make all this look so effortless and stylish,' I tell her, handing the fringe back.

'My mentor, Vapes – she was this crazy actress on my first job, said that no matter how shit you feel, always try and look your best. I try and live by that, although some days are very much harder than others.'

'Er… tell me about it,' I say, then tell them about being banished from the shop by Lorna when I went in after my operation and I wasn't looking on-brand.

'That was mean,' Tamsin said.

'Yeah, well, maybe she had a point. I should take a leaf out of your book and make more of an effort.'

'This Lorna… she *really* sounds awful,' Sian says.

'I think she means well. Maybe she's right and I'm being oversensitive.'

'I don't think so. I mean, that thing about the awards ceremony. I've been thinking about it,' Sian says and I'm both surprised and grateful she's remembered our conversation. 'I mean, if they were going, wouldn't they have talked about it? It's almost like they kept you in the dark.'

'*Exactly.*'

'And I remember, you said before about the email business…'

'Yes! It's just weird. Honestly, they're making me think I'm going mad. Because there's a read message in my inbox about the awards ceremony, but I swear I didn't see it. And Lorna just won't believe me.'

'Well, maybe they *are* messing with you,' Sian says.

'What do you mean?'

'You know I told you my job was very boring?'

'Yes.'

'Well, it was… for huge stretches of time, because I was a forensic accountant.'

'A what?'

'I had to go through people's computers and find out what they'd been up to. You'd be surprised how many devious ways people try and stab their colleagues in the back. And fucking with their emails is classic.'

'You honestly think Pierre might have done that?' I ask, remembering how I had suggested this to Tom, who thought I was being crazy.

'I promise you. Nothing would surprise me,' she says. 'But you're the boss, Keira. You have a right to know what's going on.'

She's right, I should be braver about this.

'So you go through emails and accounts?' Tamsin asks.

'Everything, but it's knowing where to look. I mean, having a careful look at the books might also be a start. If Pierre's suddenly got the go ahead to be Finance Director, who knows what his motives are?'

'But we can't just go in there and demand that Pierre shows us all of his files,' I say.

'No, of course not. I'd go in at night and copy everything to my hard drives. Dave and I always used to go into places between two and four in the morning.'

'You are a stealthy one,' Amma says, impressed.

'Who's Dave?' Tamsin asks.

Sian blushes. 'Just a guy I worked with.'

'Just a guy?' Tamsin says, probing for more.

Sian bites her lips. 'No, not just a guy. Someone… someone quite special. I can't even believe I'm actually telling you this.'

'There are no secrets in the Cancer Ladies' Running Club,' Tamsin counters with a smile and, whilst trying to get her breath and run at the same time, Sian tells us about Dave, the guy who was her partner in crime, who made her laugh and inspired her to be her best. And, even though she's running and blushing, as she recalls all the banter at work and how she looked forward to seeing him each day, we can all see how much he meant to her and how much she misses him now.

'So where is he?' Amma asks. 'This Dave of yours?'

'He was never mine,' Sian counters. 'Nothing ever happened between us. He had no idea how I felt.'

'Really? But it must have been mutual?' Amma says. 'You don't get that chemistry when it's all one sided.'

Sian shrugs. 'I guess I'll never know.'

'But why don't you contact him?' I ask her.

'It's too late. I've moved on and he's still in Bracknell,' she says sadly, although this clearly isn't true. She hasn't moved on.

'Then call him up,' Amma says, as if it's the most obvious thing to do. Which of course, it is.

'I can't.'

'Why not?' I ask.

'Because he doesn't know,' Sian says. 'You know… about the cancer. About why I left. And it'd be too difficult to tell him now.'

48

Tom takes to massaging my armpit and chest most nights for me, but despite his care and attention, my scar doesn't feel much better. Over the following week, it just feels weird. It goes really hot, then feels like there's mice skittering about underneath the surface of my skin. Then it feels like I've been stung by wasps.

I call Sam, my lovely cancer care nurse, who assures me that this is just my nerves reconnecting and not to worry. She says she'll see me when I go in for my appointment with my oncologist. I've been assigned 'Sexy Phil', as Tamsin called him.

Doctor Phillip Mayer is in his early forties and is very trim. He has a bike helmet hanging in his office and a picture of his wife and kids on his desk. Once again, another man, who I've only just met, tells me to strip off and go behind the curtain, before examining my chest. He's got a practical, comforting manner, and reassures me that I'm healing well.

We talk about why I didn't get reconstruction and how I have cold feet about more operations.

'There's no right or wrong thing to do,' he says. 'Some people choose not to have any kind of reconstruction at all. They leave things as they are, or even get a tattoo. In fact there's a very well-regarded tattoo artist right here in town who does them for free for women who've gone through this procedure.'

What? I think. Like a blue anchor? Or some hipster motor-cycle brand? Or some kind of miraculous trompe-l'œil that makes it look from a distance like both my boobs are still here?

We get on to discussing treatment and like Mr Mabiyan, Phil tells me it's got to be a long-term solution. I've got my head around this, already, so I tell him to treat away.

'Technically, you're cured,' he says, 'but there may be cancer cells floating about.'

'Then zap 'em,' I say.

'You seem very positive, Keira. I'm glad to see that you're taking it well,' he says and looks at Tom, who holds my hand, proudly. 'And given that you're healing so well, we might as well start the chemo sooner rather than later,' he says.

'Bring it on.'

However, it turns out that I've got some 'house-keeping' to do. By that, Phil means I have to have a smear test and visit the dentist, as I can't go during treatment as it'll be too dangerous to risk any kind of infection, which sounds a bit alarming. Then Sam tells me in a blasé kind of way that, because of the steroids, I'm likely to put on about a stone through the course of chemo.

A stone? I can't put on a stone. I'm already at the edge of my comfort zone. But the subject of diet and exercise leads me to the running.

'I run with another one of your patients,' I tell Phil. 'Tamsin.'

I notice a little look between him and Sam which I can't decipher.

'You probably can't say anything, right?' I surmise. 'Confidentiality and all of that?'

'Tell her I said hi,' Phil says. He smiles at me.

I like this guy. And I can see why Tamsin likes him too. I feel in safe hands.

49

Tom says I should go home and rest, but I decide instead to go to Wishwells. I've dressed up for my appointment, so I should pass muster with Lorna. After the other day, I sense that I might feel better if I try and assert myself.

However, Pierre is sitting upstairs at my desk, looking very pleased with himself. The office is piled high with cardboard boxes and I can see Lorna and Becca both trying to stack them out of the way.

'Keira,' Pierre says, jumping up and kissing me on both cheeks, like I'm a long-lost stranger. He puts Jackson down on the cushion of my office chair. 'This is a surprise.'

'Isn't it,' I say, looking at Lorna.

'How are you feeling?' he asks, but I don't want to talk about my health.

'Better, thank you,' I say curtly. 'What are all these boxes?'

'Teapots,' Pierre says, like Christmas has come early.

'Can I?' I ask, opening the cardboard box and lifting out a package from inside. It's my teapot – the shape is the same, but the china is thick and the design looks cheap. These must be the ones that Pierre has got from China.

'Don't you like them?' he asks, seeing my face.

'You can't sell these,' I protest. 'They don't look anything like Lisa's.'

'But Lisa can't match our pricing strategy,' Pierre counters, coolly in a way that sets alarm bells ringing. Does this mean he's already talked to Lisa about pricing? Do the presence of all these boxes mean he's put Lisa out of a job? My mind races with the consequences of Pierre's decision on my oldest, most loyal supplier.

'But it's about quality. It's about our brand.'

'Actually, it's about making a profit,' he says reasonably.

'I just don't like this… this whole strategy,' I tell them both. 'You've just gone on with this without any discussion.' I try and sound confident, but something about standing up to them both is making me feel shaky. 'I just think we need to stop and have a proper chat about this once Moira's back.'

I look up at them both and Lorna looks briefly at Pierre, then lowers her eyes.

'Well about that,' Lorna says. 'You see, the thing is, Keira… Moira's not coming back.'

At first I think I've misheard her. But then I see her face. 'Not coming back?'

'I didn't want to tell you before, because you've been so stressed out about your operation, but Moira has decided to call it a day with Wishwells.'

I don't believe her. I don't believe that Moira would retire, just like that, without telling me. My heart thuds.

'She didn't want to upset you,' Pierre says, looking at Lorna and then at me. 'But the truth of it is, that it rather plays in our favour.'

I stare at him, wondering what he could possibly mean. 'Without her as an overhead, we've been able to take on Tyra—'

Tyra is a *replacement* for Moira? As if that's possible.

And… hang on… has Pierre actually just described Moira as an *overhead*?

'We needed someone to cover for you,' Lorna says, pre-empting my objection.

'And we can also employ someone young and dynamic to help build the web business, too. A social media expert. We've put some feelers out already,' Pierre continues.

'You mean, you're interviewing people for a post we haven't even discussed?'

'I knew you'd be like this! Why do you have to be so combative about everything?' Lorna exclaims. 'I know you're ill, but you've got to look towards the future. We just want what's best for Wishwells.'

'You have to look long term and realise that the high street is over,' Pierre adds. Isn't that what the council guy told Brian? Has Pierre fallen for this crap?

I can't believe they're saying this. 'I don't think that's true. Didn't we just win retailer of the year?' My words sound barbed, infused with the resentment I still feel about them going to the awards ceremony without me.

Lorna and Pierre exchange a look.

'Look, I can see that work is just too stressful for you right now,' Lorna says. 'You're very emotional about everything.'

She's right. I am emotional. But that's because she's being a bitch.

50

I am so upset about Moira. How can she have just slunk out after years of service? Especially when Lorna *must* have told her that I've had cancer. How could she not have contacted me? Her lack of concern, when I thought we were true friends, hurts so very much.

I can't wait to see Amma, Sian and Tamsin for their perspective on our next run, but I have to wait my turn, as the conversation needs to be about Amma first. This week, she's lost her hair, but she's happy wearing her wig, she says, and she looks healthy and glowing.

When she turns the attention to me, it's not long before I'm off-loading about Pierre's shonky teapots and how, to my horror, he and Lorna have totally shafted Lisa and her ceramics business.

'But it's your shop. Surely you make the decisions?' Amma says.

'You'd have thought so, but they seem to be ganging up on me. And then they do this whole thing, like they're doing me a favour. That's what I can't bear. And even worse, Tom thinks they're right and I do just need to take a step back and get through the treatment. Sorry,' I say, realising I haven't paused for breath. 'I'm seriously off-loading today.'

'You're bound to be a bit frazzled by it all,' Sian says, sympathetically. 'What's going on with your treatment?'

I tell them about meeting Sexy Phil and that my chemo is going to start soon.

'Did he say anything about me?' Tamsin asks.

'Only that he said to say hi.'

She nods her head, but something about the way she looks away at the horizon makes me now remember the look Phil gave to Sam. The others don't notice. I wait for her to turn back so I can study her face, but I don't get the chance, as she speeds up in front.

'You can't get riled about the builders and then call him Sexy Phil,' Amma points out. 'Isn't that just the same thing?'

'Ah, well, do as I say and not as I do,' Tamsin says, over her shoulder, teasing her. I want to press her about Phil to check everything is OK, but when I catch up with her and run by her side, she moves the conversation on. When the others catch up, she explains that she's been on the phone all morning to her boss at the council, as they've short changed her on her sick leave pay, so I feel a bit guilty for moaning about Wishwells.

'Bloody council. And arseholes like him don't help,' Tamsin says, pointing to a newspaper on a bench we're running past. The front page has a picture of a middle-aged man on it.

'Who?' I ask, confused.

'Doug Crawley,' she says. 'He's running for Brightmouth Council Leader and then the word is, he's going to be an MP.'

'Hang on...' Amma says, slowing down, then reversing. She peers down at the paper, then picks it up and shakes it out. 'I recognise him.'

'Who? Crawley... or who's this guy?' Sian asks, pointing to the other fat middle-aged man who is laughing. He's wearing a sweatshirt with words on it. She reads over Amma's shoulder. 'Terry Douglas from Arc Contractors'.

'No, not him. Him. Crawley. He was at this political meeting I went to last year when I was campaigning for Phillada.'

'Who's that?' I ask.

'Phillada Macey. You know, she stood for the Women's Equality Party.'

'You didn't mention you were political,' I say, surprised.

'I'm not… well, I am, but no more than you, probably. I just got involved because Phillada was a great theatre supporter, so I helped her out with canvassing, that sort of thing. But then she had to pull out as a candidate because her little girl got sick. She put me forward as a paper candidate.'

'What's that?' I ask.

'They put me up as a candidate so that they could say they had a candidate – not that there was a hope in hell's chance of me getting any votes in that ward. Anyway, I was at a meeting with her at the library and Crawley was there. He sort of… well… groped me.'

'Groped you?' Sian asks.

'Well, groped is a bit much. Nothing I could slap him for. But, definitely a case of wanderinghanditis.'

We all inspect Doug Crawley's smiling face.

'He's sounds like a sleazeball,' I say. 'More like Creepy Crawley.'

'Yeah, well now he's going to continue sitting uncontested on the council,' Tamsin says, 'and put all the cuts through that will see my sick leave go.'

'We should do something about it,' Sian says.

'Like what?' Amma says.

'Well, let's think of something.' Tamsin grins with her Cheshire cat grin.

She raises her eyebrows at me, as if to challenge me, too. 'Just because we're going through cancer, we can't just roll over, right ladies? Come on. No time for slacking.'

We make it slowly around the last lap, but today there's no sprint finish to the end. When we've finished and we're walking back to the cars, I catch up with Tamsin and get a moment with her to myself. 'Is everything OK?'

'I'm sure it is,' she says, after a slight pause. 'It's just they've ordered more tests. It's never something you want to hear.'

In spite of knowing all the various risks – and, trust me, I've read enough scary stats online – I've always believed that we'll all get better. But what if we don't? What if one of us is one of those scary statistics?

I don't get a chance to say more, because Amma makes a whooping sound. She's got her phone in her hand.

'Oh my god,' she says. 'Oh my god!'

'What?'

'It's from Evan...' She looks wide-eyed at the screen, then turns it to face me so that I can read the text that is plastered in celebratory emojis. 'I don't believe it! I've got it. I got the part,' she says. Her eyes are shining. She jumps up and down, clutching her phone. She comes over, throwing her arms around me.

'The politician part?' I ask her.

She nods. 'The conflicted, complex, nuance, principled, potentially fucking career-making politician part. Yes! They start filming in three weeks.'

51

Tom has committed us all to going down to visit his parents, but when we get up the next morning to go to Devon, it seems that Tilly is not coming with us.

'I'm going to stay and look after the dog,' she says, triumphantly.

'We're taking Pooch with us,' I say, looking between my husband and daughter as I come down the stairs with my overnight case. They've obviously made this arrangement behind my back.

'Granny won't want him in her house,' Tilly says. 'Not with his bottom. Not on those carpets.'

'More like those plastic covers,' Jacob grins with relish. It's a long-standing family issue that my uptight mother-in-law keeps plastic covers on her carpets. For a long time, they wouldn't let us visit when the kids were little – even *with* the plastic covers on the carpets. 'Imagine the streaks.'

This, of course, is absolutely true, but I resent her triumphant tone and that Tom has made this decision without me.

'I told her she had to come,' I say to Tom, once she's flounced inside with Pooch, as if she – and she alone – is the only one who ever cares for him.

'She'll be fine.'

'You trust her to be home alone?' I ask him.

'Have a little faith in her,' Tom says. 'It's good to give her some independence. And I get the feeling she needs a little space.'

From me. He means space from me.

I try not to be put out and cross about it, because he's probably right, but even so, her being given permission to stay behind, when technically, I'm the one with the only valid excuse to slob around in my pjs all weekend, annoys me. It doesn't help that the M25 is at a standstill and we stare at the windscreen, the rain lashing down.

'At least Pooch isn't farting,' Tom says, as if that's an advantage. But it's no consolation.

'Shall we play I Spy?' I ask, but only half-ironically. We used to like playing games in the car, but behind us, the kids are staring at their iPads, their headphones on, their jaws slack, their faces illuminated by the screens. They don't even hear me. I can remember when they were little and they'd come into the shop and Moira would invent little games to play with them: Silly word games and hide-and-seek and they'd laugh and laugh and beg her for more.

I stare out of the window and sigh and Tom looks at me. 'What is it?'

'I just can't stop thinking about Moira,' I tell him. Because it's true – I can't.

'Not this again,' he says, annoyed and I wish I hadn't said anything. I know he's bored of me talking about work – and especially my upset about Moira resigning. 'Just ring her. Clear the air.'

'No,' I say. 'She should be the one to ring me.'

'Have it your way,' he sighs, exasperated.

It takes hours and hours to get to my in-laws. We stop at the services for a break after four hours and Tom goes inside to get some sandwiches. On the way back, I watch him shrugging his hood up.

Then his phone rings, because he juggles the shopping and delves into his pocket to get it. He's been in an increasingly foul mood with the traffic, getting road-ragey with each new set of un-manned roadworks, but now I see his face crack into a grin.

I watch through the rain-spattered windscreen as he scuffs his toe against the kerb. The same habit Tilly has, when she's being bashful. I know every single tiny body gesture of his well enough to know that he's praising whoever is on the phone. And he's getting praised back in return.

'Who was that?' I ask, when he gets back in, but I already know.

'Oh, just Janine,' he says.

'What did she want on a Saturday?'

'Hmm?' he asks, as if he hasn't heard me. He turns on the engine. 'Oh, nothing. Crack open the sarnies, love. I've got you a prawn mayo,' he says. But suddenly I don't feel so hungry.

52

Things don't improve and we're all scratchy by the time we get to Tom's parents. I watch through the glass in the door as Hilary hobbles along the hallway to the door.

'Keira,' she says, kissing me. Her face is pale and drawn, her cardigan hanging off her shoulders. I smell her familiar Dior perfume tinged with an acrid old person's smell. She used to be quite statuesque, but in the past few years she's shrunk quite a bit and is shorter than me now.

'Tilly?' Peter, my father-in-law says, not rising from his comfortable armchair in the lounge, reaching his hand out for Bea as we all bundle in.

'No, this is Bea,' I tell him, looking at Tom in alarm. It's not like his dad to forget who his grandchildren are. 'Tilly couldn't come this time,' I say tactfully whilst hastily disrobing. The sitting room is heated to approximately the same temperature as the surface of the sun.

Peter looks at me with confused, opaque eyes. 'Are you ill, Keira? Hilary says you're ill.' He sounds worried. Like I might be about to die any second. He grips both my hands, like a desperate old man. His hands are chilly.

'I'm fine,' I tell him. 'I've just got to have some treatment, then it'll all be alright.'

I'm alarmed by how much my in-laws have aged – even in

the four months since I've seen them. They were up in London on a group coach trip and we met them for a quick Saturday lunch in early December before their theatre matinee, but I haven't actually been to their home here for nearly a year. Now, my internal rant of resent and bitchiness from the car fizzles into a new kind of shocked dismay. How come they are so old and frail all of a sudden? Hilary's fall seems to have catapulted them into an entirely new phase.

Where has my father-in-law gone with his cheeky argumentative streak, who liked nothing more than a row over the Conservative party with a couple of gins? And Hilary – usually so brilliant in the kitchen, serves us up some pensioner portions of a microwaved meal. Tom sneaks Jacob some money to go with Bea to the village to get fish and chips.

Hilary – with what I now see is a very large front of her own – is determined that Tom and I 'don't make a fuss'. She won't entertain the concept of a chair lift, or to move their bedroom downstairs, although she admits that it takes them both well over an hour to get upstairs at bedtime. She won't discuss *why* she fell – which is clearly to do with her failing eyesight. Or hips. Or back. Or all of the above. And she positively clings to the walls to avoid the elephant in the room – the fact Tom's dad is definitely getting dementia. Instead, in increasingly shrill tones she insists that *'everything is completely normal'*.

Beating her at her own game of 'everything is fine', I refuse to be drawn about my cancer treatment, but after dinner, she talks me into a game of Scrabble and soon we're alone at the little round table in the bay window.

Hilary and I have had our arguments over the years both spoken and unspoken. The worst was 'buggy-gate' when she insisted on buying Tilly the most unwieldy contraption known to man and had a six-month sulk when Tom and I refused to take the said pushchair home with us (not that we could fit it in the car). Then, there's been the ongoing, unspoken beef about her being annoyed that I work at Wishwells, which apparently means that I don't support Tom in his career enough – a fiction entirely of her own making. But Scrabble is always a truce. Scrabble is how we connect.

Twenty minutes in, however, and I realise that Hilary has something to get off her chest.

'So, I looked up the percentages,' she says, squinting at her letter tray.

'The percentages?'

'You know the percentage likelihood of it coming back. Your cancer.'

Am I to understand that she's taken it upon herself to try and ascertain how long I have left on this mortal coil?

'Hilary,' I tell her, 'I don't want to know.' Even though I already do know. Even though I already do know, but have chosen to forget.

'But—'

'Those statistics apply to other people. And there's a whole load of factors involved that don't apply to me,' I tell her.

'You—'

I cut her off again. She's really not taking the hint. 'And besides, even if there was a 99.9 per cent chance that this cancer was going to come back and get me, I'd still believe that I'm in the 0.1 per cent that will be OK.'

This has ruffled Hilary's feathers.

'You can't get through it on positivity alone,' she says,

tight-lipped, as if positivity is something new-fangled and dodgy.

'I'm not. I'm getting through it with the help of an experienced medical team and the support of amazing friends.'

Back atcha.

But she's not taking it. 'I've known so many people to get it and think they're OK and then they're not.'

I roll my eyes, exasperated. 'And that's helpful to hear how?'

'Hilary?' Peter calls from his chair. 'Hilary?'

Hilary draws in a breath. 'Look, you've upset him now. He hates raised voices.'

'Poison,' I say, laying down my letters. 'That's eight and a double word score... sixteen.'

53

When we visit, we always sleep in Tom's childhood bedroom, which hasn't changed at all since he was a teenager. The maroon and grey checked wallpaper is so old it's almost come back into fashion. Hilary likes to keep it as a kind of time-frozen shrine to her mostly absent son, including the creaky bed. As I try and get comfortable in it later on, bashing the matted pillows to get some softness, I try and explain to Tom how annoyed I am by his mother's attitude. We have to whisper, so that the kids don't hear us through the wall and that in itself makes me feel even more like a petulant teenager.

'She's just trying to be helpful,' he says, unhelpfully.

'It's a bit rich, her doling out advice on how I should live my life, when she won't even entertain the idea of getting an assessment for your dad.'

'You know what she's like. You being upbeat and positive doesn't compute with her.'

'So she has to bring me down? *Give me a dose of reality*,' I say, huffily, impersonating her. 'What's wrong with being positive anyway?'

'Nothing,' he says, kissing me. 'You have to get through it any which way that works for you.'

'Thank you. Exactly,' I say, pacified that he sees it from my point of view. 'I mean, your mother wouldn't know what to make of my running mates. She'd probably think we're all doom and gloom, but she'd be wrong. Take Amma. Well, she's totally over the bloody moon. Right now, I challenge you to find a more excited and optimistic person on the planet,' I tell him.

He grunts, but I know the face he's pulling in the dark. His lawyer face. His realist's face. His face that the truth, not a fantasy, will always out.

'Be realistic. What she's doing... or planning on doing.'

'What about it?'

'She can't take the job, Keira. She can't start filming when the worst of the chemo is still to come.'

'Why not? If she feels OK?'

Tom sighs. 'Because it's unprofessional. Not to mention stupid of her to put herself under that much pressure. And if you were any kind of friend, you'd tell her as much.'

He turns over, bunching the duvet over him, so that I feel it dragging off me, across my scar and I stare at the ceiling, annoyed that he's somehow linked his mother's stubbornness to Amma. That in his mind, his mother is somehow right.

I look up at the ancient glow-in-the-dark stars that still have a vague fluorescence to them and think back to the first night I ever stayed in this house and how I'd had to sneak in from the spare room because Hilary didn't approve of us sleeping together out of wedlock.

Were Tom and I so different then? I wonder. We were certainly so full of plans. We were going to travel around the world and live a wholesome, simple life. I imagined that by now, I'd feel so strong and so free, but instead, I feel... not exactly trapped, but certainly hemmed in and caught between my grumpy teenagers and stubborn in-laws. And the worst bit is, that there suddenly doesn't seem to be that much time between now and when I'm Hilary's age.

That's if I'm actually lucky enough to live that long.

I remember running with the girls, joking about the only fate worse than getting old is to *not* get old. But Hilary and Peter aren't doing a very good job of selling me old age.

I drift off to sleep eventually, but I hear a phone bleep at three in the morning and I wake instantly. Tom is stirring.

'Did you hear the phone?' I ask.

'It's not mine,' he says, annoyed. 'Mine's on silent.'

I grab my phone. There's a text from Maria, our next-door neighbour.

I don't mean to worry you, but I just thought you should know there's something going on at your house.

I sit up in bed, my pulse racing as I think of Tilly home alone. I ring Maria, aware of how late it is – even though she's only just texted me.

'What is it? Is everything OK?' I ask, when she answers. Tom grunts and blearily sits up.

'Well, I suppose so, yes,' she says. 'Tilly seems to have been having a party and the police have just turned up.'

54

When we get home, there's a flattened-out Amazon box taped to our front door where the glass should be, and the remnants of broken bottles and cigarette butts on the lawn. The front door lock is broken. It looks like it's been kicked in.

'Wicked,' Jacob says with a grin as we start up the garden path from the car. He's delighted that Tilly is in so much trouble. He has the air of someone who'd like nothing more right now than to unfold a director's chair and click his fingers and cry, 'action'.

And, right on cue, here comes our starlet now.

Tilly takes the chain off the door and scurries backwards facing us, the mop and bucket in front of her. The hall tiles are wet with bubbly water. She stands in her jeans, dark bags under her eyes. She looks like she hasn't slept. There's a fuggy smell above the soap suds of alcohol and cigarettes. I can already see a big stain on the stair carpet from here.

'So... um... that happened,' she says.

I'm not impressed. After all, she's had time to prepare for our entrance. I spoke to her once in the night, when she was clearly pissed and once this morning before we left Hilary's to make sure she was OK, but she kept crying. The whole thing is awful – made worse because Hilary is so horrified that we've left Tilly home alone, somehow insinuating that it was bad parenting on my part. Not Tom's. Oh no. This 'debacle', as she put it, clearly has nothing to do with him at all. And then there's been the god-awful five-hour silent drive home in the rain.

Now Tilly stands before us, holding the mop like Cinderella, or Fiddler on the Friggin' Roof, like we should be the ones feeling sorry for her.

'Do you have anything to say?' Tom asks. His foot taps in a particularly ominous way, like he's a bull about to charge.

Tilly is clearly trying to gauge how much trouble she's in. She winces, looking between us. 'Sorry?' she says, as if it's a wild guess at a trick question.

'So what happened with the door?' I ask. She hasn't mentioned this on the phone.

'Oh... well... there were some gatecrashers,' she says. 'Destiny put the party on her Snapchat and then loads of people showed up. I tried to stop them. I promise I did. And Alfie did too.'

'Who's Alfie?' Tom asks.

She blushes. 'My boyfriend.'

'Your *what*?' Tom says. This is certainly news.

'Told you they'd find out,' Jacob says to Tilly, as he walks past us into the hall.

'You knew?' I ask him.

'About the boyfriend or the party?' he says, hanging up his coat.

'Either.'

'Just the boyfriend, as it happens. But I wish I'd known about the party. Was it epic?' he asks Tilly and for a split second her eyes twinkle at him.

She doesn't even need to say it, because he says it for her, 'Yeah, it was lit.'

'What kind of gatecrashers?' Tom asks, trying to keep the teen-bollocking on track.

'Just these boys… they were all about nineteen and they wanted to come in and when I told them no and shut the door, they tried to kick the door in, so I called the police and the party got shut down,' Tilly says.

'By the police?' Tom says.

'Yes.' Tilly smiles awkwardly, like this was a good thing. 'They were here surprisingly quickly, actually.'

I gather from her tone that she's expecting us to be impressed with how she handled it.

'You were bloody lucky nobody got hurt,' I say, my mind racing with all the alternative scenarios that could have played out last night.

'I mean, I know it's bad and everything,' she says, 'but actually, apart from the door, I would have got away with it.'

'Oh! Really?' Tom says incredulously. He looks round at me, as if he's expecting a you've-been-pranked film crew to appear.

'Because I'd been really responsible, actually. I photographed everything before me and Destiny locked it all away in the spare room. All your paintings and belongings and stuff. And I was going to put everything back, today,' Tilly explains, 'in exactly the right places, so you wouldn't even have noticed.'

'Can you believe this?' Tom asks me.

I can. She's 16. I had parties when I was 16 and to be fair to Tilly, this is possibly the first opportunity she's had to host one of her own. Nothing like a chip off the old block. Unfortunately for us.

'We trusted you,' Tom says. 'Do you have any explanation?'

He does this, sometimes. Just demands an explanation, when

there can't be one. Because Tilly is 16 and she has no words to justify her thoughtlessness. How can she explain the torrent of stupid decisions she's made one after the other, that have brought us to this point?

'There's no excuse, I know,' she says.

'You're grounded,' Tom says, still not smiling, his face deathly still. His 'game face', he once called it. The one he uses when he's negotiating, to let someone else know he's totally got them by the balls.

But before Tilly can respond, Bea says, 'What's wrong with Pooch?' She's snuck past Tilly in the hallway showdown and is now standing by the kitchen door. 'He's not moving.'

55

On the way to the emergency vets, I hold Pooch in my arms in a blanket in the back of the car. His breathing is laboured and he stares at me in a desperate way.

'This is going to cost an arm and a leg,' Tom says.

'What choice do we have?' I ask.

It turns out that Pooch has eaten the box of chocolates I hid under the cushion of the kitchen bench and completely forgot about. We found the chewed foil tray next to him on the floor. He's scoffed the lot – even the ones with the cherry liqueur centre. When Jacob googles how toxic the chocolate is likely to be to a dog, we all get very scared.

Hayley, the veterinary nurse who is on call at our practice looks at Pooch's notes on the computer. 'Is he up to date on his injections?' she asks.

I bite my lip. 'He's probably a bit behind,' I admit.

'But he has to have them every month,' Tom says, accusingly. 'You said you were going to sort it in January?'

'It's been on my list,' I say, defensively. Pooch has started to shake and his legs have gone weak. Hayley helps him to lie down on the bench in the surgery, and murmurs soothing words as she strokes his head.

Tom glares at me.

'I've had other things on my mind,' I tell him.

'How could you neglect Pooch?' he says in a cross whisper. My eyes sting. That's not fair.

Hayley examines Pooch and says that he'll have to stay over-night, to see what happens once they've pumped his stomach.

Pooch looks at me with weak, sad eyes and makes a little ill groan that makes my heart hurt.

'I'm so sorry,' I tell him, burying my nose in my favourite soft patch on his neck. 'You have to be a brave boy and get better, OK?'

'What's the chance he'll survive?' Tom asks Hayley, once we've filled in some forms.

'I'm afraid I can't really say.'

'But if you were to give us a percentage…'

And I can't help it… when I hear that last word, I picture his mother's face.

'It's about fifty-fifty,' she says.

We stay for a while longer whilst Pooch gets sedated and then there's no point in us being there.

On the way back to the car, Tom says, 'Fifty-fifty isn't very good. It's not something you'd exactly put the mortgage on.'

'This is why I hate percentages,' I snap – and when I look at him, I see he gets it, what he's just said.

'No, you're right,' he hurriedly says. 'Of course he'll be OK.'

We sit in the car in silence. I'm upset that he thinks Pooch's current predicament is my fault. But I'm even more upset, because it is.

Is there anything worse than accidentally hurting the people and creatures you love the most? As I think of Pooch, uncon-scious and ill, silent tears roll down my face mirroring the raindrops on the glass.

Eventually Tom says, 'It's not your fault, Keira.'

'It is.' I sniff.

He reaches out and holds my hand, but I can't be comforted.

'A boyfriend?' he says, trying to change the subject. I know Tilly's revelation is playing heavily on his mind.

'Alfie. I know. Fucking hell.'

And we both just sit there in silence, thinking it over. Trying to work out what this latest curveball means and how life just doesn't slow down. Not for anyone, no matter what's going on.

56

We all sleep badly and it's miserable in the kitchen on Monday morning without Pooch. I keep looking at my phone for news from Hayley. It's almost impossible to function with the fifty-fifty odds rattling around my head. The thought that Pooch might never come home from the vets is worse than everything that's happened to me in the past few months. Every time my mind goes to imagining a world without Pooch, I get practically winded with terror.

There's a guy from a local firm refitting the glass and lock on the front door, which will hopefully restore our security, but I still feel residually annoyed that there have been so many strangers in my home. Normally, maybe I wouldn't mind, but the sanctity of my space feels particularly important at the moment and Tilly's party feels like a violation. Particularly the bathrooms and the bedrooms. Gross. I don't even want to *think* about what might have gone on in there.

It doesn't help that Tom has claimed the angry patrician high ground, which leaves me somewhat floundering around. Because he's definitely not hearing me up there on fury heights where the cold winds of indignation howl loudly.

'Bea?' I call, annoyed that she's dragging her heels. She'll be late for school at this rate.

'Bea, come on,' Tom calls, determined to be more annoyed

than me. He's dropping her off on the way to the office and he can't be late. He's doing up his shirt and he doesn't give me my usual morning kiss.

'Bea,' I try again, a few minutes later, frowning at Tom. Her toast is getting cold. Then, growling with annoyance, I go upstairs past the workman in the hall, who says, without a glimmer of humility, 'When you're ready, I'll have a cuppa. White, two sugars.'

Tilly is kneeling on the pink fluffy rug in front of Bea who is curled up on her bed. She is only half dressed in her school skirt and dressing gown. Tilly hands Bea Mr Bluebear – a huge teddy that once went everywhere with her. Bea takes it and cries even harder. Jacob puts his hand on Bea's shoulder and then pulls a worried face at me.

'What's going on?'

I know she's upset about Pooch, but this is a little over the top.

'Just tell her,' Jacob says to Bea.

'Tell me what?'

Bea sniffs loudly and says in a little voice. 'Pooch didn't eat the chocolates.'

'What?'

'I did. Before we went to Granny's. They were under the cushion on the bench.'

Relief washes through me. Pooch isn't going to die of chocolate poisoning. The poor little chap's probably just got a bug. I scoot Jacob out of the way and sit down next to her on the bed.

'You should have said.'

'I was too...' she hiccups, 'too... embarrassed.'

'Oh darling,' I say, lifting her to a sitting position and folding her and Mr Bluebear into a hug. 'It's OK.'

'I thought you'd be cross with me, because they were your special "I'm sorry you've got cancer" chocolates,' she manages shakily.

I have been trying very hard to be as normal as possible at home, but this admission from her makes me realise once again just how much everything I'm going through is impacting the kids. How much I'm expecting them to suck up this whole experience with me.

'I don't mind you eating them,' I tell her, kissing her head. 'Honestly.'

I look up at Jacob. He's biting his lip, nervously. 'What?' I ask.

'I think we know why Pooch is poorly,' he says.

He cocks his head at Tilly who steels herself and stands up, retrieving her phone from her back pocket. She taps the screen and then points it towards me.

'I didn't see this going on, I swear,' she says.

There's a Snapchat status open and a video is playing on repeat showing our kitchen full of teenagers and Pooch guzzling a can of Guinness, to raucous cheers.

'Tilly… what the hell?'

'I know,' she says. 'They made him drink the whole can.'

'What's going on?' Tom asks from the doorway.

'Her friends made Pooch drunk,' I tell him.

'Basically, Dad, he's got a giant hangover,' Jacob says, sounding perilously close to laughter.

'It's not funny,' I snap.

Tilly is trying not to laugh too. 'Poor Pooch. He's had his stomach pumped.'

'That's it. You're grounded. Er again,' Tom quickly corrects himself, pointing his finger at Tilly. '*And* you can pay for the vet.'

'It's not my fault,' Tilly shouts, then stomps into the corridor.

'Er, well, actually, yes, it kind of bloody is,' he shouts after her. 'And you can pay for the door, too.'

'It's ninety quid all in,' the workman calls up from downstairs as Tilly's bedroom door slams.

57

When I call the vets, Hayley confirms that there wasn't any chocolate in his stomach and that Pooch has miraculously revived after a night on a drip. Hayley is perplexed, wondering what might have happened, but I'm too ashamed to tell her about Tilly's party, or that my pet is now officially an old soak.

After I've paid the exorbitant bill, I take Pooch out to the car and he jumps onto his cushion in the boot, his tail wagging. I cuddle him, holding his face and looking into his brown eyes.

'Don't frighten me like that again,' I tell him. 'We're not very good when you're not around.' Then add, 'You old pisshead.'

I call Tom and tell him that Pooch is fine, but he's distracted and the conversation is terse and short. I can tell that he's still cross even though the party incident is officially over and it pisses me off that he won't let it lie and has somehow lumped the blame on me. If I was meaner, I'd tell him to get over himself and that he is being like his mother, but that might just send him stratospheric.

Instead I remain polite, because I know exactly how this will play out. We'll all have to pussyfoot around him and cajole him back into being normal, but right now, I actually can't be arsed.

Instead, I crank up the radio and I'm nearly home, when Amma calls and I press the call button on the steering wheel.

'Hey,' I say, aloud, pleased to hear from her and grinning at Pooch in the rear-view mirror. I'm so happy to see his head poking between the back seats. 'How are you feeling?' I'm wondering how the treatment is starting to affect her.

'I can't do it, can I?' she asks, by way of reply and I know immediately that she's talking about her acting gig. I feel a lurch in my stomach remembering my conversation with Tom at the weekend and how what he said made so much sense. There's no way Amma can take a big part like that. Not now. Not with what's coming. 'Just tell me. Tell me honestly, Keira.'

I know how much it means to her. And, as her friend, I want her to be happy, but as her friend, I know I can't do that with a lie. I sigh and steel myself.

'I don't know, but I do know you need to tell them the truth,' I tell her, as gently as I can.

'Fuck!' she says. '*Fuck.*'

'I'm sorry. I know it's brilliant to be offered it, but maybe it's just not the right timing. But I know, just know, there'll be other parts.'

'Oh, Keira, but what if there aren't?' Her voice cracks and she starts to cry.

'Shall I come over?' I offer and she tearfully says yes.

'I guess I'd better call Evan and fess up,' she says, sniffing loudly.

'Do that and put the kettle on and I'll be there.'

I do an illegal U-turn at the traffic lights, feeling gung-ho. It feels good to be helping out a friend for once and being the person I used to be. I'm so much better at giving support than taking it. I stop at the florists by the station and pick up a bright bunch of flowers.

Ten minutes later, I smile from behind them at Amma, as she opens her door, but my attempt to jolly her along doesn't work.

'How was the call to Evan?' I ask her. The whole way here, I'd been hoping, just hoping that he'd tell her that, no it was fine, the producers would be cool about it, and somehow it might still work.

But instead, she shakes her head and bursts into fresh tears. She's wearing a headscarf tied over her bald head and a long black kaftan and grey cardigan which makes her look like she's in costume as a Russian peasant. She's not wearing any make-up and for the first time ever, she looks vulnerable and weak.

'You don't mind me bringing Pooch, do you?' I ask, following her inside and along the corridor. The walls are lined with framed theatre posters and there's a large wooden coat rack stacked with funky fur coats and hats with feathers on them.

Whilst my house is on the scuzzy side of shabby, her little house is definitely on the other end of the spectrum, very much more towards chic. In the open-plan kitchen, she has a pretty wooden dresser full of tastefully mismatching china plates and hooks full of floral mugs – some of which, I notice, are from Wishwells. The walls are painted a tasteful shade of baby blue.

Pooch wags his tail, sniffing around the bottom of skirting boards. For food – or Guinness? Who knows these days?

Amma slumps into a kitchen chair. She's been crying for a while, judging from the scrunched-up tissues dotted on the table. Her eyes are red-rimmed.

I pop the flowers in the sink and then sit across from her and reach out for her hand as describes telling Evan her news.

'He said all the right things... made all the right noises, but he's already written me off.'

'That's not true, surely?'

'You don't understand. You don't get offered roles like this and then turn them down.'

'Not without good reason.'

'Yeah, I've got fucking cancer,' she says, her watery eyes meeting mine.

'*Had* cancer,' I remind her.

'I don't think I'd let it register until now. And now it feels so…' she sobs, 'so fucking frightening.'

I go around the table and hug her. I really do feel her pain. Pooch joins in, nuzzling his face in between us and onto her leg and she smiles tearfully and strokes his head.

'I know. I know how you feel. But it's going to be OK,' I tell her.

'It was my dream part.'

She looks wrung out as she gets up and says she's going to make tea. 'Or maybe we should have gin,' she says. 'To toast the beginning of the end. Or Arsenic, to bring it around that much quicker.' She's attempting wry humour, but she looks too sad to pull it off. 'Or maybe we should just drink to lost dreams.'

Pooch looks at me with his big brown eyes and suddenly, I have an idea.

'Well, what about replacing it with another dream?' I tell Amma. 'How about you play that female politician for real.'

'What do you mean?' she asks, dabbing at her face with a wodge of tissue.

'Doug Crawley,' I say. 'That dickhead standing unopposed for the council. The one pissing everyone off.'

'What about him?'

'Take him on. Stand against him yourself.'

'You mean… you mean go into politics for real. Not just as a paper candidate?'

'Why not? You're smart, you're very presentable—'

'Ha!' she says, pointing the snotty tissue at her tear-stained eyes, but I can see a glimmer in them.

'Why not reinvent?' I say.

'Reinvent,' she says slowly, rolling the idea around. 'At my age?'

'Yes. Absolutely. Reinvent,' I say, warming to my theme. 'Use this crisis point as a springboard. You told me how hard it is being an actress, but how much you've always enjoyed the challenge. Well, this is going to be every bit as challenging. And you said how much you were looking forward to playing a – what was it you said? – principled politician. So do it. Fight for the equal rights you're always banging on about. Take that bastard down and take his job.'

'I couldn't just… stand,' she says. 'Just like that?'

'Why not? You're opinionated enough,' I tease her.

'But I can't give up acting. I just can't.'

'Why not?' I tell her. 'What could be a better way to spend your time than standing up for what you believe in? And it might not be so different to acting. Just think – instead of waiting for your dream role to come to you, you could just go out there and claim your audience. You're made for it.'

'Am I?'

'Yes, I absolutely think you are.'

58

The new centre – designed specifically for cancer patients – is in a swanky building next to the main hospital in town. It opened a couple of years ago, thanks to a big cash injection from Macmillan, the cancer charity. And this morning, I have an appointment that Tamsin has made with Angela 'the wig lady'.

'Oooh. Impressive. Well, this isn't what I expected, Dad,' I mutter, as I walk through the sliding doors, thinking how much this place would appeal to him with its exposed wooden beams.

In the airy atrium, there are stylish purple and green sofas dotted around and I see Tamsin sitting on the arm of one of them. She's talking to a group of women, some of whom are in gym clothes, but she spots me and waves enthusiastically, beckoning me over.

Today, along with a black tunic over twelve-hole red DM boots, Tamsin's head is covered up with an elaborate scarf tied in a giant bow at the front. She's wearing her trademark pale foundation and she has stuck on pink glittery eyebrows. If I wore those, I'd look like a drag queen, but somehow Tamsin is pulling it off.

'Ah, there she is,' Tamsin says, with her wide grin, beckoning me over. 'This is Keira from our Cancer Ladies' Running

Club,' she says, hugging me warmly – and I like hearing our little gang's name said out loud. It's like we're official and not going away.

Tamsin smells nice – of patchouli and orange and she explains that she's just had a massage. This is certainly a different aspect of Cancer World, because here a massage isn't considered 'dangerous'. I wasn't expecting this kind of vibe at all.

She introduces me to the group she's talking to. One of the women is clearly a long way through her treatment. She's wearing a shapeless tunic and her face is puffy, her eyelids look sore where she doesn't have any eyelashes, but she's fiddling with some lovely swirly enamel earrings, a big grin on her face.

'I like those,' I tell her. And I do.

'Tamsin made them for my birthday,' she says. 'Aren't they lovely?'

'Flattery will get you everywhere, Julia,' Tamsin says.

I inspect them, surprised that Tamsin has yet another talent I knew nothing about.

'In my next life, I'll be a jeweller,' Tamsin says, matter-of-factly.

'And I'm sure you'll be very successful at it,' I tell her. 'Those are fab. I'd sell them in Wishwells in a heartbeat.'

Another woman is wearing a lanyard. She looks like she's in charge and she shakes my hand.

'Tamsin was telling us all about you. I think the running is fantastic,' she says, introducing herself as Kathryn. She has dark olive skin and lovely shiny black hair. It's only now that I'm about to lose my hair, that I've started noticing other people's hair. Hers is lustrous and thick.

'It is, but I'm a little stiff,' I admit. 'Tamsin is a hard task-master.'

'Well, if you need a massage, do book yourself one in here,' she says, as if it's no big deal. I tell her what happened when I rang up the massage place in town and she rolls her eyes, as if she's heard it a thousand times before. 'Let me get you a programme.'

I leaf through the brochure she gives me listing all the things the centre offers – complementary therapies, yoga, qi gong, counselling, advice on finances, it goes on and on. The women Tamsin has been talking to all get up to go upstairs to a fitness class in the gym and they all smile and hug her goodbye. Julia kisses her repeatedly on the cheek, like you would a small child, and Tamsin laughs at her effusiveness.

I'm so supported at home, I haven't felt the need to come somewhere like this, my instinct being to shy away from anything charitable and 'free'. I've told myself that others might need it more, but actually, I see now that I've just been standoffish, thinking that if I came somewhere like this, then I'd have to admit I'm ill. But the centre is the first place I've been where I've been treated as if I'm totally normal and not going through something hideous. This is where my tribe hang out. I'm kicking myself for not coming before.

Tamsin and Kathryn give me a tour on the way to the wig-fitting room, and everyone I meet is so friendly and so can-do, I feel a profound sense of gratitude. As I see a woman trying to move on crutches, being supported by a volunteer along a corridor and Tamsin shares a few words of encouragement with her, I remember how incredibly lucky I am.

*

Angela, the centre's hairdresser, has a little salon with a dressing table with lights all around the mirrors, like it's backstage at a theatre. She sits me on the stool. Along one wall, there's a whole row of polystyrene heads, each with a different wig.

'So, first you'll need one of these,' Angela says, stretching her fingers inside what looks like the foot of a tight.

She puts it over my head and I instantly feel like an old actress getting ready to play Elizabeth the First. It's not my best look.

'So… did you have a style in mind?' Angela asks.

A bunch of silly suggestions pop into my head: mohawk, rockabilly, *Blackadder the Third*. Because there's no getting away from how surreal this all feels. But I keep my mouth shut.

'Try them all on,' Tamsin says, eagerly from the other stool. 'Come on. I want to see what you look like as Cher,' she says, grabbing the neck of the mannequin head and tipping off a long black curly wig.

I try it on. 'Oh yes,' she purrs, fussing round me. The hair blows up my nose and my head feels itchy, but soon, we're having a right laugh and she's trying on wigs too. So maybe it's OK to be silly. Maybe it's alright to have fun. *Yeah. Fuck you, cancer.*

'Oh, that's dreadful,' I laugh, as she puts on a short chestnut bob. She pulls a face in the mirror. 'Don't you think I look like a newsreader?'

'Not like any newsreader I've ever seen,' I say.

'Unless I get to announce the apocalypse,' she says. 'And here's the news with Huw Edwards in the studio and Tamsin O'Brien,' she says, doing a deadpan impression, before leaning into the mirror, as if it's a news camera. 'You're all going to die of rage virus, motherfuckers,' she says, looking manic and Angela and I laugh.

'She's mad,' I tell Angela, and she nods, but Tamsin's crazy energy is infectious.

Eventually, I plump for the wig that's closest to my own hair, although I secretly suspect that I might never wear it. It just feels too much like fancy dress, or like a deliberate disguise, when at the moment, I really don't feel like I have anything to hide. For good measure, I also pick up some soft bamboo headscarves and a tuck-in fringe, like Amma's.

As I drive Tamsin home, I thank her for today. After all, I've had loads of fun. Being tooled up for the other side of chemo, when my hair will fall out, makes the whole thing less daunting.

'It was entirely my pleasure,' she says, but her jolly demeanour fades the nearer we get to her flat. After a few leading questions, she opens up a bit more about Ian. She never has a kind word to say about him when we're out running and I wonder if it's really true that he really is as useless as she says he is. I can't imagine Tamsin not demanding the kind of support she needs, so I'm intrigued to find out more about their dynamic.

'I feel… I don't know… seeing you and hearing about how you are with Tom and your kids, I feel I've missed out… not on the kids bit. I never wanted those,' she says, 'but there's something about you that reminds me of how close we were when we were growing up. You know, me and Mum and Dad.'

'Don't you see your family?'

'Ian won't have them in the flat, and we haven't really talked much. I still send pagan cards at Christmas to wind them up. Mum's a staunch Catholic you see.'

'Do they know about… you know, the cancer?'

She shrugs, pulling down the sun visor in the car to check her make-up. 'There's no point in them knowing. It'd just open up old wounds,' she says.

59

We've agreed on our Cancer Ladies' Running Club group chat that we'll run as usual on Friday if Amma is up to it, which she says she is. I'm glad, as I've been banned from working this week and I'm pleased I'll be able to fit another run in before I start chemo. I never thought in a million years, I'd actually be relieved to be running or even to actively want to, but I find myself wishing the days away until Friday.

I want to get my best time in this week if I can as I'm sure my fitness will go down over the course of the next few months. I know the running has definitely made me feel stronger – and not just physically. Meeting the girls, being with people who understand has made me mentally stronger too.

On the morning of the run, I go to Jennifer's café to pick up Sian and stare longingly across the road at Wishwells. Lorna has redone the window display and there are lots of clothes and pashminas on display. I know it's ridiculous, but spying like this makes me feel like I'm snooping on an ex-boyfriend.

'It's ridiculous. I should just go in there,' I tell Jennifer. 'Say hello.'

'Yes, you should. I'm sure they'd be pleased to see you. Ruby was saying how worried she was about you,' Jennifer confides, but I balk at the thought of seeing Lorna when I'm in my running kit. She'd definitely tell me off again for not being 'aspirational', and thinking about this and all the things she's said makes my hair prickle.

But remembering my promise to myself not to get wound up by her, I turn my attention to Sian who is coming out from the kitchen. As we make our way to the park together, I tell her about meeting Tamsin at the centre and about Amma's meltdown about not accepting the part. Sian agrees with me that Amma should go into politics and it feels good that in our little unit, we can bolster each other up.

'Any advice for me starting chemo?' I ask, as some wise words from the horse's mouth – so to speak – is just what I need.

'One of my favourites is "Paddy's Law" from a friend of a friend of a friend.'

'Paddy's Law?'

'Don't have anything to eat that you like whilst you're having your actual chemo. You'll never be able to stomach it ever again,' Sian says. 'I used to get these chicken torpedo sandwiches from the shop opposite the hospital and now every time I go past it, I do a little retch.'

I laugh at her face. 'Seriously?'

'Seriously. And don't wear your favourite knickers. Or anything you'll associate with chemo later on. I had to throw all mine away.'

'Still, not so much of a problem with the bras, I suppose. I've thrown all those out already.' I shake my head. 'I can't believe I'm about to start,' I tell her. 'Time is so weird. Sometimes it feels like January was ten years ago and sometimes it feels like it was five minutes. It's like I've been sucked onto this conveyor belt.'

'It'll be like that for a while. And then, like me, you'll be spat out the other side.'

'I guess I just have to do it bit by bit,' I tell her. 'And not look too far ahead. Although I'm really not looking forward to losing all my hair now it's imminent.'

'I reckon your hair will go just before your second chemo – so in just over three weeks from now,' she says.

'Does *all* your hair fall out?' I ask Sian. 'You know... everything.'

'Yep, the lot. Oh, apart from the hairs on my big toes. They were like pensioners on a beach, sitting on their union jack deckchairs, watching the planes fly over, sharing a flask of tea. Other than that, I was completely beach body ready for the first time ever, although sadly without a beach to go to.'

I can't help laughing a little. 'Were you tempted to have the cold cap?' I've heard that they offer this treatment at the hospital where they make your head really, really cold before the chemo, which can stop your hair falling out. But I've never been able to drink a can of Coke without getting brain freeze, so the idea of it really doesn't appeal.

'It wasn't for me. I tried it, but it made the appointments longer and, well, I just wanted to be in and out of there as quickly as possible. Get the job done, you know? In the general scheme of things, losing my hair was the least of my worries.'

It's not going to be so bad, I think, this chemo lark. They've all done it. I can roll with it, I'm sure. Can't I?

'So what does chemo feel like?' I ask Tamsin, when we've started our run in the park. 'I mean, if you were to describe how you've been feeling?'

'Oh, well, let me see,' she says. 'Imagine being in a terrible nightclub, on a nasty pill and you've lost your friends and your shoes,' she says, 'and you've got a migraine from the noise and claustrophobia from all the people pressing against you and you can't get out.' I pull an alarmed face at her description. 'It's that. Times ten.'

'Yeah, she's right,' Sian laughs. 'It's exactly like the Nineties.'

'Oh God!'

'Well, you can't say you haven't been warned.' I'm not sure how much she's joking. I don't think she really is at all.

Amma and I are soon faster and we naturally fall in together as we go up the hill. A few weeks ago, I couldn't even face the thought of the hill, but now we're nearly at the top before I realise that I've hardly altered my pace.

I'm about to ask her how she's feeling after our chat the other day, but the workmen are heading down the path towards us. 'Here we go,' I mutter. 'Just ignore them.'

'Alright, gorgeous,' the leery one says, wiggling his eyebrows at Amma.

'Oh just zip it,' she says.

'Keep your hair on,' he says, nudging his friend. He's clearly delighted that she's acknowledged him.

'No, I won't keep my hair on,' she says, furiously, yanking off her wig. It's the first time I've actually seen Amma bald.

'Fuck!' the bloke says, backing away. He looks terrified.

'You want me now, huh?' Amma asks, jutting out her chest towards him. He spills his tea and drops his bacon sandwich.

'You lot being such a bunch of sexist wankers really doesn't help, OK?' I say, cutting in and backing her up. 'So how about fucking piping down and start showing us a bit of respect.

We've all got cancer and all we want to do is run, without being harassed.'

The builders look horrified.

'I'm really sorry,' one of the younger ones mumbles, as they stumble off after each other up the path.

Sian and Tamsin catch up and we laugh and clap.

'That was brilliant. Did you see their faces?' Sian says.

'That has made my day,' Tamsin adds. 'Good for you, Amma. And what about you, potty mouth,' she says, turning to me with a grin. 'I didn't think you were that kind of a girl at all.'

'That's the good thing about hanging out with you lot. I think I'm really starting to evolve.'

Tamsin laughs, slapping me on the back.

'The downside is that I'm going to have a wonky wig all day now,' Amma says, trying to reposition it on her head.

'Leave it off,' I tell her. 'Seriously. You look amazing.'

And she does. Her baldness shows off her refined bone structure and bright, almond-shaped eyes. It's marvellous to see her being so bold, so uncowed.

'Really?'

'Yes, really. Come on. Own it,' I say, again remembering Tom's awful phrase. You can rock bald.'

'You think so?'

'Absolutely.'

We run the last bit and across to the car park. We're all laughing so much, we don't notice the large Range Rover or the figure standing next to it, until we're a few metres away and then Amma stops, putting her arms out, as if she's just seen a tiger in the wild. We all crash into her arms and stop.

'What is it?' I ask, but then I see. The woman standing by

the car is Isabel Monroe. *The* Isabel Monroe. Even from this distance, she exudes star quality.

'Oh darling,' she says, opening her arms to Amma, as we all approach. Her eyes are twinkling with tears. 'Evan told me. I came straight away.'

60

By Saturday lunchtime, I've considered texting Amma several times. I'm in the kitchen sorting out the washing and my mind wanders away from the podcast that's playing to Amma and Isabel.

I know I'm being nosey, but I'm desperate to hear what happened after they left the park. I guess that's one of the problems with being friends with someone who was once in a TV soap – you can't help wanting to know what happens next.

Amma gave me such a grim parting look as she got into Isabel's car, her wig still off. At the time, I thought she was annoyed with me that I'd made her stay bald for the first time, right when her arch enemy – in TV soap terms at least – turned up, but now I'm not so sure. Should I have stepped in, perhaps, and rescued her? Maybe given her an excuse to be somewhere else?

I think about the friendship game women play and how Bea and Molly are enjoying a honeymoon period of their newly rekindled friendship. I dropped Bea round at Grace's this morning and she treated Bea like a prodigal daughter returning. I wonder if she's had some kind of hand in trying to get Molly and Bea to be friends again.

I suppose Bea is finding her way and will, in time, gather her essential BFFs – and maybe Molly will be one of them. Like Trivial Pursuit cheeses, she'll collect the girls to fit her own wheel of friendship. She'll spend her childhood and adult life swapping in, or keeping a selection that might include: the loyal one (who can be a bit needy), the good time one (who'll lead her into trouble), the tricksy one (with fascinating yet unsolvable problems), the bitchy one (who is forgiven because they have a heart of gold), the busy (but reliable) one and, perhaps, the intriguingly new one.

I know Grace is trying to earn her own piece of best friend pie with me, but her insistence on helping me feels so over-whelming and I don't know what to give in return. She's already presented me with a carefully worked-out rota of which school mum is doing what meals for me each time I have chemo. I have pointed out that we can really sort out food for ourselves, but she's absolutely insistent. I'm not sure how Tom and the kids are going to react to all this strange food arriving, or where I'm going to put it. I suppose I'd better defrost the freezer. Like I need another thing on my to-do list.

Tilly slopes through in her pyjamas, yawning.

'Morning,' she says.

'Actually, it's the afternoon,' I tell her. 'I thought you were coming for a dog walk this morning?'

Pooch and I have already been on our morning shamble past the park runners. He's back to his couch-potato self, snoring soundly on the armchair in the kitchen by the radiator.

'I thought I was grounded,' she says, opening the fridge and pulling out a carton of juice. She opens it and swigs from it.

'Glass,' I tell her.

'There's hardly any left,' she retorts, draining the carton and then throwing it in the bin.

'Can you wash and recycle that please,' I say, annoyed that she can't seem to get this into her head.

Her shoulders slump and she lets out an antagonised sigh.

'The future of this planet belongs to you, not me,' I point out. She rinses the carton and throws it into the recycling bucket, but it misses and goes on the floor. She catches me looking at her, groans even more and then lollops over to shove it in the bucket. If she could scrape her knuckles on the floor, I'm sure she would.

I watch her as she goes to the toaster and puts a bagel in, my heart breaking for my bouncing little girl that's still in there somewhere. I wish I could stop her making me out to be the most annoying person that ever lived, but maybe this is what being a mother to teenagers is all about.

I always thought I was quite good at parenting, but once again, just when I thought I'd got it sussed, I find that I don't know what I'm doing. I'm groping in the dark here, hoping I'm making progress, but terrified I'm going to fail. It's a tough line to tread when I'm punishing her and she's retaliating like she's the hard-done-by one.

'Where is everyone?' she asks, eventually, sitting down at the table with her plate.

'Dad's gone into the office for a bit,' I say, 'Jacob's at football and Bea has gone round to Molly's.'

'I thought she hated Molly?' Tilly says, licking Nutella off the knife. She knows how much that particular habit irritates me, but I let it go.

'So did I, but suddenly, their friendship is back on like nothing ever happened.'

Tilly raises her eyebrows. 'Well, let's see how long it lasts this time.'

'I'm not even sure why they fell out in the first place.'

'I am,' she says, then munches her bagel and I stop mid-fold of the tea towel and look at her for an explanation, but she grins. 'I'm not going to tell you. You won't like it.'

'Just tell me.'

'No.'

'Go on.'

She sighs. 'O-*kay*. They fell out because Bea told Molly that we bitch about Grace at home. I guess it's not something a kid wants to hear about their mum.'

'We don't bitch about Grace,' I say, indignantly.

'Oh, come off it, Mum. You're always saying how pushy and self-obsessed she is.'

Am I?

'Anyway, I think Bea let slip a comment along the lines of how you thought Grace's Botox was a mistake. Something like that.'

'Well, I sincerely hope she didn't,' I say, feeling a sick sense of guilt. What must Grace think of me? And she's been so kind. I really am a dreadful *cow*.

'Don't beat yourself up about it,' Tilly says, with a shrug. 'It's all blown over. And anyway, I dealt with it.'

'How?'

'I did that circle of trust thing from *Meet the Parents* and told her that what we say in the kitchen in our family stays in the kitchen.'

'Well, thank you,' I say, but I still feel ashamed. I resolve to make more of an effort with Grace.

I smooth the tea towels, whilst Tilly checks her phone. I'm

aware that this is precious time alone and I don't want to waste it. I've also promised Tom that I'll try and tackle the boyfriend issue. I let a silence stretch for a minute.

'So you and this... Alfie?' I begin as tactfully as I can.

'Oh, here we go!' she says. 'I knew this was coming.'

'I only want to know...' I say weakly, *how old he is... what his parents do... what kind of house he lives in... whether he's going to get good qualifications at school... whether he's been brought up with good manners... and, most importantly, if he's planning on plucking your cherry.* '... that you're ready for a relationship. That's all.'

'Ugh... you're so embarrassing,' she says.

'But—'

'We've been going out for three months, Mum, so yes, I'm ready.'

'Three months?' How has she kept a boyfriend under wraps for three months?

'But... but why haven't you introduced him to us?'

'I'm not going to bring him round here,' she says, as if it's the most preposterous thing in the world, 'and let him be subjected to the Spanish Inquisition from Dad. Or to have to explain you and your... you know... what's going on.'

'It wouldn't be like that,' I say, hurt.

'Wouldn't it?'

'I just... it's about your safety,' I say, trying a different tack. I wish she'd stop being so defensive and listen. 'That's my concern. That's all, Tilly. I know you think you're a grown-up, but you're still my baby.'

'Well, if it sets your mind at ease, I've gone on the pill, OK?' she says, getting up. '*There.* Happy now?'

She stomps out of the kitchen and I'm left alone, looking at her plate where she's left it on the kitchen table.

'Oh Jesus Christ, Dad,' I whisper. 'I did not see that one coming.'

61

It's Scout who talks me down... in the way only she can. In a non-stop tirade on the phone, I tell her everything that has happened since we last spoke – starting with Hilary and ending with Tilly's bombshell. She listens patiently, as I pace in my bathroom with the door closed. She interjects suitably dramatically noises, that make me know she's 100 per cent on my side.

'Hmm,' she says, finally. 'You're not having a great time, are you?'

'Oh, and there's the cancer too,' I add, feeling relieved to have unburdened myself. I sit down, exhausted, on the loo seat.

'Oh yeah... that,' she says, laughing sadly that I've added it as an afterthought.

'I'm so bored of it, Scouty. I'm so bored of all this drama. I'm not a dramatic person. I just want things to be normal, you know?'

'They will be,' she says.

'Will they?'

'Yes,' she says, gently. 'You've just got to get through the next few months, but this time next year, you'll be a new pin.'

'That feels like a very long way away.'

'I know, darling. And it doesn't help that you're getting this much stress on the home front.'

'But life doesn't stop, does it?'

'Oh Keira Babira,' Scout says, using my childhood nickname. 'I'm sorry you're going through all of this. I really want to just beam myself there and give you a hug.'

'Everything used to be so simple,' I tell her. 'Didn't it?'

'No,' she laughs. 'We always had our dramas. And for the record, you were awful to your mother when you were younger.'

'Was I?'

'Yes. You were always slagging her off.'

'I don't remember,' I say, although I know she must be right.

'So ignore Tilly. She's just lashing out. She'll come round.'

'*But she's having sex.*' I sound really horrified. 'My baby.'

'So? You had sex with Gary Stubbs when you were fifteen,' she says.

'True.'

'And you didn't tell your mother you weren't a virgin until you'd been going out with Tom for over a year, remember? You already know way more about Tilly than Eileen ever knew about you. So chill about that one. Just don't go to war with her.'

I know she's right. She might have twin boys, but her wisdom about Tilly is spot on.

'Should I tell Tom?' I ask her. 'About the pill thing?'

'No,' she says, as if I'm mad. 'Of course not.'

62

I've been reading up about how to get through chemo and, for the first time ever, I've bought a thermometer to monitor my temperature. The pharmacist at Boots was horrified when I proudly declared that I'd never once taken my childrens' temperatures, explaining that 'not believing in being ill' has been my mantra up until now. Oh, but then I got cancer. Go figure.

Rob has insisted on dropping me and Mum off at the chemo unit so that we don't have to go to war with the hospital car park. Tom's joining us after his latest unmissable meeting. I've told him that I'll be fine without him visiting, but he's insisted. It's kind of Rob and Mum to come with me, but I don't really want everyone fussing around me like this. It somehow just puts me more under the spotlight, when all I really want to do is slouch in the dark.

When we get to the hospital, I send Mum off to M&S for snacks and make my way up to the oncology suite. Unlike elsewhere in the hospital, the cancer unit has had some extra money – probably from charity – and the entrance lobby is freshly painted and jolly. You've got to love the NHS. When they get it right, it's truly an amazing institution. I'm soothed by the fact that there's jazzy music playing. Soon I'm called through to the ward beyond the double doors.

There's about fifteen chemo chairs crammed into the room with torn curtains between them, making them into cubicles. Some of the curtains are drawn, but in the open ones, I can see patients wired up to drips. There's a very old man, who has his head lolling on his chest, his mouth open.

I look away and concentrate on my chemo nurses who introduce themselves as they take me to my cubicle.

Clarrie has a grin so huge that you can't help grinning back. She's been a nurse for thirty years and is so competent and skilled that I'm immediately put at ease when she sits me in the chair and without any further ado, takes my blood. They will send it off to be analysed, just to check that my white blood cells are in good shape and I've got enough immunity to tolerate the chemo drugs.

I've been waiting for this day for so long, but now that it's here, it feels different to how I'd imagined. I'm not sure what I've been expecting – some sort of Cold War-style black and white grimness, to go with the seriousness of being pumped full of super powerful drugs, but it's not as daunting on the ward as I first thought. Through the curtains, I can hear laughter and chatting.

Sian has raved about how acupuncture can really help with the side effects of chemo and I've managed to get an appointment with a practitioner called Lara who has agreed to come to the hospital to treat me just before they start the chemo. For free, as it turns out. Funded by charity. All those people shaking buckets. It really does make a difference.

When I tell Clarrie my concern that I might have a cold coming on, she waves at another woman who has just come into the unit.

'Then you're absolutely in the right hands,' she says, introducing Lara.

I like Lara on sight. She's not wearing any make-up, her features bold and clear, and she's wearing a funky linen smock and a large gold pendant. She also smells really nice.

We talk a lot about what's happened to me so far, then she presses her fingers into my wrists and stares off towards the poster on the wall, like she's listening to me. She's reading my pulses, apparently.

'What do you reckon?' I ask.

'I'd say your spleen is a bit sluggish,' she says.

'What do I do about that?' Because, if I'm being strictly honest, I haven't got a clue what a spleen is, or what it does.

'Avoid pork and bananas,' she says.

'That's a bummer. I love pork and bananas. Although not necessarily together.'

She put four needles in me. One in my foot, two in my hand and one in my ear and leaves me to it in my reclining chair. She pops an eye mask over my eyes, so I can relax.

I feel strange whooshing sensations and my face goes hot and then cold. It's funny being aware of my blood actually moving around my body like this, like some kind of freaky little motorway system packed with its own little busy commute. I try and tune in to the other conversations going on around me, but it's hard to focus.

After a while, Lara comes back in and I tell her that I could definitely feel stuff happening. She checks my wrists again and says that my pulses are a bit better and I really do feel energised and a lot less snively, so maybe there really is something in it.

Tamsin texts.

Good luck today. Keep smiling and remember that you're on your way. Bless the drugs. They'll make you better.

Mum arrives, bustling in with a carrier bag and I smother a smile as I remember how Tom used to give her a theme tune, humming Dexy's Midnight Runner's 'Come On Eileen', whenever he saw her.

'So what snacks did you get?' I ask.

'A Daim bar, of course. Your favourite.'

Sometimes, I really could hug her. So I do.

She sits down and starts knitting next to me and soon the nurse comes along with a clattering trolley stacked with needles and gauzes and says that my bloods have come back and we're good to go ahead with the chemo. That's certainly a relief and I grin at Mum, as if I've passed some kind of test.

Then Clarrie brings another trolley and monitor and explains that she's hooking up a saline drip, which will have to run into my body, along with the drugs. She inspects the chemo drugs that have just been delivered by the pharmacy. She explains that they give a combination of drugs called a regimen, and mine's called FEC. To my astonishment, the first drip she hooks up to the stand is full of bright orange liquid.

'It looks like Aperol Spritz,' I tell Clarrie.

'It does, doesn't it,' she says. 'And it'll make your wee go red.'

'Wow.' First blue tears, now red wee. You can't accuse Cancer World of looking drab.

'How are you feeling?' Mum asks, in a concerned whisper, like I might back out and run for the hills. Clarrie watches on, an amused smile on her lips. Maybe she can see – as well as I can – that Mum is way more scared than me.

'I'm fine,' I say, surprised at how unscared I am. But then, I've talked this all through with Amma, Tamsin and Sian. And if they can do it, then so can I. 'I mean, if anything I feel lucky,' I say.

'Lucky?' Mum says, as if I'm mad.

I think about the book Billy sent me through Amazon, with the sweetest note, wishing me luck for today. It was a delightful book of illustrations called *Les Très Riches Heures de Mrs Mole* by Ronald Searle, an artist who drew an illustration every time his wife, Monica, had to have a chemotherapy session, to show his love and evoke images of their future together. This was back in the days when chemotherapy really was brutal.

'You have to think about how much money has been spent to get safe drugs that are going to make me better. And how many people were guinea pigs and had to sit in the chair not knowing whether it was going to work.'

'I suppose that's true,' she concedes.

So I say, 'Hello, magic medicine. Come and do your shizzle!' I watch the orange liquid snaking down the thin line into the back of my hand. I'm expecting it to feel warm in my veins, or tingly, like Deep Heat, but I can't really feel anything. But then, after a moment, my heartbeat flutters. There's no going back now. My body is already in an altered state. Like it was when I was pregnant. It feels momentous, just like it did when I peed each time on the little pregnancy test stick.

'You're lucky to have such a positive daughter,' Clarrie tells Mum, but mum doesn't look convinced.

Tom arrives, looking harassed, followed by Rob, who has had a nightmare parking. It's turned into quite a party. They all sit cramped together in front of me in the line of chairs with eager, watchful faces, and I'm tempted to point my finger and declare, '… and for that reason, you're fired.' Except I can't, because I'm wired up to a drip.

'I got you a prawn one,' Mum says, opening her bag and offering a packet of sandwiches to me.

'I can't, Mum,' I tell her. 'Or I'll never be able to eat them again.' It's the same reason I haven't touched the Daim bar. 'Paddy's Law.'

'Nonsense,' she says. 'If you can't spoil yourself now, then when can you?'

I almost relent and then shake my head. 'Please don't be offended, but I'd really rather you put it away,' I say, firmly. 'Or Tom will have it.'

He reaches out his hand and she hands it over to him.

'If you're sure,' she says, looking confused. Neither of us are used to me being this assertive with her.

'I'm sure.'

We settle down and I try and think of a conversation topic, whilst we all watch me being pumped full of drugs. Maybe we should have a round of 'I Spy'. Though I'm not sure 'needle', 'bloody gauze' or 'drip' would really cheer anyone up.

'Did you know Tilly's got a boyfriend?' I ask Mum. 'This is our sixteen-year-old,' I explain to Clarrie.

'Oh yes,' Mum says.

'The big fella? With the tattoos?' Rob adds.

Tom and I look at each other.

'He's joking,' Mum says, laughing. 'Oh, you should see your faces.'

63

The chemo takes hours and hours and my bum goes numb as I sit in the chair. They have to change the bag of drugs halfway through and then there's lots of faffing with the saline monitor to get the rate right. Tom has to go back to work, so Mum and Rob bring me home and I have to be quite insistent to make them leave. I do get it, Mum wanting to mother me, but I'm also a mother myself and I just want to be normal for the kids.

I'm desperate for a bath. That's one thing about hospitals – they make me itch to have a wash, no matter how spotless they are. I'm just about to retreat when Grace arrives with the first of the scheduled meals – a casserole and two lasagnes, along with a huge basket of chocolate products, all wrapped in crinkly cellophane.

She explains that it's the result of a cash collection she's gathered from all the mums at school. After what happened with Pooch and the vet, I really don't want any more chocolates in the house, but I can't tell Grace this. She's glowing with magnanimous generosity.

Bea and Molly run into the living room and I can hear them booting up Wii Just Dance, so I have to offer Grace a cup of tea. She's clearly not in a hurry to leave.

'You really shouldn't have done a collection,' I tell her. I'm very touched that everyone has been so sweet and I foggily read all the names on the get well card, feeling slightly daunted that I'll now have to contact everyone to say thank you.

'Not everyone contributed,' she says. 'You know how some people are. Mentioning no names…' She's ready to bitch about one of the other mothers, but I won't be drawn. 'How are you feeling?' she asks, her head to one side, pity etched on her face.

'Fine, actually,' I reply, honestly. 'Just a little tired. It's been a long day.'

'Well, you might feel fine now, but I'm sorry, but this is where the shit starts.'

I feel instantly annoyed. I don't want her declarations of shittiness. How does *she* know? But right away, I feel a surge of doubt too. Like what's rushing around my bloodstream and into my system might not be jolly magic medicine after all, but something irredeemably grim.

'I'm keeping positive,' I say, with a thin smile.

She gives me a look like I'm crazy for taking such an approach, but then the doorbell goes again and I look at the clock. Who has decided to descend *now*?

'You shouldn't be having so many visitors,' Grace says, making herself comfortable on the kitchen stool, not seeing the irony of this statement at all.

It's Jennifer at the front door. 'I hope this isn't a bad time. I brought you a lasagne from the café. The veggie one you like.'

'Thank you,' I tell her. 'Come in.'

Grace gets up, looking annoyed when I put Jennifer's lasagne next to her blue Le Creuset dish and the other two lasagnes on the kitchen counter.

'You'll have to freeze that one too,' Grace says. 'You must eat my casserole whilst it's still fresh.'

Jennifer looks uncomfortable. 'I didn't mean to intrude.'

'I'm touched, honestly. Thank you,' I say, deliberately.

'I think Keira needs her space. Molly,' Grace calls, unexpectedly loudly. 'Molly, come on. We're going.'

I try and half-heartedly dissuade her and get her to drink her tea, but in a minute, she's left. Jennifer is clearly baffled that her generosity has caused such consternation. I try and explain that Grace has organised a rota of food from the school mums.

'I didn't realise,' Jennifer says. 'I only wanted to help.'

'I know. And you are. Thank you.'

'You've been so kind to Sian. Running with you is doing her the world of good,' Jennifer says. 'You see, she hasn't got that many friends. Sometimes, I'm not sure whether it was such a good idea for her to move down here from Bracknell.'

'Oh?'

'But she was so poorly,' Jen goes on, 'and Mum and I were here and she was there. She didn't have a support network.'

'But she had people she was close to,' I say. 'She talks about this one guy, Dave at work.'

Jennifer looks taken aback. 'Really? She never mentioned him.'

I would have thought Sian would have said something, but she clearly hasn't. And now I feel a creeping, ugly sense of guilt that I've betrayed Sian's confidence to her sister. 'Well, please don't say I said anything. Please, Jennifer. Promise me.'

'We're friends. Of course I promise,' she says.

Why can't I keep my big mouth shut these days?

64

Jennifer has only just left by the time Tom comes in from work and so, by the time we all sit down to eat, I'm exhausted. I tell him about Grace and Jennifer and the lasagne-off. I really should have defrosted the freezer in the garage, like I meant to, because it's taken some Tetris-style repacking to fit everything in.

'I was going to make pasta,' he says, when I show him the casserole.

'We're going to have to eat this instead. It's something with turmeric. Chicken, I think.'

However, Grace's casserole is unexpectedly delicious and I text her with some emojis to declare as much. I'm sure she'll feel better, knowing we appreciate her efforts.

Afterwards, I have a bath, inspecting my bruised hands where the canula was inserted. I'm due to have a portacath fitted, which is a permanent plastic port hole that will stay under my skin for the next few months. I've been told it'll help make the administration of the chemo drugs a lot faster, so I can be in and out of the hospital in half the time. I hope it's the right decision and won't hurt too much. I sink under the bubbles with a sigh, wanting to forget it all, closing my eyes and letting the steam relax me.

Afterwards, I'm lying on the bed, when Tom comes in and lies next to me.

He holds my hand.

'How does it feel?' he asks. He means the chemo drugs. The colourful little cocktail of Fluorouracil, Epirubicin, and Cyclophosophamide that is coursing through me at this very moment.

'Hmm... a bit fuzzy. And like I'm full up. There's no other way of describing it. It's like being pregnant all over again. And a bit like I'm on a boat – you know, sort of queasy, but not quite.'

Tom says the kids are settled and he suggests that we dim the lights and listen to an audiobook and I'm touched that he can sense that I'm talked-out after today, but that I need him. I roll onto my side and snuggle in next to him.

'I worked it out,' I say sleepily.

'What?'

'The real advantage of having one boob.'

'What's that?'

'This,' I say, getting super close to him, 'there's no squished breast in the way.'

I nod off almost immediately.

65

At 4 a.m., I wake up in a full body sweat. Sweat is running down my back, all over my face. I sit up, feeling dizzy and nauseous. 'Fuck,' I tell Tom. 'I think I'm going to barf.'

He rubs my back. 'Maybe it'll pass,' he says. 'It just means the chemo is doing its job.'

I nod, fighting down the feeling of extreme sea-sickness as I grip the edge of the bed. Sweat pops out of my forehead and eyelids. I take slow deep breaths and try and visualise the magic medicine seeping through each part of my body. Eventually, the nausea gets too much and I hurry along to the landing loo.

I sink onto the carpet, cooling my back down on the tiled wall. I don't want Tom to have to listen to me in our en suite, or to be disturbed by the light. He's got so much on at work.

As I sit and contemplate how I really ought to replace the loo brush, I force myself to try and stay positive, but this is the first time my strategy has been properly tested, because I feel *fucking awful*.

I force myself to remember that, like Tom just said, this feeling means the medicine is working. I visualise sending love to my bones and organs in the form of a constant stream of pink heart emojis. Then I think about why I'm going through this. Yes, I tell myself, I'm in control.

Mothership central command: All chemo missiles armed and fired! Fuck you, cancer cells. Your asses are mine!

I remember what Amma told me: that if I'm not sick after the first chemo, then I'm not likely to be sick at all, but I feel very on the edge of purging my insides.

I blow out breaths, chilly now that my full body sweat has cooled down. I try and focus on the montage of photos on the wall. I've been meaning to replace it with an updated version, but never have. There's a picture of Dad outside the back of Wishwells with Tilly as a baby on his shoulders. And that lovely one of me and Tom, all bedraggled after a festival, with our rucksacks on.

I remember our matching rucksacks. They must be in the loft somewhere. When I got pregnant with Tilly, our travelling itinerary came to an abrupt halt. I never did get to see Machu Picchu, the Grand Canyon or the plains of the Serengeti. How did my life fly by so fast?

I get up on my knees and lean over the bowl. My mouth fills with saliva and I squeeze my eyes shut. I really don't want to be sick. It occurs to me now, why people call it a bucket list. Not just because of kicking it, but because, this is the kind of wretched moment, when you're about to fill a bucket, when your long list of unfulfilled wishes rears up.

I sit back down. Sweat beads my upper lip. My head throbs and I shiver. I don't think I've ever felt as alone as I do in this moment. I have been worried about leaving the shores of Old Keira, but this feels like I've left the entire planet.

I think of all the people I *don't* know who are going through this right now, all by themselves. All the people in the world, shivering, cramped by their own toilet bowls. Also alone.

Only we're not alone, are we? I tell myself. There are millions of us. We're not alone. Just apart.

'Dad,' I whisper. 'Dad if you're an angel, just go and give them a hug, OK?'

Because I'm not alone. I know that now as I hear the creak of the landing floorboard and my very own tractor beam comes to grab me.

'Oh, baby,' Tom says, crouching down. 'Come back to bed. It's freezing.'

I let him lift me up and I lean my head on his shoulder.

'It's going to be OK,' he says in a soothing voice. 'You just need to sleep.'

I feel weak and tearful with gratitude. For his strong arms around me and his gentle words. 'How you're feeling now… it's going to pass.'

I nod, but tears run down my face. 'You know that phrase, all at sea,' I tell him. 'That's how I feel. Untethered. Like I'm in a boat sailing away from the old me. And everyone is around me, all my friends – and you and the kids – powering the boat, but I have no idea where we're going.'

We snuggle into bed and he pulls me into a tight hug, but I'm still crying.

'And I never saw the Serengeti,' I say, through my tears.

But Tom doesn't understand. He strokes my sweat-soaked hair. 'Shhh. Come on. It's going to be OK. And, anyway, the Serengeti's dangerous. Didn't you know there are lions there?'

66

Amma rings the next morning and says that exercise will help me get the drugs through my body. We can't get hold of Tamsin or Sian, so it's just the two of us.

'It'll have to be a chat and a slow jog,' I tell her. 'I don't feel up to much.'

'A "chog" it is then. That's all I'm up for too now this second chemo is kicking in.'

Putting on my trainers is just about the last thing I feel like doing, but knowing that Amma is also feeling rough – probably much rougher than this – being a few steps ahead down what I already know is an accumulative line, spurs me on. If she can do it, then surely, so can I. And, besides, I'm also curious to hear what happened with Isabel.

It's a freezing but sunny day and I wrap up warm. On the radio this morning, I heard that snow is forecast and there's that metallic tang in the air. I've agreed to meet Amma at hers and when I park near her house, she's already on the doorstep, locking the door. She's wearing gloves with diamanté studs, designer shades also with diamanté studs, and a black hat with a huge fluffy pompom. She looks glamorous and happy, as if something has lifted.

We walk along the street to a little cut-through near the train tracks, where the leaves on the ground are crispy with frost. I haven't been up here before, but I know it'll bring us out at the big park that runs along the river into town. We jog across the zebra crossing, but then she tells me to wait. She undoes a zip in her jacket and takes out a fiver. She stops by the homeless man who is by the park gate, sitting on an electricity box.

'Morning, Bob,' she says, slipping him the fiver. 'Nice morning.'

'No, Amma,' he says, looking at the note. 'I can't take it. Not again.'

'Go and get a cuppa in the warm,' she says, smiling.

'If you're sure?'

'I'm sure. And promise me you'll book into the hostel if the snow comes.'

'You know I hate it there,' he grumbles.

'I insist. You'll freeze to death out here,' she says, giving him a look and he nods and smiles. 'Oh, and I read that book you recommended,' she says, as we pass.

Bob's face erupts into a toothless grin. 'You did?'

'I'm not usually a thriller type of girl, but you're right, it was a page-turner.'

She notices my surprise as we go into the park. 'I've known Bob for years,' she says. 'Poor guy can't get a break. It's scandalous that someone like him isn't a teacher in school. He's so bright. It makes me furious that they don't have better hostel places available. Maybe it's something I'll have to sort out.'

She gives me a knowing grin as we start slowly running together. Does she mean that she's starting to think seriously about challenging for that council spot? My heart leaps at the prospect that she's considered my idea.

I don't get a chance to ask, because she's quickly grilling me about my chemo session and how I've been feeling. It's so cold, my breath clouds into steam as I tell her. The sun twinkles on the river and two swans glide by.

'So… what happened? With Isabel?' I ask, eventually, as we pass the bandstand.

'Well, it was very interesting. Revelatory, in fact,' Amma says.

'I want to know everything.'

'I know, but what I'm about to tell you… you can't tell anyone.'

'I won't, I promise,' I tell her. 'It's in the vault.'

She nods, satisfied, and I know I'll keep her confidence. I still feel bad about telling Jennifer about Sian's crush on Dave. I'm not going to make that mistake again. 'So?' I prompt.

'Well, it was so odd at first. We sat in the car whilst she cried and cried. She said she felt so dreadful that I was going through all of this.'

'How did you feel?'

'Sort of numb, I guess. And then annoyed at her for making *my* cancer about *her*.'

'So what did you do?'

'I did that thing where I started to be sympathetic about her feelings, but then I caught myself doing it and I got pissed off and gave it to her with both barrels. I don't know… maybe it was what you said about me reinventing. Or maybe it was socking it to those builders that gave me the confidence, or maybe because she caught me bald and there was no need for any pretence any longer, but I just told her straight. About how I was chewed up that she'd got the part in that movie and had dumped me when she got successful.'

'Wow. That's brave.'

'I know,' Amma says, turning to me. 'And then… guess what?'

She's slowed and now stops. She takes some deep breaths.

'You OK?'

'Can we stop for a little bit?' she says and I nod. We sit on a bench.

'Tamsin would never allow this,' I say.

'Let's not tell her then,' Amma says, her hand on her chest. Even chogging is a bit too hard.'

'You'll be OK in a minute,' I say, guiding her through some deep breaths. She takes off her hat, lifting her face to the sun. After a while she nods her head.

'I'm OK. I'm glad we stopped.'

'So, come on. Tell me. What did Isabel say? Was she cross?'

Amma puts her hat back on and gives me a funny look. 'No. She kind of broke down.'

'Broke down?'

'Yes. She admitted to me that I was always more talented than her, and that the only reason she got that part was because she…' she turns to me and grips my arm, for suitably dramatic effect, '… she gave the casting director a blow job in his office.'

'What?'

'I know! She said he'd made it very clear that he would think more highly of her if she showed her appreciation. Then he gave her a drink and she just kind of did it. And the worst thing is that I remember! I remember how the casting guy was off. That he had a weird energy and said something to Isabel about me giving him a brush-off look after my audition. And then she got the part and I didn't think about it, but when she told me… it all made sense.'

'You're kidding?'

'No I'm not. And then, afterwards, when she got successful and Evan took her on, she felt too embarrassed and ashamed to tell me. When she met Greg, she was terrified that if she told me about the casting director, then I'd tell him and ruin everything.'

'That is some secret.'

'I know. And I'm furious. With her, for being so stupid and with that prick of a casting director who abused her. But mostly because it's such a waste. All that heartache.'

'So what happened then?'

'We went to the pub and got pissed, like we always used to. That's why I couldn't answer your text. I was mortally hungover. Turns out chemo and alcohol isn't a good combination.'

'Oh dear,' I say, laughing.

'Then we both wept a lot and caught up and she's invited me to meet Greg and her baby. She said it was such a relief to finally tell me. What a secret to carry for ten years.'

'Poor girl.'

'It's not just the clear abuse of power, though and what she felt forced into doing, it's the ramifications... the fact she's ashamed about it, and can't even enjoy her success at all, because she got it under false pretences.'

'Didn't she want to say something when the whole Me Too thing happened?' I enquire.

'No, it just made her more terrified. About then getting dragged into the papers like some poster girl. Not to mention what it would do to Greg and her baby, Bear. So there's no point in me wading in, but it has made me think more about Creepy Crawley.'

'Why? What about him?'

'Because he's just as much as a sleazeball as that casting director, isn't he? And if I was the victim of his wandering hands, then I bet he's crossed a much bigger line with women who aren't as tough as me. I mean, I don't *know* that for sure, but I wouldn't put it past him.'

'You might be right.'

'So, I've decided. I'm going to take him on,' she says, slapping her gloved hands on her thighs. 'Not just as a paper candidate, but for real.'

'Oh, yay. Go you!' I exclaim, laughing and giving her a high-five.

'It's all thanks to you, Keira,' she says. 'Or it would never even have occurred to me, but now, somehow the path seems obvious. And that's not the best bit. I called Phillada last night.'

'Who?'

'You know, Phillada? I told you about her and how I did some campaigning for her.'

'*And?*' I can't believe she's really moving on this so fast.

'And she told me that she thinks I'd be brilliant and is prepared to put her weight and entire network behind me. She's practically offered to be my campaign manager, Keira. So I can take forward and finish off what she started. Isn't that great?'

I grin at her and she stands and points along the glittering tarmac. 'Talking of which, come on. Let's see if we can run the last bit. You're right: Tamsin would never allow this level of slacking. Even on a chog.'

67

I hadn't really considered how big an operation having a port fitted would be – or that I'd need a general anaesthetic again. Yet, just days after my chemo, I find myself back in the ward at the hospital, pulling on compression socks and signing disclaimer forms.

It's weird, having never been in hospital before this year, apart from to have the kids, that there's now a different attitude towards me from the staff, like I'm an old timer. And, in a way, I've become a lot more accepting of the fact that by being here, I'm at the mercy of the system.

I wait and wait in my little cubicle, watching people in hospital scrubs pass by and lurk around at the reception area. I pay close attention, trying to figure out who is responsible for what on the ward, or if anyone is actually in charge and has noticed I'm here, but it's impossible to tell.

When the nurse finally does get around to seeing to me, she's very matter of fact and takes it as read that I know what I'm doing and that I'm used to the pre-op drill, but it actually feels more daunting than when I had my mastectomy. She doesn't offer any words of reassurance. It doesn't help that a hospital cleaner decides that this is exactly the right moment to mop the floor.

Now, a very young surgeon comes in, side-stepping the

cleaner and her mop. She's moving slowly, but resolutely and isn't going to move out of the way for anyone, including him.

Clearly in a hurry, he doesn't introduce himself. There's no mister, or surname proffered, like for all I know, he's just grabbed his white coat and marched in here, like Leonardo DiCaprio in *Catch Me If You Can*. And, OK, I don't necessarily want to be on first name terms with a man who is about to cut me open, but some kind of vaguely human connection would be nice. But that's hospitals all over for you. Most of the staff are brilliant, but some people, well, aren't.

Mr Whoever-the-hell-this-is doesn't make eye contact with me as we whizz through the options at quiz-show speed, before telling me bluntly that he's going to put the port in my chest.

But that's where I stop him. I tell him I want it in my arm. Because I'm no longer a newbie and this doctor/patient thing isn't a command structure, it's a dialogue.

'Oh, and while we're chatting,' I say, 'perhaps you could tell me your name?'

'Er, George,' he admits, with a blush.

I smile, thinking back to those builders. Christ, six months ago, I don't think I'd ever have found the courage to just stand my ground like this.

But the fact is, I've seen Tamsin's scar from her port. The scar will definitely show under a swimming costume strap and I don't want that. George reluctantly agrees to try and fit it in my upper inner arm and I can't help thinking about how blasé we're being about surgery. It's like he's a plumber and we're discussing where he should put the kitchen tap.

My cancer care nurse, the lovely Sam, appears and has a quick chat, asking me how I am, before showing me what they'll be fitting inside me. It's the first time anyone's really explained to me what a port is.

And the answer is that it's a plastic device with a long tube running off it, which will be inserted into my vein towards my heart. Sam makes it all sound very straightforward and reminds me of the benefits again – that the port will allow the chemo to go in quickly, 'like a petrol pump,' she says chirpily.

Well, I suppose that upping the mothership's fuelling capacity can only be a good thing, so I nod and very soon I'm wheeled off to theatre, trying not to think about my signature on the disclaimer forms and how, sometimes, people just don't wake up.

68

When I come to, I'm on a ward – a different one. There are definitely more unconscious and semi-conscious patients in here. I look down at the thick bandage on my arm. I can't feel very much, but I get the sense that I've been prodded about. Tom rings and says he's coming in, I beg him to stay away and to let me sleep. I've never felt so tired in my life.

For the next few days, I can barely get out of bed. I feel guilty for being so weepy and low – especially when I can't go to meet the others for a run. Tamsin reminds me by text that it'll be the anaesthetic and that we'll get together if I'm feeling better after the weekend. It doesn't help that Tom has a crazy week at the office and then – guess what? – has to work all weekend. With her. With Janine. But he promises, *promises* me, that this will be the last time. His big meeting that will settle the case he's been working on is on Monday.

I call Lorna to give her an update.

'I miss coming in,' I tell her, hoping she'll revise her opinion that I'm not terribly 'aspirational'. 'I know I've been useless,' I tell her, 'but I want to be involved. I can't just sit here and do nothing.'

She sighs. 'Well, there's a strategy meeting on Monday, I guess… if you want… you could come in for that. Then I can explain where we're up to.'

'That'd be great,' I tell her, so grateful for this bone she's throwing me.

Tilly, Jacob and Bea have been popping up to my bedroom sporadically to check that I'm alright, but when I hear a fight breaking out in the kitchen on Saturday afternoon, I force myself up. I hate that everyone is arguing over the chores I do all day every day without moaning, and annoyed, I send Tilly out with Pooch. Where Jacob's been stepping up, she's just been playing up more and more. Ducking out in the evening, doing sod all work as far as I can tell. I'm not sure where it's all leading, but I really don't have the energy right now to sort it out.

On Sunday, the kids are not impressed when I say there's only pasta for lunch and not the full roast they wanted. Jacob complains that he's still starving after he's polished off two platefuls of spaghetti and another fight breaks out over who ate the last choc ice. As usual, they've left the empty box in the freezer.

I ask them to clear the table and pack up the dishwasher and take the laundry upstairs and stick it in their drawers, but supervising all of this feels every bit as arduous as doing it. And before long I end up shouting at them to stop arguing and then everyone disperses, keen to get as far away from me as possible. So much for my happy family time.

I call Joss and tell her about how cross I am with the kids.

'I told you not to have them,' she teases me. 'I told you to cross your legs, but *would* you listen?'

I laugh, feeling cheered up by her easy banter. 'Anyway, enough about me. Tell me about the real world. Tell me about how fun your life is.'

'I can't.'

'Why not?' This is not like her.

'Being single and footloose and fancy free isn't all it's cracked up to be.'

'Isn't it? I thought you were loving shagging everything with a pulse.'

'The novelty has worn off. There hasn't been anyone who is even remotely a candidate for my dream beach wedding.'

'You can't honestly still want that?' She's always had a romantic notion of a Bali wedding – ever since she was a teenager. Her ridiculous fantasy of Mr Perfect on the white beach has always made me and Scout laugh, especially as Mr Perfect has become more and more preposterous as the years have gone by.

'No, I guess not. I just want some normality, you know? Someone to watch a box set with.'

I give her a dose of reality about the perils of long-term marriages, by sharing my woes about Tom. I know her well enough to know that she won't judge. She also thinks that I'm being ridiculous about Janine. I can't stop thinking about them being in the office together.

'Tom loves you,' she says. 'Through and through. You're reading too much into it.'

'You think?'

'I know.'

Tom comes in later on from the office. He walks in on me upstairs in the en suite and asks me how my day has been. I want to tell him that I'm fed up being the one who has to discipline the kids all the time, and I'm fed up of them never helping out unless they're told to, and then sulking when they are, but again, I just don't have the juice.

Instead, I concentrate on unwrapping the bandage on my arm as Sam, my nurse, said earlier on the phone that I can take it off and can finally have a bath. Tom stands, frozen in the door, watching me, his eyes filling with tears as we both take in how bruised and battered my arm is.

'Oh my love,' he says. To be fair, from where he's standing, he's not getting a good view.

'It'll settle down,' I say, but I don't feel as brave as I sound. Tom's horror at his one breasted, beaten up, soon-to-be bald wife hurts. I want to comfort him, but I don't know how.

'You're so brave,' he says, coming in and hugging me. His jumper is cold and I feel tears smarting. I want to tell him how I'm not brave. That feeling this terrible now only makes me focus on how much longer there is to go on this ride in Cancer World. That I feel so far away from myself… so far away from the person who could hold her family together. But he knows that. I bet he's missing me too.

69

By the morning, I was hoping to feel a bit better, but I feel wobbly as I make my way to the park to meet the girls before I go into work for the strategy meeting. I'm hoping for a much-needed pep talk about how to deal with Lorna, as I haven't told Tom that I'm going into Wishwells. I didn't want to bother him with it, when he had to get up at an ungodly hour this morning. It's his big day in court today and he should win the case, but even after the months of work he's put in, it's far from guaranteed and I know he's worried. I don't need him to have any more stress.

I also haven't told him that I had a text from my bank because a few of my direct debits have bounced. It seems that my Wishwells salary has been paid as normal, but a fraction of what it should be. Obviously, it's a mistake, but I need to clear it up with Lorna and Pierre.

Pooch hasn't been out, so I have to drag him along to the park with me. He scowls at me and makes a plaintive whine. He really doesn't like the cold.

Sian and Amma are by our bench. It's the first time I've seen Sian since my chemo, so I regale her with the details, and my operation.

'Are you OK, Keira?' Amma asks, after a while. 'You look a bit pale.'

'I think so,' I tell her, although I really don't feel great.

'Sit down for a minute,' she says, helping me gently onto the bench, 'whilst we wait for Tamsin.'

I look at the railings on the other side of the path and they blur a bit, like a TV effect. Amma and Sian sit down either side of me and Sian puts a cool hand on my head.

'You're really hot. I think you've got a temperature.'

'I feel cold,' I tell her, my teeth chattering, but I can feel sweat beading on my lip.

Amma nods at Sian. 'Come on,' she says, pulling me up.

'Where are we going?'

'I'm taking you to A&E,' she says.

'What? Don't be ridiculous.'

'I think you've got an infection. I don't know for sure, but we shouldn't muck about.'

'But...' I start to panic, remembering the stark warning Sam gave me about taking my temperature and being vigilant about infections and my white blood cell count. 'I don't want to go.'

'Tough, you're going,' Amma says. 'Who should I call?'

I wince as she takes hold of my arm as my legs go wobbly. It really hurts and she apologises. I tell her to call Mum, because Tom will still be in his meeting, and she takes charge of Pooch as Sian and I get into Sian's car.

On the way to the hospital, Sian insists that I call Sam so that she can ring ahead to the hospital, as she'll have a direct line to A&E. I get her machine at the office, so leave a message on her mobile instead. I sit in the car as we whizz straight through the lights up to A&E.

'This is ridiculous, there's nothing wrong with me,' I tell

Sian as she slows to a stop in an ambulance bay. 'I have to get to work.'

'Better to be safe than sorry,' she says. 'Go straight in and I'll park.'

'Good luck with that,' I tell her.

'Just go,' she says.

I start to walk away, but I feel really wobbly. It's like I'm very stoned. In a second, Sian's arm is supporting me and she guides me into reception.

70

It seems that Sam did get my message and rang ahead, because when I get to the glass desk, they have my name and a nurse takes over from Sian, quickly ushering me past the walking wounded waiting in the hot reception area, to a small side room. I wouldn't have minded waiting; *Homes Under the Hammer* is on the TV.

Sian leaves to park, once she's happy that I'm in good hands. My nurse is from Slovenia and has steely grey eyes, which look me up and down as she snaps on some blue plastic gloves. She takes my temperature and it's bad, just as Sian had thought.

She takes a look at my port, but even just touching it makes me yell out in agony. Giving up on using it, she makes three attempts to locate one of my veins in the back of my bruised hand, but eventually, she hits a good spot and fills up six test tubes with my blood.

'I will send them off to the lab,' she says, sticking labels on the tubes.

'How long will it take for the results to come back?'

'Should be in the hour.'

'Wow! That's quick.'

I want to wait for Sian, but the nurse says I can't be exposed to the general public, because of the risk of further infection.

Further. Yes, that's what she says. Like there's something I've already got. I'm properly spooked at how seriously she's taking this.

Down in the basement, we walk quickly through a ward, where there's people recovering from heart attacks and minor surgery. We push through double doors that say 'No Entry' to the area beyond. There's a large hub with nurses behind it, looking at computers and lots of monitors and equipment. I'm told to go into a side ward where there's a bed and I'm hooked up to a heart rate monitor. A nurse takes my temperature and frowns, then leaves quickly before I have the chance to ask her what it means.

I get out my phone, but there's no reception.

I try and get the attention of one of the nurses, who seem to be dashing around everywhere, except for near me, but every time one passes, they assure me that someone else will be here to see me soon. But it's not soon. The minutes tick by as I'm left alone and I stare at the stained wall and the sanitary bin as my panic mounts.

Eventually, a young doctor with a clipboard comes in, followed by two nurses. She reads my notes thoughtfully, then engages with me fully. I like her already.

'It looks like you have an infection,' she tells me. 'You also have neutropenia, which means your white blood cell count has flatlined. If we don't get your count back up, then things could get critical.'

'Critical? What does that mean?'

'I'm afraid there's a real danger of neutropenic sepsis.'

'Sepsis? Don't people die of sepsis?'

The doctor puts her hand on my shoulder and smiles down

gently at me. 'Don't panic. We know what we're doing. We're going to get you on some intravenous antibiotics, right away.'

I feel so helpless and vulnerable sitting on the bed, as they hook me up to a drip. And stupid. Naïve. If it hadn't been for Sian, I might be in serious trouble. Maybe Hilary was right and I can't just positively think my way through this. And the knowledge that my strategy might not work leaves me perilously close to tears.

It's decided that my port is infected, but the nurse also demands to see the burn on my thumb from Tilly's hair straighteners. I take off the plaster and see that the burn has gone green and gunky. No wonder it's been sore. And it's this realisation that my body really can't heal itself that frightens me the most.

I watch my heart rate monitor, trying to make sense of the numbers, as they check and double check the antibiotics, feeling very much that my life is in the hands of other people. In spite of Hilary's nagging voice in my head, I try and do my positive visualisations and tell myself that everything is going to be OK, but the beeping machines and rushing staff make it almost impossible.

An hour goes by and I start to fret about my life 'out there'. It feels so cut off from me in here. Has Amma managed to get hold of Mum and deliver Pooch home? Will Tilly panic when she finds out that I'm in hospital? What will Lorna do when I don't show up for the meeting? The fact I have no control over any of these things only makes it worse.

I try and close my eyes, but tears form and I squeeze them away and tell myself to stop being such a baby, but I've never been so scared. I keep thinking about what the doctor said: No white blood cells. Sepsis. Danger.

I remember enough from my Biology O Level back in the last century to know that white blood cells are fairly crucial in this sort of situation. How can my body fight an infection when it has no white blood cells?

Suddenly, I can hear nurses outside and Tom comes in. He's carrying his coat over his arm. I shuffle up on the bed.

'What are you doing here?' I ask, as he comes over and kisses me on my forehead. It's the big meeting and he should be there. Not here, but I'm so relieved to see him. I grip his hand tightly.

'Janine said Sian came to the office to find me. She gave me a lift here, actually.'

'But what about Andrew? Won't he mind?'

'We'll deal with that later,' Tom says.

It's bad enough that I'm in here with an infection, but just awful that he's walked out of his most important meeting of the year on account of me.

71

They make me stay in overnight to observe me and I try and sleep, but I'm delirious with tiredness and shock. But then, finally, my temperature starts dropping and I fall into one of those crazy deep sleeps, where it's like rising up and surfacing through black liquid tar when you finally wake.

Tom takes me home and puts me to bed. Mum – who's been up all night worrying and knitting herself sick, of course – bustles round, looking concerned. But despite everyone treating me like I'm about to die, over the next twenty-four hours, I start to feel better and better.

I steel myself to call Lorna to apologise for missing the meeting. She sounds annoyed, like I've deliberately missed it on purpose.

'It's just I'm getting very mixed messages from you,' she says. 'You say you want to be here, but then you don't show up.'

Has she not listened to a word I've just said? She obviously doesn't believe that I've been in a life-threatening situation.

'I couldn't help it. It was a medical emergency.'

'This is what I've been saying all along, Keira. You just need to stay at home and take your time to get better,' she says. 'There's nothing going on here apart from our influencers evening next Thursday.'

'I'll come in for that,' I tell her. 'Definitely.'

'If you want to,' she says, as if she thinks I'll back out. She doesn't sound like she wants me there at all.

'And... um... Lorna, we need to discuss money.' I hate having to raise this, but I explain about my direct debits bouncing, because my salary cheque was so low. 'I'm sure it's just a mistake...'

'I'll get Pierre to ring you,' she says, tightly, then rings off.

I want to discuss this with Tom, but a nagging fear fills me. Have they deliberately cut my salary because I haven't been in work? I have no idea what's been agreed about sick pay. If I have any... or what I'm entitled to. And not knowing only makes me feel more out of touch with Wishwells than ever.

But Tom is unapproachable. I get the impression that him abandoning the meeting to come to me in A&E has not gone down very well at work. He says that Janine and Dan were fine without him, but he's not giving me the whole picture. I know Dan, his colleague, gets right up his nose and that it's more than likely that Dan has probably stepped in and claimed the glory that should have been Tom's.

What I can't bring up – and I know is very much on Tom's mind – is that he's expecting Andrew to give him promotion news any moment now. The fact he hasn't is worrying, but then again, Andrew is quite capable of stringing things out.

On Wednesday, there's talk everywhere of snow, but none has actually fallen, so I dispatch the children to school. I'm getting changed for work, when Kathryn from the cancer centre rings and asks if I want a slot that's become available for a massage. My shoulders are like boards and I tell her yes please.

In the warm treatment room, Chris, the masseur, has bare

feet and rolled-up linen trousers and a smock. He has a beard and long hair and the most intense grey eyes I've ever seen.

He takes my history and asks lots of questions. I sit on his heated massage chair and he explains that he'll give me gentle acupressure. I don't mind what he does. It's just lovely to be pampered.

As he starts on my back, I can't help groaning. Under his fingers, months of tension come flooding out. At one point, I feel myself getting tearful.

'Let it out,' he soothes. 'It's perfectly normal.'

Is it? I let out a shuddery breath, as the tears fall. Then, later, he massages my scalp and when I catch sight of my reflection, my hair is standing up like I've had an electric shock, but my expression is stoned and happy. The man is a miracle worker.

Afterwards, I sit and sip herbal tea and Kathryn chats to me and I feel more like a normal human being than I have done for months.

Outside, snow has started to fall as I head to the car. I get a text from Grace saying they're letting the kids out of school early and she's picking up Bea and Molly, so I can relax for a bit. The soft, muted atmosphere of the falling snow suits my mood. I feel floaty and light.

I'm just getting into the car, when I see a woman smiling at me in the next space. She's getting out to go into the centre.

I recognise her. She was one Tamsin's friends – the one Tamsin made the pretty earrings for.

'Julia,' she reintroduces herself.

'How are things with you?' I ask.

She shrugs. 'Can't complain. You?'

'I just had my first chemo, so there's a long road ahead,

but I just had the most amazing massage with Chris. Tamsin recommended him.'

'Tamsin's so great,' she says. 'So positive, you know.'

'I know.' I smile. I really should get on, but Julia is in no hurry to let me go.

'I mean, she's so cheerful for someone with terminal,' she says.

I stare at her. 'Sorry? With *what*?'

'She's got terminal cancer. Didn't you know?' She bites her lip, seeing that I don't.

'But she's having treatment,' I protest.

'Because there might be a small chance it'll work,' she says, hurrying on, clearly worried she's let far too much slip. 'And maybe it will,' she says, brightly. 'Let's hope so.'

72

Tom, fortunately, can't get out of his meeting, so I go to see Sexy Phil for my oncology appointment alone. To be honest, I'm relieved. I'm too shaken up by what I've heard about Tamsin, and I know Tom won't understand.

Julia's words rattle around in my head. It can't be true... can it? But now, all sorts of things start to make sense... about how Tamsin has never really discussed her prognosis or treatment with us. Has she been running with us all this time – geeing us up, making us laugh, when all along she's been facing the most devastating news by herself?

I keep thinking of her the first time I met her, just before I got my own news. 'I'm not dead yet,' she'd said. But maybe she hadn't just been joking. Maybe she'd been telling me even then that it was only a matter of time before she was.

Phil doesn't seem phased, when I regale him with the infected port story and what happened at the hospital. I tell him how excellent the system was for fast-tracking me and how amazed I've been by the effectiveness of the antibiotics. But I also admit how I nearly did nothing about it and he frowns. He warns me again that throughout the chemo, the greatest danger I'll face is infection – and not the kind that I'll pick up from anyone else, but the kind that my body might easily develop all by itself. There's a lot of systems on the mothership working at full capacity, it seems. I can't take it for granted that everything will run smoothly and I realise that I'm going to have to take a lot more care of myself.

He checks my port and my armpit and tells me that the bruising should go down in a few days. My arm has gone a horrible mottled black and green colour and the bit of plastic sticking up underneath my skin is so tender, it's impossible to touch. It feels like that scene in *Alien*, where Sigourney Weaver looks down at her stomach and realises there's something inside her. Touching it makes my tummy go all shivery and weird.

Eventually, after I've told him that apart from the emergency A&E dash and near-death experience, I'm more or less fine, we get on to the subject of running.

'I heard something about Tamsin,' I say. My voice starts to tremble. 'Earlier. About her being terminally ill…?'

'Hmm,' he looks down. 'I know you're friends, but I can't discuss—'

But he's already confirmed it, hasn't he? Because he hasn't denied it. He hasn't set me right. And that's when I burst into tears. As in proper tears. Big tears. Like a kid. Because that's suddenly how I feel.

Sexy Phil's trying to say something, but I'm crying too much to hear. Sam takes me to a little side room and I weep and weep.

'I don't want her to die,' I tell her, accepting yet another tissue.

'I'm sorry you're so upset,' she says. She's trying to keep what she's saying neutral, because she's not allowed to discuss Tamsin any more than Phil, but I can see from her eyes that it's true.

And then everything's suddenly blurting out. Not just how I feel about Tamsin, but everything else too.

I tell her about Tom missing his meeting to come and find me in accident and emergency, and how difficult things are at home. How the kids are scratchy and unhelpful and even doing half the normal things I've always done as a matter of course feels like a Herculean effort. How I'm tired and sore and scared and she listens, understanding. It feels good to get this off my chest to her. Then I get on to the subject of Lorna and the tears come faster and faster.

'But it's normal for most people to give up work during chemo,' she says. 'It sounds to me, Keira, like you should really give yourself a break.'

73

The kids are larking around the next morning and I feel I should go outside and build a snowman with them, but I don't feel resilient enough for a snowball fight, and instead, I watch on from the window, blowing the steam on my tea.

I hadn't planned on going out, but I know I won't be able to last the day if I don't talk to Tamsin and she's not picking up her texts. I take some of the vegan brownies Bea has made and drive round to Tamsin's flat.

When I knock on the door, at first I think there's nobody in. I can't hear anything and there're no lights on in the window. Then the door opens and a thin man answers. He's probably no more than 40, but he looks like a 70-year-old. His skin is sallow and leathery. He looks at me suspiciously. So this must be Ian.

I explain who I am and, reluctantly, he shows me into the flat.

Tamsin is in the bedroom, under a black satin duvet. A large fluffy cat is on her lap. There's a light on a bracket with a black lampshade and a glass table piled with novels.

'Keira,' she says, but her voice is weak. 'This is a lovely surprise.'

I go to her and kiss her. Her skin looks almost translucent. She isn't wearing any make-up and I can see the veins on her skull. It dawns on me now how much her make-up has covered up before. How I might have known how ill she was if she hadn't masked it so well.

'I've been worried,' I tell her. 'I hope you don't mind me coming round. I was just passing.'

'Not at all. It's good to see you,' Tamsin says, but her chest wheezes. 'You met Ian.' He stands by the doorframe watching us. He's so quiet, I hadn't noticed he was there. I nod to him.

'You want anything? I'm going out?' he says to Tamsin, but without much conviction. 'Before we get snowed in.'

She shakes her head and waves her hand at him in weary dismissal.

'How are the girls?' she asks. I tell her about us meeting and my hospital drama on Friday. 'Been there, done that.' She nods.

'I'm so grateful to Amma and Sian. I would never have gone if it wasn't for them. I'm such an idiot.'

'No, you're not. It's hard to face this stuff.'

A moment later, we hear the front door close.

'Could you be a darling and get me some tea?' Tamsin asks, cheering up a bit. She shuffles up so that she's sitting up more comfortably.

'Of course.'

'Help yourself too,' she says.

I get up and go to the kitchen. The sideboard by the kettle is littered with pill bottles. I inspect them and see Tamsin's name on them all. I only recognise a couple of the drug names. Strong painkillers, mostly, but I can only guess at what the rest are for. I put the kettle on and go back to Tamsin.

'I don't mean to pry, but I just saw all those pills in the kitchen.'

'It's alright, Keira,' she says with a sad smile. 'Julia told me she'd let the cat out of the bag. I was wondering how long it would be before you came round.'

'It's true then? That it's… you're…'

'Terminal? Yes, it seems that the pesky cancer is back with a vengeance. It's in my brain, apparently this time. And what I've got is rare. Trust me not to have something straightforward.'

'Oh, Tamsin,' I say, reaching out for her thin hand. My eyes fill with tears. 'I'm so sorry.'

'Well, it's not exactly like it came as a complete surprise. Life *is* terminal, if you hadn't noticed,' she says, with one of her cheeky grins.

'But… what about a cure? There must be a cure?'

'Phil says the best treatment is here and they're doing all they can for me, but Ian has been doing lots of internet research.'

I want to remind her how Amma warned us not to believe anything online, but I can see from her face that this isn't the time to point that out.

'The thing is, there might be a cure in Mexico in this clinic Ian found. There's some really promising results. He really wants me to go, but we can't afford that.'

'But… if you don't, what then?'

She gives me a look. 'Well, who knows? If I'm lucky, I might get a few months.'

'A few months? To live?'

'No, to die.' Another dark grin.

'Oh Jesus.' I clamp my hand over my mouth, not wanting to face what she's just told me.

'Don't ask him,' Tamsin says, laughing at my profanity. 'Believe me, I've already done some praying and it hasn't worked. And at this point, I'm willing to try anything. Maybe Mexico is the solution.'

'If that's what you want… then, then, there must be some kind of way to get you there?'

'I'm buggered if I can think of one,' she says. 'I could beg and borrow off everyone I know, but it still wouldn't be enough.'

'Don't give up,' I tell her. 'Don't lose hope. We'll find a way.'

'All I want is some time,' she says, sadly. 'More time.'

I make her tea, but she refuses anything to eat. I don't want to leave her alone, but she says she wants to sleep and when she nods off, I leave.

Outside, in the snow, I delve into my parka pocket for the car keys. I have to tell Amma and Sian. As soon as possible.

My hands are shaking and a piece of paper drops out of my pocket and cursing, I pick it up. I'm about to screw it up and put it in the litter bin, when I see what it is. It's the flyer I picked up months ago about the charity run in April.

74

The snow still hasn't let up so it's impossible to meet for our Friday run, but the roads are clearer. I've called an emergency meeting and Sian and Amma have braved coming out to meet me at a café. I would have gone to Jennifer's but I can't risk being so close to Wishwells and running into Lorna or Pierre. Not today. I'm not strong enough to deal with them. It would be different if Moira was there, of course, but Moira *isn't* there, I remind myself, feeling the sharpness of the resentment, like a pin I just can't stop pricking myself on.

But I have bigger things to worry about today. I hardly slept last night, thinking of how alone Tamsin must be feeling. How hopeless she was. And that's when it hit me. What we could do. How we could help. How we could give Tamsin back her hope. '*With hope in our hearts and wings on our heels.*' Yes, *this* was what that dream about Nigel Havers had been about. This was what he'd been trying to tell me all along. Running had brought us together and running would fix this mess too.

But first, I have to break the news about Tamsin having terminal cancer, which I couldn't bring myself to do yesterday on the phone. Instead, I brace myself and hold hands with Amma and Sian as I tell them what I discovered yesterday. They're both as shocked as I was and devastated when I tell them about what Tamsin said about wanting more time. We all cry a bit and I hug Amma because she's nearest.

'We have to do something,' Sian says and I reach out and hug her too. I know they're both as chewed up about this awful news as I am.

Amma sniffs and blows her nose. 'But what?'

'She seems keen on this Mexico idea. Although she can't afford it. Maybe raising some cold, hard cash is the solution?' I suggest.

'But how?' Sian asks.

I spread the crumpled flyer out in front of us. 'OK, so this is a bit mad. I found this in my pocket and it occurred to me that this could be the fastest way of raising money.'

'Can we really do it?' Amma asks, picking up the flyer and showing Sian. '10K? It's a fuck of a long way and I'm not exactly at my fittest.'

'I know, but it doesn't matter how fast we get round,' I tell her. 'Even if we end up walking. It's about raising money for Tamsin.'

'Do you think she'll have a problem with it, though?' Sian asks. 'Shouldn't we check with her?'

I think for a moment. 'Yes, you're right. We should.'

I call Tamsin's number and we all listen to the phone, our heads bent towards the screen I'm holding flat in my hand. She answers and we all say 'Hi.'

'We're in the café. All together,' I explain.

'You lazy lot,' she chuckles. 'You should be out in the snow. I turn my back for one minute and look what happens!'

'We've had an idea,' Amma says. 'About you.'

Tamsin chuckles and I can imagine her Cheshire cat grin.

'Oh, I see. So you've all been gossiping.' If she minds about the fact I've told the others, she doesn't sound it. 'Go on...'

I look at Sian and Amma who nod. 'We're going to run the park 10K in April.'

'What? That's in less than a month.'

'We're going to run to raise money for your treatment,' Amma adds.

There's a silence. *Oh God*, I think. *Does she hate the idea? Does she hate me for coming up with it?*

'That's very sweet of you,' Tamsin says. Her voice is husky. 'But...'

'If we start fundraising immediately, then we have a shot at raising quite a bit,' Sian says. 'If we tap up everyone we know.'

'We'll have to really go for it,' I say. 'But between the three of us, we know lots of people – and I'll be able to contact local businesses.'

'But even if you could raise some money, can you all *actually* run 10K?' Tamsin asks. 'Any of you?'

'Well, I've never tried,' Sian says.

'Me neither.' Amma pulls a face.

'The furthest I've ever run is in the park,' I say.

'And don't forget that some of you are in the middle of cancer treatment too,' Tamsin reminds us.

'Yeah,' I admit. 'There is that little detail. But isn't it worth a go?' I tell Tamsin, trying to get her enthused. 'We might be able to get round, if you train us.'

She laughs. 'Really?'

'Keira's right. It's got to be worth a try,' Sian says.

'Yeah. Just because of the cancer, we can't just roll over and take it, right,' I say, quoting Tamsin back to herself.

'You'd really do that for me?' she asks.

'That's what friends are for.'

I smile at Amma, knowing Tamsin has been won over.

'Then, ladies, I suppose I'd better find a way of dragging myself out of my deathbed and see you in the park on Monday. Weather permitting.'

I ring off and Amma, Sian and I high-five. I beam at them.

'So... we'd better sign up,' I say, looking at the flyer and tapping the website into my phone.

75

Bea has been spending a lot of time with Molly recently, Tilly has been busy with her project at college and Jacob has been at Biffa's for the last couple of days, so that evening, we sit down for the first family meal we've all had together for a while. I've been full of nervous excitement, since meeting the girls in the café, my mind buzzing with our plan.

The kitchen is warm and cosy and I've laid up the table nicely. Snow falls softly on the other side of the kitchen window. Tom comes in the back door from his office, stamping his feet on the mat to get the snow off. He looks tired and stressed.

'It's bloody freezing out there,' he says. He gives me a perfunctory kiss and then ruffles Bea's hair.

'What's this one?' Jacob asks, lifting up the foil on the dish in the middle of the table.

'I think it's fish pie,' I tell him. 'Watch out, it's hot.'

'Why do we keep having to have all this strange food?' Tilly asks, as I put the bowl of peas on the table.

'Because people want to help. And I don't want to cook.'

Tilly nods. 'Fair enough.'

'You could learn?' I say, raising my eyebrows.

'I'd like that,' she says, surprising me. 'Alfie cooks for his parents.'

I try and keep a lid on my excitement. This is the first time she's mentioned Alfie since she last flounced off. Tom knows it's significant too and gives me a look and tries not to smirk as he washes his hands at the sink. I shake my head a fraction. If we tease Tilly, then she'll go off like a rocket.

'Oh, really?' I say, trying to sound nonchalant, like chatting with my daughter about her boyfriend's culinary expertise is something we do every day. 'What does he cook?'

I've been busy vilifying Alfie in my mind for having sex with my daughter, but this paints him in a slightly different light.

'He says he does a mean chilli.'

'I like a man who likes his spice,' Tom says, a bit too enthusiastically in a silly accent, as he sits down at the table, and Tilly rolls her eyes and the conversation moves on.

I'm annoyed, obviously, that I didn't get to pry a little bit more. From the intel I've gathered from Jacob, I know that Alfie is in the same year at college as Tilly, but that's about it. Is he tall, or short? Funny, or dull? Other than the fact we're clearly going to be seeing him on *MasterChef* sometime soon, my first born might as well be dating the invisible man.

Still, it's a start.

We all eat the fish pie and listen to Jacob giving us a blow-by-blow account of his progress on Fortnite, then Bea tells us all about what she's been learning about Henry VIII in school and the forthcoming trip to the Tower of London. The meal is nearly over by the time I get a turn to speak.

'So, I have some news,' I tell them. I do a little drum roll with my fingertips on the table, but give up, as my arm hurts. They know about Tamsin as I was upset last night after I came back from her flat, so I'm glad to be making a more cheery announcement.

Tom looks at me. 'What is it?'

I smile. 'Well… I've signed up for a charity run.'

'A what?' Tom asks. His fork clatters to the plate.

'My running group and I are doing a, wait for it… 10K charity race to raise money for Tamsin to go to Mexico for treatment.'

'10K?' Tilly asks.

'As in *kilometres*?' Bea checks.

'As in you? Jacob says. 'And you're actually planning on running it? Not catching a bus?'

'Or a cab?' Tilly adds.

'Well, thanks a bloody bunch,' I say, feeling the anger rise up inside me. 'I'd have thought you'd at least have the decency to—'

'It's alright, Mum, we're just teasing you,' Tilly says, unexpectedly wrapping her arms round my neck and squeezing me tightly for the first time in I don't know how long.

'When did you decide this?' Tom says. He's the only one not smiling.

'Today.'

'And when's the race?'

'April.'

'Well, good for you,' Jacob says.

There's a silence as Tom looks at the kids.

'What?' I ask.

Tom puts his tongue around his teeth, biding his time. 'April is not very far away. Just over a month, in fact. You'll still be in the middle of chemo.'

'So?' I tell him.

'So... only days ago, you were too weak to get out of bed. Not to mention your infected port. You're mad to even think about running a race. You said yourself that you had to take your treatment seriously – that the emergency hospital dash gave you a fright.' His words smart.

'I just want to *do* something. Something to help a friend,' I explain.

'But you hardly know this woman,' Tom protests. 'And I'm sorry that she's—'

'Dying,' I state. 'As in will be dead, unless I do something about it. Unless we all do. Me, Amma and Sian. I've got so much and she struggles, Tom, only you'd never know it. She's the bravest person I've ever met.'

'I still think you're mad,' he says.

Mad is a bit strong.

'Well, whether I'm *mad* or not, I'm doing it. And I'd appreciate it if you'd all sponsor me,' I tell them all.

Tom dumps his paper napkin on the table and gets up. 'I'm going to call Mum,' he says. He gives me a dark, furious look as he leaves.

'What's the matter with him?' Bea asks, looking at me.

'I think he's just stressed,' I tell her.

'And he thinks what you're doing is dangerous,' Tilly says.

'And is it?' Bea asks, her voice suddenly small.

'No,' I tell her, folding her in my arms. 'Not if I take the right precautions. Not if I train properly.' Not if I don't overdo it, or get an infection, or anything else that can go wrong in Cancer World. But I want her to believe me. I want to be her invincible mummy.

'I watched a YouTube documentary about breast cancer,' Jacob says, staring at the empty doorway Tom has just stormed out through. 'It's always tough on the husband.'

Right now, I don't have it in me to feel sorry for Tom. Just Tamsin. And how I pray to God that what we've promised her is something we will actually be able to do.

Shortly afterwards, Bea and Jacob find excuses to leave the table.

'I think it's good you're doing something for someone else,' Tilly says, picking up on my mood. 'I was reading about the teachings of the Dalai Lama.'

Sometimes she actually floors me. 'You were?'

'Yep. He reckons the way to find happiness is to help others,' she says.

I nod. 'OK, then. So... can you load the dishy?'

'Sure,' she says, getting up, but as she does, I can see that she's been doodling on her paper napkin.

'What's that?' I pick it up.

'Oh, nothing. It's just when you said that Tamsin wanted more time...'

'Tilly this is fantastic!' She's drawn the words, 'Time for Tamsin' in wiggly gothic letters. The more I look at it, the more it looks like a logo.

'Really?'

'Really! Can I use it?

'Sure.'

'Time for Tamsin. That's absolutely it.'

'I'll come and watch the race, Mum,' she says. 'And I'll get sponsorship, if you like. Well, we all will. Well, all maybe apart from Dad.'

She's looking at the empty doorway too. There's still no sign of him coming back. Tears spring to my eyes and I pull her into a tight hug. 'Thank you, darling,' I whisper. At least *she's* on my side.

76

Upstairs, I can hear Tom laughing on the phone. He rings off when I get into the bedroom.

'Your mother sounds cheerful,' I say, picking up my hand cream.

'Oh, it wasn't her,' he says. 'It was Janine.'

I hate overhearing that jokey, happy voice of his, when he's been so snotty with me, but I sense challenging him on this will only expose my ugly jealousy.

'She's working late?'

'Yes. I'm not sure what I'd do without her,' he says. 'It's been a crazy few days. I should be there really, but she's got it covered.'

I almost say something bitchy about saintly Janine, but stop myself just in time. There's a tense beat between us. I wonder if he's going to say more, but when he doesn't, I understand fully what's going on and that he's not talking to me about work, because if he does, he'll end up blaming me for what happened when he had to come and do the emergency hospital dash. And whilst, technically, it is my fault he didn't make it to the meeting, that wasn't my intention and he knows it.

'Did you speak to your mother?' I know I sound snippy and annoyed.

'What? Yes. I'm going to have to go down again. Probably

for a couple of weekends,' he says, climbing into bed. He puts out his light straight away. 'That's if you're OK to be left.'

'Why wouldn't I be?' I say, indignantly.

Tom doesn't say anything. I lie still in bed, silently fuming… about his mother, and Janine and how he reacted to my news about running the race for Tamsin.

'Did you turn the heating off?' he asks.

'No. But the kids are cold. I'll leave it on tonight.'

'OK. Night,' he says, rolling over.

But I can't sleep. Not for hours. Because what is happening? To us? To me and Tom? There seems to be so much we can't say to each other. I know Tom is stressed and I can't bear it that I'm the cause of much of that. I want to feel like I used to – like the old me. Old Keira used to keep the peace and put everything right. We'd never go to sleep on a row – or a non-row, like this, but this is happening more and more.

And this is before the subject of sex. Friday night is usually our night for a cuddle if nothing else, but tonight, Tom might as well be in another room.

What will it be like when all of this is over and I've finally landed on New Keira for good? And what if I don't make it, like Tamsin might not make it?

That's not going to happen. I'm not going to let that happen. To me… or to her.

The power cuts out in the middle of the night, but I mistake the faint alarm of the chest freezer in the garage for a faraway car alarm. When we go down in the morning, it's freezing and there are no lights. The icy conditions have bust open the leaky bit in the conservatory roof and the snow has got in and melted, thanks to the heating being on, which in turn has flooded the electrics.

'I thought we were going to get the conservatory roof fixed?' Tom says, an accusation in his voice. 'You said you were going to get a quote?'

'Well, I haven't had time to sort out a builder.'

He raises his eyebrows, like this is yet another thing I've failed at. Like I've had time because I haven't been at work. 'You could have done it,' I say, accusingly back. 'I don't see why it's my responsibility to do everything around here.'

'There's no internet connection,' Tilly complains.

'It's freezing,' Jacob adds. 'And there's no hot water.'

'All the food will be ruined in the freezer,' I tell Tom.

'Well, none of us wanted it in the first place,' he says, nastily.

Thankfully, on the recommendation of Jennifer, the electrician turns up at eleven. By the time he arrives, my teeth are chattering, but he's so warm and friendly and competent, I feel immediately better. I stamp my feet, as he surveys the damage and winces. Tom's right: To fix it properly is going to cost a fortune, but the electrician says he'll do a quick fix that will get us back up and running, as long as we don't mind not going in the conservatory for a while.

'I hope it's not indiscreet to say anything,' he says, as I hold the torch in the garage and he fiddles with the fuse box, 'but Jennifer told me you're going through cancer treatment.'

I told Jennifer that I didn't mind if she played the cancer card, but that we needed someone round pronto, but now I feel embarrassed.

'Yeah, well, I guess a lot of people are,' I say, trying to play it down.

'My sister had it.'

'I'm sorry,' I tell him. I'm really not in the mood to hear another cancer story. I'm too cold to sympathise about a dead sister. I don't want to hear any more about death.

'She says it's the best thing that ever happened to her,' he says, surprising me. 'She's completely reinvented herself. Dumped her husband, went travelling, lost weight and she says she's happier than she's ever been.'

'Well, that's good,' I say. 'My friend Amma is thinking about reinventing,' I tell him. And then, because we're stuck in the garage alone, I tell him about the Cancer Ladies' Running Club.

'Why don't I put in a call to my mate at the local paper? He plays football with me. He might do a piece on you. Raise awareness, if nothing else. I mean, you're trying to raise money, right? So the more publicity you get, the better.'

'Well, yeah, I mean, of course,' I say, as though I'd obviously thought of that. 'You think we might be newsworthy?'

'... Er, a 100 per cent,' he says. 'You're running through cancer treatment to raise money for your friend. That's epic, Mrs Beck.'

Despite the cold, I feel a warm glow. He's right. It is pretty epic. If we can actually manage to do it, that is.

77

I dress in my funkiest clothes for the evening at the shop. The evening at Wishwells has been going for a couple of years now. It was Lorna's idea to invite all the vloggers and bloggers to Wishwells for a private viewing of our spring collection and now it's become a permanent fixture on the calendar.

I've been so looking forward to being back, but the shop has transformed even more since the last time I was here. As I walk in, I hardly recognise the place and I feel a pang for something I can't put my finger on. Maybe it's just that these four walls have always felt so solidly mine, so much a part of my identity – like the colour of my eyes. But now, being here – I feel like an imposter. And more than that... like yet another part of me has been taken away.

I tell myself to stop being silly. Wishwells is mine and will always be mine. I can't expect it to stay the same all the time, and anyway, Lorna and the girls have clearly been working very hard in my absence, because I have to admit that the shop looks great. It's colour coordinated and has a chicness that I've never managed.

Ruby seems pleased to see me and Lorna kisses me perfunctorily on the cheek.

'You look better than I expected,' she says. I'm not sure if this is a compliment or not.

'I'm trying to keep healthy.'

'Are you still running?' Ruby asks.

'Yes… actually, I was going to talk to you about that,' I say to her and Lorna. I go on to explain about how we're going to run the 10K race to raise money for Tamsin, but as I tell them, Lorna shakes her head.

'Keira, you can't,' she protests. 'I mean, you're going through *cancer* treatment. You can barely work, let alone run.'

That's unfair. It's not like I don't *want* to work. She just hasn't let me. I feel myself bristle. I hate being told I can't do something.

'I know, but, I have to do this,' I tell her. I was going to ask her if Wishwells would sponsor me, but she clearly doesn't get it.

'10K is a long way,' she says, looking at me like I really am crazy. 'You should be looking after yourself. Taking it easy. I mean, surely Tom can't have agreed to let you go through with it?'

I realise that it's a pointless waste of time to try and make her understand. Instead, I let the subject drop and try to make myself helpful whilst Ruby circles with a very full tray of prosecco flutes.

'Isn't she gorgeous,' Becca says, with a longing sigh, nudging me, from where we stand behind the counter by the till and it takes a conscious shift in my head to try and engage with her thinking. Because she finds all these people 'aspirational', to coin Lorna's phrase, but caring, really *caring* about all this stuff is difficult for me to understand at the moment.

'Who?'

'Her. Willow,' she says, discreetly pointing. 'You know. She's that YouTuber.'

The girl she's pointing to is browsing the shelves. She's wearing high-waist jeans, flashy trainers and a little cropped puffa jacket that shows off her toned midriff. She's carrying a designer handbag over her forearm and chomps on a wodge of chewing gum. She can't be much older than 18, but I can already see she's had cheek fillers and something odd done to her lips. Her eyes are huge, with diamanté bits on her eyelashes. An enormous bouncer stands behind her, his gold-ringed hands crossed deferentially over the crotch of his shiny nylon jogging pants. He keeps his sunglasses on, even though it's five o'clock and dark outside.

Eventually, Willow comes up to the till with the things she's picked out. Of course we're not charging her, or any of the other influencers here. We're just hoping that whatever they take, they like enough to feature on their channels. I chat with her as I start to wrap her things in tissue paper.

I suddenly become aware of Ruby and Becca staring at me. Ruby coughs meaningfully.

'What?' I say.

I put my hands to my head and push back my hair, feeling self-conscious. It takes me a moment to realise that all my hair has fallen out. Literally, just like that. Where I moved it, it's just fallen down. All over the tissue paper. All over Willow's items.

Willow looks on in horror as I try and blow the hair away, but it's going everywhere. I try and salvage the situation, but she puts out one hand, with her long acrylic nails.

'It's OK, thanks. I'll leave it.'

She backs away and Becca looks at me in horror, then nods towards the staircase. Taking her heavy hint, I go to the small loo on the way up to the office and when I look in the mirror, there's a huge bald bit on the side of my head. I pull at my fringe and it comes out and falls in the sink.

I don't quite know what to do. I'm worried if I so much as move, the whole lot will drop. I touch my hair again – the lightest touch, to see if the deluge is over, but more just falls out. The small sink is full of hair now and it's all over the floor.

There's a knock on the door. It's Lorna.

'Are you OK in there?'

I open the door. Her eyes widen when she sees me.

'I know. Krusty the Clown,' I tell her. 'That was so embarrassing.'

'Why don't you go home and I'll finish up here,' she says.

'I'm sorry, Lorna,' I say. I feel I should apologise, for the way Willow reacted.

'You can't help it that your hair is falling out, Keira,' she says. 'That's what happens with cancer treatment. You can't keep pretending it's not happening when it is.'

78

I call Tom to explain what's happened on the way home.

'I want it all gone,' I tell him. 'Seriously. I want it all shaved off. I can't bear it.'

'OK, don't panic.'

'You're going to have to do it. I need you to shave it. You said you would,' I remind him. 'When the time came.'

'Don't freak out just because of Lorna.'

But I am freaking out, and he agrees to meet me at home and reluctantly promises that he'll dig out his clippers

At home, everyone gathers in the kitchen for 'the big shave'. We've talked about this in theory, but the kids are shocked that it's actually happening and that I'm so adamant about it. Jacob is late back from football, but I can't wait a moment longer. My hair is getting everywhere, in my eyes and throat. It's suffocating.

Like a gunslinger at a bar brawl, I sit astride the chair in the middle of the kitchen floor.

'Are you OK, Mum?' Tilly asks.

'I feel like Anne Hathaway,' I tell Tilly, as Tom untwists the lead of his hair clippers. 'You know, when she was playing Fantine in *Les Mis*? Remember when they hacked off her hair?'

'Oh yeah. And she sang that song...'

'I dreamed a dream in time gone by,' I sing, and Tilly joins in with, 'when hope was high and life worth living.'

I'm trying to be jolly, but Bea looks worried.

'Are you nervous?' she asks, kneeling down in front of me. Pooch is next to her.

'It's OK,' I tell them both.

'OK, really? You ready?' Tom checks.

I nod. 'I am strong, like bull,' I tell him, in a silly voice.

'Right then. Stay still,' Tom says. 'I don't want to hurt you.' The buzzers flick to life.

'Here goes,' I say.

Pooch puts his head on my knee, his brown eyes looking up.

Tom stands behind me. 'Are you double sure?' I can feel his hand shaking on my shoulder.

'Yes. Get it off.'

'I'm going to start at the back,' he says, but his voice wobbles. This is hard for him. I've been giving him buzz cuts for years, but it's weird for our roles to be reversed.

'Don't worry. You can't muck it up,' I tell him, reassuringly. 'Whatever you do.'

'Give mum a mohawk first. For a laugh,' Tilly suggests.

He shaves the sides off my hair and leaves the top, but when I try fluffing it up, I shower Bea and Pooch in hair. 'See,' I say. Its in my nose and throat. 'Off with the lot. Just do it.'

Tom puts the razor close to my head and I feel it move all over my scalp. Hair falls all around me. Bea stares on with wide eyes.

'What do you think?' I ask, when Tom has finished.

'It's amazing,' she says. 'You look like you, but different. Come and see in the mirror.'

I get up and she and Tilly hold my hands as they take me

out of the kitchen and into the hall so that I can see myself in the long mirror, whilst Tom sweeps up my hair.

'Close your eyes, close your eyes,' Bea insists and I do.

'Ready?' Tilly asks.

I open my eyes and I'm presented with myself in the hall mirror.

I look drastically bald.

'Wow,' I say, stepping closer, as if examining a stranger. I can feel my heart thumping. Part of me wants to wail, but I know I have to be strong and embrace this. For someone who isn't good at change, this is big.

Jacob opens the front door and before it's even open, I yell, 'Boots!'

I don't want a repeat of the other week when he trod mud everywhere.

But then I remember my hair and see him stopping in the doorway and I look at him, twisting my lips, waiting nervously for his reaction. He only raises his eyebrows. 'Well?' I ask.

'Ta da!' he says, taking off his hat.

He's shaved his head. As in... he's completely bald.

I put my hands to my face. 'Peanut, what have you done?'

'Bea messaged me to tell me what you were planning. I thought I'd keep you company, Mumma Bear,' he says.

I pull him into a giant hug. 'Oh, you crazy boy. What are they going to say at school?'

'I already told them. And I've got permission to take in a collection pot for your race. Anyone gives me any aggro and it's a pound for Time for Tamsin.'

We laugh and jump around and then Tom comes into the hall.

'Look at you two!' he says.

'Meet the eggheads,' Jacob says and Tilly takes a picture.

'Oh Lord. Look at us! It's not exactly the most flattering picture of me,' I tell her.

'Shall I delete it?' She sighs and rolls her eyes at Jacob. There is an ongoing family chagrin over the fact that I delete most photos of myself. In fact, there are some years where there is no photographic evidence of me being on trips away or on family holidays.

Before all this happened to me, I was under the misguided delusion that I still look the same as I did when I was 20. And therefore, seeing my slightly crinkly, jowly face and lumpy figure has always been a disappointment as it didn't match the 'me' in my head. So, on seeing a photo of myself, I've always gone: 'Eeww… who is that fat, wrinkly, old bag?' Delete. Delete. Delete.

But right now, right here, something has happened.

Because I don't care what I look like anymore. I just want to *be* in the photos. No matter how unflattering the shot.

And with this realisation comes another, hot on its heels. That I'm going to stop being nasty and judgemental about myself. From this moment forth, I'm going to look in the mirror and smile at myself.

'What are you looking so pleased about?' Tilly asks.

'Nothing,' I tell her, grabbing her and holding her tight. 'Come on, let's do some more selfies.'

'You hate selfies.'

'Not anymore.'

79

On Saturday morning, I decide to start seriously on my training programme for the 10K. Fuck Lorna. I *am* going to do this race.

Before anyone is up at home, I drive to the park by Amma's house – the one by the river. I've texted to see if she'll come with me, but she texts back to say that she can't this morning, but I'm determined not to be put off.

My plan is to blend in with the people doing the parkrun, as I know they all follow a 5K course. If I can master that, then 10K shouldn't be so hard, right?

I start off at the back, reminding myself that I have actually run three times around the other park, which must be near 4K, so this should be fine, but it's hard without Tamsin to keep up the pace.

I notice curious looks from the pack of runners, who clearly all recognise each other and can't place me. But very soon, the majority of them are far ahead. I'm wheezing for breath as I get to the first hill. Jesus, this is hard. Much harder on my own than I expected it to be. And the chemo obviously doesn't help.

I slow to a stop, my gut twisting with the onset of a stitch. I feel shaky and nauseous. Soon, the fastest runners are on their second lap and overtake me. One of them looks familiar and, as she passes in a cloud of lovely perfume, I see that it's Janine.

I've thought about her so much since that first day I saw her in Tom's office, but this morning, she looks even more gorgeous, her legs long and shapely, her lustrous ponytail swishing. She's running really fast and has barely even broken a sweat and I hear her laughing with her friend.

I don't think that she's seen me, but just in case, I run on, like I'm a regular parkrunner, but my body is screaming for me to stop and suddenly, I know I'm going to hurl. I open the top of the dog poo bin and spew up my tea and toast from this morning. Then I catch the backdraft stench and hurl again on my trainers.

Back at home, I don't tell anyone about my epic fail, but head to the bath, feeling miserable. Maybe Tom is right: I'm never going to be able to run the race, at this rate. What the hell am I even thinking?

I'm so wrapped up in my panic, that I don't twig that something's going on, even when Tilly surreptitiously changes the sheets in the spare room and I hear Jacob running the vacuum cleaner around the sitting room. It needs doing. I'm still shedding my hair – albeit the shortest of short stubble. I listen to the unusual sound of my house being cleaned by my children and raise my thinning eyebrows in tacit acknowledgement of a plan that's working.

However, I'm in for another shock. As I look down, all my pubes float to the surface of the water. It's really quite alarming. I have to sort of sieve them off the top. It's revolting. I wash my hair, but it feels so odd running my hands over my bare scalp. I get out and inspect my glistening body. I'm like a seal.

'Arf, arf,' I say to myself in the mirror, flapping my arms.

There's a ring at the doorbell and Tom yells up for me to get it. Why the fuck can't he get it?

Annoyed, I jog down in my dressing gown, wondering if it's the postman. I remember then that it's my birthday tomorrow. I've told everyone I'm not interested in celebrating until I feel well. I want the day to go unnoticed, but Tom clearly has had other ideas.

'Surprise!' Scout shouts, grinning widely.

Her being at my door fills me with a joy that's almost indescribable. As she puts her arms around me, it's like I'm a desiccated flower drinking in rain.

I've always been a sucker for *Tapestry* by Carole King and her lyrics to 'So Far Away' have always resonated with me about Scout and now I'm reminded of the line, 'It would be so nice to see your face at my door.' Because it is *so* nice to see her face at my door.

I also know how much she must have juggled to get away for the weekend and I'm touched she's made the journey to come and see me. I burst into tears and weep and weep and laugh at the same time.

80

Once I've calmed down, over coffee in the kitchen and once Tom has left us alone, she tells me she has news.

'I talked to one of my old colleagues,' she says, 'who did some digging around on Pierre.'

'Did you?' I ask. I hadn't said I wanted her to do this, but I'm glad that she has.

'And now I'm really worried.'

'Why?'

'Because nobody has a good word to say about him,' she says.

I feel something spark inside me – a flame of indignation I thought had been dampened right down.

'Go on...'

'I've asked my guy to get better proof, but he thinks it's a miracle that Pierre hasn't been prosecuted. There's all sorts of allegations surrounding him.'

'Like what?'

'Well, it could all be hearsay, of course, but there was talk of embezzling. Fraud...'

'Holy shit!'

'The thing is, Keira, I don't think you should really have him involved in Wishwells if you can possibly help it.'

I nod, but I can't help feeling that it's way too late. And I feel like a fool too. Why didn't I *know* this about him? Why didn't I follow my own gut instinct? I feel a rising sense of panic that I've left my precious business in the hands of a fraudster. And what if he's not just got his sights on ousting me, but Lorna too? What if she's in his firing line as well?

Joss arrives an hour later, bearing gifts for us all and a huge bottle of champagne. She and Scout admire my bald head and take it in turns to try on my fringe and headgear. At Joss's insistence, we go into town to go clothes shopping and they make me buy crazy trousers and a funky coat. They both completely get the idea of chemo chic when I tell them all about Amma. I've always worn grey, navy and brown clothes in the winter, but embracing colour for the first time makes me feel instantly more cheerful.

We head to the pub for post-shopping pints of lager and Joss regales us with her latest dating fiascos. I feel warm and loved and happy to be with my friends, and an afternoon not talking about cancer is just the tonic I need.

I tell them about running the race for Tamsin and how annoyed Tom is about it.

'He's just being protective, but actually, I think the race sounds like a great idea,' Joss says.

I smile, relieved to have her onside. Having my friends with me makes me feel like one of those Christmas movies where Santa's sleigh can only run on belief. I feel like their support is charging me up and bringing back some of my lost confidence.

And Joss is right: I'm not going to let Tom put me off. I tell her, instead, about the electrician and how he's offered to put in a word with someone at the local paper.

To my surprise, Joss is slightly put out that I would consider using someone else's PR contacts.

'Leave this to me,' she says. 'I'm going to call everyone I know. Oh... I just thought... Jessica at the local Beeb. She owes me a favour. Do you think your girls would do a piece for the section after the six o'clock news?'

'The BBC? You mean the TV?' I ask, incredulously.

'Yes, on the TV, you numpty,' she says. 'If you want to raise some decent, useful money for your friend, then you're going to have to PR the shit out of this race of yours, and you don't have much time.'

Later, back at home, the celebratory mood continues and we crack open the champagne – after all it's in the DNA of our relationship for the three of us to get smashed. Normally, a few glasses of fizz wouldn't touch the sides, but I keep forgetting that things aren't normal and all too soon, I feel sloshed and dizzy and when Tom suggests I go to bed at ten o'clock, I don't argue. But I hate not staying up late with my friends.

'You drank too much,' Tom says, unhelpfully, when he comes upstairs to check that I'm OK. 'You always do that with Joss.'

'I know.'

'I thought you said that alcohol was bad and that you couldn't ignore the links between booze and breast cancer?'

'That is not helpful, you telling me that right now.'

'I don't know why you do it.'

'Because that's who I am. I can't just give up drinking with them. That's what our friendship is based on.'

'You're being ridiculous. Nobody is going to mind if you don't drink.'

'I'll mind,' I say, but then I wretch as my body rejects the champagne and I have to run out of the bedroom to the loo.

Not surprisingly, with all the alcohol sloshing around my system, it's the worst night sleep I've had for months. I'm deluged with episodes of full-on body sweats as my kidneys try and process the dehydration – oh, and all the chemo drugs. And worse, so much worse, is the guilt. The insidious voice that chastises me for not saying no to all those drinks. The terrible, gnawing truth that even when I've got cancer, I still can't find the strength to look after myself.

81

When I hear people getting up on my birthday, I just want to pull the duvet over my head, but Joss and Scout are up early and I have to get up for the kids who have made me pancakes. I have to try really hard not to gag.

I open my presents and cards and it dawns on me that every card from my friends is alcohol related. Perhaps it's because of my hangover, or my realisation that my hitherto steadfast relationship with booze has hit a rocky – possibly terminal – patch, but I'm wondering when it became the norm for women to be marketed alcohol as a coping mechanism. Because, it's virtually impossible to get a funny greetings card for a woman without it involving booze, the humour spotlighting our clandestine relationship with gin, or wine, or our need to be slightly squiffy to deal with our kids... or even just life.

Tom says that he's going to cook everyone a spectacular roast for lunch and whilst he's busy in the kitchen, Joss and I discuss how to raise money for the race, whilst Scout and Tilly go for a walk with Pooch.

Joss takes it upon herself to register a web domain for the Cancer Ladies' Running Club and a JustGiving page for Tamsin. We have a long chat about whether the Ladies in our title should have an apostrophe after it and we decide that grammatically, it should. It's always been deliberately ironic to refer to ourselves as 'the ladies' and it seems silly putting it in print, but Joss is deadly serious. It's weird when you see your friends in their work capacity. She's quite a hard taskmaster and I can see why she gets her way in her PR agency, as I'm soon dutifully doing everything she says. The copy we cobble together is rough, but it's better than nothing and Joss assures me we can change it later.

Her enthusiasm, however, is grating on Tom, who is distrustful of the whole Mexico plan of Tamsin's, when this isn't a treatment path that her oncologist has recommended. And he's still worried about how fit I'll be for the race. I don't tell either of them how bad yesterday's run was.

'I'm just going to take it day by day,' I tell Joss, so that Tom can hear. 'I'm going to plan to do the race and if I can, I can. If I can't, then that's just the way it's got to be. But I'm not going to not try.'

But despite this, over lunch, Tom continues to remain tight-lipped.

'It's pretty impressive,' Scout says. 'I mean, I thought you hated running, you know, ever since…'

She fizzles out and she and Joss share an amused look, as they both take long sips of wine.

'Since what?' Tilly asks, picking up on the vibe.

'Don't,' I say. 'Don't you dare!'

'I didn't say anything!' Joss says, putting her hands up, but she and Scout both know all my secrets and when they glance at each other again, I know that the cat is out of the bag.

'I won't say anything,' Scout says, almost into her glass, colour rising in her cheeks. 'If you don't want me to.' Then she looks up at Tom. 'You must know this story?' she says, incredulously.

Tom shrugs. 'I honestly have no idea what you're talking about.'

So now, Jacob and Tilly really want to know and giving me a look that says she really has no choice but to tell it, Scout recounts the horror story of sports day 1984.

Tilly, Jacob, Bea and even Tom (who is amazed that I've never shared this story with him) laugh and clap, as Scout recounts how I bounced over the line.

'The whole school saw,' Scout says, giggling and glancing guiltily at me.

'Did you ever get to go out with the guy?' Tilly asks, agog at this less-than-flattering story.

'No,' I protest. 'As if I would after that.'

'He was a knob, anyway,' Scout assures her.

'I wish I'd been there. It sounds so funny,' Joss says, laughing along with the others.

'Yes, very funny... bloody hilarious,' I say, getting up and starting to clear the table.

Now that I'm an adult, looking back, I can see why they're laughing, because someone being that stupid and delusional and getting caught out is funny, right? Only it's not funny. Because it was me.

Even decades on, I feel butterflies in my stomach and my throat go tight as I stand by the sink. I resent them for teasing me – and for telling my family.

Usually, I'd be able to handle it, but it's not a joke. Because what they don't mention is how, afterwards, I had a full-scale panic attack behind the sports hut.

Tom senses that I'm a bit upset and I'm grateful to him for moving the conversation on and I sit back down at the table.

He gives Joss and Scout an update on his parents – both of whom they've known since we've been together. They don't let on for a second how much I've bitched about Hilary to them. Tom tells us all how Zippo is going to help him install a stairlift for them.

'Is Zippo single now?' Joss enquires. There's always been a little bit of chemistry between them. Tom tells her about Lucy and she looks deflated.

'You wouldn't seriously consider Zippo, would you?' I ask, as we clear up the table later and she shrugs. He hardly qualifies as Mr Perfect.

'Maybe,' she says. 'He was always pretty fit when we were younger. Shame he likes younger women.'

'*You* like younger men,' I tell her. 'You can't have it all ways.'

There's a ring at the doorbell and I groan, knowing it's probably Mum and Rob, but it's Amma.

'Happy Birthday,' she says, kissing me. She looks amazing in a vintage suede coat coupled with a 1950s leopard print turban with a big fake jewel brooch on the front. I'm so glad to see her. I'm so glad she doesn't come loaded with information grenades from the past.

'Come in, come in,' I tell her.

She's bought me a scarf, along with an assortment of fake eyelashes and Tilly helps me apply some. She's a little bit starstruck by Amma, especially when she starts talking about Isabel and how she's agreed to help promote our cause.

'She's on the PR junket at the moment for her latest Netflix series,' Amma enthuses, 'but she says she'll do her best.'

It's weird seeing her with Joss and Scout, but they all get on, as I knew they would. Joss shows Amma the JustGiving page we've cobbled together and she makes a few suggestions, before airdropping her some photos from her phone of us all.

'They're great,' Joss says. 'Put them up on The Cancer Ladies' Running Club page, Keira.'

She says this, like it's the easiest thing in the world and I nod dumbly. But inside, I feel a sickening sense of dread that I've committed to getting a website up and running. How the hell am I supposed to do that?

'Looks like we can't back out now,' Amma says to me, and I wonder if she's feeling as nervous about the race as I am.

82

The next day, it's time for my second chemo. Tom seems relieved that I've told him that Mum is coming with me. I don't let on that I've told another fib. Because I've told Mum that *Tom* is coming with me today, so she can go to her Pilates class.

It's ridiculous I've had to resort to such subterfuge, but today I need to be alone. The chemo suite is chatty enough as it is, without other people staring at me, when there's absolutely nothing to see. And, to be honest, I'm quite looking forward to sitting down in a chair away from everyone.

In the chemo suite Lara, the acupuncturist is waiting for me. She looks concerned when I tell her about my infected port and what's happened since she last saw me. She doesn't need me to tell her that I'm tired and stressed. Everyone who comes here is. I'm also aching all over from my run and feel wrung out with my hangover. I don't tell her about getting pissed on Saturday night. I'm too ashamed. However, the acupuncture make me feel like I'm a bit more on track.

As Clarrie wires me up for the chemo drugs, I tell her about the 10K run and how we're hoping to raise money for Tamsin.

'Oh, Tamsin, she's quite a character,' Clarrie says, with a chuckle. 'I'm not so sure about her partner, though.'

'Ian? You've met him?'

'He's come in a couple of times, but he always complains about something and Tamsin has to cover for him.'

Clarrie gives me a sceptical look. 'But is that what she wants? Or is she doing it for him? I shouldn't really say this, but between you and me, I see this all the time with people in Tamsin's position. Their loved ones can't accept what's going on, so they throw money at the situation, thinking it'll help. Sometimes, though, it just makes things worse.'

I nod, taking this sobering perspective on board. I can't help thinking about Tom's misgivings about Tamsin's proposed treatment plan in Mexico. What if he's right? And what if Clarrie's right and we're only going to make things worse? But it's too late now, I tell myself. We're on a path and we can't stop now.

'But, you know, it's their relationship and there's no manual for how to help your partner.'

'How many relationships survive this whole cancer thing, do you reckon?' I ask, ominously thinking of how strained things are between me and Tom.

'From what I see, if relationships are strong, then sometimes, going through cancer makes them stronger. But sometimes it breaks them. And if the relationship is weak, then it breaks very quickly… or can mend. I've seen it all ways. But every relationship is tested by this.'

It's true that this whole cancer thing is harder than I thought it would be. I mean, it would be bad enough dealing with my situation at work with Lorna, Tom's work, the kids – not to mention adding Tom's ailing parents into the mix, so I guess it's hardly surprising that we're a bit grumpy with each other.

'I wish Tamsin had more support from her family,' I muse as Clarrie inspects the drip going into my port.

'Yes, well you can't help wondering what that's all about,' she says.

'If you had a child you didn't speak to, but they were sick, then wouldn't you want to know?'

'Of course,' she says. 'Who wouldn't?'

83

After what Clarrie said, I make an extra effort to be chipper and positive when I get home. I'm grateful for the moussaka from one of the mums at school, but even more grateful that Tilly has taken it upon herself to heat it up and Bea has made a salad to go with it.

When he gets in from work, I make a point of telling Tom how much I appreciate how much he's doing and how special he made my birthday. And he, in turn, apologises for being snappy. And in an instant, our bad vibes are gone – like they always are, when we remember to be kind to each other.

In bed, we cuddle and I want to feel everything is back to normal, but it isn't. Not quite. Not when I haven't brought up the subject of Janine. I don't tell him that I saw her on my run on Saturday.

'How was your mum today?' Tom asks.

'Hmm?'

'At the chemo session?'

I have my face on my chest so he can't see my expression. Should I continue with my lie? Because if I tell him the truth, he'll be offended.

'She was fine,' I say, mentally crossing my fingers.

'Interesting,' he says, and in that instant I know he's caught me out. 'She texted me to ask how I was getting on in the hospital and if she and Rob should pick us up.'

'Oh,' I say.

'Why can't you just be honest, Keira? Life would be a lot easier if you were,' he says.

I look up at him. 'I didn't want you to be offended that I wanted to go on my own.'

'If that's what you want, then... fine.'

'I wish I could make you understand.'

'I said it's fine.'

I lie back down on his chest, but it's not fine. He's not fine.

I feel stupid for being caught out and I blush. There's something so childish about lying, but I knew it would be like this – that he'd take today as a rejection. We're supposed to be doing this whole cancer thing together. That's what we'd agreed and we both know I've broken our pact.

I'd been hoping my positivity would get things back on track and we'd be more connected, but now I know that a shag is completely out of the question when Tom yawns, stretching up to switch off the light. He turns away, shifting me from his chest and fakes going to sleep.

By the time I wake up the next morning after a fretful night, he's gone.

After each chemo session, I have to inject my own stomach with some stuff called GCSF or Granulocyte Colony Stimulating Factor which is supposed to gee up my white cell count recovery and I have a plastic bin for my discarded syringes that I'm keeping in the utility room away from the kids. Pooch watches me as I pinch a big wodge of my stomach flesh – 'my roll', as that doctor described it back at the beginning – and inject myself. This feels like a very weird addition to my morning routine.

'It doesn't hurt that much,' I tell him. 'Don't look so worried.'

Joss rings as I'm having breakfast, although I'm not really getting my toast down. Everything tastes a bit weird and the toast feels like sand in my mouth.

'It's happening,' she says.

'What's happening?'

'The Beeb. They've bitten. They want to film you tomorrow at the park. Can you gather the gang?'

'What… I mean… they… they're going to *film* us?'

'And interview you, yes. About the race. About Tamsin.'

'Oh.'

'You don't sound very happy about it.'

'I am, I am. Thank you, really,' I hurry on, but I'm already panicking. We're going on TV? About Time for Tamsin? About the race that I have no idea whether I'll be able to complete?

'Have you got the webpage up and running? I need to get the details to Jessica.'

'No. Fuck. I haven't had a chance.'

'Keira,' Joss says, 'come on. You've got to think of the PR opportunity.'

The next day, I make a big effort with my appearance, donning my new trousers, turban and tuck in fringe and do my best to 'own' my new look, as I go into town to Jennifer's café. I need to talk to Sian about the website. I don't have a clue where to start and maybe she can help.

But Sian isn't working for Jennifer today and, now at

a loose end, I steel myself and go into Wishwells. I want to clear the air after my embarrassment in front of Willow the other day.

'Oh, get you!' Ruby says, doing an air circle with her hand in front of me. 'Funky, funky. I like it a lot.'

'Thanks.'

'And, Keira, guess what?' Ruby says, her eyes wide.

'What?'

'Come and see, come and see,' she says, making me come over to the iPad by the till. She's grinning. 'I rang up Willow and explained about… well you know… about the hair thing and what was happening with you.'

'Did you?'

I feel bad Ruby felt she had to apologise on my behalf and that she's had to lay bare the details of my cancer treatment.

'She was super sweet about it. Anyway, look!'

I see what she's pointing to. A picture Willow has posted on Instagram showing one of our throws, some candles, gloves and earrings and on her YouTube channel, she's described Wishwells as her 'fave' shop.

'That's great,' I say, relieved that my faux pas has resulted in an unexpected plug. Ruby grins, delighted too.

'Oh, Keira. You're here,' Lorna says, coming in through the back door.

'I just stopped by,' I tell her and she nods, taking in my outfit, but she doesn't comment.

'Come upstairs,' she says.

'It's really good that Willow posted that,' I say, following her up the stairs, but she doesn't say anything. She's clearly not as enthusiastic as Ruby.

In the meeting room I can see that she's got something on her mind when she shuts the door.

'Look, Keira. After everything that's happened, Pierre and I were thinking that it might be an idea for you to take a step back for a bit. In a more formal sense.'

'What do you mean?'

'You popping in like this isn't working for anyone. I think you should stay away until you've finished your treatment completely.'

'But that will take months.'

'Some time away will do you good. Do us both good.'

She's talking about her and me. There's a beat as we both acknowledge that the conversation we've been putting off having, is now here.

'I haven't meant for there to be bad feeling between us,' I tell her.

'I know, I know. It's not about the cancer, Keira, it's more... well... I just think that if we're not seeing eye to eye, then maybe we should shake things up a bit.'

'What do you mean?'

'I've been thinking that perhaps Pierre and I should take the business forward together. Without you.'

I feel like a stone has plummeted into my stomach. My cheeks burn and my mouth goes dry. I can't believe she's saying this. I can't believe she'd even have the nerve to suggest it. She rubs her finger on the meeting room table. So much for Pierre being the baddie. She's even worse.

'But Wishwells is mine,' I manage.

'Well, I know it was your idea in the beginning, but...' She bites her lip. I can see she's wrangling with something. 'But the thing is, Keira, Pierre wants to buy you out.'

'Buy me out?'

She picks up an envelope from the table. 'There's a very reasonable offer in here for your shares. I mean, after the forecasts were so wrong, it's not amazing, I'll grant you that, but we all agree that it's fair.'

'We?'

'Pierre and I talked to Clive and Richard. It's a unanimous decision by the board.'

She looks at the floor, rather than face me. 'Just take it and think about it.'

84

Her offer, of course, is pitiful and does not remotely reflect the fifteen years of hard work I've put into Wishwells. But the much bigger issue is, that regardless of what she's prepared to pay, I'm incensed that she's even considering trying to get me out of my own business. And I'm hurt to my core that she's consulted the board about this devious plan of hers, behind my back.

It would all be easier, of course, if I could off-load any of this, but I'm too shocked... too numb to tell anyone what Lorna has done. Apart from Tom, maybe, but he's still a bit frosty after my lie. And anyway, in his current mood, he's really not going to see how I feel about this. For all I know, he'd probably tell me to take Lorna's offer. And I can't. I just can't.

Can I?

Because now my head flips the argument around. Maybe Lorna is right and we're not seeing eye to eye and for me to take a step back might make sense. Maybe this treatment is going to take a lot longer and be a lot tougher than I thought it would be. Maybe work is going to be too hard. Maybe the old kick-ass Keira has gone forever...

Joss interrupts my yo-yoing panic by texting to ask if I've set up the website. I haven't had a moment's headspace to think about the race, but now her text sends me into a spin.

I'm desperate to back out, wishing that I'd never agreed to do this at all, but it's too late. And anyway, there's Tamsin and her terminal diagnosis. What right do I have to complain about my First World problems when she's facing *that*?

It's Jacob who saves the day. He sits up with me at the laptop in the kitchen, and eventually we have a Cancer Ladies' Running Club website, with a link to the Time for Tamsin page. Tom comes in from work late, clearly furious that I've commandeered that he has to heat up his own dinner, but I'm determined to crack on.

When I finally make it to bed, Tom's already asleep and I'm glad. I can't bear to tell him about Lorna and Pierre and what they've suggested. I run our meeting over and over in my mind, cursing myself for not ripping up the envelope in front of Lorna. Cursing myself for meekly taking it and saying that I'd think about it. Because that's as good as saying I acquiesce, isn't it?

The next morning, when we meet for our interview with the BBC, Amma is looking more glamorous than I've ever seen her. She's in a blue and silver running kit with matching trainers. She's wearing enormous glittery earrings beneath her cap.

Sian has picked up Tamsin on her way and I wave at them. Tamsin looks thin in her running kit. She's without make-up for once.

'What, no eyes?' I tell her.

'I thought about it,' she says, 'but I think "cancer victim" is more convincing.' She says cancer victim on an inhale in a silly voice and I laugh and so does Sian. Tamsin is not a victim of anything.

Jessica arrives with the cameraman and a sound guy, who is holding a big fluffy boom. He's wrapped up in a huge parka jacket, like he's come to the arctic.

'I've never been on TV before,' Sian says.

'Me neither,' I admit.

'You'll be fine,' Amma says, clearly keen to get on film. She flashes her best smile at the cameraman, who hauls the camera onto his shoulder and I see him blushing.

Jessica, the presenter, talks to us about the various shots she'll want. When she discovers that I'm going through chemo too, she persuades me to run with Tamsin without my hat and wig.

'In for a penny, in for a pound,' Amma says, stripping off her wig and joining in too. We let out a whoop. It feels oddly liberating, like we're going topless and about to jump into a pool – which in a way, I guess we are.

'I feel like the odd one out now,' Sian says.

There's a few false starts, but then we jog together along the path. The cameraman follows alongside us, holding the camera as steadily as he can. The sound guy blunders after with the boom, trying not to put the shadow of it in shot.

'So, Keira,' Jessica says. 'Tell us about the Cancer Ladies' Running Club.'

I'm not sure why I've been nominated as the spokesperson. I'm out of breath from the running, but I try and smile. My cheeks are pink and I know I'm sweating.

'We're all having cancer treatment,' I gasp. 'Well, Sian has finished.'

'You've just had chemo, is that right?'

'Yes. A few days ago.'

'That's amazing,' she says, shaking her head, as if the mere fact I'm out is astonishing, or maybe, like everyone else, she thinks I'm barmy.

'We're all friends, because of the running. That's why we're determined to help Tamsin,' I say. 'She's the one who got us all started. Who keeps us going.'

'And you're going to be running *ten kilometres* to raise money for Tamsin, is that right?' Jessica asks. The way she says it makes it sound like even more of an impossible feat.

'Yes. That's the plan.'

'Regardless of what happens to me,' Tamsin says, 'running with these girls has been my lifeline. The thing that's got me out of bed.'

She means it.

'If we can inspire even one person to give it a go – to get outside and get some fresh air, whether they've got cancer or not, then I'm happy,' she says, but almost as soon as she's said it, I know she's going to have to stop because she's so out of breath, and I look at Jessica. She holds up her hand and we all slow down.

'That's brilliant,' Jessica says. 'Thank you all so much. That's all we need.'

Later on, the kids all gather to watch the broadcast at home on the sofa. It's only a minute or so section on the local news, but the cameraman has made us all look good in the morning light, although I still can't get over the shock of seeing myself bald. The film cuts back to the studio and the newsreader has his finger on his chin in a contemplative look.

'That's certainly very inspirational,' he says. 'And you can find out details of the race on our website.'

It's just as well I managed to send the link to Joss in time. Let's hope it works.

'You looked amazing, Mum,' Tilly says, clapping her hands.

'You think so? You don't think my bum looked too big?'

'No!'

I remember my resolve to be kind to myself. I'm not going to pick apart how I look on TV. Anyway, I don't need to, as Mum rings seconds later.

'Did you see it?' I ask.

'You could have worn that nice wig,' she says. 'You didn't have to look like…'

'Like what? Like a cancer victim?'

'Like that other girl. Like Tamsin. Like you're the same.'

'But I am the same as her,' I protest, standing up. 'In this, anyway. That's the whole point. We're all in the same boat. Standing up to this thing… facing it together.'

Tom gives me a warning look, but I've had enough.

'Well, I think you look better with the wig,' Mum says and I make a furious growl.

'Can you just stop being critical for one minute,' I snap. 'And be supportive? Because until you can, I don't want any more of your negative comments, OK?' I end the call and throw the phone on the sofa, like it's scalded me.

'Wow,' Tilly says, 'you really socked it to her.'

Tom's eyes are wide, his eyebrows raised.

'Don't look like that. Like I'm in the wrong,' I snap at him. 'She's so bloody negative. I mean, why can't she be supportive?'

'Maybe because she's right for once and you running in your state is a stupid idea,' Tom says.

'Oh fucking hell,' I yell and stomp upstairs.

85

I'm still brooding on Tom's disapproval and my phone call with Mum the next morning. Tom and I have hardly spoken and Mum hasn't called and I haven't rung to apologise. But for once I'm going to stick to my guns. It's hard enough living with my own doubts, let alone theirs.

Jacob is at the kitchen table on the laptop when I come down.

'Hey, Mum. Guess what?' he says, distracting me from my internal rant at Tom.

'Hmm. What?'

'You know we put that contact widget on the site?'

'Did we?' I'm not sure what a widget is.

'There's been hundreds of hits on the website and loads of enquiries. People want to join your running club. And sign up for the race.'

'Really?' I say, coming over and reading over his shoulder. There's loads of messages... some of which make my heart beat faster, like from Sarah W.

You are so brave... so inspirational... I want to run with you too.

Count me in, I read from Lindsay C. *I finished treatment a year ago. Seeing you on the TV was just the kick up the bum I needed. I'm off to buy trainers.*

'We'd better put something up,' Jacob says.

'Can you... I don't know... thank people for getting in touch maybe. Can you do that?'

'And shall I let them know they can join the club?'

'Do you think people are serious?' I ask him.

'I can put a pin in a map and put it up showing where you meet?' he says, helpfully.

'Yes, do that,' I say, like I know what I'm doing.

I don't think for a second it's going to work, but on Friday, even before I approach our bench for our run, I can see that there are twenty or so women milling around. Some of them are wearing headscarves and hats and are clearly going through treatment, others look like experienced runners.

Sian breaks away from the group and comes to find me.

'Isn't this amazing!' she says, hugging me, her eyes bright.

I hear a whistle – the kind the builders make – and I see Amma has helped Tamsin climb onto our bench. She has her fingers in her mouth and whistles again. 'Welcome, welcome, everyone,' Tamsin calls. She's absolutely in her element. 'Welcome to the Cancer Ladies' Running Club. I'm Tamsin, this is Amma, Keira and Sian, our founding members.'

I count the women who have come. There are twenty-six new members.

And that, in itself, feels like a victory. Sod Tom. Look at this! And this is just the beginning.

'Let's do some warm-ups, and then we'll go twice slowly round the park.'

We set off and I look up, watching the builders on the roof watching us. For once, they are silenced. But the women aren't.

343

There's Julie and Maddie, Laura, Hannah and Scarlett – to name but a few, who all regale me with their cancer treatment stories. I'm touched and humbled and so amazed that so many of them have turned up. Even though I've only just had my second chemo, I'm soon dispensing bits of wisdom about how to get round the park, like I'm an expert runner, which of course I'm not, and soon I'm breathless and waving people on ahead of me. I watch as Sian leads the big group on our route.

'We're going to need T-shirts,' Amma calls to me. She's at the back of Sian's pack. 'This lot are all going to run the race with us next Sunday. Isn't that great?'

I smile and nod and wave for her to go on. Tamsin is at the back and I run very slowly with her.

'I'm so slow,' I tell her. 'So out of breath.'

'It's the chemo. It'll pass.'

'You think?'

'Stop beating yourself up, Keira,' she says. 'Because you should be happy. This turnout is amazing,' she says, her eyes shining.

'It's all down to you,' I tell her. 'You inspired people.'

'I did, didn't I,' she says, with her Cheshire cat grin.

86

I'm in such a good mood after seeing all the women in the park, that I decide to ring Tom. I tell him that I'll see him at home later. I need to tell him about Lorna's proposal. I need to come clean about Wishwells, but he announces that he can't because the whole of Bryant and Woodruff are going out to celebrate winning the case. The settlement has just come in and he's very relieved it's gone their way.

'I won't be long. We're just going out for a few drinks,' he tells me on the phone.

'Oh. OK, then,' I say.

'Why don't you come along?' he says. 'We're going to the Hare and Hounds. Come on, Keira,' he cajoles and I know this is a peace offering.

'OK, I'll come along and say hi. Just for a bit,' I tell him, trying to sound much more confident than I feel.

But I'm nervous about going out. I don't want to look bald and dowdy next to Janine. It's left to Bea to give me fashion advice, as I fling outfits out of my cupboard onto the bed. There are so many of my clothes I can no longer wear. Lovely tops that are too low cut, trousers that I can't squeeze over my bulky hips. Despite my vow to be kind to myself, there's nothing more dispiriting than trying on cherished clothes that don't fit.

Eventually, I plump for jeans and a leather jacket and on

Bea's advice, I put on the wig and lots of bright lipstick and big hoop earrings. I feel like I'm in deep disguise by the time I leave.

I'm later than I intended as I push through the door of the pub and see that the bar is crowded. Janine is standing next to Tom. She's wearing a sassy grey suit with a low V-neck top, which leaves nothing to the imagination. It's very windy outside and I've had to clamp my hands to my head to stop my wig flying off. I check myself in the pub mirror by the door.

'Oh, you've had your hair done,' Janine says, as I come over. Tom smiles at me and touches my arm, but he doesn't kiss me. 'It really suits you.'

'Thanks,' I say, feeling frumpy. She must know it's a wig, right? Tom must have told her. Is she taking the piss? Surely not?

I don't get a chance to ask him, though, as there's laughter and he gets sucked in to the conversation and I tell him that it's OK and I'll get my own drink.

I'm waiting at the bar for my lime and soda, idly looking across to the other side of the bar, feeling like a spare part and wishing I hadn't come, when I notice a couple in the corner and something about them makes me do a double take. The guy is trailing his finger along the woman's face and they're laughing in the candlelit corner. The man kisses the woman and pulls away and in that instant, I experience a flash of recognition. It's Ian.

Tamsin's Ian.

The couple kiss again. This is clearly not a new relationship. There's something about the way they are together – how they now smile at each other and clink pint glasses – that makes me think that this has been going on for a while.

I stay rooted to the spot, watching Tom and his colleagues laugh. He puts his hand on Janine's shoulder as they both crack up about something, then I look back at Ian, fury rearing in my chest. Tamsin warned us that he was a dick, but I never expected him to be *this* much of a dick.

Tom doesn't notice that I slip away from the bar. I walk hesitantly at first, just to make really sure that I haven't made a terrible mistake. But as Ian sips his pint, I speed up, before I lose my nerve.

'Ian? It's Ian isn't it?' I say, approaching the table.

He looks at me, trying to place me and then he gets it and, for a second, he looks like a little boy.

'Please don't tell her,' he says.

He means Tamsin.

'What's going on?' the woman asks. 'Who are you?'

I ignore her and instead challenge Ian. 'How could you do this to her – when she's going through so much? When there's Mexico. What about Mexico?'

I feel choked with an indignant emotion I can't name.

'It's not easy on me, you know,' he says. 'It's really tough for the other person. People don't realise.'

How dare he say that? About the other person. About himself. About... well, about other people in his position. People like Tom. How dare he suggest that what they're going through is anything like as tough as what Tamsin, or me, or any of us is facing? How fucking *dare* he?

'You'd better tell her,' I say, in a low, shaky voice. 'Or I will.'

I sound convincing, but I'm not sure this is true. I can't tell Tamsin what I've seen. Not when she's pinning her hopes on the treatment that this dickhead has found.

'What's going on?' the girl-woman says.

Finally I address her. She's got very obviously home-dyed hair and she's much plumper than Tamsin. Her breasts spill out of her round-neck T-shirt. 'His partner is going through cancer,' I say. 'In fact, she's at home *right now* probably feeling shit, whilst you're here snogging him. Just so you know.'

I walk away, imagining the explosion behind me. Or maybe there isn't one. Maybe she already knows. Either way, I'm glad the people sitting at the tables next to them overheard.

What a snake-in-the-grass wanker. And what a vile, partner-stealing bitch. They're lucky I didn't say more.

87

I need a few moments to compose myself, so I go into the ladies' loo. I'm washing my hands, when I hear a flush and Janine comes out of the stall. She flicks her hair over her shoulders and grins at me. She really does have the most perfect skin.

'I'm so pleased you're here,' she says. 'I know it means so much to Tom.'

How does she know what me being here means to my husband?

I'm still shaken up by confronting Ian and the horror of his infidelity and what it means for Tamsin and now, her knowingness infuriates me. I watch as she lifts up her arms behind her head and ties her lustrous thick hair into a loose ponytail. I hate the fact that she's flaunting her hair, right in front of me.

'I'm so glad the case is over,' she says.

'Me too,' I manage. I can't stop staring at the thin sliver of toned waist on show, as she completes the ponytail.

'It must have been hard for you Tom working so much at weekends. I mean, I've hardly seen my friends. I'm really not used to working weekends, so I'm looking forward to a lie-in tomorrow.' She smiles widely and I nod. 'I envy that, you know.

That understanding. You two must be very strong.' She pulls a kind of sympathetic face.

'We are,' I nod, but my heart is pounding. I feel like the rug is being whipped out from underneath me, as I find myself opening my mouth and saying, 'That said, you know we're only strong up to a point. I mean, I really wouldn't tolerate Tom being unfaithful to me.'

She looks confused, but I meet her eye levelly. 'Just so you know.'

I go back to Tom and make my excuses to leave. He double checks that I'm OK, but I tell him that it's been a long day and I want to lie down. He kisses the side of my head. Janine watches us with a cross look on her face. There's no sign of Ian and his girlfriend.

Out in the car park, I try and compose myself. I've done the right thing, haven't I? Warning Ian and warning Janine? She won't say anything to Tom, I'm sure, but I still feel nervous that I've spoken up.

In the car, I turn on the radio and Dolly Parton's 'Jolene' is playing and I let out an exasperated snort.

'Is that you, Dad?' I say out loud, marvelling at the irony of the song about a woman begging another, younger woman, not to take her man.

At home, I wonder whether I should call Scout to find out her views on what I've done, but decide that I'm better off going straight to bed. I don't want to go into the nitty-gritty of what happened tonight with anyone. And besides, I was right, wasn't I?

I lie on the bed, feeling worried and anxious and try to

meditate and I don't think it's working, but then I wake up with a jolt. It must be a few hours later. Tom is sitting on the end of the bed. He's still in his suit.

'You're back,' I say, sitting up.

'What did you say to Janine?' he asks. His voice is low and ominous.

'Nothing,' I tell him.

'She's thinks you're under the wrong impression about her,' he says. He doesn't turn around to look at me. 'You know, you should get your facts straight before you accuse people, Keira.'

'I didn't accuse her of anything.'

Oh this is bad. I know this is really bad. My throat goes dry. I've never heard him speak to me in this tone of voice. Guilt pulses through me like a hot flush.

'Have I ever given you cause to distrust me?' he says.

'No,' I say in a little voice.

'But even so, you decide to embarrass me in front of my colleagues.'

'I didn't, I…'

'So you didn't say anything to Janine in the loo?'

I swallow hard, trying to remember my exact words. Maybe I wasn't threatening in the round-about way I've convinced myself I had been. I guess Janine must have been pretty offended by me being so direct. Offended enough to tell Tom.

'Not really.'

'Yes or no, Keira.'

'Yes,' I say and his shoulders slump. 'It's just that she's so *lovely*—'

'Yes she is lovely and clever and bright and young. And she's also gay. And has just got engaged to her partner.'

What?

Oh fuck, oh double, triple fuck. I remember Janine now in the park, running with another woman. Her partner.

He stands up.

'Where are you going?'

'I want a drink. Alone,' he says, pointedly.

88

Tom doesn't come to bed and he leaves early again the next morning to visit his parents. I get up and try and talk to him, but he won't talk to me. He's never left the house with such a bad vibe between us and as I watch the car speed off in the slush and he doesn't turn back, I feel bereft.

Bea stands next to me at the front door. 'Daddy left without me pinch punching him,' she says and I have to battle down tears. 'Is it an April fool?'

'No, darling,' I tell her.

'When will he be back?'

'Soon. He's had to go and help Granny for a while.'

With Tom away, it's hard to sort the kids out by myself, especially when Mum is still not talking to me and doesn't answer my calls. How have I managed to alienate the two people who I rely on the most? It doesn't help that I'd thought I was on top of this chemo, but now the effects of it rear up. I know that this is the low point of the cycle, but the last time I was here, I was in hospital getting antibiotics, so I haven't yet experienced how the chemo would normally work.

I remember what Tamsin said about being stuck in a club as that hemmed-in feeling besieges me. I feel bone tired and aching with it, like my skeleton is trying to escape through my skin. And, without Tom to soothe me, I feel tearful and weak.

'You said you were fine,' Jacob says, when he catches me at the kitchen table, my head on my arms.

'I was.'

'Come on, keep your chin up, Mum,' Bea says. 'You're positive, remember?'

She says this as if it is something I'm not allowed to deviate from, but I see now that my relationship with Tom is the bedrock of everything. Without him at home, I can't find the strength to be positive.

We eat bread and cheese for lunch – it's all I can muster, but it sticks in my throat. The cheese tastes like sandpaper and my mouth has erupted into painful ulcers. I feel bloated and miserable and when Amma rings to tell me that the race is a week tomorrow, I burst into tears. As I wipe my tears away on a tissue, my eyelashes go with them.

I tell her that I am literally falling to pieces and then recount what happened on Friday night and what I said to Ian.

'I wish I hadn't said anything,' I weep to Amma on the phone.

'You had to say something,' she counters.

'Not really. I should have kept my big mouth shut. Ian is all Tamsin has and now I've put a bomb under him at just about the worst time.'

'I'd have done the same thing,' she reassures me, but I can't be comforted.

'I just keep fucking everything up,' I tell her.

'No, you don't. Come on, Keira. This feeling will pass. Stay strong. You're going to be fine. You just need to get practical.

Firstly, you need to get some fresh pineapple – that'll sort out your mouth, then have some ginger tea, if you feel a bit nauseous, and thirdly go outside. Go for a walk. Keep moving. One foot in front of the other, remember?'

89

By Sunday, Tom still isn't back and everyone is stressed. Tilly has a meltdown about her textiles project and I have to stay up late to help fix it. Not that she's grateful at all. I even go up in the loft for her to get some fringing which I know is on the old sitting-room lampshade.

I can't stop thinking about what Clarrie said. About how even some of the strongest relationships are broken by cancer. What if that's me and Tom? What if we can't get past this current impasse?

Our relationship has always been so happy, so tender, so full of joy, but now that golden light has been dimmed by recent events, I'm starting to see the clutter that is lying around in the shadows – resentments that I now see are like packing boxes in the loft. I don't want to start digging into their contents, but I can see their dusty labels: his mother, his bad habits. I sense the pile of old grievances in the boxes, like folded moth-chewed blankets, each one dangerous to air: how it's always me that has to sort out arrangements for the children, me that does the planning for our holidays, me that does everything around the house...

But then I stop myself going down this track. Because if I start to unpack any of those boxes, then he might start unpacking his own boxes – and, if we both start unpicking and unpacking, then everything will crumble. I know that.

I'm about to renegotiate the ladder down, when I spot a box of letters that Tom and I wrote to each other when he was away at law school, and take them down to our room.

By six o'clock on Sunday, Tom still hasn't rung, so I dial his parents' number.

'Hi Hilary,' I say, annoyed that I'm having to talk to her. I feel nervous… like the teenage me ringing up Tom at home. 'Is Tom there?'

'No, he's gone out with his father. Zippo,' she calls, 'what time will Tom be back?'

'Zippo's there?' I ask. No wonder Tom hasn't given me a second thought all weekend.

'Yes, do you want a word?'

'Yes please,' I say.

Zippo comes on the phone. 'How you doing, darling?' he asks.

His tone is light and breezy and I find myself crying.

'Hey, hey, hey,' Zippo says. 'What's up?'

I tell him about Tom and what happened at the pub and what I said to Janine.

'And now he's so cross with me.'

'You should cut him a break. Him not getting that bump-up has hit him hard. As well, as you know… everything else.'

Cancer, he means. *Me.*

But then I actually listen to what he's said. 'Did you just say bump up? You mean, he didn't get the promotion?'

'To partner. No, Andrew gave it to that guy Dan, apparently. It's tough on Tom. His pride is hurt, you know.'

'He didn't tell me.'

'Well, you're going through so much, he probably didn't want to worry you.'

I nod, dumbstruck. Tom has always shared everything with me before and the fact that he's felt he's had to keep this news under wraps is awful. I wonder how long he's known, or worse, whether him leaving the meeting to come and see me in hospital sealed his fate.

We chat for a while longer and I ask him about Lucy and he sighs.

'It's nice to be here for a bit,' he says. 'Have an excuse, you know, to spend a bit of time away. She's quite intense. She wants… I don't know what she wants.'

'She's young,' I point out. 'She probably wants a baby.'

'No,' Zippo says, as if I'm mad. 'She knows I don't want kids.'

'Does she?'

'Sure she does,' he says, but he doesn't sound convinced.

'Have you actually sat her down and told her that, in so many words?'

'Not in so many words, but she gets my vibe.'

'Well, sometimes, you can misjudge someone's vibe,' I tell him, thinking of my all-too-painful experience with Janine. 'You need to be honest with her. You can't keep stringing her along. It's not fair. Her fertile years are running out.'

Zippo makes a harrumphing sound. 'Why do you always have to be the one to talk sense to me?' he says.

'Because I'm old and wise,' I tell him. 'You should try someone your own age,' I add. 'You'd be surprised how well you'd get on.'

I haven't read the letters Tom and I sent to each other nearly a quarter of a century ago for so long, that it feels like time travelling, as I sit in bed and touch the ink pen on the envelopes, remembering the thrill of his letters coming through the letter box at Mum's house. How I'd look forward to each one and cherish every word.

We don't write letters now and it occurs to me, as I read our words to each other how bold our declarations of love were, how simple our lives were when we had everything to look forward to. I find the insert of a homemade mix tape with one letter and remember the tracks from the long-dead tape and how they must have been lovingly recorded.

Let's never be one of those couples, I read in my own hand, *who forget to tell each other why they love each other.*

How old fashioned our courtship seems now – on paper for a start and not in texts! – but how lovely, too – our future full of high ideals. When I read about Tom's student concerns – how his workload is overwhelming – I smile to myself about how little has changed. He always was a swot. He always did ten times more than was necessary.

Perhaps I'm being impatient, wanting Tom to get over his disappointment at not getting the partnership straight away. Come to think of it, maybe I'm being impatient with Mum, expecting her to keep up with how I'm changing. And most of all, I'm being impatient with myself – wanting all of this to be over, wanting my body to mend itself.

90

The next morning, I park by the post office to post the long, heartfelt letter I've written to Tom late into the night. I've said so many things that I should have said before. How I'm truly sorry and ashamed that I ever thought he might find Janine attractive and that I hadn't meant my comment to her to come across in such an aggressive way, but that I was shaken up after my confrontation with Ian. I know my letter will make Tom feel better and get us back on track, but as I post it, I still feel bereft that he's not here. Without him, it feels like everything is unravelling.

I'm just getting back into the car, when I see a familiar figure coming out of Starbucks across the road. It's Andrew Woodruff, Tom's boss, and without giving myself time to back out, I lock the car and dart across the road between the traffic.

'Hi, Andrew!' I say, as if this is a chance encounter.

'Keira,' he says. He's dealing with his coffee, so he doesn't kiss me. There's an awkward moment. Andrew is in his sixties and today he's wearing a long coat which hangs over his shoulders over his pinstriped suit, so he looks rather like an off-duty vampire. He looks down at me with beady eyes.

'Tom's still away,' Andrew says. 'So I hear.' There's a note of disapproval in his voice.

'Yes. He's in Devon with his parents.'

'Hmm,' Andrew says, his lips pursing.

Wow, this man is irritating. No wonder Tom finds him hard to deal with.

'I heard that you didn't promote him to partner,' I blurt. I look at him accusingly.

Andrew looks put on the spot. 'I just don't think it's Tom's time, that's all.'

'His time? But nobody could have worked harder than him.'

He stares at me, his eyes suddenly cold. 'You say that, but there's been some times recently, when I've not been convinced of his commitment.'

'Oh, what? You've punished him because he left that meeting?'

'It was rather awkward.' Andrew scratches the side of his face.

'He left because of me? Because he put *his wife* first?'

He looks a bit ashamed now. 'It's not like that, Keira.'

'It is from where I'm standing. Do you have any idea how incredible Tom has been? He's been working flat out, on top of which, he's been coping with his mother being practically crippled, his Dad getting dementia, not to mention his wife going through cancer treatment.'

His eyes flick to mine and there's a beat.

'Cancer?' he asks.

And then I understand. Andrew… here… now. And Janine… there in the pub. Tom hasn't told them. He hasn't told any of them.

'Didn't you know?' I ask, aghast.

'No, I had no idea,' he says. I can see him raking my face, looking at my wig… finally understanding. His cheeks colour. 'Cancer? Oh… oh, Keira, I'm… I'm so sorry.'

It's typical of Tom and how professional and discreet he is not to have told Andrew what's going on at home, but I'm still amazed he's kept it under wraps. Or felt that he had to.

'Don't you think it's awful that you've created a culture at work where Tom felt he *couldn't* say anything?'

Andrew looks flummoxed.

'One in two people will get cancer in their lifetimes, Andrew. You might get with the programme and start cutting people like Tom some slack?'

I know with this last sentence, I've said too much. That there will be ramifications and consequences, but sod it. I believe in what I've just said. The corporate culture Andrew has created is shocking. And if Tom decides to leave because of it, then I'll support him all the way.

I only wish I could tell him this, but then I remember that he's not speaking to me.

91

I park in Wishwells, steeling myself to face Lorna. I've been chewing over and over what she offered me, but I know I can't let her push me out of the business. Besides, with Tom potentially out of a job, once he finds out what I've said to Andrew, there's no way I can leave. I have to grovel to her and find a way to get my job back.

Lorna looks horrified when I walk in through the back door. She races into the corridor to try and stop me from coming through to the shop. Behind her, there's a man in a grey suit with a retractable tape measure and a clipboard.

'What are you doing here?' she says and her voice says it all. She actually tries to bar my way as I get nearer to the shop and there's an unseemly tussle.

'What's going on?' I ask, finally pushing my way onto the shop floor and the man looks up.

'Ah, you must be Miss Wishwell,' he says, in a weasley voice. He has a bushy moustache.

I almost correct him and tell him my married name, but something about this has my nerves on edge.

'Yes, and you're…'

'Oh. Derek Anderson. I'm from Brightmouth council,' he says. 'Just looking around to finalise the schedule of dilapidations.'

'The schedule of what?'

'Keira, just leave this to me,' Lorna says, but she sounds panicked. She has her thumb and fingers on her forehead.

'Since the break clause has been exercised in the contract and we're taking the building back, I'm just assessing the damage. You'll have to return it to how it was, of course.'

I stare at Lorna and notice her cheeks flushing.

'You've given up the lease?' I ask.

'Yes, that's correct,' Mr Anderson says. 'This whole stretch will probably go now.'

'Go?'

'The redevelopment. It's going ahead. Arc Contractors won the bid.'

I stare at Lorna, my heart pounding. My mouth has gone dry.

'What have you done?' I gasp.

'We don't really need the shop,' she says. 'It's not making much profit. And we can make so much more online.'

'No, Lorna. Just no. Fuck you,' I shout. 'This is not happening.'

I stride over to the man and rip the clipboard from his hands. 'Leave,' I shout, pointing at the door. Then I stride over and rip open the door so violently, the bell breaks from its mooring.

'Just calm down, Keira.'

'I'm going,' Mr Anderson says, putting his hands up in surrender.

'I'm so sorry,' Lorna says to him, picking up his clipboard. 'My colleague is very emotional. She's got cancer.'

'Don't you dare bring that into this,' I shout.

'Please calm down, Keira.'

But I feel waves of shock pulsing through me.

'I'll be back,' Mr Anderson says, 'when you've sorted out your differences.' He scowls at me and leaves quickly through the shop door.

I feel like I'm having a panic attack. 'I can't believe what you've done,' I say, choked with tears. 'I can't believe you've sold out Wishwells behind my back. You can't do this. You can't—'

'The board will back me and Pierre up,' Lorna says, her voice steely. 'Pierre has already spoken to them.'

She stands with her hands akimbo, challenging me. I make a gargled cry and then run out of the shop, across the road to Jennifer's café and I'm properly shaking.

'Keira, what the hell's the matter?' Jennifer asks.

'There's a man in from the council. They've broken our lease. They are getting rid of Wishwells behind my back.'

Sian comes out of the kitchen. She holds me as I cry.

'They can't do that, Keira,' she says.

'They already have.'

'Which means we'll all go,' Jennifer says, her face ashen.

'What the hell are we going to do?'

'Leave this to me,' Sian says.

92

Much later that night, my fury has hardened and I'm completely up for Sian's stealthy plan. A fox crosses the empty car park behind Wishwells as she and I arrive in her almost silent electric car. My heart is pounding as I open the back door and disable the alarm. I'm terrified we're going to get caught, but Sian seems confident.

'Is there CCTV?' she asks and I nod, going into the shop to turn it off. It's rigged up to a dedicated laptop and Sian suggests that if we have time, we have a look through it.

We go up the stairs, without turning on the lights, using the torch from my mobile phone. Sian has a large black rucksack with her and she moves quietly and efficiently, clearly having done this before.

Upstairs, the office has been rearranged and my desk has been shoved in a corner, boxes of merchandise piled on top of it. I open one of the boxes and see a teapot with Jackson's face emblazoned on it. I'm sorely tempted to hurl it through the meeting room window.

'Which one should I start on?' Sian asks, nodding to the computers, and I show her to Lorna's desk.

The screen flicks into life and the Wishwells logo is reflected in Sian's glasses as she sits in Lorna's seat.

I wring my hands, feeling sick to my stomach that I've agreed to this. I have no idea what she'll find, but the feeling that it's all too late persists.

This is my own fault, I tell myself. I should never have allowed Pierre in. I should have stood up to Lorna sooner. Should have… should have… my mind goes crazy.

Leaving Sian to it, I head downstairs to look through the CCTV, but I'm not sure what I'm looking for. I stare across the moonlit floor of the shop, remembering Dad being here so clearly that my heart contracts with longing. It's the middle of the night, but without Tom, I simply can't process all of this. I yearn for someone to back me up and tell me that I'm not crazy.

Then I remember that there *is* one person I can call.

'Hey, sis,' my brother Billy says, smiling on the WhatsApp call. It's such a relief to see his face. He looks tanned and happy and I can hear the kids in his sunlit garden in Sydney. 'What time is it there?'

'It's half two.'

'Can't you sleep?' he asks and I shake my head, overwhelmed with tears. 'Hey… what's wrong?'

So I tell him. I tell him about Lorna and Pierre and about how they've treated me and how I'm going to lose Wishwells and I don't know what to do.

'I just didn't think she'd ever do something like this to me,' I say, so relieved to let it all out.

'Well, it's no surprise to me,' Billy says. 'Lorna always was a bitch. Why do you think I ended up running away to the other side of the world?'

Something goes clunk in my head as I try to compute what he's just said.

'But I thought… I thought it was an amicable split between you two?'

'Amicable?' he laughs. 'She undermined me and undermined me, until I just had to get away. She made me think I was nothing… less than nothing.'

'Why didn't you say anything to me?' I say, aghast.

'Because you always think the best of people and, at the time, you thought she was chocolate. And she'd done such a good job of convincing you that I was a total stoner. Would you really have believed me over her?'

'Keira, come and see this,' Sian says, whispering down the stairs.

'I gotta go,' I tell Billy and quickly dry my eyes. His revelation about Lorna is all I need to convince myself that I'm right to fight for Wishwells.

'What is it?' I ask Sian going back to the office.

'Well… you were totally right about the emails,' she says. 'I've been looking through Lorna's history. She's been copying you in on things and then deliberately moving the messages to read.'

'You can tell that?'

'Oh yes,' Sian says, gleefully, her hands not leaving the keyboard. 'You'll be amazed what I can tell. It seems your friend Lorna has been very busy behind your back.'

'She's not my friend,' I say, feeling better than I have done all day.

93

The next morning, I'm utterly shattered, having only got back with Sian at four, but Pooch very insistently nudges me out of bed. Tom walks in, just as I'm about to leave for the park. As soon as I see his face, I know he hasn't received my letter. There's so much I need to tell him... about Lorna and Sian going into Wishwells, but I see straight away that he's still fuming about Janine and he doesn't want to communicate with me at all.

'How did it go with your parents?' I ask.

'There's still lots to do. I'm going back down on Thursday night.'

'Thursday? For how long?'

'Probably the weekend.'

What the fuck...?

'But it's the race on Sunday. Joss is coming down and—'

'So you'll have plenty of support. You don't need me,' he says, cutting me off. 'I'm going to the office and I'm already late.'

He doesn't kiss me. He doesn't explain. He doesn't pet Pooch, who looks at me with confusion.

'Bloody hell,' I mutter, furious that my plan hasn't worked.

I don't have a chance to tell Tom about the letter, or to fill him in on my outburst at Andrew. He leaves to go to the office and he comes home when we're all having supper. He's his usual smiley self with the kids and they don't notice how off he's being with me. If Andrew has said anything to him, then Tom doesn't let on.

When we clear up, I try and talk to him, but he sighs. 'I'm very tired, Keira,' he says. 'It was a long drive.'

'I know, but… can't we talk?'

'Not tonight,' he says in a way that tells me he really wants to be left alone.

I'm about to say more, but my phone pings with a text. It's from Amma.

Have you seen the JustGiving Page?

I log on to the iPad, listening to Tom jog upstairs. We're already at 58 per cent of our target. I take a screenshot of it and send it to Tamsin and Sian on our WhatsApp group. Tamsin sends back a clapping hand emoji. I wonder how she's getting on with Ian and whether he's said anything about me meeting him in the pub. I wish that night had never happened. I wish I'd never seen him – or said anything to Janine.

But my sorryness over my mistake about Janine has been overtaken by a more resentful feeling. I'm annoyed that Tom has chosen to be with his parents, rather than me this weekend. I bet Hilary blames me for Tom not making it to partner. That's if he's discussed his career with her – which is more than he's doing with me.

I want to be happy about the race, but I can't. I'm anxious about it in so many ways, not least of all because Tom won't be there. I cajole Bea into asking her dad about what's going on down in Devon, but Bea is confused that I won't ask Tom myself.

'Mum wants to know what's going on with Granny?' she says the next morning, as Tom is tying his tie in the kitchen. Tom gives me a dark look.

'Are you two having a row?' Jacob asks, his eyes brightening. 'Wicked.'

'Just forget it,' I snap, dumping the tea towel on the table. 'I'm sick of this.'

I go upstairs and a few minutes later I hear the front door slam and I know that Tom has left for work.

94

I call Sian but she says she hasn't got much for me yet and she'll need longer to go through everything she's downloaded. I know we've got evidence that Lorna played around with my emails, but as Sian says, Lorna's clever and if it came to it, she could easily explain that away. I have this horrible, insidious feeling that Lorna's won and I don't have a leg to stand on with the board. Not when she's been so seemingly supportive towards me. Not when she's made so much of the mistakes she thinks I've made.

I'm finding it really hard to focus on anything at all with so many unanswered questions going over and over and over in my mind. Has Tom had to suck up Dan's promotion and accept that Dan, who is fifteen years younger than him, is now his boss? Is he going to take it, or leave? And if he leaves, what then? What's he going to say when I tell him about Wishwells? Because if we're both unemployed, then we really can't afford to live in this house. In fact, we really can't afford our lifestyle, full stop.

And, on top of all that – how the fuck am I going to run a 10K race, when I'm this wrung out and exhausted?

I spend most of the next twenty-four hours feeling wretched, but Tom fails to notice how terrible I'm feeling. Instead, he leaves to go back down to Devon, with a stern warning that if I insist on doing the race, then on my own head be it. He doesn't even wish me luck.

Tamsin has assured me and Amma that we'll be fine, but *will* we be? I try and carb load with one of the traybakes from the freezer, but it's not very nice and I feel queasy as I go for a lie down on Friday night.

I'm trying to meditate, to summon up some kind of positive thoughts to beat the black fog of gloom that seems to have descended, when the phone pings with a text from Amma.

ARE YOU WATCHING THIS? In capitals. NOW. BBC1

I get up and fling my dressing gown on. The kids are slobbing on the sofa.

'Hey, Mum – are you feeling better?' Jacob asks.

'Quick, quick, give me the remote,' I tell him, holding out my hand.

'What is it?' Tilly asks.

'Shush,' I tell her, flipping over the channel.

'We're watching that,' she protests, as I turn off their programme, but I ignore her.

I lean forward, watching the chat show. Isabel sits demurely on the sofa, with her husband, Greg. They are mid-chat about baby Bear and his antics.

Graham, the host, nods and consults his card.

'So this latest Netflix series is getting loads of hype,' he says, 'and rightly so. It's essentially about friends who fall out and make up. Has that happened to you?' he asks, with his trademark Irish charm. 'I mean, you must have loads of friends who are *sooo* jealous of you. I'm jealous of you, being married to him.'

Isabel laughs her sexy laugh. She clutches Greg's hand on the sofa and smiles at him. He looks suitably bashful, but that only makes him more handsome.

'But seriously – you have it all, don't you. Your beautiful son, perfect marriage, amazing home, Hollywood on speed dial. You're probably hard to be friends with?'

She laughs and shifts again. 'Maybe I am, but what does it all mean without friends? I'm lost without my girlfriends. And this was brought home to me recently, when I discovered my best friend had been going through cancer treatment, and I didn't know.'

'Heavy,' Graham says, with a grimace to the camera.

'You'd think it would be, but Amma is just amazing. She's absolutely my inspiration. She's got this group together of women who are all running, despite going through treatment.'

'Mum! That's you!' Tilly says, jumping along the sofa to perch next to me.

'I know! I know. Shhh.'

'I thought cancer treatment is supposed to be horrendous?' Graham asks.

'It is, but Amma says that if you can run through cancer, then anything is possible. She's running a 10K race to raise money for one of the women in their group. Honestly,' Isabel says, hand on her chest, 'she's amazing. And Amma, if you're watching, I love you.'

'Aww, bless,' Graham says. There's a smattering of applause. Greg looks on proudly.

'Are you going to join in with the run?' he asks Isabel.

'Yes, absolutely,' she says. 'Anyone who wants to join the

Cancer Ladies' Running Club, come along, or sponsor us –
look up Time for Tamsin.' She looks at the camera with her
shameless name dropping.

'You'd better stick to plugging the show,' Graham says, with
a laugh. 'Or you'll be deluged.'

95

Joss arrives on Saturday lunchtime and she's high on the back of Isabel's plug. She's declined to run the race herself though – opting instead to smoke in the garden and engage Tilly in a long chat about mascara. I try not to feel miffed that they are flaunting their long eyelashes in front of me, when my own eyelashless eyes feel red and sore. But then, I suppose they're not 'flaunting' at all really, are they? They're just blinking. It's just me who sees it that way.

Still, it's not all bad. Joss has a cosmetics client and she's brought a whole range of red lipsticks, which she insists I try to find the right shade. I've never worn red lipstick with the confidence Joss has, but there's one shade that works and Tilly and Joss force me to look in the mirror and tell them how kick-ass I think I look. I lie to them both. I look dreadful to me. I look sick and tired and worried and 'Sexy Lady' lipstick is not going to cut it. Not even close.

I barely sleep and on Sunday when I hear the dawn chorus, my stomach clenches and I get up and throw up in the sink in the bathroom. When I look at my reflection, there are dark circles under my eyes.

At six-thirty, Joss comes in with a cup of tea and opens the curtains. It's a glorious clear spring day.

'It's perfect weather for the race,' she says. 'And guess what?

Jessica is going to be there for a follow-up piece. She's just texted. So you'd better get up and get ready for the cameras. She says she'll be there at the start and the finishing line. Isn't that great?'

'Joss – I can't. I mean, I really can't do it,' I say.

'Nonsense,' she says, failing to pick up on how serious I'm being. 'Is this about Tom? Because *sod* Tom and his sulk. You're doing this race, whether he likes it or not. You can do it. Now chop, chop. Up you get.'

The sun is belting down from a powder blue sky, daffodils bloom in the grass verges as we drive to pick up Tamsin. Joss has gone early to schmooze with the TV crew and is meeting us at the park. Jacob has gone over to Biffa's and says he'll be in the park for the finish line and Bea went over to Molly's last night, where Grace says they're perfecting a banner for us. It's down to Tilly and I to go over to Tamsin's to pick her up.

We find Tamsin in a fluster, trying to perfect her make-up, shaking with nervousness and with strong painkillers she's taken to get through this morning. She's resplendent in running kit, her black wig in place under her cap, her eyes an array of silver and purple. There's no sign of Ian. Neither of us mention him. I wonder if I should say something, but I can't.

Kathryn at the cancer centre has given Tamsin a wheelchair and although she doesn't strictly need it yet, Phil has suggested that she gets used to using it. Tamsin hates it and doesn't want to bring it at all when Tilly suggests that we do.

'I'll be watching the race with you,' she says, in a firm, calm way that impresses me. 'We can be quicker seeing Mum and getting between the different parts of the race if we take it. You can push me in it, if you really want?'

In the end, Tamsin relents and we set off, but my heart is hammering at the thought of how much they're expecting from me. I just want to go home and pull the duvet over my head.

'What's the matter?' Tamsin asks me, as we set off.

'I just don't think I can do it. It's so far.'

'Oh shut up, Mum,' Tilly says. 'You're being so dramatic. Besides, you can't back out now.'

96

I have never seen the park so crowded. The cars have spilled out along the row of poplars and there's a warden who guides us into one of the last spaces. There are people everywhere in running kit, limbering up. Tents have been set up around the edges of the start area to take people's belongings. 'Eye of the Tiger' blares from the loudhailer.

I call Sian, although it takes a moment to get reception.

'Where are you?' I ask her, blocking my ear and pressing my phone against the other, trying to locate our meeting place by the tree. It looks all different now there are so many people.

'Keira,' she shouts. 'You're not going to believe this. We've already run out of Time for Tamsin T-shirts.'

'What? Where are you?'

'You see that giant queue?' she yells. I can. There's what looks like several hundred people all waiting patiently. 'I'm at the front of that. All these people have turned up to run. For us! For Tamsin.'

Tamsin, Tilly and I can't believe it. We walk along the side of the queue trying to get to Sian, but people realise that it's Tamsin and applause starts and I see Tamsin put her hand on her chest and then she starts hugging people in the queue. She's rarely overwhelmed, but I can see she's very touched. Tilly walks deferentially behind with the empty wheelchair.

At the front Sian and Amma are waiting, along with Isabel, who looks tiny in her running gear and a lot plainer than I remember her.

'Oh, look. You're here,' Tamsin says, shaking her hand. 'I'm honoured we have such a celebrity in our midst. You were so wonderful on the TV.'

'I think you're the star of the show today,' Isabel says, demurely, kissing Tamsin's cheek.

Suddenly, the photographer from the local press is there, and now a man with cans and a giant boom, and a man with a microphone with a fuzzy top.

'Who's in charge? Who has organised all of this?' he says, pushing through. 'Darren from Park FM. Who can say a few words?'

Sian points at me. 'Keira.'

'Keira,' he calls, and suddenly I hear reverb over the giant speaker as the song finishes.

'I'm here with the Time for Tamsin runners. Can I have some noise people?' Darren says and the crowd all cheer. 'Welcome, welcome everyone. Keira, I understand you and your friends are taking part in this race to raise money for Tamsin's treatment?'

He points the microphone in front of my face. I'm usually so nervous about public speaking, but Tamsin's eyes lock with mine and there's her Cheshire cat smile.

'That's right. We're raising money for this amazing woman,' I say. 'Our inspirational friend, Tamsin.'

'And is it true, you're all running through cancer?'

'Yes, lots of us are going through cancer treatment. I'd have never got into running if it wasn't for Tamsin. Being here… seeing so many people coming out to support us, is just incredible.'

'And it's quite a crowd that have gathered today,' Darren says, nodding and winking at me in approval. 'Look here, we have our very own celebrity in our midst. Isabel Monroe everyone.'

There are cheers and a few wolf whistles from the crowd. Isabel smiles, like an actress at the Oscars.

'You're too kind. Too kind.' She beams. 'But really, this is not about me. I'm delighted to be part of the Cancer Ladies' Running Club today along with Amma, my best friend.'

Amma grins at her. Like me, she's wearing large shades and bright red lipstick and she's not wearing a wig – only her cap. When I first met her, she was so keen for her cancer treatment to be secret, but today, she looks relaxed and happy. She says that this lot of chemo drugs has not been so bad to deal with, although she's still a bit breathless. Unlike me, she seems super confident about today.

'Are you a runner?' Darren asks Isabel.

'We'll find out, won't we?' she says, with her husky laugh. 'I hope so. I hope I can get round.'

As do I… because suddenly I'm gripped by it again. A terrible, terrible sense of foreboding. Because… what if I screw this up? What if I fail again… right in front of the cameras?

'And Tamsin,' Darren asks, leaning down to talk to Tamsin, who has now settled herself in the wheelchair. 'How are you feeling?'

Tamsin takes the microphone from him and there's a pause.

'Annoyed that I'm not able to run with all these lovely people,' she says.

'You're a long-distance runner. Is that right?' Darren says. 'And with a bit of luck, with the money raised for your treatment, then you will be again.' The crowd cheer again.

Tamsin bites her top lip, before smiling, but her eyes flick towards me. He doesn't have a clue about the complexity of her diagnosis or the treatment she's contemplating – or if it'll work. She takes the microphone back from him. 'But I want to say…' she begins, but then she chokes up. I've never seen her cry before. She takes a breath. 'I want to say thank you. To you all for being here. But mostly, thank you to my friends.'

97

Darren and the warm-up team gee us all up, then the BBC crew are upon us.

'It's so lovely to see you again, Keira,' Jessica says. 'We've got a tracker on you, so we'll save the main interview for the end of the race.'

They're going to track me?

'How are you feeling?' she asks, but I can't actually speak.

'She'll be fine,' Amma cuts in. 'We'll run together,' she adds, but I'm starting to feel really dizzy. Amma gives me a reassuring smile, but I can't smile back. I'm too intimidated by how together she is, how confident and happy, even though she's got even more chemo on board than me. I feel like I'm falling apart.

There's lots of communal shouting and more 'Eye of the Tiger' blasting, before we're all corralled into the starting pens and then a claxon sounds and everyone whoops and starts walking towards the starting line, but my feet won't move.

'Come on, Keira,' Amma calls, but I shake my head, tears starting.

'I can't do it. I won't be able to get round.' I start shouldering through the crowd. I just have to go. I have to get away from here.

'Keira, wait,' Amma calls, but I shake her off. I'm nearly at the back of the runners, when I'm stopped in my path. It's Joss. She grips my shoulders.

'What the fuck are you doing?' she asks. 'Where are you going?'
Amma runs up too. And Sian.

'I can't do it,' I say, with a sob. 'Everyone is going to laugh at me and I'm going to fuck it up.'

Joss looks at me for a long moment and she's about to speak, but then she nods.

'Listen to me. It's not 1984 and you're not that little girl anymore, Keira,' she says, looking into my eyes. 'You're brave and you're strong. And you've got this. Nobody is laughing at you. Everyone wants you to succeed. And if you don't try it, you'll never forgive yourself.'

'Come on. Let's feel the fear and do it anyway,' Amma says. 'There's still time. Let's catch up.'

'Please,' Joss says. 'Do it for me. Do it for Amma and Sian. And Tamsin.'

I take in a raggedy breath and then Sian and Amma hold my hands and we run now to the start line to catch up with Isabel.

'See, we can do it,' Amma says, encouragingly. 'It's just one foot in front of the other.'

'Don't think about the distance,' Sian says, but it's hard not to. We have to go all the way around the park – twice – then finish by the bandstand.

But she's right. One foot at a time. Soon we're over the starting line and Sian and Amma let go of my hands. Maybe Joss is right. Maybe I *can* do this. If I just keep going. If I just don't stop.

By the first hill, I'm over-heating and I strip down to my running vest. Then I take off my hat. I don't care who sees me bald. The wind on my bare scalp feels mercifully cool.

'Let's keep chatting. It'll make it easier,' Sian says. 'Come on, Amma, tell us about the big career in politics. How's it going?'

I can tell she and Amma are worried about me.

'Well, it's going to be tough going up against Doug Crawley. He has a big old boy's network behind him – and funding of course,' Amma says. 'He seems to have loads of money.'

'Where's that from?' Sian says, distractedly, looking at me.

'No idea. He just got back from Portugal. They say he has a big villa out there by a golf course.'

Sian's stride falters for a moment.

'What is it?' I ask her. Her brain is clearly whirring.

'Just… nothing…'

'Oh look. There she is,' Amma says and I can see her waving at Isabel, who has waited for us.

In a moment, in the crowd, I've lost sight of Amma and Isabel and then Sian is with me, but then there's a moment of confusion and I look around and she's gone too.

I hear Amma and Sian call my name, but there are too many runners between us – many of them from the Time for Tamsin team, and I wave to her and yell that I'll catch up, but I'm not sure that's going to be possible.

And I know they want to help. I know they want to support me. But I'm glad we've split up, because I need to do this alone. For me. By myself.

Runner after runner overtakes me, but then I feel a tap on my shoulder. A woman in a Cancer Research T-shirt passes me. She turns back to face me.

'Keep going,' she calls. 'I'm clear. Two years.'

'Me too,' another woman says, who has heard the exchange. 'Five years. Don't stop believing.'

A few minutes later, it happens again and then again. 'Fifteen years', 'Clear four years,' I hear women say and each time it's like a little sprinkle of fairy dust is wafted down on me. All these women… who are all surviving… no, scrap that. They're not *surviving*, they're positively thriving on the other side of cancer.

A woman now falls into step next to me at the water station.

'How you doing?' she asks, as I glug down from the plastic cup that a volunteer hands to me.

'I'm hot,' I pant back. 'Other than that, not too bad. I'm just trying to put one foot in front of another.'

'Well, good for you,' she says, setting off at the same pace as me. She clearly wants to chat and that's fine. Anything for the distraction of the pain of running and how far I've still got to go.

The woman has lustrous dark, curly hair and lovely skin and a kind smile. 'I ran all the way through my treatment,' she says.

I look at her, surprised. I see now that she's probably a bit older than me, but she seems to be glowing with health. '*You* had cancer?'

'Stage three, but I made a full recovery,' she says. 'I've been clear three years now. And let me tell you, life is better than ever.'

'That's good to know.'

I tell her about Tamsin and why we're running today and I tell her, too, about my diagnosis and treatment, but talking is hard and I'm slowing down.

'There will be moments when you feel like you're stuck in the middle of it all and there's no way out,' she says, 'but, believe me, there really is light at the end of the tunnel.'

Her friendly manner and wise words, feel like they are nourishing the very core of me and I thank her, but I'm aware she's almost walking now, because of me.

'Don't let me hold you up,' I tell her, eventually. 'Please, you go on.' I feel guilty that she's taking the time to run and chat with me. She smiles and waves and I watch her speed up towards the park entrance.

I have to walk for a while and I muse on how nice the lady was. It's not my internal demons that stop me now, though, just the chemo. I breathe through it, trying to summon the spirit of Nigel Havers.

'*Come on, Keira. Let's do it,*' I say, imagining Nigel by my side. '*One foot in front of the other.*'

I force myself to run on, but it's the slowest run ever. It doesn't matter. I'm moving. But just the other side of the park gate, I see the lady who chatted to me again. There's a bit now where we have to run along the road and back into the park by the other gate.

'Are you OK?' I ask, confused as to why she's stopped.

'Actually, I was waiting for you,' she says. And I'm about to tell her to go on without me, when she draws me to one side, out of the flow of runners. 'Hang on. Stop a minute.' I'm grateful for the break, but confused. 'I want to tell you something.'

She leans in close to me, as the other runners pass us, but I don't care. I feel held by her stare. Her eyes are a lovely shade of green. 'When I was going through treatment,' she says, 'this thing happened. A lady in a café – a complete stranger – seeing I was at a low point came over to talk to me. She said that she'd been watching me and knew what I was going through.'

I nod. I'm not sure where this story is going. But now the

woman unearths a necklace from beneath her running top. It's a pretty little butterfly on a silver pendant.

'And this lady took off the necklace she was wearing, *this* necklace, and handed it to me saying it was a little butterfly of hope and she wanted me to have it.'

The runner now reaches behind her neck and undoes the necklace. 'And I've been wearing it ever since. And I knew I was wearing it today for a reason. Because *you're* that reason.'

She reaches out and puts the butterfly necklace around my neck. I'm so stunned by this amazing story and her gesture that I hardly react, but I'm sure my mouth must have fallen open. I put my hand over the butterfly. She puts her hand over mine.

'This is now *your* butterfly of hope. To remind you that everything is going to be fine. Better than fine. That you mustn't give up hope, or believing that you will be out the other side of this experience, and richer for it. Because you will.'

'Thank you. Thank you so much,' I tell her. I feel choked up.

'You can pass it on, too, when you feel you want to. But it's right that it's yours for now.'

She hugs me tightly and when she lets me go, I see that her eyes are damp with tears. And then, a second later, she's off and I realise that I don't even know her name.

98

I run on in a trance. I'm so emotional and elated, I've almost passed Jacob before I realise it's him yelling at me.

'Mum, I've got you jelly babies.' He's leaning over the barrier on the side of the road, waving a packet at me. 'I'll have a red one,' I tell him, collapsing against the railing, and he fishes one out for me. 'I must look like a jelly baby myself,' I joke. 'I feel like one.'

'Nonsense, keep going,' he says. 'You're doing brilliantly. Bea is up ahead. Look how much money, already,' he says, shaking a bucket with a Time for Tamsin logo sellotaped to it.

'That's amazing, peanut,' I say, leaning in to kiss his cheek. He flushes in front of Biffa.

As I come along the road to the gate where Amma talked to the homeless man, I hear Bea before I see her, as she's leading a chant of 'Go Keira, go Keira.' She's made a huge banner with giant yellow letters and I wave. There's a few of them from the dance school and one of the kids has one of those rattle things that he makes a noise with, waving it around his head. Another has a whistle and another a horn. It's quite a cacophony.

I stop for a minute to kiss Bea.

'Have you seen Sian?' I yell. 'I lost her.'

'She's just gone by. If you hurry you'll catch her.'

I speed up, mentally summoning Nigel Havers again to

keep me going. And miraculously, a few minutes later, I find Sian, as well as Amma and Isabel. I'm so relieved we're finally all together.

Breathlessly, I tell them about the woman and the butterfly of hope necklace and they are amazed by it too, and then there's only one kilometre to go and we try and speed up together. We go on a big loop of the park and there are crowds lining the railings. I've never heard so much clapping and cheering.

And then, by the bandstand, I see Tilly waving. Tamsin is in front of her in the wheelchair.

I run over with the girls.

'Lift me up, lift me up,' Tamsin says, struggling up and Amma and I grab her, her arms over our shoulders.

'Let's do this thing,' she says.

'It's just one foot in front of another,' I tell her. 'Believe you can do it, and you will.'

She runs at our pace for the final stretch to the finish line. I can hear Darren yelling down the microphone and the crowd is roaring as Sian puts her arm around me, and Isabel around Amma and together, the Cancer Ladies' Running Club fly over the finish line.

99

My knees do that funny wobbly thing you see marathoners do, as I get over the line, but I'm absolutely elated, as I'm handed my finishers' medal and a foil cape to wear.

Darren is there and I hear over the tannoy, 'The Cancer Ladies' Running Club, everyone. They did it. Let's have some applause.'

I can hear the crowd cheering and Amma, Sian, Tamsin and I all hug each other. Then the man from the press is there and we pose, holding our medals.

Then Jessica is there, filming us. 'How do you feel?' she asks. 'Did you think you'd be able to do it?'

'No!' I laugh. 'It's a miracle I got round. I never thought... I never really thought I'd make it to the end.'

I laugh and hug Tamsin and Amma again. I can't ever remember feeling like this.

'Oh. My. God...' Sian says.

'What is it?' I ask, following her gaze to where a man is pushing through the barrier and out of the crowd towards us.

'It's him.'

'Who?' I ask.

'It's Dave.'

Dave, Sian's old colleague, is around the same height as her. He has a friendly face and is wearing a baseball cap, which he now takes off to reveal gingerish thick hair. He smiles, nervously, his soft eyes glued to Sian.

'What are *you* doing here?' Sian asks, her hand on her chest. Dave leans forward to kiss her cheek and from where I'm standing, I see him close his eyes for moment, like he's breathing her in.

'Sian, I had no idea,' he says. The two of them stare at each other. 'And then Jennifer, your sister, she found me.'

'Jen did?'

'She told me about your running friends and how you'd talked about me.'

'You told Jennifer?' Sian says, looking at me and then at Tamsin.

'Nothing to do with me,' Tamsin says, putting her hands up defensively. 'But very nice to meet you, Dave. We've all heard a lot about you.'

'It was me,' I volunteer. 'I told Jennifer. I'm sorry.'

Sian's face was crimson from running, but now it positively glows.

'Don't blame Jennifer. She just wanted to do the right thing,' Dave says. 'And then, just after she'd got in contact, I saw Isabel on the TV and put two and two together. I never knew why you'd left. I thought it was because of me.'

'No,' Sian exclaims. 'Of course it wasn't because of you!'

'Lianne never said that you were ill. If I'd known... oh Sian, I feel so bad you went through all of that...'

Dave and Sian step closer to each other and hold hands briefly and I look at Tamsin and wink at her. Her eyes are shining. Neither of us could have imagined such a happy outcome for Sian. For a second, I think Dave is going to kiss her, but suddenly Jennifer is there with Bea. Their banner looks a little worse for wear. Bea runs into my arms.

'You did it,' she says. 'I'm so proud of you, Mummy.'

'Oh, you found Dave,' Jennifer gushes, pushing through to kiss Sian. 'You did amazingly. All of you.'

Sian turns to me. 'I can't believe he's here,' she says.

100

Isabel and Amma soon leave together and I squish everyone in to the car and drop Tilly, Joss, Jacob and Biffa outside our front door, and then take Tamsin home. I'm dying for a bath and I wish Tom was home and I wouldn't have to make food, but there are no lights on in the house and his car isn't on the drive. I still can't believe that after everything I've been through today, he hasn't been there for my moment of triumph.

I finger the butterfly necklace and picture the woman's face, telling me not to give up hope. I'm longing to tell Tom about her – how amazing and truly life-affirming today has been, but then I remember how cross he was about me doing the race and my heart hardens. If he's at his parents and has read my letter and is still in a sulk, then I really don't know what more I can do.

Tamsin's flat is also dark and she fiddles with the thermostat on the wall, and I hear the heating going on.

'Will you be OK?' I ask as I follow her in and store her wheelchair in the space she's made in the hall. 'Where's Ian?'

She doesn't turn on the light.

'I know you know, Keira. About him. About her.' I feel my stomach churning. 'He told me.'

'Oh, Tamsin, I'm so sorry.'

She turns to face me. 'I can't blame him.'

'I can.'

'It's tough. Too tough on him. He's not strong.'

'But he should have tried to be,' I say. I can't believe she doesn't resent or blame him.

'I always knew he was weak, deep down. It's not a surprise that he shipped out when the going got tough.'

I'm glad she doesn't blame me for the split, but the resignation in her voice saddens me. I want to ask her what this means now and what she'll do about going to Mexico, but I can tell she's way too tired for this conversation now.

'You're lucky, Keira. Having a stand-up guy, like Tom,' she says. 'He's definitely a keeper.'

'Ha,' I counter, bitterly. 'You know, he missed it, today. The race. Tom. He didn't come. Deliberately. He was so cross about me doing it. He thought I'd damage myself.'

'So, you proved him wrong,' she says, with a chuckle.

'He won't see it that way.'

'Oh, come on. Don't be so hard on him.'

I help her into her bedroom and then run a bath for her. I almost can't bear to leave her by herself after today, but she insists that I go home to the kids and that she can manage. She grunts with exertion as she kicks off her trainers.

'What a day,' I tell her, trying to cheer her up and keep her focused on the positives.

She nods and smiles. 'It was quite a turnout, wasn't it?'

'I didn't think I'd do it,' I confess. 'I nearly didn't.'

'You can do anything, Keira,' she says. 'Don't you know that, by now? You're so kick-ass. Remember the builders?'

I do remember standing up to the builders in the park – and standing up for myself with the surgeon who did my port.

'You even stood up to my bully, Ian. So why you don't...'
She fizzles out.

'Go on... say it,' I urge.

'It's just... you won't stand up to Lorna. When she's about to take everything you've worked so hard for.'

'I know, but there's nothing I can do.'

'There's always something you can do. You're resourceful, Keira. Don't let her win.'

We talk for a while more and I tell her about Sian looking through the files at work and finding nothing. I feel very close to crumbling – to telling her how bereft I feel that I'm about to lose Wishwells.

But I can't break down. Not when the emptiness of her flat is like a noise. Instead, I beg her to come home with me. To come and stay for as long as she wants, but I know she won't. Her bravery is admirable, but she shouldn't be alone. Nobody facing what she is should be alone.

She says again that she'll be fine and she's going to have a long soak in the bath. I tell her I'll make my own way out, but as I leave, I notice there's an address book by her phone. I flick through it and then I find what I'm looking for. I take Joss's red lipstick out of my fanny pack then rip the race number from the front of my shirt and write down Tamsin's mother's number on the back of it.

101

Back at home, I park on the drive and I close my eyes. I'm exhausted – physically and emotionally. Tamsin's words run round and round in my head.

She's right, of course. I haven't stood up to Lorna, but without Tom's backing and without a leg to stand on, I'm not sure what I can do.

There's an old Harley on the grass verge and I see Maria's lights on next door. I wonder if she's finally got a new boyfriend. I hope so.

The elation I felt at running the race, the shock of all the people who ran feels overwhelming and the sadness I feel for Tamsin feels so raw that I really have to brace myself to go into the house and face the kids. I know they want me to be cheerful, but I feel wrung out.

I hear voices, as soon as I open the front door, then Jacob calls out.

'We're in here. Dad's home.'

Tom is in the kitchen with Zippo and I realise that it's Zippo's bike that I'd seen on the grass verge. Have they honestly come from Devon on his clapped-out old Harley?

'Look who's here,' Joss says, her cheeks pink as she stares at Zippo. I can see she's skittish and flustered in a way I've never seen her before. Zippo looks different too. He's shaved his hair off and the earrings have gone. He looks more like a grown-up than I've ever seen him look.

Tom stands up – with difficulty, as he's wearing too-tight leather trousers, which are obviously Zippo's, and in two steps he comes over and picks me up. He hugs me in one of his special bear hugs. He smells of diesel and dirt. 'I tried to get here sooner,' he says. 'But the car broke down. Zippo brought me and we came as fast as we possibly could, but I'm so gutted I wasn't there in time to see the end of the race.'

He lets me go and Zippo hugs me now. 'It sounds incredible. Well done, K. Proud of you, babe.'

'We're over 300 per cent,' Joss says. 'That's ten grand already, we've raised.'

I nod, hardly hearing her, staring at Tom, wanting an explanation.

'I got your letter,' he says and I nod, but I'm close to tears. 'We came as soon as I read it. Mum forgot to give it to me. Can you forgive me for being such an arse?' he says and then I start sobbing.

Upstairs, once I've composed myself, I get into an Epsom Salts bath and Tom sits on the edge. His face is wind-blown and I know he's exhausted too.

'Can you take those disgusting trousers off,' I say, laughing.

He nods and starts disrobing.

'Those two are getting on like a house on fire.' He's talking about Zippo and Joss, and I smile. We both raise our eyebrows at each other.

'I know,' I say. 'But what about Lucy?'

'She's history,' Tom says. 'So he's a single pringle ready to mingle.'

I laugh. 'Don't jinx it.'

I sink into the water with a sigh.

'Is that good?' he asks, and, oh, it is. I feel like every worry I've ever had is slowly dissolving away.

'Like you don't believe.'

He smiles down at me, his eyes soft. And there he is, my Tom.

'So… how have you been?' I ask.

'I've missed you.'

'I've been here,' I tell him.

'I know. But my head's been all over the place. I was just so angry about being put out to pasture. After everything I've put into that firm. Although, surprisingly, after promoting Dan, Andrew seems to have got cold feet about it and wants to find some way of promoting me too.'

I tell him about meeting Andrew in the street and what I said. 'Are you cross?'

Tom laughs. 'No, actually, I'm glad you said something. I'm glad you stuck up for me.'

'You're worth sticking up for,' I tell him and my voice cracks.

He nods and then tells me about the situation in Devon and how he couldn't come back because he was getting his dad into the system and getting him monitored by doctors for his memory loss. Zippo and him have spent the weekend finishing the stairlift for them, even though Hilary's knee is getting much better. Tom has even talked to them about the future – about getting in carers when the time comes.

'Mum only remembered your letter at seven o'clock this morning.'

'I see.'

'And then, when I read it, I realised… well, I realised

everything. Because everything you said was spot on. I so wish I'd been there, Keira. I wish I'd seen the race. I'm so proud of you.'

And then he leans over and we're kissing and I pull him into the bath with me.

102

After the bath, I sleep for the whole evening. Tom brings me some supper and I can barely wake up to eat it, but when my mobile rings at midnight, I wake up immediately. Something must have happened to Tamsin.

I turn on the bedside light and pick up the phone. Tom groans, squinting in the sudden light.

It's Sian.

'Hey,' I say, blearily. 'How are you doing?'

This must be a call about Dave.

'I've got it,' Sian says. She sounds excited.

'What? Got what?'

'What are you doing now?'

She's not making any sense. 'I'm sleeping?'

'It's the thing Amma said – about Doug Crawley having a golf club villa. It's just been niggling at me and I realised why.'

'Why?'

'Can you get me into Wishwells?'

'Now?'

'I'll meet you in the car park in ten minutes.'

I ring off.

'What's going on?' Tom asks, as I get out of bed and start to get dressed.

'If I tell you, will you promise not to be cross?'

He sits up. 'Uh-oh,' he says. 'What's going on, Keira?'

'If you come with me, I'll explain on the way.'

By the time we arrive at Wishwells, Tom is dumbstruck.

'You mean to say, she wants to buy you out? And not only that – she's going to get rid of the shop?'

'That's about the sum of it.'

I tell him about what Sian found out the first time she was here.

'They really did mess with your emails?' he says, incredulously and I nod. 'But that's so evil.'

'I know. I thought I was going mad, but that thing about the rent... I really *had* never seen that email.'

'Oh, Keira – I'm so sorry you've been going through this all alone. I had no idea.'

'I haven't been alone,' I tell him. 'Not really. I've had Sian and Amma and Tamsin.'

'But even so... I should have listened. I feel dreadful.'

'I just can't lose this place, Tom. It just means too much to me.'

'I know, darling. I know.'

Sian is waiting with a torch and we creep in through the back door of the office and I disable the CCTV. It feels like we're burglars – even with Tom with us. Up in the office, Sian gets to work on Pierre's computer. She's clearly got the bit between her teeth.

'Shit, he's changed the password,' she says, before rolling up her sleeves and hitching her glasses up her nose. Her face shines blue in the light of the computer.

We watch her concentrating.

'She's good at this,' Tom whispers.

'She's amazing.'

Sian bites the end of her tongue. 'That should do it,' she says. And then a few moments later, she grins. 'I'm in. Now then, let me see,' she says, scrolling through emails. 'Let's have a look at the company bank accounts. Have you got the login details?' she asks me.

I go to my desk and dig out the diary that's still in the drawer to give her the online banking passwords.

'That's a relief that Pierre hasn't changed those. So, Keira, when was the last board meeting?' she asks, her fingers flying over the keys, and I flip through my diary, remembering the date. Remembering that Lorna changed it so that I'd miss half of it.

'There, look,' she says and Tom and I go around to have a look at the screen. 'There was a payment made in and it went straight out. But it was from a Portuguese company OportoGT. I noticed an email from OportoGT to Pierre in the trash folder and then when Amma said about Doug Crawley having loads of money and having just come back from Portugal, I suddenly remembered.'

'Remembered what?' I ask, confused.

'That very first time we saw a picture of Crawley in the paper. Do you remember? When Amma first pointed him out, when we were running? And there was a photo of Crawley shaking hands with the guy from the developer – Terry whatshisname, from Arc – the guy who got the council contract?'

'Vaguely?'

'Well *that* guy was wearing an OportoGT sweatshirt.

I remember it clearly. He had the logo on it. So OportoGT and the council developer are linked. It was too obscure to be a coincidence. And OportoGT gave Wishwells money.'

'It's twenty thousand pounds,' I say, astonished. 'Do you really think that was some kind of bung?'

'It looks like it,' Tom says.

'So Crawley must have got the developer to bribe Pierre to let go of the lease.'

'But why?' Tom asks.

'For their new development, of course.'

But at that moment, I hear something on the stairs. Sian switches off the torch and we all stay frozen.

'There's someone coming,' I whisper.

My heart pounds and I hold on to Tom. What if it's Lorna, or worse… Pierre?

Then the light goes on in the office and I cry out as the person carrying a large torch drops it with a clatter.

And then I see who it is.

'Jesus Christ you scared me,' I gasp.

'Keira – what the hell?' Moira says.

She looks at me and then Tom and Sian and then back to me. 'Brian rang me from down the road. Mine was the only number he had. He said he thought there were intruders.'

'And you came alone?' Tom said. He looks at me. It's typical of Moira to be so brave.

'Brian's downstairs,' she says, distractedly, but she's staring at me.

'Keira… what on earth has happened?'

'Oh, Moira,' I gasp. And then I run to her and throw myself into her arms.

Tom goes down to tell Brian that everything is OK and he's to go back home, whilst Moira and I talk rapidly, my words spilling over each other. She strokes my hands over and over as she listens.

'Oh my poor love, I had no idea you'd been ill.'

'But Lorna told me you'd decided to leave? She said you'd just left and didn't want to tell me yourself.'

'No! Nothing of the sort. She fired me. Just after Christmas. Well, she fired me saying it was your idea and you didn't want to tell me yourself. And that's what hurt so much. That's why I had to go away. Because I was so upset thinking that you could do that to me.'

'Oh, Moira,' I cry, stroking her familiar gorgeous face. 'You really thought that? All this time?'

'Keira, I'm so sorry.'

'I can't believe Lorna did that to you two. She's something else, isn't she?' Tom says, coming back in and overhearing the end of this conversation. 'Looks like she had us all fooled.'

'Well now her number's up,' I tell her.

'It certainly is,' Sian says. 'I'm just going to print out this stuff. It's all here, Keira. All the proof you need.'

103

We get back at three in the morning, but I hardly sleep and I know Tom's brain is whirring too. When the light creeps in through the curtains, I put on my dressing gown, but as I come out of our room to go downstairs and put the kettle on, Zippo appears on the landing. With all the high drama in the night, I'd forgotten he was here.

It looks like he's spent the night in the spare room with Joss. And looks jolly smug about it too. He's got a towel wrapped around his waist and he stretches up and rubs the back of his head, before wincing at me.

'Morning,' he says.

'Morning,' I say.

'Don't say anything.'

'I wouldn't dream of it,' I reply, with a grin. 'Two teas?'

I go downstairs and I'm still smiling to myself, as I make four cups of tea, for me and Tom and for the new lovers. Pooch pants and licks my hand and I let him out and watch as he circles round and wees on the patch of crocuses that have come up in the middle of the lawn.

I finger my butterfly necklace that the runner gave me during the race, and I feel a profound sense of gratitude. I know that my journey in Cancer World is to be continued and there's a long way to go with treatment, but after the detonation of my diagnosis into my life, I can feel the pieces settling. And I remember what the butterfly necklace runner said, about having hope.

I close my eyes for a second. 'Thank you, Dad,' I say, remembering how I wanted him to make things better, that first day I sat on the bench in the park. And how Tamsin came running into my life. I think of everything that has happened because of her and how close I feel to her and my running friends, especially after yesterday.

Then I go to my bag in the hall and take out my race number and, picking up the phone, dial Tamsin's mother's number.

I watch the sun coming up over the shed, bathing the garden and the budding trees in light. I take a deep breath and find myself listening to a ringing tone and then saying,

'Hello, is this Shirley O'Brien?'

'Yes.'

'You don't know me,' I tell her, 'but I'm a friend of Tamsin's.'

Zippo and Joss leave very soon after they're up, refusing breakfast. Joss gets onto the back of his motorbike for a lift to the station.

I want to talk to her, to find out how she's feeling and what happened during the night she's spent with Zippo and what it all means, but she's blushing and bashful and unlike I've ever seen her before and I know I'll have to be patient and wait until she tells me in her own time. Tom and I watch from the doorway, bemused as she puts her hand up in salute and he knows I'm itching to call Scout to tell her this – the juiciest of juicy bit of gossip.

Tom has asked Mum to come round and he sings her Dexy's

theme tune, 'Too-Ra-Loo-Ra Too-Ra-Loo-Rye, Ay?' as she rings the front door at noon. I can't help laughing. She is holding a peace offering of an apple crumble and kisses me on the cheek.

'I hear you did very well in the race,' she says, in her pious voice, but it's the closest thing to praise I'm going to get.

'I'll put a tenner into the fund,' Rob offers, kissing me.

'Thanks,' I tell him. 'Every penny helps.'

Tilly takes Rob's coat and everyone goes into the kitchen, but Tilly holds me back.

'So… um, I was wondering… would it be OK if Alfie comes over today?' she says.

'Sure. That'd be lovely. He can come for lunch too, if he likes. That's if I'm not too embarrassing? I check.

'No, Mum,' she says, with a grin. 'Actually, I think you rock.'

104

Tom agrees to come with me to the emergency board meeting that I've called at Wishwells on Tuesday morning. I've dressed in my only power suit – and after much deliberation have got my wig on, as well as some of Amma's false eyelashes. Tilly has helped me fill in my eyebrows, so that they look natural and not like slugs, which is how they look if I do them. Despite starting out sleep-deprived, bald with greyish skin, the transformation is miraculous and I feel kick-ass and strong.

We meet with Clive and Richard in Jennifer's café first for a full debrief where Sian gives them a damning account of what's been going on in Wishwells for the past few months and they, like Tom are shocked and stunned by Lorna and Pierre's duplicity and lies. Sian looks very pleased with herself as I thank her and give her a hug by the café door, holding on to my wig so it doesn't go wonky.

Clive is so impressed with her work that he wants her to work with some of his other companies.

'That's amazing… he's serious about giving me an actual proper job,' she whispers to me.

I'm delighted for her, but not surprised. She deserves it.

'Aren't you going to go back to Bracknell, though?' I ask her.

'To my old job? No way?'

'But what about Dave?'

She grins widely. I know they've been in almost constant contact since the race. 'He wants out from there and a change of scene, so we're already talking about him moving down here. And if I have work lined up, then that'd be perfect.'

'So it's all falling into place,' I say. 'I'm so happy.'

'Oh, Keira,' she says, giving me an extra squeeze, 'I can't thank you enough. Now go get 'em.'

I feel shaky with nerves, but Tom squeezes my hand as we head over the road. 'Go for it,' he says. 'Let rip. I've got your back.'

I don't speak to Lorna when we get into the shop. I don't trust myself not to lose it with her and I keep my head down as Clive, Richard, Tom and I all head up to the meeting room. My heart is pounding, but I feel steely and strong. I know that I have all my ducks in a row.

'This is ridiculous,' she blusters, watching us all go. 'What the hell is going on?'

The issue we're here to discuss first and foremost is Pierre's underhand dealings about the shop, but it's *her* betrayal that galls me the most. I realise as she squares up to me how intimidating I've always found her, but today, I'm determined not to let her get to me.

'What's going on? Why is Tom here?' Pierre asks as we get upstairs to the offices.

'In a legal capacity,' I counter, brushing past him and Becca into the meeting room.

Lorna makes eyes at me, like I'm completely out of order for involving Tom… which is a bit rich coming from her and what she's allowed *her* husband to do.

'Nobody has broken the law,' Pierre says, with a guffaw, as

if I'm being ridiculous. I have to bite my tongue. The *arrogance* of the man.

When everyone is finally in the meeting room, I close the door, eyeballing Becca so that she goes back to her computer and minds her own business and then stand at the top of the table. Clive, Tom and Richard sit, but they don't look at Pierre or Lorna as they take their seats. There's a stress ball on the table and Pierre picks it up and chucks it nonchalantly between his hands as he reclines in the chair, like this is some kind of low-level brainstorm.

'So what's all this about? Why the long faces?' he says, hoping, no doubt, to charm his way out of the situation, but I remain standing.

'Well, first off – we're here to discuss the lease,' I say.

'What about it?' Lorna asks, innocently, as if our showdown in the shop never happened.

'Pierre has acted completely outside his remit,' I tell her. 'Nobody ever agreed that he could break the lease.'

Pierre looks cornered, but shakes his head, bluffing it out.

'Oh that. You're still cross about the shop going? I heard there was a scene.' He pulls a face at Lorna and then slaps the ball into his palm. 'You know the strategy is to go online,' he says. 'It makes financial sense to close down the shop and actually, Keira, for your information, everyone agreed.'

'*I* didn't agree. I'd never agree to letting my shop go – and you know it.'

He frowns at me and shakes his head. I'm amazed at his thick skin. At his belief that he is going to actually front this out.

'The thing is, Pierre, you told us very specifically that you'd discussed it with Keira,' Richard says. 'Which doesn't appear to be true.'

'Clive, Richard, let's just be reasonable about this,' Lorna appeals.

'Talk to Keira, not to us,' Richard says, curtly.

'This is absurd.'

'It's not absurd. Pierre has lied, repeatedly,' I say, sternly. 'In order to shove me out of my own business. Which is why he has to go. Right now.'

Pierre shakes his head, as if I'm being ridiculous. 'You can't just—'

'I can and I am. Pierre, you're fired.'

'Now steady on,' Lorna says, appealing to Clive now.

'Lorna, given the circumstances, Keira is perfectly within her rights to terminate his employment,' Clive says.

'What circumstances?'

Clive nods at me and I reach into my bag and slide two of the dossiers over to Pierre and Lorna.

Pierre finally leaves the ball, and with a weary sigh leans forward. He takes the dossier and pulls it towards him.

'What's all this then?' he says, but as he flips it open, I see his jaw tighten.

'I think you both know what's in there – but just to be clear, taking a bribe from the developer was a shitty move.'

'I did no such thing,' Pierre says.

'Err… actually, yes you did. It's all there, in black and white,' I tell him.

'But how?' Lorna asks, scanning through the damning pages and then looking up at me with new eyes, but I ignore her for a moment, concentrating on Pierre who now stands.

'I don't know where you've got this, but—'

'Oh, this is just *some* of the damning evidence I have… because there are also some rather alarming allegations from your ex-colleagues in the city. And should they choose to reopen that case with this fresh evidence of your recent behaviour—'

'You can't let her speak to me like this,' Pierre shouts.

'Frankly, Keira can address you any way she likes,' Clive retorts. 'I'm surprised she's so calm.'

Oh, I'm calm. You bet, I'm calm.

Lorna is on her feet. 'You can't just—'

'Pierre, unless you really want to thrash out right here and right now just what *level* of fraud and deceit you have carried out in my premises, before I call the police, I suggest that you get out,' I tell him.

For a second, he looks like he's going to try and continue to argue his way out of it, but then he turns and walks out.

'Pierre!' Lorna calls, horrified that he's leaving.

'You can't do this,' she yells at me.

'I just did,' I tell her. 'And now, we're on to you,' I say. 'And oh, what you have done is so much worse.' My voice wobbles, but I stay strong. 'You were supposed to be my friend, but you stabbed me in the back. What you don't seem to understand, Lorna, is that this is *my* shop, *my* business and you trying to take it away from underneath me would have been bad enough, but you using my cancer diagnosis to accelerate your plans is just… evil.'

Her mouth moves, but she doesn't speak.

'You fired Moira, causing her untold distress and then you tried to make out that I was going mad, but all the time, you were tampering with my emails.'

'Yes, I think the technical term for what you've been doing to Keira, Lorna, is gaslighting,' Tom says, backing me up. He gives me an encouraging look.

'Which is particularly despicable, given what she's been going through,' Richard adds.

I'm glad for their back-up, but I don't need them. Lorna's cheeks are red. Her eyes fill with tears as she finally meets my steely glare.

'So I want you to listen carefully, because this is what's going to happen. My lawyer will be in touch about my own "reasonable offer" to buy out your shares,' I tell her, referring back to the derisory offer she gave me. 'And in the meantime, you can take your awful Jackson merchandise and your shitty teapots and fuck off out of my shop.'

105

I call Tamsin and leave her a message to tell her about my triumph at the board meeting, but she doesn't call back. On our group WhatsApp, Amma keeps us informed of the money going up and up on our Time for Tamsin page, but Tamsin only adds thumbs up emojis.

I'm worried about her, but I'm too busy at Wishwells, trying to calm things down after the board meeting showdown. Now that Lorna has gone, Becca has decided to leave too and Tyra, the new girl with her, but I can't say I'm sorry. It's all very dramatic, but I feel a new strength returning, now that I've been vindicated.

Ruby is deeply apologetic, weeping and weeping as she tells me how awful it was to have to have lied to me about the awards ceremony and how conflicted she felt about Lorna's behaviour, but I forgive her and give her a big hug.

Like me, she's over the moon to have Moira back, who sets to work restoring the shop to how we both want it. Some of the clothes stay, but with Moira back in charge, it feels as if the soul of Wishwells has returned. She's in a fabulous mood and reveals that, despite everything, she did have a nice time on her cruise. She even met someone: Oscar, a Danish potter and she's glowing from her holiday romance. Tilly and Jacob tease her about him when she comes round for dinner to show us her pictures.

I call up Lisa and tell her what's happened and reinstate her to make our ceramics.

'I'm so relieved to hear you say it,' she says. 'Not just for me, but because it's the principle that counts. People love Wishwells because it's not only full of beautiful things, but full of lovely people too. That's what makes shopping special. Not clicking on a screen. What's human about that?'

I couldn't agree more.

After the race on Sunday and my showdown with Lorna, it feels like such a milestone has been reached, that I'd almost forgotten that the bulk of treatment is yet to happen. But, as it turns out, chemo number three feels easier than the others – or maybe I'm just too tired to work myself up about it. Somehow, the chemo feels less important than other things going on in my life. I snooze this time, as Mum knits next to me.

Afterwards, I go onto our group chat and see a message from Tamsin.

Can you come round? All of you? Tonight?

Sian says she's around and agrees to pick up me and Amma and take us both round to Tamsin's flat.

At her flat, Tamsin greets us at the door and gives each of us a hug. She's wearing a long black robe and a black turban and her face is painted in its usual insane colours. She looks very cheerful. I'm last and she holds my shoulders and looks into my face.

'You are a good friend, Keira,' she says and I swallow hard, so relieved that she's not cross with me. 'You did the right thing.'

416

'You mean your mum? She got in touch?'

'Yes.' She smiles. 'Yes, and it's so wonderful to have her back. I thought I didn't need her… but I was wrong. But you knew that, didn't you?'

I nod and hug her. 'That's what friends are for.'

The others are already in the kitchen as I walk in.

'This is my mum, Shirley,' Tamsin says, limping into the kitchen and holding on to the door frame.

'You must be Keira,' Shirley says. She's got a harrowed, grey face, but her eyes are soft and just the same colour as Tamsin's. 'I'm so grateful that you rang.'

'Not as grateful as me,' Tamsin says.

I hug Shirley, who says she's going to get tea for us all.

Tamsin limps from the kitchen to the living room.

'What's wrong?' I ask her. 'Why are you limping?'

She grins at me. 'This is why I wanted you all to come round,' she says. 'I've got something to show you.'

'What?' Amma asks, confused.

Tamsin undoes her robe and takes it off. Underneath, she's wearing running shorts and a top.

'Look,' she says, turning round.

On her calf she has a new tattoo, which is covered in cling film. It says 'The Cancer Ladies' Running Club' – made to look like a motto. Red hearts and blue butterflies swirl around it.

'Oh my goodness! That's amazing!'

'Really? You hate tattoos, Keira,' she teases.

'I know, but it's fabulous.'

'I've been in the chair for two days,' she explains. 'I used the last of my savings.'

We all admire her tattoo and then Sian picks up the cat and it purrs loudly and Tamsin sits on the sofa.

'So, what's the plan for Mexico?' Amma asks, perching on the arm of the sofa. 'Now we've got the money for you.'

Tamsin bites her lip. 'So... about that...'

She sounds shifty and I see in an instant, as her eyes dart away from mine, that she's changed her mind.

'Is it still what you want?' I probe, but I think I already know the answer.

'I thought I did, but actually,' she gives a big sigh, 'I'm not going.'

'What?' Sian asks. 'But we raised all the money.'

'And I'm beyond grateful to you. To you all, to everyone who put their hand in their pocket, but you see...' She closes her eyes, as if this this going to be a hard thing to say and we all lean in, as she opens her eyes and spreads her hands out on her knees. 'Mexico was Ian's idea. And I had to go along with it because it was what *he* wanted and I was too weak to stand up to him and then when you said you were raising money, it all spiralled out of control. Believe me, I was so touched that everyone wanted to help. But the thing is I love my medical team here and I also know that there's no better treatment to be bought anywhere else in the world. I know Phil is treating me in the very best way possible and doing all he can for me. So, no, I'm not going.'

'But doesn't that mean...?' Sian starts.

'You wanted more time,' Amma continues.

Tamsin smiles at us all. 'Look, I thought having a terminal diagnosis would mean that I had to count the days before I die, but I'm living better than I have for years. I have my family back and I've let Ian go, but most of all... I have you.'

Amma looks at me and her eyes fill with tears. She takes Tamsin's hand.

'I always wanted to be a leader,' Tamsin says. 'I always dreamt of having my own running club. And thanks to you, I got it. I even got the ink to prove it.'

'Oh, Tamsin,' I say, sinking down beside her and taking her other hand. I can tell she means it and she's made her decision.

'Stop it. No tears. Come on, cheer up,' she says, but I can tell she's choked up too. 'I'm not dead yet.' And there's her Cheshire cat grin. 'You can save your tears for then. But between now and then, for every second I have remaining, I'm going to do the things that make me happy and be with the people I love.'

Sian kneels on the floor next to Tamsin. 'Fair enough.'

We all have a group hug.

'Oh and the money…' Tamsin says.

'Oh yes, that,' Amma says. 'You've got quite a war chest. What will you do with it?'

'Oh, don't worry. Plenty,' Tamsin says, happily. 'I want half of it to go to research, so that other people in my situation will have a better chance of survival than me. And I want the other half to go to the hospice. You know they rely on fundraising for three quarters of their income and so if the Time For Tamsin money can go anywhere, it can help St Margaret's stay open.'

'It sounds like you've got it all worked out,' I say, relieved that she's made this plan and she's back in control of her future.

'I have, but I want you to promise me one thing,' she says.

'What's that?'

'For you all to keep on running together. Keep the Cancer Ladies' Running Club alive. For me.'

And we promise that we will.

106

Despite my delight at being back at work and the crisis at Wishwells being over, the following two months still turn out to be the hardest of my life. It seems that the final rollercoaster on the chemo ride in Cancer World is the hardest of all.

Soon, I completely understand Tamsin's analogy about being trapped in a noisy club, coming up on a bad pill, when there are whooshes in my head that make me feel dizzy and sick. I'm wrung out and have to surrender quite often, taking to my bed, when my bones ache too much for me to stand. I'm assaulted by relentless toe-to-scalp hot flushes that make it impossible to sleep and the scar on my chest and arm throbs. I just want it all to be over and by the last chemo, I've barely had any up time, when I've felt even vaguely normal.

But my family, along with Sian, Amma and Tamsin, bolster me up through it all and I still manage to make it into the shop, where I can forget all about the cancer. There's been a collective sigh of relief from everyone on our stretch of high street, that the council's plans have been scrapped for the time being and there's a sense of calm returning after a storm. Lorna and I have only spoken through lawyers. I don't care what's happening with her and Pierre, although I've heard a rumour that they've separated.

Moira and Ruby are doing a great job running the shop for me and Moira has set up a 'cancer corner' selling Mum's knitted knockers. We've started to talk about how we manufacture some 'butterfly of hope' necklaces.

And even when I'm feeling utterly wretched, I still haul myself out to run with the girls every Friday morning. Tamsin comes on a couple of outings too. Her condition seems to be stable for bit, although she's shockingly thin.

Our running group is quite big now – over twenty regular members, sometimes as many as thirty – and I've met so many fascinating and inspirational women through it. But the most inspirational of all is Amma.

When Sian and Amma did some more digging around, they discovered that Doug Crawley's wealth had come directly from OportoGT, who in turn bankrolled the council's development company. The whole enterprise was thoroughly crooked.

Thanks to Sian's evidence, Amma managed to completely discredit Crawley and her campaign is going from strength to strength. She went on to accuse him of sexual harassment and as a result of her bravery, many more women have come forward with much more serious accusations. Creepy Crawley, is now being held over multiple counts of sexual harassment.

Despite all my bitching about tattoos, I have to have three of my own before I have my radiotherapy which starts on a bright June morning. A very competent radiographer administers a little ink dot each side of my chest and one in the middle of what was once my cleavage.

I'm to have twenty sessions of radiotherapy in a row and clear my diary to focus on getting back and forth to the hospital on time. I'm really lucky to have Mum and Rob on hand to help drive me and we're soon used to the drill.

On the fifth session, I disrobe in the dark suite, hang up my bra and T-shirt on the back of the chair in the small changing cubicle. I glance at myself in the mirror. My eyes are super itchy and red, and without any nose hairs, my nose drips constantly. I'm bloated, but, I note, as I take off my bamboo headscarf, some hair has grown back on my bald bonce. I look like a patchy, fluffy chicken and I run my hand gingerly over the new hairs.

'You thought I was no spring chicken,' I said to Tom this morning. 'But you were wrong.'

It's good to joke about my diminished physical state, but there have been times when it's been impossible to keep up my positivity, especially when, each week, it feels like bits of me are falling off. I inspect my nails which have all gone a funny brown colour and they're all loose. It's like having false nails that are about to come off and it's hard to pick anything up.

'Come on. You're nearly there,' I say to my reflection. 'You can do this.'

On the radiotherapy bed, I shuffle down on the instruction of the nurses. My bottom has to be in exactly the same place each day and they line up the lasers using the tattoos on me, so the radiotherapy can be fired at my chest.

So that they don't zap my heart, the nurse puts the breathing apparatus in my mouth and then slides on the goggles over my eyes and puts a peg on my nose. She puts my arms above my head and I fight down the feeling of claustrophobia as she potters around me, sliding the giant machines into place.

Inside the goggles, I am now looking at a computer screen which shows a graph. My breath is represented as a red line and the nurse makes the final adjustments. Soon an alarm sounds and the nurse and radiotherapist scurry from the room, so they aren't affected by the radio waves.

I can hear the nurse's voice over the intercom and she gives me my cue. I have to take a deep breath in, which makes the red line on the graph go up to a horizontal green line. I have to hold my breath until a light in the bottom of the screen goes on and I let out the breath. I have to do this six times whilst the radiotherapy rays start zapping my chest, seeking out the last of the rogue cancer cells.

Yeah, *fuck you*, cancer cells. I think. Because I have won, I remind myself. The mothership is strong. With a combination of surgery, chemo and radiotherapy, I sincerely doubt that there are any cancer cells left in my body. If there are – then hats off to them, but I reckon I've quashed the rebellion and I'll be climbing up mountains when I'm 90. No, sod that. I will be climbing up mountains as soon as possible. As soon as I'm fit.

It's all part of the landscape on New Keira. I've changed many things about my life since the beginning of the year, the first being a habit to attend to my wellbeing on a daily basis. I've discovered qi gong, which is like Chinese yoga and it baffles me that I didn't make time for some meditative headspace before. I like the idea of qi – of life force, that is all around us. As the dark machines move over me, in my head, I say the mantra I say every day to keep myself on the right track.

Just for today, I will not be angry. Just for today, I will not worry. Just for today, I will count my many blessings. Just for today, I will do my work honestly and just for today I will be kind to every living creature.

Then I breathe out.

107

Outside, Mum is waiting for me in the waiting room.

'How did it go?' she asks.

'Five down, fifteen to go,' I say. 'Can't complain.'

She nods and puts away her knitting and we walk out through the long corridors to the car park where Rob is waiting and I tell her how it feels good that the end of my trip to Cancer World is almost in sight.

'You know, I couldn't be like you are. The whole thing – the whole cancer thing – it terrifies me.'

'I'm sure you could get through it,' I say, astonished at this admission from her. 'I mean, it's bad, but it's not the worst thing that could have happened. Because it didn't happen when I was young and single, or trying to get pregnant. And it didn't happen to one of the kids.'

'It happened to one of my kids,' Mum says and I see a rare emotion cross her face. I grab her and pull her into a hug.

'I'm honestly OK, Mum. I promise. I'm going to be fine. And it'll just be something that happened. A long time ago.'

And I hope to God, that this statement is true.

Because, of course, it's not true for Tamsin. I find out she's finally gone into the hospice from Shirley who rings on Friday and asks if I'll go in to visit.

Tilly, who has done some volunteering at St Margaret's hospice offers to come with me and I'm glad that she does. I'm worried about seeing Tamsin so depleted and ill, but actually, although she looks frail, she's still smiling. She's wearing a purple tie-dyed robe and fluffy socks.

Tamsin is full of praise about the nursing staff and the facilities as if she's in a five-star hotel. The staff love her, obviously, not least of all because the Time For Tamsin money has helped so much. But when Tilly finds out that Tamsin and Shirley have mostly been holed up in this little room together, Tilly insists on taking Shirley on a tour. She says there's a whole stack of books and games Shirley must see and Tamsin puts in a request for Trivial Pursuit.

I glow with pride as I watch Tilly chatting easily with Tamsin's mother as they walk away. I admire her for instinctively knowing that I wanted to be alone with Tamsin and that Shirley needed a break.

'How are you doing?' I ask Tamsin, reaching forward and grabbing her thin hand. Her silver rings are loose on her fingers.

'And now, the end is near, and I must face, the final curtain…' she sings, trying to do a Frank Sinatra impression. 'Oh for God's sake, don't look so scared, Keira,' she says. 'It's only death.'

I laugh. 'Only death! Only you would say that.'

I don't want her to die. I wish she had more time. 'Are you scared?' I ask her. 'About when it happens… you know, at the end?'

'A bit, but part of me is very curious. It's just the next adventure. The next part of the run that's over the horizon.'

'That's very brave of you.'

'Well, maybe I am brave now. It's just a shame I wasn't for so long,' she says, with a sigh. 'If only I'd realised sooner that life is a gift, not a given. Always remember that, Keira. For me. Don't take one single day for granted.'

108

One Year Later

Amma and I haul each other up over the last grassy tufts and stop next to Sian, taking in the view. The sky is an infinite powder blue without a cloud in sight. We've nearly completed our charity walk which has brought us over the stunning South Downs to this point, where the Seven Sisters stretch out in both directions, the green grass giving way to the sheer chalky cliffs that plunge to the glittering sea.

We're footsore and weary, but we're all smiling as we fill our lungs with the fresh air. I have taken to yomping up hills with gusto since my treatment finished, but today's walk has been particularly enjoyable. And it's satisfying to know that when we've completed it, we'll have raised thousands for the hospice in Tamsin's memory.

'Shall we do it here?' Amma asks. 'I don't think Shirley and the others are far behind.'

'I reckon it's a good spot.'

Amma has just come back from a well-deserved week with Isabel, Greg and Bear in their villa in Greece. Her hair is curly and lustrous and her skin glows with health. She's ready for the final push of her campaign and I have absolutely no doubt she's going to get her seat. She has my vote for sure and it's not just me. The press love her and she's always on TV, talking about how she's impacted the homeless crisis in our area. She hasn't said it out loud, but I reckon she's got her sights set on Westminster.

Dave stops and puts his hand on Sian's shoulder, leaning forward. His knees are pink from being out in the blazing sun all day. Sian smiles down at him. Thanks to Richard and Clive, her freelance work has really taken off and Dave has moved from Bracknell and is now working with her. They've just had their offer accepted on a lovely flat by the park.

We sit on the grass and I gently lower my rucksack to the ground. From inside, I take out the plastic tub containing Tamsin's ashes and Amma, Sian and I stare at it.

'Is that her?' Dave asks, and I nod.

'She would have loved this,' Amma says, turning her face into the breeze. 'I can't help feeling she's here with us.'

'I know what you mean.'

And I do. I quite often get the feeling that Tamsin is watching over me. I've had several dreams about her and Dad being together, laughing in the camper van, off on a road trip having become firm friends. Each time I've woken up smiling.

It's a year since she died, but her death – although sad – wasn't a traumatic event. She was so happy in the hospice in those last weeks and we all took it in turns to go and see her. I gave her the first of what has turned out to be many new ceramics pieces – a 'Time for T' mug, which Tamsin adored.

In return, Tamsin gave me a beautiful pair of earrings on the day my treatment finished and I'm wearing them today.

It helped that I knew that Tamsin wasn't daunted about dying at all, which made it bearable for us all when she slipped away quietly in the night, with Shirley holding her hand. Shirley said she died with a smile on her face.

The funeral, in accordance with Tamsin's wishes, involved a party with a rock band. She had a cardboard coffin and we all wrote messages on it in felt tip. My message was to thank her for her words of wisdom – that life is a gift, not a given. And, just as I promised her, I've tried to remember that every day since.

'Up here,' I call, waving to the crowd coming up behind Jennifer, who arrives now and breathes in a big breath.

'Check out that view,' she says, with a grin.

The people who ran the Time for Tamsin race, and are now firm members of our ever-growing Cancer Ladies' Running Club, are all here, as well as Tamsin's mum, Shirley.

I wave now, as I see Tom, Moira and the kids coming from the other direction. He's come by car and has parked at the bottom of the hill. He's carrying a cool box and the kids have the bags with the cakes and sandwiches we've made for the ceremony. Jacob has the folding camping table, which he's carrying with Tilly's boyfriend, Alfie. I'm glad Jacob's hair has grown back and his fringe is flapping in his face. My hair is taking a little longer, but it's getting there.

Pooch runs ahead and I bend down to pat him. 'Hey, fella,' I say.

Moira is soon up the hill with the first of the bags. 'What a day for it.'

Pooch licks her hand. They get on famously and Moira was the first to offer to look after him when we go away. We've managed to get the kids out of school ten days early and next week, we're all off on a two-month adventure, before Tom, Janine and a few others launch their new legal start-up.

We're flying to Asia, to see Thailand and Vietnam, then we're going on to Bali to meet Scout, Mart and the twins for Joss and Zippo's wedding. Then we're flying for the last two weeks to Australia to see my brother Billy and my nieces and nephews. I can't wait.

Joss, in fulfilment of a long-held wish is finally getting her beach wedding in Bali. Scout and I are going to be her bridesmaids, which we both find both flattering and hilarious. Joss and Zippo have been inseparable ever since the day of the race and they were engaged six weeks later. They were always pretty good individually, but together they are wonderful. Having known each other vaguely at uni, they both admitted that they've always fancied one another, so maybe they were always meant to be. She says he is her Mr Perfect and I believe her.

'You've all done amazingly well,' Tom says, catching up with Pooch and hugging me.

'It's been brilliant,' I tell him. 'Thanks for bringing the stuff.'

Jacob, Tilly and Alfie set up the table and Tom unpacks the bottles of champagne and Bea carefully lays out the glasses in rows. It's a shame Alfie's not coming on our trip. I know Tilly is going to miss him desperately, but she's determined to come on our adventure. We've all been talking about nothing else for weeks.

Soon, there are about twenty of us gathered, and Tom and Bea hand out glasses of champagne.

'Do you want to say something?' I ask Shirley.

'No, you do it. You'll know what to say,' she replies.

So I tell the story of how I first met Tamsin and how she inspired us all to run and how the Cancer Ladies' Running Club is still going to this day, because of her.

'She was someone who really knew how to live,' I say. 'Which is why Shirley says we must set her ashes free. So that she's out there in the universe, smiling at us with that grin of hers.'

Fortunately the wind is blowing out to sea as Amma and I step forward, and with a huge cheer from the crowd, we release Tamsin's ashes into the wind. We watch as the grey cloud flies up, then sinks below the level of the cliff, almost like the wave of a hand.

'Goodbye, my dear friend. Go with hope in your heart and wings on your heels,' I say.

Then we put our arms around each other and then Shirley and Sian join us and we stare out towards the horizon for a long moment, the sun warming our faces.

Author's Note

Whilst this is very much a work of fiction, Keira's diagnosis and treatment is informed by my own experience of going through breast cancer in 2017. I wanted to write about what happens to a person during this process, but I'm very aware that each patient's diagnosis and treatment plan is completely different. Fortunately, cancer treatments are changing and improving all the time and my greatest hope is that the treatment I've written about in this book will soon be a thing of the past.

I'm hugely indebted to the many people who put me on the path to recovery, including Ros Choate, a fellow mum at the school gates and a fitness instructor who suggested, when I first got diagnosed, that I join her group of recovering-from-cancer runners. Personally, I couldn't think of anything worse. I wanted to crawl under the duvet and stay there, but I was cajoled out onto the seafront and soon met the amazing gang of women who inspired this story and to whom this book is dedicated.

A few months later, after training and some serious bolstering, we all took part in the Brighton Marathon 10K. It was just before my third session of chemo and I was running bald, but just as it happens in the book, I was soon overwhelmed with messages of love and support from the other runners.

I really did meet the woman in the story who told me that she'd run all the way through her cancer treatment. She waited for me at the last turn of the race and stopped me to describe how, when she'd been at her lowest point, a stranger in a café had given her a little silver butterfly pendant: 'A butterfly of hope,' she'd called it. The runner then took off the same pendant, saying she'd been wearing it for three years and it was now time to pass it on, and she put it around my neck. She told me it was now my little butterfly of hope and that I must keep the faith and believe that my life would be better than ever out on the other side of cancer. We had a hug and a few tears and off she went.

I never even knew her name, and I doubt she'll ever know that her random act of kindness inspired this whole story, or that I still wear my little butterfly necklace every day – a talisman to remind me of that extraordinary, life-affirming moment; to remind me to be positive and to look forward, not back, because, you know what? Her words absolutely came true. So, wherever you are, butterfly lady, I salute you.

Acknowledgements

Firstly, I'd like to thank my very clever, insightful, persistent agent, the very wonderful Felicity Blunt and her assistant Rosie Pierce, along with everyone at Curtis Brown, including Jonny Geller, who told me that *The Cancer Ladies' Running Club* would be a good title for a book. I'd also like to thank my publishing fairy godmother, Vivienne Schuster, for her love and her tough love too, and for helping me turn some rambling diary entries into a proper novel. I'd really like to thank Jodi Fabri and Sarah Harvey in Foreign Rights for taking this book out into the world. Thank you to all the editors who have bought the book for translation. I'm truly touched that this story resonated with you.

When the book auction happened for this book, I was overwhelmed with the messages I got from the publishers (people in publishing really are lovely), but none more so than Emily Kitchin at HQ, who went above and beyond to really prove how much she got this book. I've been lucky enough, whilst Emily has been on maternity leave, to work with the fabulous Katie Seaman, who I'd really like to thank for her friendship and support. The whole team at HQ are simply outstanding and I'm so proud to be your author. Thank you especially to Lisa Milton, Melanie Hayes, Jo Rose, Joe Thomas, Melissa Kelly and the fantastic sales team, Fliss Porter, Harriet Williams, Samantha Luton, Darren Shoffren and Hannah Avery.

I have been lucky enough to be a writer for twenty-five years and I'd like to give a big shout out to my fellow authors, particularly the ones who read early copies and have lent their support. I'd like to thank all the book bloggers and reviewers too, whose dedication to reading and reviewing books is invaluable to us authors. I'd also like to thank my early readers, particularly Shân Lancaster and Susan Opie.

This really is a story about friendship and I am blessed to have friends from all parts of my life who have supported me during my whole career, but especially during this book and everything that led to it. I'd like to take this opportunity to thank Anna, Ceetah, Clare, Dawn, Harriet, Harry-Tights, Katy, Lesley, Nicky and Ruth, as well as my Brighton gang, particularly Bronwin, Eve, Lizzie and Louise too, for marching Ziggy and I over the downs. Thank you to Ros and my running girls, obvs! You rock. And Jo for getting me playing the piano duets and Alice at Posh Totty for helping me with the Keira storyline.

Thanks to my Mallorca besties, Toni, Pebbles and Beccy, Ien and Annie too, for lending me the four-leafed clover. Thanks, too, to the mums at St Paul's – Mette, Orshi, Madoka and especially Suzanna (who is nothing like pushy Grace). Thank you, too, to the lovely men in my life who keep me smiling: Paddy, Fortithsby-Smythe, Kev, Giles, Rupert, Pete for all the compilation CD's – and Chris for making me sing in full Freddie Mercury get-up when my hair had just grown back.

I would like to thank the wonderful staff at the Montefiore hospital who restored me to rude health – especially my oncologist, David Bloomfield, and surgeon, Charles Zammit. I'd particularly like to thank Maria Daultrey, Beccy Bloomfield, Lynette Awdry and the amazing nurses who saw me through my treatment with love and laughter: Sarah, Michelle and Clare. I'd like to thank Jo Darling, my acupuncturist, and Peter Deadman, who brought qi gong into my life.

Thank you, of course, to my family: my wonderful sister, Catherine, who was legendary throughout my treatment and through the writing of this book; thanks to Dad and Dianne, Aunty Liz and Aunty Merryl and my fabulous cousins. And to my darling daughters, Tallulah, Roxie and Minty – your love and smiles have always kept me going.

But the biggest, deepest, most heartfelt thank you goes to the love of my life, Emlyn. When you signed up for the 'in sickness and in health' bit, I bet you weren't expecting it to be so dramatic! Turns out, though, you are the best husband in the world and I am a very lucky girl.

Lastly, thank you to *you*, dear reader. I really hope you've enjoyed my book.

Q&A with Josie Lloyd

The Cancer Ladies' Running Club was informed by your own experience of cancer. Was it hard to write about something so close to you?

I think it was more a case that I couldn't NOT write about it. I started a diary when I was going through treatment, mainly to process what I was going through. I've always found writing to be the best (and cheapest!) form of therapy. After a while, taking an objective look at the material I had, I realised that I'd written lots of interesting stuff and I wanted to share it. There's lots about Keira's treatment that is based on my own experience and it does feel a bit scary to put those personal details out there, but it matters to me that the book is honest and authentic.

Keira is a busy wife, mother and business owner. Was it important for you to have a relatable character to show how cancer touches so many of our lives, and for readers to follow that journey?

Absolutely. I think the thing about getting a cancer diagnosis is that it rips the rug from under your feet. I wanted Keira to be at the top of her game, in the prime of her life – or so she thinks. She's running a successful business, she's a great mum, wife, friend and she feels like she's got it all. It's only when she gets a diagnosis that she realises how much she has to lose. I wanted to portray how scary that feels, because it's sometimes not until you have that moment and you come face-to-face with your mortality that you realise what really matters. Going through cancer treatment feels like you leave behind everything about your life you knew and loved and you're on a journey, but you have no idea where you're going. I wanted the readers to experience that with Keira. By the end of the book, she's learnt to look after herself and has come to a different understanding about what it means to live well.

The running club and those new friendships becomes such a positive force in Keira's life. When times are tough, what helps keep you going?

I'd say that, without a doubt, my family and friends definitely hold me up when times are tough. I certainly couldn't have gotten through my own cancer experience without them. However, it's also really good to find new people going through the same thing. They are often the greatest solace. I'd also say that keeping a sense of humour is vital. One of the things that I found when I had cancer was that people expected me to suddenly be quite serious – and I'm not a very serious person. My instinct when times are tough is always to make a joke, and that gallows humour the running girls share in the book was very much based on the banter we had out on our runs with the real-life running girls I met when I was going through treatment.

What advice would you give for anyone inspired to take up running after reading the novel?

Just do it. That's it. It's not a big deal. It's as easy as putting on a pair of trainers. Lots of people make excuses not to run, but the barriers before and during running are mostly mental not physical. If you tell yourself you're going to do it, you will. There are brilliant programmes available, like Couch to 5K, which really work. The most important thing is to practice running – little and often. Don't flog yourself around the park and hurt yourself. Start off running and walking and congratulate yourself on what you achieve. Running is a habit, just like any other. The more you do it, the easier it becomes. I think taking up any form of exercise puts you back in control of your health and that can feel very empowering.

What is the main thing you hope that readers take away from the novel?

I'd like it to be a moving, informative, but ultimately uplifting read, not just for people who have had cancer, but for everyone else too. Everyone who (like me) was terrified of even the word 'Cancer'. Because with one in two of us set to get cancer in our lifetimes, and one in eight women getting breast cancer here in the UK, it's a subject that needs some debunking. We need to get talking about it, sharing our experiences and making it less scary. Because it's not all bad news. With our excellent health service and amazing treatments, many, many people are not only surviving cancer, but positively thriving because of the experience of going through it.

Can you tell us about what you're writing next?

Yes, I'm very excited by my next project. It's about a group of very different women, who take to the cold water together and through their friendship come to a new understanding about their issues. It starts in 2020 and again, I want it to be an honest look at what's going on right now, but with an uplifting feel to it. It's very much about what we've gained, rather than lost in these times of Covid – such as a new sense of community as well as an appreciation of nature. I live in Brighton and I've always been a warm-weather swimmer, but in 2020 I joined the ranks of the Dry Robe wearers and started swimming in the winter. I'm now addicted, so I have plenty to write about.